C000109519

THE
IMPRESSIONIST
MURDERS

THE IMPRESSIONIST MURDERS

WILLIAM CODY SARGENT

Copyright © 2019 by William Cody Sargent.

PAPERBACK: 978-1-950540-76-1
EBOOK: 978-1-950540-77-8

All rights reserved. No part of this publication may be reproduced, distributed, or transmitted in any form or by any electronic or mechanical means, without the prior written permission of the publisher, except in the case of brief quotations embodied in critical reviews and certain other noncommercial uses permitted by copyright law.

Ordering Information:

For orders and inquiries, please contact:
1-888-375-9818
www.toplinkpublishing.com
bookorder@toplinkpublishing.com

Printed in the United States of America

Acknowledgements

While writing this novel, the following people were either instrumental or supportive when I needed them.

My wife Ginger, whose ideas always inspires me.

Vicky Swafford, who taught me everything I know about telling a good story.

Tabitha Cash, who I lean on sometimes too much.

John Williams, a good friend who seemed to know the answers when I hit a brick wall.

Dene Tham, whose wisdom has never failed me.

CHAPTER *1*

Friday June 6th 2003

Minute Maid Park, Houston, Texas

Omar Abuo lay face down, watching his brother's blood pool and commingle with water from the sprinkler system, then snake an eerie trail to the drainage grate a few feet away. Through one eye he could see the fireworks display streaming over the stadium walls in a luminous cascade oft plumes and brilliant fire bursts, reds, blues and greens. The sound of each burst echoed off the buildings and parking garages surrounding Minute Maid Park.

He struggled with the tightly wrapped duct tape around his wrists, ankles and mouth, but it was no use. He watched the killer drag his brother's lifeless body into the darkness and stay there for what seemed like an eternity. How long before he would come for him? It was only a matter of time, he thought. What was he doing to Youssef's body? If he could only see; if he could only turn himself in that direction; it seemed hopeless.

He wanted so desperately to touch Youssef's hand one last time in a venial attempt to somehow explain how this had happened and that it wasn't his fault. He knew that if he could just talk to Youssef he could make him understand.

As tears spilled from his eyes, his mind raced with thoughts and scenes from the past. The most vivid and daunting were the warnings from his mother that slashed at his heart like a serpent. She had spent more than two days pleading with her two young sons not to go to America. "What's wrong with the universities in

Alexandria and Cairo?" she asked repeatedly. "You're unprepared for the decadent life styles that the Americans live," she reasoned. When all else failed she warned them, "There will be consequences and retributions from God for your refusal to listen to the voice of wisdom and reason."

He should have known that her words would someday become the nails in his coffin. Suddenly, without warning, the killer was on him, turning him over. For the first time he could see the killer's face. His body was covered in Youssef's blood, but what was the man wearing? It looked like a jumpsuit of some sort made of clear plastic. The killer grabbed him by the lapels of his jacket lifting his torso off the concrete. Just as his head involuntarily arched backward from its own weight, the killer swung the curved blade weapon cutting his throat just as he had Youssef's.

For a moment there was a sound like air escaping from a congealed or bubbling liquid. Aside from that, the only recognizable anomaly was an involuntary twitching of his left eyelid. He could feel the killer removing the duct tape from his ankles and wrists and for a fraction of a second he wanted to command his brain to react, to kick, or to attack his killer with his freed hands. He could do neither. The last clear thought that his mind registered was a lament that he hadn't listened to his mother. He closed his eyes and quietly died.

When the fireworks display was over, a bank of lights on the north side of Minute Maid Park came on, lighting the walkways and the concrete sidewalks along Crawford Street. It would take another eight minutes for the crowd to spill out of the stadium and into the surrounding streets and find the slain bodies of Youssef and Omar Abuo.

Richey Sneed snorted his last two lines of cocaine off a mirror from his wife's handbag. Beverly Sneed had gone into a Stop-And-Go to use the restroom and pick up a couple bottles of cheap wine from the cooler. She gave the attendant her last twenty dollars to pay for the wine and a package of Marlboro Lights, then staggered out the door and headed for the van where Richey was waiting.

"Hey genius," she started. "You got any bright ideas on where our next money is coming from? And don't even think about me turning tricks for it, cause I just got my period, and I ain't doing it tonight," she snarled through the open window.

Richey Sneed hadn't heard a word she said. The buzz from the coke had taken him out of any meaningful reality and dropped him in a place where nothing else mattered, and common audible sounds didn't exist anymore. Beverly unscrewed the cap from one of the bottles of Boone's Farm and turned it up. When she set the bottle in her lap, it was half-empty. She looked at it listlessly, lit a cigarette, and punched her husband in the stomach. "Wake up Richey. You lousy piece of...," she stopped in mid-sentence when she noticed the mirror from her purse in his lap.

"I do not believe this." She frowned and punched him again. "You snorted the last of the coke, didn't you? I don't believe you did that, Richey. What about me? Do you ever think about me? Where's mine? Wake up, Richey."

She licked her index finger and ran it across the face of the mirror then stuck it in her mouth. It wasn't enough, the kick wasn't there and she needed a bump. She punched Richey again and took another shot of Boone's Farm then flipped her cigarette out the open window, wiping at the corner of her mouth with the back of her hand.

"Wake up Richey," she yelled. Before she realized what she was doing she poured some of the wine over his head and watched it spill over his face and onto his chest. His eyes opened with a venomous glare. It was a mistake and she knew it instantly. He slapped the bottle out of her hand then slapped her face. Her reactions were too slow to see the coming blows. She tried to slide out of the seat and into the back of the van but he stayed on top of her, slapping her again and again. She held her hands in front of her face, pleading with him to stop, but it only made him more violent and aggressive.

When she finally slid her way to the back of the van with nowhere else to go, he put his hands around her neck and began choking her. Her body was heaving and slithering from side-to-side across the floor of the van like a wounded animal. He ripped open her blouse exposing her breasts and lacy white bra. Suddenly her defensive posture changed and she smiled a devil's smile. Then before he knew what she was doing she drew him close and kissed him hard on the lips.

"Come on baby, you want to rape me? Do it, do it now," she taunted him, knowing that the coke he had just snorted would yield him impotent and unable to perform.

He leaned back away from her, still holding her blouse in his hands. He wiped the sweat and wine from his forehead while releasing her and falling against the wall of the van. He lay dazed and unmoving, unable to form a coherent thought, ashamed of his wrath and violence against his wife.

"It's okay baby. I know you didn't mean it, I know you'd never hurt me. I shouldn't have poured the wine on you. We just need to get some money, that's all, so we can have a little party. You got to think, baby. Where are we going to come up with enough money to last us for a while? Think Richey, think," she coaxed him.

He wiped at his face with the palms of his hands then ran his fingers through his hair. The coke was still zapping him. He shook his head in an attempt to clear the cobwebs and bring himself out of the stupor.

After several moments he sat up on the floor of the van and wiped his eyes with a paper towel he found on the top of a tool tray. He blinked several times then looked at her as thoughtfully as his brain would allow.

"I know where to get the money," he said, blowing his nose on the paper towel. "I know where we can get all the money we'll need for a long time to come." He watched her face in the dim light as a trickle of blood moved from the corner of her mouth onto her chin. He ran a thumb across her face smearing the blood, then pulled her to him and kissed her softly on the lips before letting her go.

4

At that moment two teenage boys in a purple Dodge Avenger convertible pulled into the parking lot and circled the gas pumps before parking a few spaces from the van. The top was down on the convertible and a song was playing loudly on the stereo. It was an old song by the Eagles, "Life in the Fast Lane". Richey Sneed listened to the lyrics for a moment then looked at his wife, a smile covering his face.

"Ain't it hell living in the fast lane?" he said. "Now let's go get that money."

Redhawk Simmons was a man with a vile and pernicious past. His Chiricahua Apache ancestry could be traced to Cochise, one of the most legendary of all the Apache. He seemed to wear his abhorrent nature like an inexorable badge of honor. In and out of one prison after another, his last stint landed him in Huntsville, Texas, serving a twenty-year stretch for manslaughter. One more brush with the law and he'd be locked up for good, he told himself.

But with prison overcrowding in Texas as bad as it had ever been, he saw a light at the end of the tunnel when he was offered parole. He served ten years of his sentence and was released to a halfway house in Houston. Upon arriving at the halfway house a thought crossed his mind about taking a path that many of his ancestors had taken when the Calvary or Texas Rangers were on their heels and head straight for the border of Mexico just a few hours away. But for reasons he was never fully understood, he decided to give the halfway house a chance and forget about Mexico at least for a while. The only problem he could see now would be staying out of the local bars, and away from the troubles that always seemed to track him down like a fugitive.

Over the next two years he worked at menial jobs, none lasting more than a few months at a time. But in January of 2002, he got a job with the Alabama Coushatta tribe just outside of Livingston, making hunting knives for sale in the tourist shops on the reservation. It was the only thing in his life he had ever been good at. And because of his heritage and ties to western folklore and the mystic persona of Cochise, the sales of his custom knives soared over night, and the money began pouring in.

In January of 2003, The Houston Chronicle ran an article on the Coushatta Tribe, about their struggles with the State legislature, which for years had denied the tribe's requests to reopen the casino they had built on the reservation just outside of Livingston. The article didn't do a thing to help re-open the casino, but it showed a number of photographs of products sold by the Tribe. Among them was a set of engraved Bowie knives, made by Redhawk Simmons that would later be adapted for national sales to knife collectors from Maine to California.

The recognition Simmons received from the newspaper article and later on from the Internet, took the small knife making operation to heights that no one on the reservation could believe. The phones never stopped ringing with new orders. And it seemed as if no price was too much for one of his custom-made knives. What had started out as a struggle for survival had turned into an overnight success!

When Simmons first began working in the tiny shop behind the main showroom, he offered knife sharpening as one of his services to help pay the bills. Hunters would come from all over east Texas to have Simmons hone a razor-sharp edge on their favorite skinning knife. But now because of the influx of orders for his custom-made knives, he was seriously considering curtailing or discontinuing the service of knife sharpening altogether.

Simmons had always been the consummate loner, never socializing or dating much. But now it wasn't just the Indian population that called him by name or looked on him with the reverence and attention he knew so little about. For the first time in his life, rich, white men were calling him Mr. Simmons or Mr. Redhawk, and waiting hours to speak with him or have him show them one of his knives.

Everyone seemed to know about his being an ancestor of Cochise, and the legends that followed his name. People clambered for his autograph on something he had made or sharpened, almost as if he were a rock star. He soaked it all in and began to recognize the same customers buying his products over and over, even becoming friends with many of them, which seemed odd and a little disconcerting at times, given his previous history with strangers.

But of all the customers whom he became acquainted with in his newfound popularity and trade, one troubled him more than all the rest.

The man came in every few weeks and always with the same knife. It had an unusual curved blade, sharpened on both sides like a dagger or sword. The man rarely spoke, and almost never stayed in the store while Simmons sharpened his knife. He just appeared, collected a claim-check, and quickly left the store. A few days later he'd reappear to retrieve his knife. He always paid in cash and never left an address or phone number where he could be reached.

No one had ever had such a negative effect on Simmons, not even when he was in prison. It was like dealing with the Devil himself, Simmons had told one of the workers at the store. Anytime the man brought the knife in, Simmons sharpened it as quickly as he could so that he would be done when the strange man came back for it. He wanted the knife and the man out of his presence and out of the store as quickly as possible. It was a sensation Simmons had never dealt with before, on any level, adversarial or otherwise. It was pure unadulterated fear, and it shook him to the core of his being.

Nizar Kheif inhaled the aroma of the flowering citrus groves that flourished along the Awwali River, lingering as long as he could in the place where he'd grown up as a child. But as the sun began to rise, and the sounds of night faded, he pulled on his backpack and headed for Beirut. Before the sun set that evening he boarded a plane for New York City. A day later his journey would end in Houston. Over the next five years he would attend the University of Houston, earning a degree with honors in structural engineering.

After graduation, and the termination of his educational visa, he was offered a position with Brown and Root; an engineering and construction company based in Houston. And, because of the nature of the project he was assigned to, he was granted a work visa and later, an opportunity to apply for citizenship.

The project would allow him to work with people from the Texas Highway Department, The Department of Transportation, and the Army Corp of Engineers, in the design and construction of several major bridges spanning the Houston Ship Channel. Over the next twelve years his dedication to the project gained him recognition as far away as Austin and the Governor's mansion. Governor Ann Richards had sent him a letter personally acknowledging his perseverance and dedication to the projects, and the State's appreciation for his service.

Kheif also received letters of recommendation for his citizenship. With the right people pulling the right strings, he was a United States Citizen before the project reached the halfway point of completion. It was all he needed to send for Marta and begin planning the wedding he had waited for most of his life.

Over the next ten years Kheif and Marta had three children and bought a home in Pasadena which was close enough to the last bridge of the project that would span the ship channel on Highway 146, near Laporte. It was one of the largest suspension bridges in the southwest and brought Kheif even more notoriety and a hefty raise in pay.

Kheif was good with money and, although conservative, he managed to build a sizable portfolio with stocks and cash holdings in excess of two hundred thousand dollars by the end of 1999. It was just enough to capture another of his dreams he'd had since he was a young boy growing up on the Syrian border. He wanted to own his own business.

In May of 2000, he purchased a convenience store in northeast Houston, on Aldine Mail Route, across from a Library and Aldine

High School. He moved his family from Pasadena into a rent house behind the store and he and Marta started to work. In the months ahead, they transformed the rundown location into a clean and viable place of business. They called it The Pit Stop.

Operating the convenience store was a lot harder than Kheif had expected, and the money didn't come as easily as he thought it would. There was always something broken or in need of repair and every penny they made had to be plowed back into the store to keep it clean and looking presentable. And, to complicate matters, the long hours and lack of money were draining on the marriage. With Marta working days and Kheif working until midnight every night, they had little time for each other and almost none for the children.

Things had deteriorated to the point that in October of 2002, he entertained selling the place to an investor and going back into the engineering business. But someone suggested that he start cashing payroll checks for the hundreds of workers from the nearby factories. After several meetings with his bank and attorneys, he pledged the last of his stock portfolio for a sizeable loan, and went into the check cashing business.

Kheif and Marta were skeptical at first. It seemed like such an insignificant thing, cashing payroll checks. They charged one-percent of the total check amount for each check they cashed. Most of the checks were between three hundred and six hundred dollars. The average take was four dollars and fifty cents per check. They cashed over eight hundred checks per week. And once the workers had a pocket full of money, they almost always bought something before leaving the store.

By June of 2003, the convenience store was clearing more than twenty thousand dollars a month. And there was plenty of money to hire two clerks to work the day shift, so that Marta could spend more time with the children and cook Kheif's favorite meals before his shift began in the evening.

Richey Sneed flipped the indicator switch up, veering right onto Highway 59, northbound. He lit a cigarette, turned the radio down, and started talking to his wife.

"Listen to me," he said, shaking her on the arm. She had been staring out the window, half asleep and half in a malaise brought on by the wine. She rubbed her eyes and turned to face him but she didn't speak.

"Look, I know this place. It's on Aldine Mail Route, about six miles from here. The place is owned by some rag-head named Kheif, or something. He cashes payroll checks for all the businesses around there." Beverly Sneed lit a cigarette and looked at him as if he was speaking a language she'd never heard before.

"I'm so sure this rag-head is going to be cashing checks on a Friday night, at midnight. You're not thinking right, Richey," she almost shouted.

"Calm down, baby. That's just it, he does cash checks on Friday night. That's why we got to get there in the next twenty minutes, stick the place up, and get out, before they get off. Remember that big machine shop on Winfield road? Your cousin Harlow used to work there. Don't you remember? We picked him up there a few times," he said. She was listening now, but none of what he was saying made any sense.

"The second shift gets off at eleven. There must be a hundred guys with checks to cash, and only one place in town to cash them and buy beer that late on Friday night. That rag-head has got stacks of cash just waiting to be picked up," he said.

She took a long drag on her cigarette and allowed the smoke to drift out of her mouth and nose when she talked back to Richey. "So you're saying we're going to rob this place now, tonight? You're coked-up and I'm half wasted on wine and meth, and this is your bright idea?"

"You got a better one? What's your plan for the weekend? You think your brother is going to give us enough of his stash for us to get by all weekend? The answer to that question is no. We don't have much of a choice, as I see it, do we?"

"Does this guy have a gun? What if you go in this place and this guy has a gun? What happens, Richey? Promise me you're not going to kill this guy. If you kill this guy, they're going to kill us; you know that don't you, Richey?" "Yeah, I know the consequences for armed robbery and murder in this state, but we ought to be in and out of there in ten minutes. Look, here's the deal: We have to go in through the rear of the store because he's got surveillance cameras facing the cash register and front door area of the store."

"Are you sure they're the only cameras in the place? Do they have an ATM machine? I know that anywhere there's an ATM they film your transactions." "The ATM is in the back of the store and away from the front; they won't be able to record what we're doing from the ATM camera. Just don't go to the back of the store. Stay away from the ATM," he raised his voice.

"Oh Richey you can't plan something like this on a whim," she said, leaning back in her chair. She took another pull on the cigarette and threw it out the window, showing her disgust with his plan to rob the store.

Richey pulled the van onto the shoulder of the freeway and stopped. He lit a cigarette, tossed the pack on the dashboard of the van and folded his arms as if he were contemplating the speech he was about to give her.

"Look baby, the only reason you ain't climbing the walls of this van is because you swigged down a fifth of wine. But that's going to wear off in a few hours and you're going to want something more than wine. Now, I need to know what you want me to do. We don't have time to debate this. I know it's a spur-of-the-moment kind of deal. I know it's risky, but I don't have any other answers on how we're going to come up with more money at ten o'clock on Friday night. Talk to me, baby; 'cause I'm all ears."

She stared out the window at the shacks and dingy buildings fronting Crosstimbers Road. From the overpass of the freeway she could see into the sparsely lit neighborhood and rundown businesses along the frontage, and she knew that it was drugs that had destroyed most of the lives of the people who lived there. The scene was depressing, but not nearly as depressing as the thought of curtailing the addictions that ravaged her body and spun both their lives so out of control.

"Okay, Richey, I know we got to do it, but please baby, don't kill anybody."

"I ain't going to kill anybody. As long as the rag-head is cool, I'll be cool. Okay, this is how we play it. We go in through the back; you hold the gun on the rag-head while I cut the cable on the cameras. Once I'm done I'll take over, you go back to the van and be ready to drive. Make sure to move him away from any buttons or silent alarm switches, make him stand in one place until I'm done."

"How long will it take you to cut the cables?"

"Only a matter of seconds, you'll only have the gun for a minute or two at most. Once I've cut the cable, I'll take the gun, get the money, knock out the rag-head, and we're gone. We head back downtown where we can score enough drugs to last us for a while. What comes next is we have a nice long weekend in the country. Maybe we'll go over to Garner State Park and rent one of those cabins, maybe do a little fishing," he said, a broad grin covering his face like he was talking about attending a church social.

"It sounds too easy," she said looking out the window again.

Richey Sneed didn't say another word. He lit another cigarette, started the van and headed for Aldine Mail Route.

Redhawk Simmons turned out the lights, then locked and bolted the storefront. It had been a long busy day and he thought he needed a drink. But he knew he couldn't do that and get away with it. What he really needed was a day off, maybe a few days to do some fishing or hunting for that big buck he'd seen two days ago as he drove onto the reservation. He couldn't believe he was starting to think and act as someone who wasn't a miscreant or wanted by the law.

He stepped out onto the redwood decking that ran between the store and the three-room house the Coushatta's had built for him as a reward for his hard work. The night was warm and clear and the smell of honeysuckle and night blooming jasmine filled the night air with sweetness he had never known before. He looked at the stars through the canopy of tall pines and another smell tickled his senses. It was the searing of white bass and onions in a frying pan on his stove.

Simmons opened the cottage door and stepped inside just in time to see Renee Harjo walking away from the table she had just set. Having a woman in his life was another thing he was learning to accept, but it came a lot easier than all the other changes he was facing.

He met Renee in his second week on the reservation. She worked as a tribal social worker and lived on the reservation working with troubled teens and unwed mothers. They had little in common aside from the fact that they had lived most of their lives as loners, until now. Maybe it was her kindness or gentle spirit that he enjoyed. Whatever the virtue was, it affected him in a way he couldn't explain and yet had no intention of changing.

"I'm running late, Redhawk," she apologized. "Why don't you wash for dinner and watch the news or something? Everything should be ready in fifteen minutes," she yelled from the kitchen.

"I could smell the fish cooking from the store. I hope it taste as good as it smells," he said. He listened for her to say something but when she didn't he headed for the restroom to wash for dinner.

When he walked back into the living room Renee had turned the television on and the ten o'clock news promo was on the screen. He sat on the couch as the anchorman begins to speak.

"This just in, channel 2 news has just learned that the bodies of two men have been found just outside the stadium complex at Minute Maid Park. The men have yet to be identified but sources close to the crime-scene said the men are believed to be Arabs. Both men had their

throats cut and sources believe this could be the work of the person or persons responsible for the deaths of at least three other men of Arabian decent over the last four months. We'll keep you posted as this story develops and will attempt to have an interview at the scene before this broadcast ends."

Simmons moved to the edge of the cushion, and with the remote control in his hand, punched the button that turned the set off. He swallowed hard running his hands through his hair. He held his hands in front of him watching them shake uncontrollably. He stood and walked to the front door, then back to the sofa, and after a second, back to the front door. He had never wanted to run from any place so badly in his life.

But that wasn't the answer and he knew it. If the strange man brought the knife in tomorrow to be sharpened, he'd know for sure that he was the killer, because he had done it three times before. It didn't make much sense to get paranoid before then, he told himself. Simmons closed his eyes and tried to think of other things, quiet things, and peaceful things. It was something he'd learned to do in prison when he was thrown in solitary confinement, otherwise known as the "hole". He almost jumped out of his skin when he felt a hand latch on to his shoulder.

"I didn't mean to startle you, Redhawk," she said softly. "Are you alright? Is something wrong?" She walked around to the front of the couch and kneeled in front of him. "I've never seen you act like this, Redhawk."

"It's nothing," he waved a dismissive hand through the air. "I must have dozed off and was having a bad dream or something," he lied unconvincingly.

"Well, come to dinner. I've been calling you for the past five minutes. You looked as if you were in a trance or something. You frightened me," she said patting him on the shoulder.

"It was just a bad dream, that's all," he said. "Just a bad dream."

Richey Sneed cut the Master Lock on the back door of the convenience store with a set of bolt cutters from his toolbox. When he pulled the hasp away from the metal loop the door opened of its own accord. He sat the bolt cutters against the outside wall and stepped inside the darkened storage room; Beverly Sneed mirrored his every move.

The storage area extended the whole length of the store providing rear access to the coolers and enough storage space for supplies to keep the store stocked for several days. There was also an office and a set of restrooms along the back wall of the space. Directly across from the rear door was a set of double doors leading to the store itself. The door on the right had a one-way mirrored glass in the upper portion of the door so that anyone working in the rear of the store could see anything happening at the register and down the two rear aisles.

Richey stopped at the mirrored door, took a deep breath and for a moment watched a woman in a floor length brown dress, counting a large stack of bills behind the register. If anyone else was in the store he couldn't see him. He turned and handed Beverly the 9mm Tarus semi-automatic. She wasn't very thoughtful of the situation or of her surroundings.

She took the handgun, burst through the door and immediately began shouting at the woman behind the counter. And although the woman was temporarily startled by Beverly's sudden emergence, she began yelling back at Beverly in a language that neither she nor Richey understood.

Richey moved to the first of the two surveillance cameras mounted high on the wall to the right of the swinging door. He climbed the shelves and cut the cable on the first one. But before he could reach the camera on the other side of the swinging, mirrored door, the screaming woman emerged from behind the counter and struck Beverly across the face with a long heavy, wooden rod.

The blow knocked Beverly into the shelves running along the back wall of the store, sending cans of evaporated milk and jars of baby food and formula flying in all directions. The woman charged

Beverly and was poised to hit her again when Beverly started firing the 9mm. The first round went through the acoustical ceiling tiles and imbedded itself somewhere in the roof of the building. The second round caught the woman in the right front shoulder, throwing her to the floor behind the cash register.

Beverly was holding the weapon with both hands when she managed to get to her feet. Before Richey could say a word or move towards the fallen woman, Beverly had lunged to the edge of the counter and pumped two more rounds into the bleeding woman. The woman never moved again.

Just when Richey thought it was over, from the back corner of the store, a middle-aged man holding a half-gallon of milk dropped the carton to the floor and made a dash for the front of the store. When he made the turn around the back row of shelves, Beverly pointed the gun in his direction, firing two rounds that hit him squarely in his chest. The man's dead body skidded to a stop just before it hit the counter, his head almost touching the feet of the dead woman.

Richey couldn't believe what had just happened. In the blink of an eye two people were dead, killed by a woman who couldn't stand the thought of someone being killed in the robbery. He had to get the gun out of her hand before she shot him, he thought. He called her name, but she didn't answer.

She just stood there like someone frozen in cement.

Slowly, he climbed down from the shelf, talking softly to her as he moved. Finally she looked at him and dropped the weapon to the floor, her mouth gaped open in disbelief. She looked ghastly, he thought. Her face and left eye were swelling from the blow the woman had given her, and her nose was dripping blood from the fall.

"Richey" she started to scream his name as the realization of what just happened seized her.

She didn't stop screaming until Richey grabbed her, shaking her violently. Then before he knew it he was holding her tightly, trying desperately to calm her enough to get her out of the store before she became totally hysterical.

He let her go for a moment and grabbed the stack of cash from the counter, stuffing it into a large paper bag. He retrieved the 9mm from the floor, took Beverly by the hand and headed for the rear of the store.

Just as he moved through the mirrored door he saw the rear door opening and the woman's husband rushing into the storage area. Richey was glad he hadn't turned the lights on in the storage area, as it gave him an edge the Arab didn't have. When Richey reached the storming man he jumped high, dropkicking the man in the chest, knocking him into the door jam. The momentum of the kick threw him forward again and Richey hit him across the top of his head with the butt of the 9mm. The Arab never saw the blow coming and lay on the floor unmoving and bleeding profusely.

Richey threw the bag of money through the open window of the van and helped Beverly into her seat, buckling her in tight. Seconds later, he had the van on Aldine Mail Route turning right on John F. Kennedy Boulevard. He heard sirens when he reached Beltway 8, but he was too far away from the crime scene to be associated with the robbery. He looked at Beverly and touched her cold hand, searching for the right thing to say. But before he could find the words, she vomited on the dashboard and a second time out the window of the van a few moments later.

CHAPTER *2*

Wade Gorman had heard the whispers around the station. He knew how things got started. A rumor here, a tiny bit of fact there, and before the truth had a chance to surface, the story was circulated that his wife had left him and cleaned him out financially. When the story did finally make it back to him, he was amazed at how accurate the rumor mill had become.

It was true that his wife of fifteen years had left him. But the estrangement and subsequent asset split, for the most part, had been arrived at, and agreed upon by both parties. Those same parties were also consenting to the divorce. There were no children in the marriage for anyone to fight over. And what money and property they had amassed seemed fairly easy to divide.

Since she was the one who had been transferred to Seattle, she couldn't very easily keep or use the house and furnishings in Houston. And he wasn't interested in selling the home he'd worked so hard to build. So, except for two thousand seven hundred dollars in his checking account, she took the sum of twelve years of savings by the both of them, which totaled almost three hundred thousand dollars, and headed for Seattle, leaving him the house and everything in it. Its net worth was somewhere in the neighborhood of three hundred thousand dollars.

There were no hidden lovers, no back alley, sultry romances to be uncovered or fought over. It was so simple it was almost frightening. They came to an impasse in their lives, calmly discussed the options, and decided to split it all right down the middle. It was a divorce made in heaven, he told one of his neighbors.

Now that it was over, he could put in the hours he wanted; be as ambitious as he pleased or do nothing at all, if that suited him. But Gorman loved to work. He was already one of the first black Captains in the department, but he had his eyes set on The Chief of Police position. And he felt sure he'd get it after Bill White was elected Mayor of Houston in November; it was just a matter of time, he thought.

It was after ten o'clock when his phone rang. He answered it on the second ring recognizing the voice on the other end as Gloria Bonds from dispatch.

"Captain, I'm so glad you're still here. This has been a night from hell.

There must be a full moon or something," she started.

"What's the problem, aside from the fact that we live in one of the largest cities in the country, and people like killing each other?"

"There's been a double homicide at Minute Maid Park and it looks like someone almost cut the heads off of two Arab guys, and left them in a fenced area on the north side of the ballpark. There are a dozen uniformed officers on the scene doing crowd control. They really think one of the detectives needs to see this before the crime scene becomes any more contaminated. And Sir, if that's not enough, we've got three other shootings, two robberies, three domestic disturbances, and two bar room brawls, but no one left that's qualified to take this one. Can you get someone? Or, do I need to call someone else?"

"Call Clayton and Stillwell and tell them to get down here now," he told her.

"Stillwell won't be back from vacation for another week, Captain. I'll call Detective Clayton and tell him what's going on," she hesitated and cleared her throat as if there were more she wanted to say.

"Spit it out, woman, what on your mind?"

"Well Sir, I wanted to say that I'm sorry about what happened between you and your wife, I'm sure things will get better for you, but don't bury yourself in this job, it's too much. You're working all these hours and I'm just afraid you're going to flame out. Do you know what I mean, Captain?" Her voice was quivering as she spoke. Gorman knew that the woman had had a huge crush on him for years. But he couldn't bring himself to get close to a woman who weighed over three hundred pounds and spent all of her free time at the wrestling matches.

"Thanks, Gloria. You're very kind but believe it or not, I'm not miserable. I'm even working a few of these cases myself while everyone's either on vacation or at that symposium with Mayor Brown," he said.

"I didn't mean to intrude, Captain Gorman. Please let me know if there is anything I can do for you...anything at all." She disconnected the line.

It was 10:30 when Clayton called back.

"I need you to come in, Clayton. What on earth is that noise? You're not in a night club, are you?"

"Not at all, I'm at a Three Doors Down concert, Captain. The song you're hearing is called "Kryptonite". What's up?"

"I need you to get to the station as quickly as you can. I want you and Stillwell to concentrate on these Arab killings; we may have a serial killer working Houston and I want it stopped. From what I've been told it appears that two more persons of Arab decent have been killed tonight. We're going to be in a lot of trouble with the press if we don't stop this guy and do it soon."

"I don't know whether you know it or not, Captain, but I'm off duty, and I'm on a date, and Stillwell is on vacation with some tuba player," he rolled his eyes at the thought of his partner shacked up with a musician.

"I don't care if she's on tour with Ray Charles. You find her and get her back in town. I want everybody working till we catch this guy."

"You got to understand Captain, I'm off this weekend. And this good looking blond in a tight red dress is supposed to be going home with me and sleeping in my bed tonight. There's not going to be a lot of fun happening in that bed if I'm not there, Captain. I know you know what I'm talking about," he whispered to Gorman.

"Just put a lid on that for now. I want you here in thirty minutes and I'm tired of yelling at you with all that noise in the background. Just get rid of miss hot pants and get in here, now!" Gorman said, slamming the phone in its cradle.

Delores Rucker loved everything there was about being a cop. Her career started with the HPD Forensics team, mainly because her degree was in pre-med and Forensics seemed a natural fit. After the first eighteen months in Forensics, she used her friendship with Leona Stillwell to get into the Police Academy, and because of her education and the fact that she had worked in forensics, the move to Homicide as a second grade detective under Ross Clayton and Leona Stillwell seemed only a natural progression. But after three years on the force working to help solve some of the highest profile cases in the city's history, she decided to fulfill a promise she had made to her father just before he passed away.

Tom Rucker, her father, worked in a small town mortuary in Galveston. But his dream had always been to be a Doctor of Pathology in Dallas or Houston, performing autopsies on murder victims, helping the police solve horrible crimes, writing opinions and pioneering new procedures for after life studies. But because of his wife's untimely death, he was forced to leave medical school and take a job in his hometown where the mortuary provided him with adequate living accommodations, a steady income, and a decent place to raise a daughter who loved him.

Now Delores Rucker was within eighteen months of having what her father had always wanted for himself and later on for his daughter, a doctorate in pathology. All that remained was six more months of intern duties, and a year of residency. But she was burned out and in desperate need of a break; so she had taken the summer off to rest and regroup.

And aside from rest, she needed money; so her plan was to earn a few bucks working either at The Houston Police Department (HPD) or at one of the many summer jobs offered on the Baylor Campus.

Her dorm room was small, resembling a mid-level motel room. It had a place to study, a place to shower and take care of the necessities, and a place to sleep. There was what resembled a couch on the back wall and a portable television set, which she rarely watched, that set atop a small refrigerator that was almost always empty.

For the first time in months everything she owned was cleaned, ironed, and stored away neatly. And her room looked the way it did when she moved in. She lay on the couch and turned on the television set and within minutes was sound asleep. The phone must have rung a dozen times before she awoke, found it, and said hello.

"Delores, thank goodness you're there. I need your help," Clayton started. "Who, who is this?"

"It's Ross Clayton. Did I wake you? I don't know why, I just thought you'd be studying, or something."

"I'm not taking classes this summer. I need some time off and I need to earn some money if I want to continue to eat next semester," she said, covering a yawn with her hand.

"Well maybe the timing is good then. Stillwell is off on vacation with that idiot she's dating, and Gorman thinks we've got a serial killer running loose. Can you help us for a few weeks? It would mean a lot to me."

"When is Stillwell coming back? And the guy she's dating is not an idiot, Clayton. Idiots don't play with the Houston Symphony Orchestra. He might be a nerd, he might not dress very well, but he's no idiot."

"She's supposed to be back a week from Monday, but Gorman wants her back now. I think it would be better if you call her and tell her Gorman wants her to cut her vacation short and come back right away, and tell her I've asked you to help us with this serial killer thing too."

"Ross Clayton, I thought Leona Stillwell was your best friend in the whole world. Why do you want me to call her?"

"I don't seem to have much patience when it comes to her tuba playing friend. I somehow manage to say the wrong thing," he said.

"You think? First of all, the man doesn't play a tuba it's an oboe. There's a difference, I think. Do you have a number where she can be reached?"

"Are you going to work with us or not? Because if you are, I need to pick you up in twenty minutes and get over to Minute Maid Park. You can call Stillwell on my cell phone from the car. C'mon, D, this is important."

"The killing took place at the ballpark?

"That's what they tell me."

"Are you going to pay me overtime?"

"Yeah, whatever you want; I just need your help."

"I'll be ready in ten minutes," she said, hanging up the phone.

Before Wade Gorman reached Minute Maid Park, his cell phone rang and Gloria Bonds started talking as soon as he said hello.

"Captain, we've had a robbery homicide with two killed, at a convenience store on Aldine Mail Route. Uniformed officers are on the scene with the forensics people but their asking for a detective or a supervisor. Can you take it?"

"Yeah, I'll take it. What's the name of the place?"

"It's called The Pit-Stop. The address is 2415 Aldine Mail Route. Thank you, Captain Gorman."

Gorman called Ross Clayton on his cell phone and explained that he wouldn't be meeting them at the ballpark. He took Washington Avenue to Interstate 45, and when he reached the loop he headed for Highway 59, taking the north exit. It took another twenty minutes to reach Aldine Mail Route and find the convenience store.

It was eleven twenty-five when Gorman pulled into the parking lot and got out of the squad car. He pushed his badge holder in his jacket pocket and headed inside. The glass front doors were in the open position, and cold air was streaming through the open doors when he walked inside.

Carlin Belichec, the Harris County medical examiner, was leaning against the front counter digging in the bowl of his pipe with a small pin-knife.

Belichec was tall and balding and always appeared to be under-nourished. He was wearing a blue pinstriped shirt and a blue and turquoise bowtie.

"Wade Gorman, I haven't seen you in a month-of-Sundays. How in the world are you?" He held out his hands in Gorman's direction.

"Never felt better, Doc, how have you been?" The two men shook hands then embraced briefly.

"This is a little past you're bedtime, Doc. What gives?" Gorman looked at his watch as if he were checking the time.

"Same as you, I suppose. Seems we're all running a little short staffed these days. Sorry to hear about you and the wife. But you don't seem any worse for wear. Is everything okay, Wade?" A troubled look covered the Doctor's face.

"It's all good, Doc. We're both happy now. Now, tell me what we got here."

"From what we've been able to piece together, at least two people came into the store from this back door," Belichec walked Gorman halfway to the door showing the cut lock on the floor. They were standing just inside the storage area. "This swinging door was closed, so the robbers got a good look at everything inside the store before they came in. Once inside one of them cut the cables to the surveillance cameras while the other set out to grab the money. That's when the action started." The two men were standing back at the bodies when Belichec picked up a bloody wooden rod from the floor and showed it to Gorman.

"It appears that the woman behind the counter stepped out here and whacked one of the robbers with this wooden pole. There's blood on it and I'm sure it came from the robber who was trying to collect the money. I think it was at that point the robber started shooting.

24

We found six shell casings from a 9mm. Both victims have been shot with what appears to be the same gun, but we won't know for sure until ballistics looks at it."

"What about this guy? Why was he shot?"

"Don't really know. But it appears that he was running at full speed when the shooter clocked him. He must have skidded two feet or more before stopping here. Neither body has been moved; they both bled out where they lay."

"How much money would a convenience store hold this late on a Friday night? Probably not more than five or six hundred at the most," Gorman speculated.

"How about forty five thousand?" Belichec said, waiting to see the expression on Gorman's face.

"Say what? I've got to get my hearing checked. Did you just say forty five thousand dollars? Why would they have that much money in the store? No wonder they were robbed."

"I talked to the woman's husband. He was just loaded into that ambulance," Belichec pointed to an ambulance in the parking lot with its lights flashing. "If you want to ask him any questions you'd better do it now."

"Has he been shot? Is he coherent?"

"He came in just as the robbers were on the way out. He says he didn't see much before one of them kicked him in the chest and hit him in the head with something heavy. From the looks of the wound I think it was the butt of the 9mm but I'm not for sure. He needs to get to the hospital, so you'd better hurry." Gorman began moving in the direction of the ambulance before Belichec finished telling him about the man's injuries. Gorman pounded on the rear door of the Ambulance then opened the door.

He stepped inside the ambulance and sat quietly for a moment as the EMT finished inserting an IV tube in the man's arm.

Gorman put his hand on the technicians back and began talking to the wounded man.

"Sir, I'm Captain Wade Gorman with HPD. Can you tell me anything about the men who did this? Were they black, white, Hispanic? Were there just two? How many did you see? Gorman pulled a small spiral notepad from his jacket and was poised to take notes and, for some reason, felt uncomfortable looking at the man. When he did finally look into the man's face, it was the picture of hate.

"It should have been me instead of my Marta. I want these people brought to justice. Bring them to me, Captain, and I will kill them myself. My Marta was a kind and generous woman. She didn't deserve to die at the hands of these criminals." Gorman thought he was about to say something else when he suddenly stopped speaking and breathing. His head jerked back in several violent gasps for air.

The EMT moved in front of Gorman and began inserting a long clear plastic breathing tube in the man's throat. He said something to the driver then looked back at Gorman. "If you're going with us close the door. If you're not you need to get out now. We have to get him to the hospital now or I'm afraid he's not going to make it."

Gorman pushed the door open and stepped out of the ambulance. As he closed the door he thought of something he wanted to ask the EMT, but before he could open the door again the ambulance was gone. He stood there for a moment attempting to digest everything that just happened. He was still puzzled by the question he wanted to ask.

He met Belichec coming out of the store as four men with metal stretchers wheeled them inside the store to collect the bodies.

"Is there any reason you want to keep the bodies any longer?" he asked. "No, I think the bodies can go. What I do want is any DNA we can get off of the club the woman used on the bad guy, and I want everything in the place dusted for prints, especially these cans. It looks like the shooter was knocked into these cans. He might have left a print on one of them. Has anyone looked at the surveillance tapes? If not I want the tapes sent to my office. What about the rest of the family?"

"There are three children all under twelve years of age. Their grandmother is with them, but she doesn't speak much English. I'm not for certain that the old woman knows for sure what's happened. We need to get someone out here from CPS who speaks Lebanese to make sure everything is okay, and they can get to and from the hospital. I'm worried about their father; he took quite a blow to the head." Belichec lit his pipe and blew the smoke away from Gorman. It hung in the air for a moment then dissipated.

"You still off the cigarettes?"

"Four years now, but I still think about them sometimes," Gorman said. The two men moved to one side of the door as men from the corner's office wheeled the bodies outside and rolled them to a waiting vehicle. When the forensic team came into the parking lot, Gorman stopped Ed Martin, the man in charge and handed him his card.

"Ed, I guess I'll be working this thing personally, so would you please make sure that I get everything as soon as you have it? I want it all; fingerprints, ballistics, I know DNA will take a while, but do what you can, okay? The people who did this are well on their way to getting away with a big haul and murder," Gorman said.

"You got it Captain, it's good to be working with you again," Martin said, in a deep southern drawl.

Gorman walked back through the store looking for anything that he or Belichec might have missed. He couldn't put his finger on it, but something was bothering him, and he didn't want to let it go. But without any witnesses or even anyone who got a look at the car the killers were driving, there just wasn't much to go on. His only hope was that something would turn up with the fingerprints or the blood on the wooden rod.

He thought about Clayton and Rucker working the downtown crime scene at Minute Maid, and decided that if he hurried he might be able be of some assistance there before they were done. He shook hands with Belichec, got in the cruiser and headed for the street.

Just as he pulled onto Aldine Mail Route he remembered what had been troubling him for the last half hour. He looked back at Belichec, who was getting into his Suburban and just as he was about to turn back into the parking lot, an eighteen wheeler hauling forty-foot joints of heavy wall pipe, plowed into the passengers' side of Gorman's cruiser.

The drainage ditch on the other side of Aldine Mail Route was fifteen feet deep and thirty feet wide. Gorman's Chrysler rolled over once on the street before it reached the guardrail of the drainage ditch, then in the flash of an eye, the car flipped over the guardrail landing upside down in the drainage ditch. Gorman was unconscious when Belichec and the forensics technicians reached the bottom of the ravine. He would have died if they hadn't been there. Because in less than one minute, what water there was in the ravine quickly flooded the cab of the cruiser through the broken windows and was drowning Gorman in less than a foot of water.

Ross Clayton waited for the light trucks to back into place. When they hit the switches turning on the floodlights the area around the bodies lit up like it was the middle of the day. For a moment he and Rucker seemed mesmerized by the crime scene, neither wanting to be the first to make a comment on what they were seeing.

The bodies were lying on a grassy embankment near a brick building used to house lawn and garden equipment for the stadium. The building was partially under the stadium seats on the north side, near Commerce Street, an area away from the main flow of pedestrian traffic around the ballpark. Whoever the killer was had gained access to a fenced area, restricted to the public.

At first glance it looked like the two men had wandered into an area away from the noise of the crowd and simply fallen asleep. The body on the left lay on his left side, using his left arm as a pillow, and his right arm tucked under his chin. Except for the massive loss of blood visible on the ground, you couldn't see that the man's throat had been cut. The body on the right lay on his back with both arms propped under the back of his head as if he were spending a leisurely afternoon resting. The man's shoes were off, lying just to his left side, near his waist, no more than a foot from the body. A sweat-stained old hat covered the man's head and eyes, as if shading him from a noonday sun.

Rucker started to move in for a closer look, but stopped when she saw the lines of blood spatter streaking from one side of the concrete walkway to the other.

"They were murdered here, then drug to the embankment and staged like that," she said.

"D, I've seen this particular scene before," Clayton said, trying to maintain his composure. "My mother wanted me to be a refined and well-rounded young gentleman. So the summer before I started college, my folks sent me to Paris for a couple of months. They paid for one of those extensive museum tours with my own personal guide. I must have spent weeks with Monique dragging me through one art museum after another." Clayton made a face when he said the woman's name.

"Are you going to tell me what this is, or do I have to go to Paris to find out?" Rucker asked.

"The scene is from a painting by Vincent van Gogh; it's called *Noon, Rest from Work*. It was painted in 1890 and is one of his more famous works. But I've seen this scene painted one other time, a lot more recently," he told her, with a look that made her shudder. Rucker started toward the bodies.

"Hold that thought, I want to get a good look at the bodies. There's got to be a piece of evidence on these guys somewhere. Give me a bit, will you?" Rucker said. Clayton nodded and headed in the direction of two uniformed officers.

"Do you think you guys could give us a hand?"

"We're here to do anything we can," one of the officers told him.

"I want to canvas the area twenty-five feet on either side of the bodies and all the way to the street. Make sure we have enough cops to keep everyone away from the crime scene, other than that, I need to have everybody looking for anything that might have been left by the killer. So far this guy hasn't made any mistakes. But if there is anything here, I want to find it," he said.

Thirty minutes had passed when Rucker turned off her flashlight and stood up, stretching the kinks out of her back. She and Clayton met a few feet away from the bodies. Clayton listened intently to what she had to say.

"First of all there's no sign of any struggle, which seems really odd unless these men knew the killer, or unless he killed them one at a time, which is what I suspect he did."

"What are you saying? You think he had them in custody and maybe brought them to this spot one at a time?" Clayton asked.

"Yeah, maybe, at least that's the way it looks. What I am sure about is that whoever did this was strong. He was physically strong enough to almost decapitate these men with a single blow, and he had an extremely sharp weapon."

"Like a razor or a medical instrument?" Clayton suggested.

"I don't think it's either. The blade is too broad. I think it's a sword like weapon with a curved blade, possibly one that's been sharpened on both sides. Once the killer had them on the ground he let them die before he moved them again. With their temperature and lividity being what it is, my guess is they were killed between nine and ten o'clock. It didn't take long for them to die either." Rucker looked away from Clayton, lost in deep thought. Then she started again.

"The blade severed the esophagus, the trachea, the sterna-mastoid, the sterna thyroid, the external jugular, the posterior external jugular and internal jugular. Unconsciousness came in a matter of seconds and death in a minute or so. The only thing holding their heads on their bodies is the muscles and nerves in the back of the neck. If he'd been standing an inch closer he'd have cut the head clean off."

"What about all of this blood, the killer left his footprints everywhere. Can we use any of that?

"I think that he's obsessed with these murders being perfect. I think he was wearing plastic booties, the kind used in hospitals. I found fragments of a blue, cloth-like plastic in several of the tracks.

I think that it took so long to stage this thing that he put on a second pair when he noticed the first pair was wearing thin. Our killers a perfectionist," she said.

"That's for sure," Clayton agreed. "Did you get an identity?"

Rucker handed Clayton a plastic bag from under her arm containing the men's wallets, keys and other personal effects.

"They were brothers, Youssef and Omar Abuo. I think they're Egyptian, and I think they've been in the country for a few years. The dates on their drivers' licenses indicate they were issued at the same time. Did you guys find anything?"

"Nothing that hasn't been here for a few days. We'll check it all out anyway; I'll give it to the forensics people if they ever get here. Did you find anything else on the bodies?" Clayton asked.

"I found a powder like substance on both men's shirts," she said.

"Powder, like cocaine?" Clayton asked.

"I'd be willing to bet it's not cocaine. It had an odd smell to it; I really don't know what it is," she said. "I taped it and got as much of it off their shirts as I could. I also bagged the hat. I'm fairly certain the man wasn't wearing it when he came here. I think it belonged to the killer so we should have it checked as well."

"Did you find anything else?"

"Like what, a painting?" Rucker looked at Clayton like she was waiting for the rest of the story.

"Yeah, exactly like a painting. Let's see it, what does it look like?"

Even though it was a warm night, Rucker was wearing a white, waist-length nylon windbreaker. She'd become accustomed to wearing it, because the hospital and morgue were always colder than she could stand. She reached inside the jacket and pulled a rolled piece of canvas from an inside pocket and handed it to Clayton. It was wound tight with a rubber band in the center and bagged in a clear plastic bag.

"Do you think we ought to unroll it here or wait until we can check it for prints?"

"Did you touch it?" Clayton asked.

"One corner is all. Just enough to slip it into the baggy and then into my jacket," she answered.

"We probably ought to wait till we get back…"

Before he could finish his sentence his cell phone went off. He pulled it from his belt and started talking. The conversation didn't last but a few seconds. When he closed the phone he motioned for one of the uniformed cops to come over.

"We have to leave, now. Captain Gorman's been in a bad accident, forensics teams and coroners are scattered all over town so we need some of you to stay here until they get here. Tell the medical examiners that we've released the bodies. The investigation is done. Cover the bodies and turn off the lights until they get here. And don't leave the scene unattended, not even for a minute. Are we on the same page about that?" Both officers nodded and Clayton and Rucker walked away.

Small drops of rain began pelting the concrete as Clayton reached the squad car, when he remembered the bagged evidence, painting, and the driver's license of the two dead men. He looked around the area and saw an old friend from his days in uniform. The man's name was Sergeant Aaron Phillips. When Clayton started in his direction Phillips got out of his cruiser and met him half way.

"Good to see you, Clayton." The two cops shook hands then started walking in the direction of Phillip's cruiser.

"I hate to ask you to do this, but I just got word that Gorman has been in a bad accident and I feel like I ought to be at the hospital when he comes around."

"Just tell me what you want me to do," Phillips said. Clayton handed him the license and the bags of evidence.

"I need you to find out about next-of-kin for these two men and get the information back to me ASAP. Get somebody to notify their families; maybe someone from the medical examiner's office can do it if you don't want to. Secondly, I need you to carry this to forensics. There's probably no one around at this time of night but post it on the door and sign my name to it. Run it through NCIC, have them do whatever they need to do, but find me a print on it. They'll know what to do with the taped specimens. Tell them I'll be there by noon tomorrow. Can you take care of those two things for me?"

"Consider it done," Phillips said staring at the driver's license. "But this is going to cost you a steak dinner," he said.

"Then you consider it done," Clayton said. He turned and walked away.

Leona Stillwell was tall and slender and even at two thirty in the morning was drop dead gorgeous. The young bellman that helped her out of the taxi smiled broadly, holding onto her hand an instant longer than he should have. Stillwell flashed him a quick smile then headed for the lobby of the Waldorf. The doorman opened the door for her then stood there watching as she walked away.

She had left her date at the Metropolitan Opera, ostensibly because of a sick headache. But the truth was brutally simple. She'd had enough of musicians, and opera, and ballet, and Broadway musicals to last her a lifetime. And she'd had enough of Leland Combs, the man she'd been dating for the past few months.

She met Combs at a fund-raising event for Bill White, who was running for mayor of Houston. He seemed charming enough at first, and offered her a glimpse into the Mercedes and Polo culture she knew so little about. And when he suggested they spend a couple of weeks taking a bite out of the Big Apple, it sounded like a vacation she would enjoy. After all, her life could use a little culture, she thought.

Now, all she wanted was a Margarita with salt around the rim, a bowl of nacho chips and a dish of hot picante sauce for dipping. And her choice of music would be Texas Swing or a Louisiana Zedico, something where the fiddle wasn't called a violin and dancing was enjoyed because it was fun, and not an event.

When she passed the front desk the clerk called her by name, and when she stopped he handed her a piece of paper with a note written on it that was blatantly quick and to the point.

"Call Delores Rucker at once, it's an emergency".

She hadn't heard from Rucker in a couple of months, but she was one of her closest friends and on occasion the only friend she could talk too. Her mind raced with thoughts. Had something happened to Clayton? Maybe he'd been hurt and was unable to make the call himself? If it was an emergency why didn't he call, they were partners after all. What if he'd been shot? She prayed silently that nothing had happened to him as she fumbled for her cell phone.

The thought never crossed her mind that she was praying for the very person who was responsible for her running off to New York in the first place. She needed a break from her partner and his constant barbs about the new man in her life. Why did he find it necessary to trash a good and decent man like Leland Combs? At least Leland was educated and respectable. Everyone in the department knew Clayton for the "air-headed Barbie Dolls" he dated. The thought of him with someone like that made her want to throw up, she thought. "God, please let him be alright," she whispered.

Rucker answered the phone on the third ring but before she could say anything Stillwell hit her with a litany of questions.

"What's happened? Where are you? I'm going to be sorry I left Houston, aren't I? Just tell me, is Clayton okay?" she asked desperately.

"I'm at Herman Hospital," Rucker started.

"I knew it. How bad is it? Rucker this ain't cool..."

"Stop, Leona. Just stop. It's not Clayton," she whispered into the receiver. "It's Gorman. He's been in a bad traffic accident. They've got him in surgery right now. The doctor said he's got several broken bones and some lacerations but they believe he's going to be okay. I think you really need to come home. We need all the help we can get, Leona."

"How did the accident happen?"

"He was on a case."

"A case? Why was the captain working cases? Are things really that bad? "It's pretty bad, Leona. The mayor has got a quarter of the department on a motivational seminar and a lot of officers are out on vacation." "Is something wrong with Clayton? Why didn't he call?"

"I think he thinks you're upset with him."

"Well if I wasn't before, I am now. Let me talk to him," Stillwell insisted. "Do you think that's such a good idea right now? You know how much he thinks of you. Why don't the two of you just admit it?" "Admit what?"

"Why don't both of you admit that you're crazy about each other, and the two of you hook-up. I'll bet he's better in the sack than Roland?" Rucker could hear Stillwell chuckling in the background.

"D, you know his name is not Roland. Now you're sounding like Clayton. Please put him on the phone."

"Well, if you don't want him, can I have him? I haven't been on a date in so long I was thinking about asking him out."

"If you value this friendship..," Stillwell could hear Rucker snickering on the other end.

"Hang on a minute, silly," Rucker interrupted her. Keep your pants on and I'll get your partner. Are you coming home or not? We need you to come home; the department is really short handed."

Before Stillwell could say another word, Rucker walked past a sign hanging on the wall that read, "No Cell Phones" and motioned to Clayton who was in a conversation with a group of other cops. When he got to the hallway she handed him her cell phone and whispered, "Its Leona."

"Hey partner, how're things in the Big Apple?" he asked.

"It's okay. Is Gorman going to be okay?"

"I think so. The orthopedic surgeon came out a little while ago and said that it's going to be a while. The damage to one of his legs is extensive and he's going to need about three units of blood. There have been twenty cops giving blood in the last two hours, so I think we've got that covered. Did Rucker ask you to come home?"

"Yes, she mentioned something about it. Why didn't you..." before she could finish her thought, Clayton started talking again.

"Look, you're my partner and I only want the very best for you. I should have never said what I did about Leroy. If he makes you happy, I suppose I should be happy."

"What time is it there in Houston?" Stillwell asked.

"Just after two, why?"

"I was just wondering what time the B.S. stops piling up. You know that man's name is not Leon, or Leroy or whatever you called him."

The two cops were laughing so hard that people around them were beginning to stare.

"If you'll call me when you've got flight arrangements, I'll pick you up in the morning," Clayton told her.

"Yeah, I should turn in and try to get a little sleep. I'll get the first flight I can. Give the Captain my best."

Richey Sneed paid the desk clerk for four nights and left another hundred for a deposit on the phone, and for any charges he might have on the pay-per-view movie channel. Richey explained to the man that he and his wife were just starting their vacation and did not want to be disturbed because she'd been in an automobile accident earlier that day and needed to rest. The man pulled the cash box from beneath the counter, stuffed it under his arm, handed Richey a printed list of restaurants in the area that delivered to the rooms, and then quietly disappeared through a door partition made of colored beads hanging from the door jam.

Lightning streaked across the horizon as Richey stepped out onto the blacktop and headed for the van. Beverly Sneed had passed out in the passenger's seat and could have passed for dead had anyone been around to see her. She hadn't moved in more than an hour and her breathing was so shallow that there was almost no movement in her chest.

He tried to tell her that the cocaine was uncut and high-octane stuff, but she wouldn't listen. She tore into the bag like a ravenous animal, snorting three lines before he could stop her. When the drug hit her, she checked out of reality, and never moved again. That was over two hours ago. Maybe she overdosed one too many times, he thought. Maybe she was dead, he thought.

He looked at the sky again as the first raindrop patted his forehead.

He found the key to the room and opened the door. The room smelled of cleaning fluids and stale cigarette smoke, but it could have smelled like a sewer for all Richey knew. His olfactory senses hadn't worked in years, or at least since he learned to snort cocaine.

The rain was falling harder as he stepped back outside to retrieve Beverly and the luggage from the van. Just as he opened the passenger door, Beverly's head twisted in the direction of the open door. The sight of her bruised face shocked him and he moved her face out of the shadows to get a closer look at the damage.

Her left eye was swollen shut and the dark bruise covering her eyelid ran to the hairline. The bridge of her nose was laid open, swollen and oozing blood. Her left eyebrow had been cut almost in half, and was crusted with coagulated blood. He shook her couple of times in an attempt to wake her but it was futile. He hefted her onto his shoulder and walked her inside laying her on the bed. He knew for sure now she was alive because she opened her eyes long enough to vomit in a bedside garbage can. When she finished she rolled over and instantly fell asleep.

When he finished unloading the van, he locked and dead-bolted the door then opened the tote bag containing the stolen money and drugs he'd purchased earlier, and began assembled them on the table in front of him. He twisted the lid off one of the bottles of OxyContin and popped two of the tablets in his mouth washing them down with a glass of water from the restroom.

When he finished counting the money he wrote the amount on a piece of stationary from the table drawer, $37,850.00. It was more money than he'd ever had in his possession at any one time in his life. And when he added that to what he'd paid the drug dealer they had netted just over forty-four thousand from the heist. The downside was that his coked-up wife had killed two people in the process. And unless they got out of Texas and soon, they stood a good chance of dying at the hands of the Texas Department of Corrections for what they'd done.

He massaged his temples in an attempt to relieve the headache that had been pounding a space behind his eyes for the last hour. He popped another of the OxyContin and as he washed it down he heard the squealing of breaks in front of his room. When he stood to check it out, the first wave of the timed-release drug hit him. He was dizzy and light-headed, he moved unsurely to the window, pulling the curtains back. He was just in time to see a red Mustang with a bashed-in rear quarter panel on the drivers side pull into a parking spot on the other side of the lot. He recognized the car from somewhere, but the drugs and his exhaustion wouldn't allow him to recall where.

He thought about it for a moment then decided that it was foolish to be suspicious about the Mustang; after all, no one knew he was there. He closed the curtain and staggered back to the table and began dumping everything back into the travel-bag. He heard music coming from a passing car in the parking lot. It was a song by Credence Clearwater Revival called *"Who'll Stop the Rain?"* When he picked up the bottle of OxyContin he unscrewed the lid and took another capsule. Before he placed another thing in the bag, he laid his head on the table and closed his eyes. The last thing he would hear before passing out was a line from the song playing in the distance.

"And I wonder, still I wonder,
Who'll stop the rain?"

CHAPTER 3

There was a hazy, almost obscure white light coming from somewhere up above.

Thank God it was there, because without the light he'd have surely panicked, making his injuries even worse than they were. He knew the Marines were coming; he could hear them in the distance. That was a good sign, he thought, at least he could still hear. But would they be there in time to save his life? He had no way of knowing that, or the extent of his injuries. The only thing he was absolutely certain of was that he was in a lot of pain, and fighting for every precious breath.

Exactly what happened? Gorman wondered. He didn't know. One minute he was dressing for breakfast, the next minute everything around him was mangled and obliterated beyond recognition. There must be hundreds of pounds of concrete, lumber and steel on top of him to cause this much pain, and for it to be so dark, he thought. How long had he been like this, he tried to put it all together. Any attempt at understanding seemed daunting and hopeless.

He tried desperately to move his legs and then his arms, but it was no use. The fall must have knocked the breath out of him, and his mouth seemed incredibly dry, tasting of dirt and plaster. He fought to pull air into his lungs, when it was obvious that he wasn't breathing. Suddenly, a hand was on his face wiping at the debris, and then it was digging in his mouth, extricating the plaster and dirt, allowing enough air into his airway to keep him from choking to death. He began to gag and heave. He fought back the urge to swallow. His eyes and mouth began to water as he choked on the foulness.

A voice from above him was speaking to him again, coaching him, pleading with him to hold on. Then the strangest thing happened. He felt the dampness of a cool moist cloth on his forehead and the softness of a woman's hand inside his own.

"Mr. Gorman, Mr. Gorman," the pleasant voice called again and again.

"I'm Lance Corporal Gorman," he weakly managed to say.

The light in his eyes was much brighter now, if he could only focus on something, if he could only see the woman behind the lovely voice calling his name. He squinted at the light as highlights began to form and reassemble out of the haze.

"Mr. Gorman, I've taken your breathing tube out. Can you take a deep breath for me?" the voice asked.

Gorman felt soft hands tugging at his sleeves, and then suddenly something wound tightly around his arm, squeezing and tightening its grip. Now, he was keenly aware of the pain racking the left side of his body when he tried to move. His face contorted at the stabbing pain.

"I was just taking your blood pressure, Mr. Gorman. Can you open your eyes?

"What happened to the barracks," Gorman asked.

"You're not in a barracks, Mr. Gorman, and you're not in the Marines anymore. This is Herman Hospital in Houston, and I'm your anesthetist. I'm Dr. Carol Morgan," she said. Gorman's eyes opened and for a moment it was as if he were trying to focus on an object on the wall that was both allusive and unattainable. He blinked several times before finally honing in on the image of the woman who had been calling his name.

"I thought for a moment I was back in Beirut and it was 1983 again," he said reflectively.

"That was twenty years ago. Were you actually there?" Carol Morgan asked.

"Yeah, I was. I was buried under six feet of rubble after the terrorist bombing. It took almost twenty hours to dig me out. I could have sworn I was there all over again; it seemed so real. What happened to me?" He tried to sit up but quickly realized he couldn't.

"I don't know all of the details, but I know you were in an automobile accident late last night," she said. Gorman closed his eyes straining to remember the events that landed him in the hospital for the second time in his life.

"I want you to stay awake if you can. We're going to move you to a private room, very shortly. You've got a lot of people who have been waiting most of the night to see you."

"What time is it?"

"It's morning. You've been with us most of the night and you've had extensive surgery on your left leg and arm. We're going to keep you in traction for a couple of weeks. But right now we need to get you out of recovery and into a private room. Do you understand what I'm telling you? I don't want you to become alarmed when we start moving you."

"I'm nauseated," he said.

The staff wasted little time in transferring Gorman to a private room on the third floor. Over the next two hours a dozen cops wandered in and out of his room to visit and to express their concerns for his plight. He slept for an hour and at ten a.m. awoke, reeling in pain. Thirty minutes later a nurse loaded a syringe with Demerol and pumped it into his hip. Stacy Cromberg walked into the room as the nurse was leaving.

Cromberg was smiling until she saw the pain on Gorman's face. She walked to the bed and made an attempt to hug him without making the pain worse.

"I'm sorry, Captain Gorman, I didn't know you were in traction. I know you must be in a lot of pain and need to rest, so I won't stay. I was just worried about you."

"It's okay," he said, waving his good hand in the air. "I'm glad you're here. I want you and Delores Rucker to work on this double homicide that I was on last night when I got hurt."

"Sir, D Rucker is back at Baylor. You must not be thinking so clearly, sir." "No, no, she's taking the summer off, and is going to be working with us for a couple of months. I've also called Stillwell back from her vacation and I'm ordering you back from this seminar thing. Rucker and Clayton were here most of the night so they probably won't be in to the department until later. Find them and tell them what I want everyone to do."

"Whatever you say, Captain." Cromberg gripped his hand and was about to leave but he wouldn't let her go.

"I'm not through," he said, releasing his grip on her hand. "Find my notebook. It's in my squad car or my clothes. Then I want you to talk to Belichec. I remember now what happened last night. I was headed back to ask Belichec if he remembered smelling something strange on the husband of the woman who was shot. I couldn't place the smell last night, that's why I was going back. I wanted to see if Belichec knew what the smell was. It's probably nothing but I want you two to interview the guy. He was hurt pretty bad so I'm sure he's in the hospital somewhere. You and Rucker find him and get all you can from him."

When Gorman stopped talking, Cromberg knew the narcotic had started to take affect, because Gorman's eyelids were sagging and his speech had become increasingly slurred as he instructed her. She kissed him on the cheek and left the room. Gorman never knew she was gone.

It was almost noon when Rucker and Clayton walked into the department. Neither of them had gotten to bed until almost six a.m. It was just after four when they allowed the two cops five minutes with Gorman in the Recovery Room. He never knew they were there.

"Have you heard from Stillwell yet?" Rucker asked through a sleepy yawn. "I don't look for her to call until after noon."

The two cops didn't waste any time getting to Art McDonnell's lab to have a look at the painting taken from the body of Omar Abuo. When they walked into the lab they saw the painting unrolled and pinned at the corners, lying in an enclosed glass cubicle that resembled an aquarium and used for uncovering fingerprints. The hat from the scene was in a second cubicle. When McDonnell saw them walking towards his lab, he opened the top of the glass enclosure and lifted the painting out, laying it flat on the counter top.

"I assume this is what you guys are here to see? But before you get your hopes up I want you to know there are no prints on it or the hat. Not one. I've tested them nine ways from Sunday and there's nothing on them."

Clayton and Rucker stood quietly, studying the painting. It was an impressionist work, depicting a wooden cabin boat in the middle of a lake or waterway with a landscape of green trees and rolling, grassy terrain in the background. The boat's reflection on the water was beautifully mastered and the pastel colors were stunning.

"Is there anything unusual about the painting?" Rucker asked.

"It's a splendid copy, if that's what you mean. I looked it up. It's a copy of a painting by Claude Monet painted in 1874, called "The Studio Boat." I'm not much of an art aficionado, but I'd say it could be worth a good deal of money if it were for sale."

"Anything else?" Clayton asked. "Is there anything special about the paints, or the strokes, or when it was done?"

"Like I said, I'm not an expert on paintings or artists, for that matter. I can tell you that it's painted with oils and linseed based painting mediums and given some time I can probably tell you the company responsible for manufacturing the paints and oils. But if you want to know about brush strokes and artist style, you need to get over to the Art Museum on Bissonnet and see Lund Corbel. He's a buyer for the museum and an expert on paintings, more acutely, on reproductions of this nature. I know this because I play racquetball with him once a week at the downtown YMCA."

"What about the two strips of powder I taped off the bodies at the scene?" Rucker asked.

"It was talcum powder. But not just any talcum powder, it's the kind of talcum found in more expensive surgical gloves," he said.

"There was a very slight smell to the powder. Can you tell me what that was?"

"Turpentine," he said flatly.

"Turpentine? You mean like the stuff my dad used to clean oil off the garage floor?" Rucker looked at him, quizzically.

"Exactly like that. My guess is that your killer is an artist, obviously a very good artist, and he uses old fashion oils and paints and solvents, like Turpentine."

"I thought I smelled something from pine trees," Rucker said.

"What do pine trees have to do with it?" Clayton asked.

"The resin or sap from several groups of conifers, or pine tree resin, is the main ingredient in making Turpentine," Rucker said.

Art McDonnell handed the painting to Rucker, and then stuffed his hands in his lab jacket. He stood there staring at her like there was something more he wanted to say but the words wouldn't come. Clayton thanked him for his help and the two cops turned to leave.

"Aren't you enrolled at Baylor?" he asked just before they reached the door.

Both cops turned and looked back when he asked the question.

Rucker handed the painting to Clayton, suggesting that he should go on and she'd catch up.

"I'm not attending class this summer. Actually I'm working here to make a few extra bucks. Why do you ask?"

"I was, uh, I was thinking," he stuttered slightly. "I was thinking that maybe you'd like to go out for dinner sometime; if you have time, I mean." He was nervously rocking back-and -forth on the balls of his feet as he asked the question.

"Art, are you asking me out on a date?"

"Well, yes. If you're not too tied up with the case, maybe next Friday night we could go out for dinner or a movie or something?"

Rucker pulled a note pad from her back pocket, scribbled her phone number on it and handed it to him.

"Call me on Wednesday or Thursday and I'll let you know how it looks. It sounds nice," she said.

Just as she handed him the piece of paper, a handsome, young street cop walked in and handed Art McDonnell a brown evidence folder. The man looked at Rucker and smiled broadly, her eyes locked on his nametag, which read, Jay Grimes. She winked at McDonnell and followed the uniformed officer into the hallway, watching him as he walked away. "Why couldn't he ask me out?" she asked herself.

When Rucker got back to Ross Clayton he was on the phone with Stillwell. She walked across the room and poured a cup of coffee. When Clayton turned around she held the coffee pot in the air asking if he wanted a cup. He shook his head no. When he hung up the phone with Stillwell, Stacy Cromberg walked into the room.

Delores Rucker and Stacy Cromberg had a lot in common. They were both still under thirty, they were both single and constantly looking for someone with a ring and a proposal. They were both extremely intelligent and they were both fearless in the face of danger. The main clear likeness about the two women was the way they dressed. They both wore jeans and flats and cotton blouses that downplayed their figures. Neither wore much makeup and both had short-cropped hair that hugged their necks.

The two women hugged briefly, and then Clayton and Rucker listened as Cromberg told them about her meeting with Gorman.

"I was really looking forward to working with you on this painting thing. It sounds like my kind of case. But I can't say I'm not happy about working with my old running buddy again either," Rucker told Clayton.

"I'm sure I'll need your expertise again before this is over. So, you guys are set? You're lined out and know what to do?" Clayton asked.

"Gorman wants us to find his notes and talk to Belichec. It's as good a place as any to start," Cromberg said.

"Well, Stillwell just called and said that her plane has landed. By the time I get to the airport she'll have her luggage and be ready to go. Let's check in here on Mondays, Wednesday, and Fridays to compare notes. Other than that we'll keep in contact by cell phone. You ladies have a nice weekend," Clayton said, and walked away.

When Richey Sneed awoke he rubbed his eyes, remembering how fitful and dysphoric his night had been. It had been a night filled with dreams. Not the kind of dreams that you want to talk about or re-live in the morning. It was the kind of dreams that extrapolate bits and pieces of our innermost fears and obstruct that part of the brain that is responsible for rational, decent thought.

In one of his dreams he was being tortured by an entity or demon that he could neither see nor hear, and yet the demon moved and handled him as effortlessly as a strong man might move a small child from one chair to another.

The demon stripped him naked, and then poured honey over his head and chest. Then took him to a room cluttered with old furniture and wooden chairs that were broken and in need of repair. The demon placed him on the floor in the center of the room in a sitting position, with his knees drawn up under his chin and his hands clasped together at his ankles. His feet remained exposed and flat on the hardwood floor.

He was then duct-taped in that position with several rolls of gray tape. His mouth was stuffed with cloth and taped shut, but his eyes were not covered so that he could see what was happening in the room.

The demon lit a small fire in a corner of the room and left it to burn at it's own pace, without an accelerant. A few moments later, a large diameter, clear plastic pipe was lowered from an opening in the ceiling, stopping just above his ankles. For a moment the presence of the plastic pipe confused him, until he saw a single, red fire ant scurry down the pipe, drop onto his ankle and disappear beneath the duct tape.

He managed to crane his neck to see the top of the plastic pipe. There were so many fire ants heading in his direction that he could not see through the pipe where they were crawling. Over the next twenty minutes more than ten thousand ants would follow the trek of the first one, until every centimeter of his body was covered with stinging, devouring ants. He began to pray for the fire in the corner of the room to hurry, and incinerate the room completely.

Why couldn't he just sleep the night off the way Beverly had? She hadn't moved an inch all night, he thought. He rubbed his face and walked over to the bed turning on the bedside lamp. The night's rest hadn't provided any miracle cures for the wounds on her face. The cuts and swelling seemed to have worsened, if anything. He looked closely at the gash in her eyebrow. "That should have been sewn up," he whispered aloud.

He lit a cigarette and turned off the lamp, but continued to stare at his wife while she slept. She was tall and big-boned, but shapely with an hourglass figure. She had full lips and piercing bright blue eyes, when she was sober. Her hair was the color of honey, shoulder length, and it often obscured a tattoo of red roses and green vines that wound down from the center of her neck encircling her left breast and ending with a red rose at her nipple.

Her skin was flawless and soft. He loved the warmth of her next to him at night and the smell of her body after she showered. He loved touching her and making love to her in the mornings before the drugs and booze had taken control. Just as he ran his hand across the fabric of her panties, he glanced back at the table where he had restlessly slept the night away.

The travel bag was not on the table. He sat up and crushed the cigarette out in a bedside ashtray. Then he saw it. The window above the air conditioner had been knocked out, and the carpet in front of the air conditioner was covered with shards of glass and parts of the metal framework that had been holding the glass in place. He ran back to the table, as if his presence would cause the bag to somehow reappear. It didn't.

He ran back to the bed shaking his wife awake. He pulled her upright in the bed, yelling to the top of his lungs for her to awake and explain how this could have happened. But before she could say a word or react to the dilemma, it hit him, as coldly and plainly as any truth ever had.

The person that ripped them off was whoever was driving the red Mustang in the parking lot last night. It was the same red Mustang with the dented rear quarter panel that he'd seen in the parking garage of his drug dealer's high-rise apartment downtown. If he hadn't been so hell-bent on getting loaded last night he would have put it all together then and could have confronted the driver.

The facts were painfully simple, he thought. Either his dealer had seen the report of the robbery on television and put someone on him to take him down, or someone was hiding in his dealer's apartment and saw all of the money he was flashing around and took it upon himself to follow, and rob him. No matter how it went down, someone was going to pay.

Clayton could see the exhaustion and fatigue in Stillwell's face when he picked her up just after two p.m. at terminal C. And she didn't waste any time telling him she needed some rest.

"Look Clayton," she started as soon as she got in the car. "I've been up most of the night and running like someone possessed, all morning, and quite frankly, I'm beat. Would you be okay if we run by to see Gorman and then take me home? I'll be ready to go Monday morning."

"Hey, it's Saturday, not much happening on Saturdays," he said. It was a meaningless observation that would come back to haunt him before the day was over.

It took an hour to get to Herman hospital for their visit with Gorman. And for some reason he was in a foul mood while the two cops were there. It made leaving the hospital a lot easier than it could have been. By the time they pulled into Stillwell's driveway in Spring

Branch, it was almost five o'clock. He carried her luggage up to her door then went back to wake her up. He opened her door, knelt down beside her and tugged at her arm.

When her eyes opened she smiled at him in a way that he had never seen before. It wasn't playful or lustful or even appreciative, it was a smile of innocence and vulnerability, the kind of look that most men fall in love with. It was such a beautiful moment Clayton was almost at a loss for words.

"You fell asleep as soon as we left the hospital," he said softly.

"I'm sorry I didn't feel like working today," she almost whispered.

"It's okay," he said, extending his hand.

Stillwell's heart fluttered when she took his hand. Like a schoolgirl, she released it as soon as she got out of the car, not knowing what else to do. Clayton walked her to the top of the stairs and when the awkward moment came, he patted her on the shoulder and with a boyish grin said. "Hang in there, pal, things will look brighter tomorrow."

The look she gave him after that brilliant proclamation was one he had seen before; it was a look of disgust. But it was too late to fix it, he thought. Stillwell fished her keys out of her purse and without saying another word went inside and locked the door behind her.

Clayton stood there for a moment with a bewildered look on his face then started slowly down the stairs. Was something happening that he wasn't aware of? Had his partner of almost four years just made a pass at him? One thing he was absolutely certain of, he'd never seen that look on her face before, not even with the men she was dating and seemed to care about, he thought. That look could have melted steel, he said to no one.

It was a long drive back downtown to the station, and he couldn't get her out of his thoughts. He had never thought of Stillwell in a romantic way before, at least not until today. His mind raced, recreating the scene on the porch; "Hang in there, pal," oh yeah, oh yeah! That ought to pretty much sew up any future romantic encounter. Of all the stupid things to say, he thought. The woman is up all night, she flies almost two thousand miles because her partner asked her to come home, she looks at you with those gorgeous eyes, begging to be held, and the very best you can come up with is, "Hang in there, pal." You're an idiot, Clayton. Look the word up in the dictionary and there will be a picture of Ross Clayton, he said aloud.

He saw the envelope as soon as he got off the elevator and walked past Gorman's office. It was taped to the wall of his cubicle with his name printed on the front. When he opened the envelope it contained the drivers' licenses of the two men who had been murdered at Minute Maid Park, and a hand written letter from his friend Aaron Phillips. The letter read:

> *Ross, I hooked up with Denise Cortez from the medical examiners office and we drove to Clear Lake to the home of Youssef Abuo and then to the home of Omar Abuo. Both families live in Clear Lake, in the Bay Oaks subdivision.*
>
> *I don't know what I was expecting, but I was surprised to find that both women were Anglo-American, and both were devastated by the news. It was one of the most challenging things I've ever done. I hope I never have to do it again.*
>
> *I figured you'd want to talk to the wives at some point, so I've left the phone numbers on the back of my card. Good luck with the case.*
>
> *If I can be of any further help to your investigation you know where to find me.*
>
> *Sincerely,*
> *Aaron Phillips*

Clayton felt bad that he had leaned on a fellow employee to handle a dirty job that should have been his. He remembered just how bad those assignments could be. It was just a few months ago when he had to break the news to a mother that her son had been shot down outside a South Houston nightclub by a drive-by shooter. He remembered it so vividly because the woman had a heart attack on the spot and nearly died. He laid the envelope on his desk and checked his watch; it was almost seven o'clock and he realized that he hadn't had dinner.

All in all it had been a fairly rotten day, he thought, but there was one more thing he wanted to do before calling it a day. He wanted to drive by the Fine Arts Museum as Art McDonnell had suggested and see what time they opened on Monday. He wanted to show the paintings left by the killer, to Lund Corbel to see if he recognized the work or he could provide any insight as to the kind of person they were hunting.

The weather had turned clear and hot again after the morning rains, but a steady northern breeze and lower humidity than normal, kept temperatures bearable, making for a pleasant evening, he thought. He headed south on Main Street until he reached Bissonnet and turned right. The Fine Arts Museum fronted Bissonnet, taking up the entire block between Main Street and Montrose Boulevard.

Clayton squinted to read the timetables printed on the front of the building.

It was useless, he thought, the lettering was too small.

He parked next to the curb on Bissonnet and got out. He had made it half the way across the street when one of the plate glass windows on the left side of the main entrance exploded with what sounded like a small bomb. Clayton recognized the sound as coming from a handgun. An alarm sounded somewhere in the building and from the Montrose side of the museum a security guard was trotting around the corner.

"Stay in your car sir," he yelled to Clayton.

Before he got the words out of his mouth, another two shots rang out and the glass in the right entrance door shattered onto the sidewalk. The security guard leaped onto the sidewalk thirty-feet from the door lying perfectly still. He watched Clayton pull his badge and 9mm Beretta and charge to the right of the other door. The security guard had yet to move, refusing to cast himself in harm's way.

"Do you have a key to this door?" Clayton asked the security guard.

Two more shots echoed from the building. Clayton looked at the security guard cowering on the sidewalk, fumbling with a set of keys attached to his belt. He sized up the two holes in the glass. The one in the door was too small for him to go through, but the one in the glass panel beside the door had blown out an area large enough for him to waltz through, he thought. He darted past the shattered glass door and ducking slightly, jutted inside the building.

He made his way to a black reception desk to the left of the door, taking cover behind it. The room was expansive with stairs and passageways leading in at least three directions. He couldn't see the ceiling of the room but emergency lights and stairwell lighting fixtures let him know that the room was at least thirty feet high.

Suddenly another volley of shots rang out to his left. He moved to a corner and peered down a long corridor of inclining stairs and an elevator on the side. He started in the direction of the shots when a man and woman started climbing the stairs and running in his direction. The woman appeared to have been shot in her left shoulder and the man was carrying a blue steel revolver and pulling the woman as he ran. Clayton dropped to one knee and drew a bead on the man with the revolver.

"Police, drop the weapon," he yelled. The couple continued to climb the stairs.

"I won't tell you again. Stop and drop the weapon, now," he yelled distinctly. Suddenly the man and woman stopped, realizing that they were about to be shot. The woman fell to her knees, moaning and sobbing from the wound in her shoulder. The man held the revolver in the air, allowing it to dangle freely from his index finger.

"Toss the weapon away," Clayton told him. The man did as he was told and Clayton moved in.

"You've got to stop him," the man said kneeling to attend to the woman.

"Tell me in as few words as you can what's going on here?" Clayton said. The man pulled a handkerchief from his pocket pressing it against the open wound in the woman's shoulder. He looked back at the badge hanging from Clayton's jacket pocket and started to talk.

"This is Diana Taylor and I'm Mark Donaldson; we both work for the Museum District. We've been spending a lot of hours lately on an Egyptian grant that will...," Clayton held a hand in front of his face to stop him from going any further.

"I don't need to know about that. Who is shooting, and why is he shooting?" Clayton asked.

"It's her husband; he thinks we've been having an affair. He's been threatening me for the last few weeks. That's why I bought this gun and got a concealed carry permit. He's crazy, officer," Donaldson said.

"Call an ambulance for her and get her outside the building. Call 911 and tell the dispatcher that Detective Ross Clayton requests backup, and that shots have been fired and give them the address. One other thing, what does Taylor look like, and how many other people are in the building?" Clayton asked. His wife pulled herself to her feet making a strange face at the question.

"He looks like the Incredible Hulk, he's big and he's very strong. Please be careful, I don't want him to hurt anybody else," she said.

"Oh this just gets better all the time," Clayton whispered. "What about the people. How many people are in the building?"

"The museum closed about twenty minutes ago, at seven. There were a few people in the cafeteria and a few others in the bookstore when the shooting started. This is a huge place, Detective, and there are a lot of places to hide and a lot of concealed passageways. He could be anywhere?"

"Just get her outside and do as I told you," Clayton said.

He made his way to the bottom of the stairway then headed into a long tunnel-like corridor that was lighted with soft, mint green lights and painted walls giving off the allusion that you were walking through a soft green cloudbank. When he got through the green tunnel he entered another tunnel that was a soft crimson color and painted walls to match. But before he could get out of that tunnel he heard someone talking just outside, in another room or corridor.

"Is that you, Taylor?" Clayton yelled.

"Who's asking?"

"Detective Ross Clayton, HPD."

"I don't have any beef with you, Detective. Just let me finish my business with that bitch, and I'll turn myself in. Or maybe I'll just shoot myself and save the taxpayers a lot of money. As long as she's dead, I really don't care." "You know I can't let you do that, and I really don't want to shoot you either, but you're not leaving me much choice," Clayton said trying to reason with the man.

"Let me ask you something, Taylor."

"Yeah, what's that?"

"Did you catch your wife in the act with Donaldson?"

"What do you mean? Are you asking me if I caught them naked, in bed?" "Yeah, that's precisely what I'm asking you," Clayton said. "No, I didn't. I ain't seen Paris either, but I know it's there."

"So you don't think you're acting just a bit hastily? You have to admit that there is a good possibility that your wife has done nothing wrong at all."

"You're pissing me off, Detective."

"I can't imagine rational thought having that affect on you, Taylor. It's fairly obvious that you've let your jealousy get the best of you. Why don't you stop acting like a spoiled child and come on out?" Clayton said, hoping to force him into making a mistake.

The next thing Clayton knew the man stormed into the crimson colored tunnel. The lumbering giant was everything his wife had described and more. Taylor was at least six-foot, six inches tall, and roughly three hundred twenty-five pounds of solid muscle. The Mauser .380 semi-automatic, looked like a cap pistol in his massive hand. He had curly black hair and a round face with bushy eyebrows and perfect white teeth, clinched in a snarl. His massive arms and neck were cordoned with bulging veins and sinew, from years of lifting weights.

When the man shot past the opening to the tunnel Clayton tripped him. It seemed like a clever idea at the time, until the man latched onto Clayton's arm and both of them tumbled to the ground in a mass of flailing arms and legs tumbling over-and-over. Both men lost their firearms in the ensuing entanglement, which ended with both men lying on their backs with their feet almost touching the others.

Clayton ran his hand across his forehead; a lump was forming and there was a throbbing pain coming from his left ear. Out of the corner of his eye he saw the big man working himself upright. Clayton rolled quickly, first to his knees and then to his feet, but he was unstable at best. The big man took advantage of Clayton's awkward stance, shoving a massive arm under Clayton's armpit and flipping him through the air as if he were part of a circus act. Clayton landed on his buttocks, jarring him senseless. His six-four frame rattled to the bone.

When the big man moved in to finish the job, Clayton spun in a half circle and kicked him in the right kneecap. He heard the man's kneecap pop when his hard-sole shoe connected and saw the man cry out in pain. He got to his feet and lunged for Taylor but the man was quick to respond, grabbing Clayton around the neck and holding him in a headlock. As Taylor rammed his fist into Clayton's face again, and again, blood splattered the walls and floor of the darkened room.

Just when Clayton thought it was hopeless, he released his own body weight, which caused Taylor's knee to buckle in pain, allowing Clayton to sag below the man's waist and giving him access to Taylor's exposed groin. Clayton sprang up with a balled fist in the center of the man's scrotum. Taylor gasped for air like a mortally wounded animal and went down in a mass on the floor, jerking and winching uncontrollably.

Tears rolled from Taylor's eyes as the blow rendered him helpless and defeated. He lay in the fetal position while Clayton handcuffed him from behind and then retrieved the two handguns. It was twenty minutes before Taylor was able to walk. Clayton could hear the HPD sirens in the distance as he walked Taylor down the dimly lit corridors and into the main lobby where it had all started.

Just as Clayton and Taylor stepped outside, the scene around the Museum resembled that of a training exercise for a natural disaster, it was organized pandemonium. Diana Taylor was being loaded onto an ambulance while the attendants crouched as if they were in a war zone with bullets flying around them. Two additional ambulances were waiting in the wings on Main Street. And the HPD SWAT Team had officers kneeling on both sides of the shattered glass panels and others scurrying to and from support vehicles in the street.

And at lease three of the city's news agencies were set up in the church parking lot across the street to film the gunfight in the event that it spilled out into the streets. The security guard that had been cowering on the ground while Clayton went inside the building was now pointing animatedly in the direction of the Museum while giving an interview to a Channel 2 news reporter.

Clayton shoved Taylor in the direction of the SWAT team leader then headed for the squad car where Mark Donaldson was sitting. One of the SWAT officers spoke to Clayton as he walked away.

"Detective Clayton, do you need medical attention?" He ordered one of his men to have an EMT look at Clayton.

Clayton never acknowledged that the officer said anything to him; he just continued moving in Donaldson's direction. When he got to the squad car Donaldson rolled the window down and looked at him as if he were looking at a deranged man who had escaped from custody.

"You don't look so good, Detective," he said.

"I don't feel so good either. The beating I took was meant for you. The only reason I came by here for was to find Lund Corbel. Do you know where I can find him?" Clayton asked impatiently.

"Lund Corbel is off until Tuesday," Donaldson said, a confused look on his face. "You need to have someone look at those cuts on your forehead," Donaldson said.

Reporters and cameramen surrounded Clayton as he walked away from Donaldson. But before he could say anything Delores Rucker grabbed him by the arm and pulled him out of the crowd while Stacy Cromberg stepped in front of the cameras to answer any questions.

"Man, am I glad to see you," Clayton told her. "What are you doing here?" "I suppose I could ask you the same question. It looks like every cop in Houston is here," she looked around at the scene. "We were eating at a burger joint down the road when all of the calls started coming in. Stacy was going to run me home when the dispatcher said that you requested backup. Looks like we got here a little late to help with the fight, but maybe I can look at your head while I'm here," she said.

Clayton sat in the back of the ambulance and went over the events inside the museum while Rucker put five stitches in his forehead and two more in a cut just above his left eyebrow. His cell phone rang just as she was finishing with the first one. He fished the phone out of his pocket and said hello. It was Leona Stillwell.

"You don't have enough on you're plate that you got to get involved in some domestic disturbance? I don't know what to think about you, Clayton. Are you alright?"

"Yeah, I'm fine, now. Cromberg saved me from the reporters and Rucker is sewing me up."

"Let me talk to Rucker," she said. Clayton handed Rucker the phone as she snipped at a black thread just below his hairline.

"D, when you get through sewing him up will you make sure he goes home? He doesn't live two miles from there but he's liable to get in a riot or another gunfight before he gets there. I woke up a few moments ago to go to the bathroom and when I get back to bed I see Clayton with this guy in handcuffs on the TV and Clayton's face is all bloody. He's a crime scene waiting to happen. Promise me you'll take him home," Stillwell said.

"Don't worry, I'll get him there," she said, handing the phone back to Clayton.

"Will you promise me that you'll go home and calm down for the rest of the weekend? I need the rest and I don't want to worry about what you're doing the whole time I'm trying to sleep. Will you please go home?" she pleaded with him.

"I promise I'll go home. Thanks for calling," he said as Rucker started on the second laceration.

Redhawk Simmons walked through the store with a stringer of white bass and Perch almost dragging the floor. He stopped to talk with one of the attendants who was closing windows and locking doors for the night.

"That's a nice stringer of fish, Redhawk. You gonna need some help cleaning them?"

"Nah, you go on home. Was it a busy day?"

"We had quite a bit of traffic this morning but it's been really quiet since about four, maybe two or three customers at best."

"Have you seen Renee?" Simmons asked.

"She was in about an hour ago looking for you. I told her you hadn't made it back yet but that was probably a good sign that the fish were biting. I guess she was getting worried or something."

"Anyone asking for me today?" Simmons asked, not really wanting to know the answer.

"I don't know. I opened up this morning, worked a couple of hours then had to leave. I got back just after four. Little Twin worked most of the day, but had to leave a couple of hours ago. So she'd be the one to ask. No one asked for you by name while I was here. We can call Little Twin if you want. Sounds like something important."

"No, no, that's okay. I've got to go to work on these fish," he said. Simmons waved a dismissive hand at the attendant and walked through the screen door onto the redwood deck. He could see Renee through the living room windows watching the news on television. She must have heard him walking on the deck because he hadn't taken two steps when she turned and saw him heading her way. She got up quickly and stepped onto the deck to say hello.

"I been worried about you, big man," she said with a broad smile, her long, raven black hair shining like polished steel in the moonlight.

"I've been aiming to get me one of them cell phones," he said, as if he were describing an object in the future. "I just never had too many people to call that's all."

"You want to do the scaling inside or outside?" Renee asked.

"The smell won't bother you if we do it inside?"

"I've been around men scaling and gutting fish all my life. You've gutted these already so let's scale them inside. At least the mosquitoes' won't carry us away," she said.

For the next hour the two made small talk as Redhawk scrapped the scales off the fish and filleted the larger ones while Renee washed and wrapped them for the freezer. After they cleaned the counters, dumped the garbage and stored everything away, they took a shower together. It wasn't until she was washing his back with a soapy oversized sponge, that the tension of the last few days and the anticipation of the evil one coming back into the store again left his thoughts completely. It was a good feeling. It lasted less than five minutes.

Redhawk Simmons had never cared much for romance or the entanglements that came with it. But Renee Harjo was unlike any woman he'd ever been with, and it was more than just her physical beauty or the fact that she could cook like a chef that he was infatuated with. There was nothing fake or plastic about her, and she worked harder than any person he'd ever known. She was honest to a fault and genuinely concerned about the welfare of others above that of her own.

He watched her running a comb through her hair while standing in front of the mirror as he toweled himself off behind her. He moved in close to her, kissing her on the shoulder. She closed her eyes, nuzzling herself into him. He kissed her again at the base of her neck then again softly just below her ear. He could feel her breathing accelerate watching the rise and fall of her breast in the mirror.

Suddenly she shivered, her eyes widened and a frown covered her face like a bad memory of an unmentionable event that awoke and disturbed the beauty of the moment between them.

"What's the matter," he asked abruptly.

"I'm, I'm sorry, Redhawk. I just remembered that creepy man," she said. "What man? Someone was here? Someone was at our house?"

"Yes. Just after dark this man walked through the store and stepped out onto the deck, like he owned the place. You know me, I hear everything, but he was already at the door of the house before I saw him standing at the screen door," she said, and shook herself again.

"What did he look like?" Simmons asked impatiently.

"Like a creep."

"Tell me everything you can remember about him. It's important, Renee," he said. She didn't say anything for a moment. She wrapped herself with a blue towel and sat on the side of the bathtub deep in thought.

"He was close to your height, but not as big," she started. Her brow furrowed like she was struggling with the recollection.

"Go on; tell me everything you can think of."

"His skin was dark but he wasn't black, and he wasn't one of our people either. I couldn't see the top of his head because he wore a hat with a wide brim, but what hair I could see was black as coal. He had mean eyes and even when he smiled he looked like he was up to something. And something else that disturbed me about him was that he wouldn't look at you in the eyes for very long. His eyes were always darting around like he was looking for something to steal or taking an inventory of things that didn't belong to him. Does he sound like someone you know?"

Simmons walked away from her into the bedroom and slipped on a clean pair of denim jeans then walked into the living room and set on the couch in the dark. He sat on the edge of the cushion with his forearms on his knees and his hands clasped together as if he were waiting for the man's knock at any moment. For the first time in over six years he wanted a cigarette and a fifth of whisky so badly he couldn't think clearly.

When Renee came into the room she was wearing a white silk robe and slippers, and she had tied her hair in a ponytail. She kneeled in front of Simmons and held his hands.

"What's going on, Redhawk? This is the second time in the last few days you've had this look on your face. I'm not used to seeing that look on your face. You never struck me as the kind of man who was afraid of anything. What's happening, Redhawk?"

He wanted to tell her to shut up and go to bed. He wanted to leave and get to the liquor store on Highway 59, and buy the whisky and cigarettes before they closed. But what he did next surprised not only Renee but him as well. He sat her on the couch beside him and told her everything he knew about the man he believed to be responsible for the Arab killings in Houston.

After he was done, they agreed that the clearest course of action was to drive to Houston first thing Monday morning and tell the authorities everything he had just told her. Simmons sat silently for a moment after they finished talking and watched Renee slip the rubber band off her ponytail and flip her hair in the air with her hand. She stood without saying a word and took him by the hand to the bedroom and made love to him as she had never made love to any man before.

CHAPTER 4

Richey Sneed stood in the hallway just outside the dealer's apartment. He looked at the nickel-plated Colt Diamondback, .38 Special in his gloved hand, flipped open the cylinder then quickly closed it. He hated the thought of walking into a gunfight with a six-shot revolver. Knowing that the men on the other side of the door would be armed with Mac 10 automatic machine pistols and 9mm Berettas with fifteen round clips. His only chance was to get inside and catch them sleeping or high, hopefully both.

He sat the .38 Special on the floor and inserted a thin metal lock-pick into the key-way. When he turned the handle the door opened. It wasn't locked, he whispered to himself. He retrieved the revolver and quietly stepped inside the room closing the door behind him. It was dark and still and deathly quiet in the room, which seemed odd to him because he had never been in the apartment when there wasn't music playing or a television blaring from one of the rooms. He stood with his back hugging the wall allowing his eyes to adjust to the darkness.

Maybe no one was home, he thought. Maybe they had snorted the uncut Cocaine the same way Beverly had and passed out for the night. Maybe someone was watching the whole thing unfold and was about to fill him full of lead as soon as he made an aggressive move toward the interior of the apartment.

The apartment was spacious. The front door opened onto a living room filled with expensive furniture. There were two brocade silk sofas sitting face-to-face in the center of the room. A glass top coffee table with heavy wrought-iron legs sat between the two sofas. Matching high-back wing chairs sat side-by-side on the far end of the sofas and a massive entertainment center covered the wall to the left of where he was standing. Tiny blinking LED lights from the stereo, CD player and wide-screen television, reflected off a floor-length mirror on a wall that jutted out and formed an opening for the dining room and a hallway leading to other rooms in the suite.

He moved into the living room passed the sofas, and stopped just inside the dining room. The dining table was made of dark oak and was at least twelve-foot long, with four high-back cushioned chairs on each side of the table and another at each end. A vase of fresh-cut flowers sat in the center of the table and the aroma of the arrangement filled the dining room with the smell of spring.

A columned opening forming the back wall of the dining room led onto a long, rolled-glass atrium running the full width of the apartment. There was another entertainment center on the end wall, a customized pool table in the center of the room, and several low-back leather bar stools sat around the pool table. At the end of the room closest to the dining room, was a wet-bar with barstools and enough liquor lining the walls behind the bar to serve everyone in the building.

Sneed peered into the atrium and then stepped inside. He was startled by the sound of something rolling on the ceramic tile floor. It was a sound that he was all too familiar with. He stooped to pick up the spent cartridge and found a half-dozen more in close proximity. His heart began to pound so loudly that he was afraid the sound could be heard outside his body.

He looked behind him, and then stood up, taking a deep breath, tightening his grip on the .38 special. There was no movement anywhere in the room. He headed toward the entertainment center. When he was twelve feet away, he could see the bodies of two men sprawled in the floor and dark circular pools of what he knew was blood glistening from the downtown lights streaming through the glass walls of the room. His heart continued to pound.

He remembered where the light-switch was for the light above the pool table. He made his way to it and flipped it on. The light in front of the entertainment center was still quite dim, but it was enough for him to recognize the bodies of his drug dealer and bodyguard laying facedown on the floor. The cartridge he had taken from the floor he held in the light checking the markings; it was a 9mm.

As he moved in for a closer look at the bodies he saw an automatic pistol lying on the floor between the two men; the slide was locked open indicating that the weapon had been fired until it was empty and then tossed onto the floor. He stepped over the drug dealer picking up the weapon. He recognized the grip of the weapon. A tiny chip of the checkered wooden grip was missing and he knew without question that it was the same 9mm that Beverly had shot the two people in the convenience store with. What a break to find the weapon before the cops arrived, he thought. Now if he could only find his drugs and money it would be a great day, he thought. He released the slide on the 9mm and stuffed it into his belt, pulling his shirt over the exposed grip. There was an arched entrance behind him leading to a hallway and the rest of the apartment. Attached to the hallway were a laundry room, a kitchen, two restrooms and three bedrooms. He moved quickly into the laundry room turning on the light. When he found nothing there he moved into the kitchen and flipped on the light switch.

The woman lying in the floor was not the woman he was looking for. He knew the dealer's girlfriend who had been in the apartment the last few times he had been there, and this wasn't her. As soon as he found the drug dealer and the bodyguard dead, he just assumed that the girlfriend had bought it as well. Maybe she was in one of the bedrooms, he thought. Now, there was one brutally inherent fact that he was absolutely certain of. Whoever had done this was someone to be reckoned with, someone who had no qualms about killing everyone in the place to preserve his anonymity. The murders were sudden and very brutal.

The way the woman was laying with her legs and feet twisted awkwardly beneath her back, told him that the killer had forced her to get on her knees before shooting her point-blank in the chest. The white cotton nightshirt and panties she was wearing had absorbed enough of her own blood that it looked crimson, except for the black powder burn between her breasts from the weapon being held so close when the killer pulled the trigger.

His first thoughts were to get out of the apartment and get as far away from Houston as he could. But with no money or drugs he and Beverly wouldn't last another day. He turned the kitchen light off and headed back into the hallway checking each room as he went.

When he reached the master bedroom at the end of the hallway he flipped on the light and stood there in the doorway trying to make sense of what his eyes were seeing. Someone had taken a heavy blunt object or sledgehammer, and knocked gaping holes from floor to ceiling in every space between the metal wall studs. Everything in the room was covered in white dust from the shattered drywall. Then something caught his eye on the floor of the closet. He walked across the room and peered inside.

It appeared that the money had been stored in the back wall of the closet and covered with drywall, plaster and paint for safekeeping. The money must have been wrapped in bundles with a red waxed paper wrapping. There were pieces of the wrapping paper on the floor and several discarded bills in varying denominations still stuck to the wrapping paper. He picked up all of the discarded bills that he could find and stuffed them into his rear pocket. When he walked out of the closet he noticed two things he hadn't seen when walking through the room the first time. There was an antique chest of drawers on the back wall that had all of the drawers pulled out and strewn around the floor. Secondly, on the corner of the dresser, nearest the closet, was a heavy gold class ring covered in dust from the demolition of the room.

He carefully plucked the class ring from the dresser studying every detail of it. It had a viridescent stone with an inscription around it that read, Smiley High School, Class of 1990. An inscription inside the ring read, "Congratulations to Anthony Degas from Mom". He tossed the ring in the air, caught it and stuffed it into his pocket. He knew the dead men in the atrium and neither of them was named Anthony Degas. And whoever had placed the ring on the dresser did so before going to work on the walls.

He moved on to the antique chest where the drawers were scattered around the floor in front of it. He sat on the edge of the bed in an attempt to understand what had happened, and then he noticed that each of the drawers had a hole in the center-top of the drawer where a locking device had been. Someone had used a tool to shatter the locks on each drawer. Then they pulled each drawer from the chest, unloaded its contents into another container and carried it with them. It had to be where the dealer kept his drugs, he thought. 'No way had they killed three people for some clothes,' he told himself.

Before he had a chance to think about the drugs being gone or what to do next, he heard a noise coming from the living room. Someone turned the stereo on, and a White Snake song called, "Here I Go Again" was blaring loudly from the speakers. His heart began to race; his pulse quickened. He pulled the .38 Colt from his belt and jotted back down the hallway, waiting by the doorway leading to the living room. He saw a tall blond woman whom he recognized as the dealer's girlfriend walk through the dining room and into the atrium. If he was ever going to get out of the apartment without being seen he had to do it now, he thought.

He made a dash for the front door, opening it and going through it in one fluid motion just as the woman began screaming from the atrium. The last thing he heard as he pulled the door closed and headed for the stairwell was part of the song's lyrics blaring from the stereo.

"Hear I go again on my own,
Going down the only road I've ever known
Like a drifter I was born to walk alone,"

"Baby, if you only knew how true that is," Sneed said, as he opened the door to the stairwell and hurried inside.

Ross Clayton sat up in bed, picked up the bedside clock radio and stared at the digital readout, which told him that it was ten o'clock. He knew it had to be morning because of the brightness of the room and his need for coffee. It had been a fitful night full of the aches and pains from the beating he had taken the night before, but it could have been worse he thought.

He rubbed the sleep out of his eyes and thought of Stillwell and Gorman, his two closest friends. He hated the thought of anything coming between him and Stillwell because in a time when so few people could be trusted, the one person he never doubted was Stillwell. And even though she was upset with him for some reason, he knew deep down inside that she felt the same way about him.

He worried about Gorman because he knew he'd just gone through a rough divorce, and that if the rumors floating around the department were true, he'd been virtually cleaned out by his ex-wife. Now, with the accident and Gorman looking at a lengthy hospital stay, his frame of mind had to be in a precarious state at best.

He pulled the phone from the nightstand and punched in Stillwell's number; she picked it up on the first ring. Her caller ID must have told her it was Clayton because she answered the phone with a question.

"Are you in a knife fight or a bar-room brawl?" she calmly asked.

Clayton chuckled when he heard the sarcasm in her voice. "You're not cutting me any slack at all, are you?"

"You don't need any slack. What you need is to be placed under constant surveillance by a team of Special Forces," she said.

"Look, I didn't go to the museum to get into a fight; it just happened. And I didn't call you to get in a fight either. I was calling to see if you'd like to have lunch and go see Gorman afterwards. I don't want to fight with you. Besides, in the condition I'm in, I'd probably lose."

"Are you picking me up or do you want me to meet you somewhere?" "I'll pick you up in an hour or so," he answered.

"Don't stop anywhere on the way over here. I don't want to be waiting all day to eat while you're tied up in a running gun-battle or something," she said. Clayton laughed at her taunting mood and hung up the phone.

Over the next thirty minutes he showered and combed his hair but his face was too tender to shave, so he left the stubble. He dressed in a pair of forest green trousers and a mint-green Polo shirt, with a caramel colored tweed jacket and matching loafers. When he walked through the living room, his housekeeper turned and smiled at him, then quickly frowned when she saw the bruises and stitches on his face.

"Are you alright, Detective Clayton?" she asked with a Spanish accent. "I'm fine, Maria."

"Can I fix you something for breakfast? You must be starving." The woman continued to look at him as if he needed medical attention.

"No thanks, I'm meeting Stillwell for a lunch. But I want you and Julio to take the day off. We talked about this before, don't you remember? The two of you work hard enough during the week; you don't need to be working on the weekends. Here's what I want you to do. I want you to go to Pappas in the Village and have a nice lunch on me. Tell Ray to put it on my tab. Everything is okay, and I won't be home until late."

"Are you sure? I don't mind cooking," she followed him into the kitchen.

Clayton turned and smiled at her.

"Do you like Pappas?" he asked her. "What's not to like? Of course I like Pappas."

"Then find Julio and go. Don't work anymore today." "Is that what you want?"

Clayton put his hand on her shoulder in an expression of sincerity. "That's exactly what I want. Live a little. Okay?

"I'll find Julio," she sighed.

Clayton's parents had hired the pair when he was seventeen and they were in their early thirties. Maria cooked and cleaned house while Julio Duarte' took care of the grounds and maintenance of the automobiles. They had no children and lived for years in an apartment above the garage. When Clayton's parents were killed in a plane crash in Scotland the two asked if they could stay and work for him. Clayton was a junior in college and needed all the help he could find taking care of everything his parents had left their only son.

Over the next couple of years he convinced them to move into the house and occupy the end of the mansion that had once belonged to him while he was growing up. Clayton moved into a remodeled master suite that had belonged to his parents, and from there the three of them lived in reasonable harmony for the next eleven years.

Clayton inherited just over thirty million dollars when his parents died. That amount had grown to over forty million the last time he'd checked, which was January first, when the accountant sent him the investment portfolio updates, taxes and yearly financial statement.

The truth about Ross Clayton and the way he lived his life was relatively simple and uncomplicated. He never thought much about being wealthy, or about the prestige and clout that his money could buy. He rarely carried cash, and almost never went shopping in a mall. He liked being a cop and being around cops. And aside from spending money on clothes he had only one extravagance in his life. He loved Jaguar Automobiles.

His everyday car was a silver XJ Super 8 with a custom package that he dropped an additional fifteen grand on at the dealership. But the love of his life was a fire engine red, 1992 XJ 220, twin turbo, two-door sports model that looked more like a Ferrari than a Jaguar, and always drew a crowd where ever he parked it. He pulled the keys from the pegboard on the wall and got in, gunned the XJ 220s state-of-the-art turbo-charged engine, and in seconds was headed to meet Stillwell.

Renee Harjo went to early mass and had to stop herself from telling the priest about Redhawk's premonition and the strange man who had been haunting him the last couple of months.

After church she chopped up onions, carrots, and potatoes and tossed them all in a cooking bag along with seasonings and a two-pound rump roast, and set it all in the oven then set the timer and heat to go off in a couple of hours. She placed a pan of water on one of the burners to boil the ears of corn she'd picked up at the store on the way home but decided to wait until the roast was almost done for that.

She changed into her gardening clothes and stepped out onto the porch and walkway to access the planting she had decided to do along the walkway and flowerbeds next to the cottage. It was well before noon when she looked into a cloudless blue sky and brushed the hair off her forehead and fitted a red bandana around her hair to hold it in place while she worked. She could hear Redhawk grinding away on something in the workshop behind the store.

Over the next hour she dug a trench along the redwood decking then planted monkey grass in the trench at one-foot intervals from the cottage to the workshop. After watering the new plants she went inside to check on the pot roast. The smell of the simmering meal hit her as soon as she opened the door and her empty stomach let her know it was past time to eat.

She washed her hands and face and then the ears of corn and dropped them into the pan of water on the stove and turned on the fire under it. When she finished setting the table she poured tea from the refrigerator over two tall glasses of ice cubes and was about to carry one to Redhawk when she turned suddenly to see the man she'd described to Redhawk standing suspiciously at the kitchen window staring at her.

She dropped the glasses of iced tea onto the floor and screamed loudly hoping Redhawk would hear her and scare the man away when he came running from the workshop. She stood away from the window frozen in fear, not knowing what move to make next, or if she should make one at all. Then she thought about Redhawk. He might need her help if there was a confrontation with the strange man; she knew she had to move. She headed for the front door, but before she took the first step she pulled a butcher knife from a drawer near the sink, gripping the handle tightly as she walked.

Before she reached the front door, she could hear talking and what sounded like laughter coming from the deck where she had planted the monkey grass. Her steps quickened, and when she reached the door she was almost at a full run. She burst through the screen door holding the long knife high in the air.

It took several seconds for her brain to collate the scene as it was being played out before her and to turn off the danger alarms that cause each of us to react to what we perceive as a harmful situation. She stopped running when she saw the two men hugging and slapping one another on the back like they were long lost friends. She was six feet away from the pair still holding the butcher knife high in the air when the men stopped hugging and turned to face her. The looks of confusion on their faces gave way to laughter as Renee tossed the knife onto the grass.

While the men laughed and talked about her holding the knife in the air, Renee turned and, without saying a word, went back into the cottage to clean up the mess she'd made dropping the glasses of tea onto the floor. Redhawk and the strange man were not far behind. The talking and laughter stopped as the two men stepped inside the cottage and heard the sound of broken glass being tossed around in the kitchen. Redhawk came into the kitchen alone.

"Renee, Renee," he called her name as he stepped into the kitchen, sheepishly holding his baseball cap in one hand and the butcher knife in the other.

"I'm sorry if you were frightened by my friend. If I'd known he was the one that came by, I could have cleared this whole thing up. He was my cellmate in Huntsville; we bunked behind bars for six years together. He was the eyes in the back of my head while I was in the joint, Renee. He's my friend," he explained.

"What's his name?" she asked.

"Snake, Snake Lopez," Redhawk said blankly.

"Snake? Well that fits…snaking around my window like that. That fits," she said, dropping the last of the broken glass into the wastebasket. The longer the two looked at each other the harder it was to hold back the laughter. Over the next thirty minutes, proper introductions were made and she asked Redhawk's friend if he liked pot roast and if he'd stay for lunch. She knew the answer before she asked the question and immediately began setting another place at the table. Things are sure getting interesting around here, she thought to herself.

Stacy Cromberg waited in front of the office of admittance for Delores Rucker who was walking to Herman Hospital through the labyrinth of underground tunnels that traversed Houston's Medical Center. When she arrived they went in together and spoke with an obese woman in a wheelchair about obtaining Wade Gorman's personal effects. The woman disappeared through a corridor behind her desk and thirty minutes later immerged from a doorway adjacent to her office, carrying a blue storage container with a clear plastic cover.

"Before I can release any of this to you I'll have to have the paperwork signed and dated by Mr. Gor-Man or his next of kin," she said in an irritating, nasally voice.

"We are this man's next of kin," Rucker said.

"It says here on his admittance form that this man is African American. Don't neither one of you look African American to me," she said with a sneer.

"This badge says I'm African American," Cromberg said, holding her badge in front of the woman's face. The woman made a face and was poised to pursue the argument with Cromberg, but for some unknown reason pushed the plastic container across the desk and crossed her arms as if she were witnessing a crime in progress.

The two cops pulled the clear plastic wrapping off the top of the container and began sifting through the contents. The container held a pair of black wingtip shoes, a pair of black sox, a blue, red, and beige striped tie, several writing pens, a wallet and pocket change, and the item they had been instructed to look for; a leather, ringed notebook with Gorman's name engraved on the cover.

Cromberg opened the notebook and read Gorman's notes aloud. "The crime scene, Two dead, one male one female, both lying face down, the male victim is Lee Denton, he appears to have been shot while running from the crime scene. The female victim is Marta Kheif, she and her husband, Nizar Kheif are the owners of the store. It appears that Marta attempted to fight off the perpetrator with a wooden pole until he shot her at almost point blank range. It is apparent that the assailants used the rear of the store for entrance because the lock had been cut with bolt cutters. I had conversations with Belichec and Ed Martin at the scene and will need the following information:"

A) Need the DNA results from the blood on the wooden pole

B) Need the results of the fingerprinting efforts on the cans of milk and baby formula that could have been handled by the perpetrator.

C) Check area hospitals for injuries consistent with someone being beaten with a baseball bat.

D) Need the ballistics reports on the rounds fired from the weapon used in the robbery.

E) Go over film from the surveillance cameras tape.

F) If possible, question the husband. Why wasn't he in the store instead of his wife? He had to see something when he was confronted by the assailants as they were leaving the store, what was it? He seemed to be extremely hostile towards everyone at the scene.

G) What was the strange odor on the woman's husband?

H) Make sure to go over the crime scene photos, see Ed Martin.

"It looks like the Captain was on top of things, and we've got our work cut out for us," Rucker said, after listening to Cromberg read Gorman's notes.

"What do you want to hit first?" Cromberg asked.

"We're not going to get a lot accomplished today because it's Sunday. I can check with the paramedics and find out where they took Mr. Kheif and we can go talk with him. Let's take this stuff up to Gorman's room, leave it, and then go make some phone calls."

"I think it's a good place to start," Cromberg agreed.

Ross Clayton looked at himself in the mirror then ran an index finger across the stitches that stopped just before reaching his scalp. The wound was still swollen, and felt tight and warm to the touch, but when he ran his fingers through his hair it fell naturally across the wound, obscuring it. The skin around each of the cuts had taken on a purple hue with a hint of yellow around the edges. He washed his hands and dried them quickly with towels from the dispenser, then headed back into the restaurant where Stillwell was eating desert.

When his waiter saw him coming he met him before he got to the table and handed him a silver tray with the bill on it and started to walk away. Clayton pulled his American Express card from his wallet and dropped it on the tray without looking at the bill or thinking about the cost of the meal.

"I need a gift certificate too. You know...one of those credit card looking things. It's a gift for a friend of mine at the department." He spoke to the waiter as if they were old friends.

"How much?" the waiter asked.

"How much what?"

"How much do you want the gift certificate to be worth?"

Clayton absent-mindedly tousled his hair. "I'm sorry, Mike. I wasn't thinking. Make it for two hundred dollars and put it in an envelope or something." The waiter nodded and walked away.

When he reached his table Stillwell was raking her fork across what was left of the crumbs from a slice of carrot cake with Carmel topping. She started talking before he sat down.

"Clayton, how often do you eat here?" she asked.

"I don't know. Every chance I get. Why?"

"It's expensive," she whispered.

"Not really. There must be a hundred restaurants more expensive than The Taste of Texas," he said, waving a dismissive hand through the air. "I thought you liked this place?"

"It's great; I just hate to think of what your monthly charges are for eating here all the time. It's got to be six or seven hundred bucks a month?"

"I don't have a lot of things to spend my money on, and besides it's close to your apartment and they have great service here. Why all the concern about money?"

"I guess I shouldn't be worried at all, it's just that you always seem to be out of money and I worry that we could eat somewhere a little less expensive, that's all."

"I'm not out of money, Leona. I just forget to go to the bank and grab some cash. Don't think for a moment that I'm out of money. It's just easier to use the card than to carry around a lot of cash. Are you ready to go?" He saw the waiter coming with his card and gift certificate.

Clayton signed the card receipt and stuffed the envelope in his jacket, then escorted Stillwell to the front door. The valet took his claim check and hurried out the door to retrieve his Jaguar.

"Where are the Impressionist paintings you've been telling me about?" Stillwell asked.

"In our office. Why?"

"Can we go see them?"

"Sure. But are you sure you want to work today? I was thinking maybe we could catch a movie or maybe drive down to Galveston or something, then go see Gorman later," he said.

"I'd like to see the paintings first, maybe formulate some ideas about how to catch this guy. Do you mind? We've still got lots of time to do things later," she said.

"I don't mind at all, I like working on Sunday," he said sarcastically.

The valet pulled the Jaguar under the veranda and when he opened the door an old song by Otis Redding, called, *These Arms of Mine,* came over the car's sound system. Clayton slipped on his sunglasses and held the passenger door open for Stillwell. She gave him a casual smile.

"Wow, Otis Redding and gallantry, what more could a woman ask for?"

Delores Rucker called the Houston Fire and Rescue dispatch command center, and was told that Nizar Kheif had been taken to Herman hospital. The dispatcher went on to tell her that he remembered the event because Kheif came to when they were wheeling him into St. Lukes and refused treatment in a hospital bearing a Christian name. Rucker hung up the phone and smiled at Cromberg.

"We don't have far to go," she said.

"He's here at Herman?"

"That's right. And get this; this man's wife had just been killed in a hold-up and he was beaten half-to-death and he refused treatment at St. Lukes because it had a Christian sounding name. He sounds like a pip of a character," Rucker said, making a face.

Cromberg phoned the hospital operator and was told that Nizar Kheif was in room 427. They packed Gorman's things back in the plastic bag and headed for the elevator. When they reached the room they could hear the sounds of children talking and a television playing the evening news. Cromberg knocked on the door and turned the knob.

"Mr. Kheif, I am Detective Cromberg and this is Detective Rucker with HPD. We need to ask you a few questions if we can." Cromberg said, clipping her badge back onto her belt.

"I prefer to speak with a male officer. It is my custom." Kheif said with an indignant sneer.

"I'm sure that if you were in your own country or your hometown you could speak with a man whenever you wanted, but your not, and we're not, so let's get on with it, please. Do you mind asking everyone else to step out side?"

Kheif said something in Arabic to the old woman and children and they wasted no time in clearing the room. In seconds they were gone. When Cromberg looked behind her at Rucker, she mouthed the word "Wow" with her lips.

"Mr. Kheif, we're terribly sorry for your loss, and we're sorry to have to be talking to you so soon after the death of your wife, but the quicker we get the answers we're looking for the quicker we'll catch the people responsible."

"Just do what you came for and get it over with," he said impatiently. "Mr. Kheif, do you or your wife usually work nights?"

"I usually work nights but I overslept and was taking a shower when the robbery occurred."

"So your wife was just in the store for a short time. How long would you say she'd been in the store before you came in?"

"No more than two hours," he said, looking away from Cromberg. Rucker was standing at the foot of the bed and up until now hadn't said a word.

"Mr. Kheif, the perpetrators cut a lock on the back of the store. Was that something you always did? Did you always keep a padlock on the rear door, and if so, why?" Rucker asked.

"There is a space between the store and our home large enough to park several cars. Our house is on the other side of that space beyond the cedar fence. Anyone could sneak in the back and steal us blind and we would never know they were there. There are thieves everywhere you turn in this neighborhood. We always kept it padlocked."

"Have you been robbed before?" Rucker asked.

"Only once, a drunken man robbed us once. The police caught the fool before he could get two blocks away. He was on foot and stopped to have one of the beers he stole from the cooler."

"Any reason to believe this person had anything to do with this robbery?" Cromberg asked.

"This was a man and a woman, I think. From the second I saw them in the dim light they appeared to be much younger than the old drunk. They both had long hair and tee shirts. I suppose they could have both been men. One of them jumped up and kicked my head against the door jam. I thought for a moment I was dying. If I would have been five minutes faster maybe I could've saved my Marta," he said, again avoiding eye contact with either of the cops.

"Is there any chance you might recognize either one of them if we showed you some mug-shots?"

"No, I only saw them in the darkness for a fraction of a second. Then he kicked me and now I don't remember anything."

"How many employees do you have," Cromberg asked.

"Two. They both work the day shift."

"Any reason to suspect either of them?"

"Absolutely not. They are my people. They are God-fearing Lebanese people, not one of your criminals," he lashed out at the question. "They have both been here to see me and are certain to attend the funeral home to see my Marta. They would not have shown their faces if they had had anything to do with this horrible crime. They are sick because of this crime."

"Just one more thing, Mr. Kheif, Can you think of anyone in the past that you might have had problems with in the store? Anyone have a grudge against you or Marta for any reason? Can you remember kicking anyone out of the store for stealing or being unruly? Please try to think, Mr. Kheif," Rucker coaxed him.

The man looked away from the cops at an imaginary object on the wall and didn't move or speak for several moments. When he finally decided to speak again his recalcitrant nature resurfaced and he lashed out at the two cops. The man's eyes were wide and flashing with hatred.

"I know what the police officials must think of my Marta. There was a man assigned to her case. I know this because I spoke with him in the ambulance on Saturday night. Now he's moved on to something more important than the death of my Marta and they've given the case to a couple of second-class subordinates. I'm burying my Marta tomorrow, I think I can expect nothing from you, so please leave me with my pain," he said, crossing his arms and staring at the wall.

Before Cromberg could clear her head enough to digest the baseless attack, Delores Rucker moved to the side of the bed where the man had turned his head and she bowed to the same level, so that they were eye-to-eye.

"Let me tell you something you arrogant ass," Rucker was speaking distinctly, forming each word in an attempt to keep this adversarial relationship at arms length and still drive home her point. "The man who was working this case was broad-sided by an overloaded pipe truck fifteen minutes after he left you. Now he's in traction with broken bones all over the left side of his body. He's here, in this very hospital as we speak. But he thought enough of you and your wife to fight through the pain and keep working the case with us as his arms and legs. And even though you think we're second-class individuals, we're good enough to find these people and bring them to justice. What I most regret is that we can't arrest you for blatant ignorance."

Rucker straightened her back, turned and walked out of the room. Cromberg gave Kheif a menacing glare, closed her notebook and followed Rucker into the hallway. Rucker motioned for the children and the old woman to go back into the room but never said anything to them.

"Thanks," Cromberg said.

"For what? I probably just got myself a good reprimand or a suspension." "Not from me. I think you deserve a reward. I'm buying dinner."

Stillwell's eyes moved from one painting to the other, intrigued by the beauty of each work.

"Well, I have to admit you were right. These paintings are breathtaking. I don't know much about art, but I know the difference between a master and a hack. The man's surely no hack, Clayton. Tell me again the story behind each of these," she said.

"I really don't know where to start."

"Start at the beginning. I haven't been here in ten days and I don't remember any of this catching my attention before I left. So just start at the beginning." Clayton took his notes from his desk and started scanning them.

"We believe the first murder happened a couple of months ago. Rhodes and Brunner caught the case. The man's name was Assam Huleyus, he was born in Lebanon and he would have been thirty-four on his next birthday. Huleyus owned a small convenience store on North Main in the Heights. Rhodes and Brunner worked it as an attempted robbery that went bad. Or at least that's the way they saw it at first. But as they got into the case it was clear it was something else."

"Why would they think that? What was missing?"

"Huleyus was killed in the rear of the store as he came out of the restroom. A number of patrons were caught on tape taking cartons of cigarettes, food, beer, you name it, but none of them were made for the murder. Forensics believes that the killer came in through the back door of the store and left the same way."

"No leads?"

"Nothing, No fingerprints, no footprints, no witnesses, no trace evidence except from the people looting the place. Robbery arrested a half-a-dozen people that the camera caught on tape coming and going into the back room where Huleyus was laying in a pool of blood. I guess one of them finally got a guilty conscience and made the call. The coroner said he'd been dead for at least three hours before it was reported. The looters were just coming and going like it was a free-for-all."

"It's nice to know we live in such a compassionate society," Stillwell said. "Go on, what else happened?"

"That's pretty much it for Huleyus. He left a wife and two children devastated by the killing."

"Were they ever suspected of anything?"

"They were visiting his sisters' home for a birthday party for his niece. His sister lived in Dallas. When Rhodes and Brunner went to the house the neighbors told them that she was away in Dallas for a few days. When they did come home it was like the end of the world. Not only did their stories check out, they drew a blank everywhere they went. No one could come up with a plausible reason why anyone would want to kill Huleyus. They worked the case for several weeks and it went nowhere."

"When did the second killing occur?"

"A little over a month after Huleyus was killed." "Was it the same M.O.?" Stillwell asked.

"Yeah, they've all been the same. The killer is wielding some sort of knife with a curved blade."

"So which was the first painting and who found it?"

"That would be this one," Clayton said pointing to the painting by Van Gogh.

The painting was a recent reproduction of an 1886 Vincent Van Gogh, *Montmartre Near the Upper Mill*. The painting is of a chilly winter's scene with cut glass lamps on high poles running along a bridge or boardwalk, a misty lake or seascape in the background, and bundled sightseers burgeoning the cold of the day in the foreground. Stillwell held the painting at arms length admiring the scene as Clayton told her about the murder and how it was found.

"The painting was found on a man named Scheib Al Kour who was killed on Washington Avenue near the downtown post office. Rhodes and Brunner never thought much about the painting until the third body was found on the old abandon bridge that crosses the San Jancinto River on Interstate 59 near Kingwood. The county installed lights on poles down the center of the bridge that look exactly like this painting. The bridge isn't used for traffic anymore so if you walked across the bridge, and you were dressed to suit the 1880s, it could look exactly like this, if you used your imagination," Clayton said pointing to the lights in the painting.

"What was the man's name found on the bridge? Was he killed the same way?"

"Akbar Aggerwal," Clayton answered, stuttering with the pronunciation of the name. "And yes he was sliced up just like the others."

"I can only guess that he had this painting on his person somewhere?" Stillwell asked while holding the second Van Gogh in front of her face. "I don't get it, Clayton. You said that this painting looked somewhat similar to the scene if you were standing on the bridge on Highway 59. But if you look at this painting of these men are sleeping on an embankment in a hayfield, a person would never have guessed that the bodies would turn up at a place like Minute Made Park. I mean, this is a stretch even for someone with a vivid imagination," Stillwell wrinkled her brow at the thought.

"It is. Until you look at the crime scene photographs. It looks so much like the painting it's unreal." Clayton sifted through a stack of photographs that Rucker had taken of the Minute Made crime scene until he found what he was looking for. He held the photograph beside the Van Gogh reproduction then looked at Stillwell to see her reaction.

"If you didn't know better you'd think that someone from Hollywood worked on this for hours to make it look the same. Even down to the old hat and shoes. They were obsessed with matching the crime scene with the painting."

"They were obsessed with more than that," Clayton said.

"Yeah, what else?"

"They were obsessed with committing a perfect murder. Our killer even wore paper shoes to keep his footprints out of the blood. And when they became too contaminated, he put on another pair. We were there for several hours and found nothing of any substance."

"So, what do you make of this painting that came from the Minute Made Park murder?" Stillwell asked.

"Well, our painter is certainly a versatile man. He's not just good at recreating the works of Van Gogh; he does Monet with the same acumen and dedication to detail. Look at this," Clayton said, handing her a copy of the Monet and the painting made by the killer.

Stillwell laid the painting and photograph side-by-side studying each detail in silence. "Clayton, I'm just a country girl, and the truth is I probably wouldn't know a Monet if you slapped me with one, but this painting, this painting is beautiful to say the least. We need someone who knows about these things to look at what we've got. There can't be that many people who can paint like this."

"Now you know why I was at the Fine Arts Museum. Art McDonnell said this guy Lund Corbel is an expert on impressionist works. He won't be in until Tuesday so I figure we can run down some of the wives and talk to them. We may get a lead there."

Stillwell didn't say a word. She just continued to stare at the paintings while Clayton spoke.

"Are you okay?" Clayton asked.

"Oh, yeah I'm fine. I just can't get over how anyone with so much beauty in his hands could have so much hatred in his heart. It doesn't seem possible for the two to co-exist in the same body," she almost whispered. "So, let me ask you a question," Stillwell said, laying the painting back on the tabletop.

Clayton put his hands in his pockets and looked dryly at the paintings. "I'm listening," he said.

"Do you think these paintings are clues or some sort of elaborate hoax?" I mean, are we supposed to go traipsing all over Houston and Harris County looking for a scene that resembles this boat and countryside?"

"I think if we find something that resembles this boat and countryside, we'll find another person of Arab descent with his throat cut," Clayton said.

CHAPTER 5

Anthony Degas and Clyde Bonner counted the stacks of money for the second time. Including the $37,850.00 they'd taken from the junkie and his wife at the motel; the total take from one nights work was just over a million dollars. And the drugs from the antique cabinet were worth another half-million at least. It was the kind of night that people wrote legends about, Bonner had boasted.

Clyde Bonner was a short, hawk-faced man with a ruddy complexion and thin lips. He had bushy eyebrows and brown eyes that always looked as if he had just awakened from a deep sleep or a drug-induced malaise. He had a full head of wavy brown hair that curled on his forehead and on his neck. His arms and shoulders were covered with prison art and gang tattoos. On his left hand he bore a scar from a gang initiation where a glowing-hot ice pick was driven through his hand for the right of entry into the gang. Any show of fear or pain by the inductee was grounds for retribution by the other members and considered as an act of cowardice by the gang members.

Anthony Degas did not possess the macho image or the tough persona that Bonner exuded, but in many ways he was more dangerous and more lethal than Bonner ever dreamed of being. Degas had been part of a Marine recon outfit in the second invasion of Iraq, and had killed at least forty men along the roads leading to and from ambush alley. It was on the suspicion that he had shot down four unarmed prisoners whom he was escorting to a rear interrogation area, that he was court-martialed and summarily discharged dishonorably from the Marines. Even though it was never proven conclusively that he was responsible for their deaths, they nevertheless died while in his custody.

Degas wore an inverted ball cap to cover his shaved baldhead. He had close-set eyes as blue as an early morning sky, and a square jaw that somehow didn't fit with the rest of his facial features. His skin was leather brown except for a white scar that skirted along the right side of his lower jawbone stopping at the center of his chin. There was no fat on his body and, with the exception of a slight limp in his left leg; he was a perfect physical specimen.

Bonner leaned back in his chair, lit an unfiltered cigarette, an inhaled the smoke deep into his lungs, then blew it out above his head. He let the cigarette dangle from his lips and crossed his arms as if he was about to say something more intellectual than Degas was capable of understanding.

"We gotta get out of Dodge, you know that, don't you? I don't know about you, but I ain't going to take no lethal injection for what happened last night. They put us onto the junkie and all that money he was flashing around then demand half of our take, after we take all the chances. No way we gonna stand for that." He flipped an ash into a glass bowl then took another drag on the cigarette. "Now we can split up or we can go together, but one way or the other we got to get out of the Lone Star State of Texas as soon as we can. Our only hope is that the cops find the junkies' gun and assume they made the hit."

"Hey man, I got nothing holding me here," Degas started. "I want to take my mom some money this afternoon, and then I'm ready to split. Where are you thinking about going?" Degas asked.

"You still got your passport?" Bonner asked.

"Yeah, I got a passport," Degas said, lighting his own cigarette.

"I'm thinking Rio," Bonner said.

"Rio, as in Rio Grande, Mexico?"

"No, you idiot, Rio as in Brazil."

"I don't know, man. I don't even know where Brazil is," Degas said. Bonner shook his head and crushed out his cigarette. "Look, let's do this right. Let's get cleaned up and get some new threads and buy the tickets through a travel agency. We'll have them book us in a fine hotel close to the beach maybe even find us a nice bungalow somewhere and just kick back, living like kings."

"Man, I like the way you think. Let's do it," Degas said, flipping an ash at an ashtray. "What do we do first?" he asked.

"First things first, let's stash this money somewhere and get some rest. It's been a long night. Then we clean up, go to the mall and get some new threads, new shoes, luggage anything we want. Then tomorrow we hit a travel agency, make all the arrangements and let's say by Thursday, we're out of here. You should have plenty of time to come up with a story to tell your mom, leave her some cash and we're gone. No one knows a thing about nothing. Are we cool?" "Yeah man, we're cool," Degas said, offering Bonner a high five and smiling broadly.

`It took Richey Sneed less than forty-five minutes at the Harris County Library in Humble, to find an address on Anthony Degas' mother. It took another thirty minutes to find the wood framed home on Fawnridge Street. When he knocked on the door he heard a dog barking in the background and the smell of eggs and bacon coming from inside the house.

"May I help you," Silvia Degas asked as she opened the door.

"Yeah, my name is Chandler Thomas. I went to Smiley High School with Anthony. I haven't seen him in years until just the other day I saw him at the mall in Humble and he asked me for a job. He said he'd been in the service and that he was looking for a job. I think I may have something he might be interested in," Sneed lied convincingly.

"I doubt seriously that you've ever seen my son. And I'm even more certain that you never went to Smiley High School, since for the last twenty years the school has been predominantly Black and

Hispanic. You're either a cop or someone Anthony owes money too, so you either show me a badge or get off my property."

The woman stood there for a few seconds waiting for the man to make a move. When he didn't repudiate her statement she began closing the door in his face. Before she realized what was happening the man burst through the door knocking her to the floor. When she saw the pistol in his hand she never moved or said another word until she was told to do so.

Richey Sneed stepped out onto the porch and motioned for Beverly to pull the car around back and come inside. Sneed kept his eye on the woman while he waited for his wife to hide the car. When he saw her rounding the driveway he stepped back inside the house and pointed the 9mm at the woman's forehead.

"I'm only going to ask you this once, you lie to me, and I'm going to shoot you. Do you understand?" The woman nodded yes but still never opened her mouth.

"Where is Anthony?"

"He's running with that hoodlum friend of his, Clyde Bonner. And if I know Clyde Bonner, they're up to no good," she said, convincingly.

"When's the last time he was home?" Sneed asked.

"Two or three days, maybe longer. He'll be back when he gets hungry or runs out of money."

Beverly Sneed opened the door and stepped inside. She turned her head away from Degas' view while walking through the living room and into a hallway leading to the kitchen.

There was a coffee pot perking on the counter, an open newspaper on the bar and a skillet on the stove that appeared to have been used to cook the eggs and bacon. There was a half-eaten piece of toast on a saucer near the newspaper, an unfiltered cigarette dangled from a tin ashtray.

"There's no one here," Beverly Sneed called out as she hurriedly checked the rest of the house.

"Are you expecting anyone besides Anthony?"

"I'm not expecting anyone at all. I live here alone. Anthony drifts in once or twice a month and stays for a few days at a time. My husband's been dead for two years," she crossed herself and set up on the floor.

"Then you won't mind if we wait here for Anthony to come home. You see what's happened here is that Anthony has helped himself to our money and drugs and we want them back. Our beef's not with you, so as long as you don't create any problems for us, we won't shoot you, could it be any clearer than that?" Sneed asked.

"Are you going to kill my son if he comes home?"

"As long as I get my money and drugs, I'm not going to hurt anyone. If I don't get what I want, someone has to pay," he said.

"I have five hundred dollars in my dresser, you can have it all if you'll just go and leave Anthony alone," she said.

"I'm afraid that five hundred dollars is not going to cut it, Mrs. Degas. If you want to help out, you can fix my wife and me some breakfast. If you don't want to do that I'm going to handcuff you to something in your room so you can be quiet. You do right by me and I'll do right by you."

"I'll be glad to fix you something to eat," Mrs. Degas said.

The dark man pulled his Sujjada from the closet and spread it out before the window on the east side of his house and began to pray.

"My God, I am all alone in this hideous land filled with infidels. I need your strength to continue on with the task before me. Give me thy strength I pray for the great work that I must do, and bless me oh God with the hand of thy greatness. Grant me thy wisdom oh God that I might be a powerful force among the infidels. Grant thy blessings on me that thy will be done and the infidels be dammed.

In Allah I bless,

The man carefully rolled the Sujjada and tied the ends in place for storage. When he emerged from the closet he pulled the curved blade knife from its sheath and examined the blade. Just the slightest movement against the blade could cause serious damage, he thought. But he should probably have it sharpened before the trial of God, he thought. He slipped the knife back into the closet and closed the door.

It was 10AM Monday morning when Ross Clayton walked into the courtroom for the arraignment of Marvin Taylor. He took a seat near the front of the gallery to watch the proceedings unfold. Twenty minutes later two guards escorted Taylor into the courtroom and left him alone in an area designated for those filing motions or pleas before the court. He was still walking with a slight limp and the bruises on his face looked a lot like his own.

Taylor was wearing an orange jumpsuit that was at least three sizes too small for his massive body. The sleeves dug into the muscle in his arms and the zipper on the front of the jumpsuit was pulled to its limit from the man's broad chest. Taylor turned to look around the courtroom and when his eyes met Clayton's, he quickly looked away.

As the room began to fill with other prisoners, lawyers, bailiffs, stenographers, and clerks, Clayton noticed a well-dressed man standing at the rear of the courtroom with a handful of forms clad in a light blue binding. He looked around the room as if he were unsure if he was in the right courtroom. Suddenly he began walking in the direction of Marvin Taylor. Just as he reached Taylor he handed him the document he was carrying, leaned over and whispered something in Taylor's ear.

Taylor looked at the man with sad eyes and then scanned the papers he had just been handed. Clayton watched the proceedings with a special interest because he knew what the powerful man could do if he was prodded toward violence. Before Taylor could say anything, the man turned and walked away just as quickly as he had appeared. Seconds later, Judge Russell Slay Cash entered the courtroom and the bailiff called everyone to attention.

The court clerk began reading the case docket and when Taylor's name was called he stood and calmly said, "I'm here, your honor."

It seemed that everyone in the courtroom was waiting for Taylor's attorney to appear and enter a plea of some sort on his behalf, as was protocol with an arraignment. When it was obvious that no one was coming on behalf of the defendant, the judge dropped the papers he was reading and looked at Taylor like he had wandered in from another planet.

"Mr. Taylor, do you have legal counsel?"

"No, your Honor, I do not," he said with his head bowed.

"Then we will postpone your arraignment until this afternoon and I will, in the meantime, appoint an attorney to represent you. Bailiff, please escort Mr. Taylor to a holding cell and notify legal aid." The bailiff nodded.

Since becoming a detective with HPD, Clayton and Stillwell had been to hundreds of arraignments and had witnessed many strange and unusual conversations between judges and the accused. In one form or another he had heard some of the most incredulous fabrications ever spun by members of the human race. But in all that time he had never witnessed what was about to happen between Marvin Taylor and Judge Cash.

Clayton wasn't sure if the papers Taylor was holding had anything to do with it or not, but in a display of self-deprecation and contrition the likes he had never seen before, Taylor eloquently addressed the court concerning his misdeeds.

"Your Honor, if I might have your forbearance for just a moment," he said. "Mr. Taylor, I hesitate to speak with you at any level without you having the benefit of an attorney present."

"Your Honor, I hereby, wave my right to have an attorney present at this proceeding. And I'd like to enter a guilty plea for the crimes with which I've been charged. I realize now that I've been a foolish and ignorant man, and that my problems are of my own making. There's no need for a costly trial to determine my contributions or my guilt in this matter; I am guilty, and there is no doubt to be uncovered."

"Mr. Taylor, what do you do for a living?" the Judge asked.

"I teach world history and coach the varsity football team at Douglas Mac Arthur High School; or at least that's what I did before this happened, your Honor."

"I don't think that you fully grasp the gravity or the depth of the charges that have been leveled against you, and are before this court now for consideration, Mr. Taylor. It's clear, or at least it is to me, that you're under some sort of emotional strain and should reconsider this course of action." Taylor put his hands behind his back still holding on to the divorce papers.

"I've had all weekend to think about this, Your Honor. Just a few moments ago I was handed these papers," he held the papers in front of him now for the court to see. "These papers say that my wife is filling for divorce. Two days ago, I almost killed her, and this police officer here," he said as he turned and motioned in Clayton's direction. "It seems to me that if I don't do something to stop the wrong I've done, and do it now, there may not be a next time. This officer could have shot me, if he had been so inclined; I was armed and had already shot my wife. Instead, he disarmed me and brought me in, and I realize how wrong I've been. The law says that I've got a right to a speedy trial and the judgment that follows. If you please, sir, I'd like to get this over with and get on with what's left of the rest of my life."

The judge looked at Clayton and then at Taylor and then at the assistant district attorney who had yet to say a word, and then whispered something to the bailiff. Then without warning slammed his gavel on the bench and said, "This court stands adjourned for thirty-minutes."

Clayton left the courtroom, purchased a cup of coffee in the downstairs lobby and called Stillwell at the station to let her know what was going on, and that he'd be there as soon as it was over. The truth was there was no reason for him to stay, since there were no pleadings for or against the accused, and no need for his testimony. But he had to see how this was going to play itself out. And even though he had a host of newfound respect for the man who'd almost beaten him to death, he wanted to see that the man received help with his problems and in the reshaping of his future. If that included an amount of time spent in incarceration to get the help, then so be it.

When Clayton made his way back to the courtroom, it was clear from the people milling about the hallway that the thirty-minute break was going to be considerably longer. He didn't have to look at the clock on the wall to know it was time for lunch and that whatever he was going to do he needed to do it now. He bought a ham sandwich and a Coke from the vending machine and a newspaper from the kiosk on the first floor and carried it back to the courtroom, found a place on a bench down the hall and made the best of the wait.

When he came out of the restroom at 1:15, the hallway was empty and the doors to the courtroom were closed. He hurried back through the double doors just in time for the judge to re-enter the courtroom and start talking as if he'd never left.

"Folks, I want to apologize for the delays this morning and for the unusual nature of the proceedings thus far. It is very rare that we have to deal with this level of honesty from a defendant. Not that everyone is dishonest, but almost no one wants to go to jail. I have spoken at length with the ADA and I believe we are in agreement and can proceed." He turned and handed the clerk a folder then looked at the clock at the rear of the room as if seeing it for the first time.

"Mr. Taylor," he said, leaning back in his chair. Marvin Taylor stood and lowered his head.

"I have spoken with some of your co-workers at the high school where you work. The general consensus from that group of people is that you work too hard; you strive for excellence, and you're part of an increasingly pervasive culture that is addicted to the use of body building steroids. I am amazed, that with your level of education, that you were either unaware of or unconcerned with the plethora of data available on the dangers and effects of HGH and other anabolic steroids."

"Are these things true?"

"Yes, your Honor, they are," Taylor said, solemnly.

"In light of this and the fact that you have no attorney, I'm going to offer you one last chance to put this off until you can acquire or have legal counsel appointed."

"No, your Honor, I want to do this now," Taylor said.

"That being the case, and in agreement with the ADA, I sentence you to ten years in a state correctional facility. Additionally, I am probating nine years of the sentence, so that you will serve a maximum of six months in the county hospital or jail and afterwards, you will perform six months of community service from a list of occupations that we will provide you with. Additionally, you will refrain completely from the use of steroids in any form. If you have one incident, or perform any act of violence that violates the terms of this ruling you will serve every day of that ten-year sentence. Do you understand your sentence as it has been read to you?" the Judge looked at him sternly.

"I do, your Honor."

"Then you are to be taken into custody and you will begin your psychiatric evaluation immediately. Do you have any questions?"

"No, Your Honor."

"Then I sincerely hope I never see you in this court again. We are adjourned one hour for lunch," the Judge said striking his gavel.

Clayton left the courtroom wondering how he would ever explain what happened to Stillwell or if he fully understood it himself. One thing he was absolutely certain of, he thought, there was nothing boring about it.

It was 1:45 when Stacy Cromberg got a call from a Detective Ryan Archer whom she knew vaguely from her stint on nights. He told her that was working a triple homicide in a downtown penthouse just off Interstate 45 and South Main. She took down the address as he talked to her.

"I hear you're working that double homicide that Gorman was on when he got hurt?"

"Yeah, you heard right, what's up? Cromberg asked.

"We got three dead on our end in what appears to be a drug deal gone wrong. We had ballistics check all the slugs fired in the apartment. Your case came up. It was the same 9mm used in your holdup Saturday night. We think you got a real shooter on your hands," he said, clicking his chewing gum as he talked.

"Can we take a look at the crime scene?" Cromberg asked.

"Sure, the bodies have been removed, but if you'd like I'll walk you through it."

"We can be there in thirty minutes."

"You got it, we'll meet you there," he said and disconnected.

Cromberg gave Rucker the details as they headed for the apartment building.

"So, let me see if I got this straight. Our shooter does a convenience store on Friday night, and then shoots up an apartment building on Sunday?" She asked.

"Yeah, I know it doesn't sound right. Archer said the guy was a big time dealer; maybe the shooter goes there to settle a loan or a recent buy and thing somehow get out of hand. The guy goes berserk and does everybody in the apartment," Cromberg said.

Rucker stared out the window watching the billboards pass, her brow furrowed in deep thought. Even without talking about it they both knew that even habitual criminals rarely commit violent crimes so close together and with such flagrant disregard for human life.

"You know, if this is the same shooter, we got a really bad character on our hands," Rucker said.

"Yeah, if he's killed five people in two days he's not going anywhere without a fight. He enjoys it," Cromberg said.

"I don't know if he enjoys it like you say, but I know one thing for sure." "Yeah, what's that?" Cromberg asked.

"He ain't afraid of riding the needle," Rucker said.

Snake Lopez and Redhawk Simmons ate everything that Renee had fixed for supper, and then drove off the reservation for a case of beer, which kept the stories going until four in the morning, when she insisted that everyone go to bed.

It was almost two in the afternoon on Monday when the two men finally began to stir. Renee had left a note on the kitchen table that she had to drive two women from the reservation into Houston for an MRI at Ben Taub Hospital and that she wouldn't be back until around five at best.

Redhawk searched the bathroom drawers until he found a new toothbrush, disposable razor, and deodorant, and stacked them on top of a set of towels and headed Lopez in the direction of the bathroom. While Lopez showered and shaved Simmons scrambled eggs and fried bacon then stacked it high on plates from the drain board and served it with the last two beers from the refrigerator. The two men ate like they were in a contest to see who could pile up the most cholesterol in one sitting.

"Redhawk, you got any money?" Lopez asked.

"Yeah, man. I'll get you whatever you need," Simmons said. "I'm doing really well for the first time in my life. How much you gonna need?" Simmons asked.

"No man. I ain't looking for no handout. I just thought if you had any money we might run over to Louisiana and do a little gambling," he said with a childish grin.

"You're trying to get me in trouble now," Simmons said.

Lopez was just about to say something else when the phone rang and Redhawk headed to the living room to answer it. He picked up the receiver on the second ring knowing it would be Renee calling in to complain about being up all night.

"Is he still there?" Renee asked without saying hello.

"Yeah," he said not knowing how to take her attitude toward his friend. "He's still here. We just got finished with breakfast. You'll have to pick up more eggs and bacon from the store on your way home."

"Is he going to stay another night?" she asked apprehensively.

"What's up, Renee? You seem to have your feathers ruffled for some reason. The man is my friend."

"Can he hear what I'm saying?"

"Look, Renee, you know this is a small place," he whispered.

"Well don't talk just listen," she said.

"Alright."

"I don't know if this will make any sense or not, but I'm worried. Things have been going so well for us for the first time in our lives. Neither one of us has ever had much of a home and certainly no one to share it with; I just don't want anything to spoil what we have together. Does that make sense to you?" she asked.

"All he wants is to spend a little time together. He wants us to go over to Louisiana to do a little gambling. Is that so bad?" Redhawk whispered.

Renee Harjo could feel her pulse skyrocket. She took a deep breath and calmly spoke into the receiver.

"Redhawk, you know that's a violation of your parole. Anybody sees you in a place like that and you're back to the pen. Is that what you want?"

"No baby, I've been working hard, a day off can't hurt," he said, sheepishly.

"Do what you got to do, Redhawk. I was only thinking of us, and what we have together. I don't want to spend the next ten years of my life looking at the man I love through steel bars," she said sternly.

"I'll be home early. I'll give him some money and he'll be gone. I promise." Redhawk waited for her to plead with him not to go, but instead all she said was that she'd see him when he got home and hung up the phone. Redhawk turned to Snake Lopez and gave him a wink and said, "What do you like to play, craps or blackjack?"

Anthony Degas and Clyde Bonner slept until three in the afternoon, then drove to the Galleria mall and parked in the Macy's parking garage. They spent six thousand dollars on clothes and shoes in Macy's and another twelve hundred at the Foot Locker, on Air Jordan sneakers and official NFL jackets displaying the Miami Dolphins, and the Dallas Cowboys logos. But the shopping spree didn't end there.

In an expensive boutique that specialized in gaudy personalized jewelry they each bought a gold chain that looked more like a rope than it did a necklace. Then Anthony Degas bought a solid gold Masonic Lodge emblem for his chain that was no less than two inches in height, even though he was never a Mason or had any idea what the emblem stood for. He told Bonner that people would think he was an engineer when they saw the compass on the emblem.

Clyde Bonner bought a diamond-studded earring in the shape of the letter B and a custom made Texas A&M belt buckle with fourteen diamonds on the face of it. Then to prove his loyalty to the A & M banner, he bought an eighteen-carrot gold class ring with the letters A and M encrusted in diamonds on the sides and a solitary diamond stud for the center mounting. When the store manager asked Bonner if he was a part of the Corps while he was at A&M, Bonner gave him a silly grin and said, "Anthony here was in the Corps, they wouldn't let me join 'cause I didn't have no high school diploma."

They spent so much money in the boutique that Degas had to go back to the car for another four thousand dollars to pay for the Tag Heuer watches that each of them purchased on their way out of the store. The manager of the store waited for them to get out of sight then picked up the phone and dialed the operator. He was just about to ask to be connected with the police when his brother tapped him on the shoulder and told him that the two men had spent just over fifty thousand dollars in cash in less than one hour. "They were probably wealthy Rap stars, or actors from out of town," he said, hanging up the phone.

When they got back to Bonner's car and were about to leave the parking garage, Bonner suddenly killed the engine and lit a cigarette. He sat there quietly puffing on the cigarette and staring at the concrete wall in front of the car as if he'd just been struck with a slice of knowledge so intellectual and so enlightening that he wandered if Degas would ever be able to fully grasp the meaning of what he was about to say.

"We can't fly to Brazil," he said finally.

"Who's going to stop us from going to Brazil? Until they pin them murders on us, we can go anywhere we want," Degas said flatly.

"Have you ever flown on a commercial airline?"

"Man, I've flown all over the world. You think we walked to Iraq? I spent a week in Amsterdam and a week in Rome too," he boasted.

"How much money were you carrying on those trips?"

"I don't know, maybe two thousand bucks. I had a lot of money stacked up in combat pay. There sure wasn't no place to spend it in Iraq, at least not where I was."

"There's a lot of difference between two thousand and a million dollars. They're not going to let us leave the country with a million dollars in cash. They're going to confiscate our money then put us in lockup until we can prove where we came up with that kind of money. We can't pull it off," Bonner said reflectively.

"So how are we going to get to Brazil and live in one of them bungalows?" Degas asked.

"The only way is by boat. We can take one of them ocean liners to Rio. All we got to do is buy some nice luggage. We cut the liner out of the bottom of one of the suitcases; glue envelopes stuffed with money to the bottom then cover the whole thing with cardboard, slip the liner back on and sew it to the sides. If they x-ray our luggage it will show up as clothes and nothing else. They won't search our luggage like their doing now in the airports since nine-eleven. Let's go back inside and buy some luggage."

"I'm sure glad you thought this thing through. I never been on one of them ocean liner boats. They got places to eat on there?" Degas asked.

Bonner rolled his eyes and got out of the car.

Clayton found Aaron Phillips's mailbox and dropped the gift certificate for the Taste of Texas restaurant and a note thanking him for taking care of talking to the two women whose husbands had been murdered at Minute Made Park. As he was walking in the direction of Stillwell's cubicle, she darted around the corner with a handful of papers and started talking as if he'd been there all morning but she had just noticed him.

"Ah Clayton, good news. I tracked down Lund Corbel and he can see us first thing in the morning at the museum. I also spoke with Anna and Courtney Abuo, they have agreed to see us this afternoon and not wait until after the funeral tomorrow. They want to do whatever they can if it will help find their husbands' killer."

"That's refreshing. Sounds like you've been busy."

"That's just the beginning. I've also got us appointments with Assam Huleyus's wife and Scheib Al Kour's wife and sister, after we see Lund Corbel in the morning," she said, while slipping out of her flats and into a pair of dark blue high heels. Clayton couldn't help but notice that she was dressed differently today, not in her usual slacks and matching jacket.

Stillwell was dressed in a knee-length, navy blue skirt with slits up both sides. Her blouse was baby blue, short sleeved with navy blue and a lighter blue piping on the sleeves and collar. The ensemble clung to her shapely form like a plastic suit, accentuating every curve perfectly. Clayton had noticed no less than four other detectives who were passing by, either turned their heads or stopped somewhere in the office to take a closer look. She was breathtaking, he thought, and found it hard to take his eyes off her.

"Are you ready?" she asked.

"Yeah, sure, I'm ready," he replied.

"Are we going in the Jag or the cruiser? I checked out a cruiser because I didn't know what time you were coming back and thought I might have to go it alone."

"Let's go in the cruiser, I want to go over the notes on the first two cases in a little more detail. I'll read; you drive."

Stillwell took Louisiana Street through town and then turned on Pease to enter the freeway system taking Interstate 45 South at the interchange. Clayton sifted through the folders containing the notes written by Detectives Rhodes and Brunner, sharing the most important details with Stillwell while she drove. The trip to Clear Lake took just over thirty minutes and she exited at NASA Road 1.

The house on Meadow Lane was an expansive two-story Tudor with a circular drive and sidewalk winding to the front door. A black Thunderbird convertible was parked next to the sidewalk. Stillwell pulled the cruiser behind the Thunderbird and both cops got out, walking slowly to the front door.

Anna Abuo opened the door and stepped in front of the two cops offering her hand to Clayton and then to Stillwell.

"We've been waiting all afternoon. We thought when Miss Stillwell called you'd be here sooner," she said.

"It's my fault," Clayton said. "I couldn't get out of court. I apologize for any inconvenience I may have caused you."

"We're very sorry for your loss, and we know this is a difficult time for you so we'll do this as quickly as possible. Is your sister-in-law here?" Stillwell asked.

Anna nodded and led them through an octagon shaped entry hall and into a spacious living room with expensive furnishings and a baby grand piano in one corner. Courtney Abuo was standing when the cops entered the room. Her face was drawn, she had dark circles under her eyes and it was obvious that she'd been crying for some time. She dabbed her nose with a Kleenex from a box on the coffee table and shook hands with Clayton and Stillwell.

Anna offered them coffee and when they declined sat by her sister-in-law on the sofa. She was wearing gray pants with a short-sleeved matching top. She had perfectly manicured nails and hair and every move she made was as if she had been rehearsing for this scene all of her life.

Courtney Abuo looked like an abstract painting of confusion, pain, and shattered emotion. She hardly looked at the cops when they sat down, and when she did it was with sad eyes, drained of a sense of being. She was dressed in blue jeans and sneakers with a dark blue blouse, a leather handbag sat on the floor next to her feet.

"Our notes indicate that you all met in college?" Stillwell started the questioning.

"That's true; we met at Berkley in 1990. Youssef and Omar had just arrived in this country and, because of our mutual interests, we became close friends within weeks of the first semester," Anna said. "Courtney and I had grown up in southern California and both wanted to be astronauts. But the fact of the matter is we were better at math and physics than we were at the physical requirements of being an astronaut."

"You said that the four of you had similar interests. What interests were those?" Stillwell asked.

"Aeronautical Engineering, metallurgy, quantum physics and chemical engineering. Each of us acquired positions with contractors here in the NASA complex. For the last five years Courtney and Omar have worked with Morton Thiokol, Youssef and I with Lockheed Martin."

"Were any of you working on anything that would attract international interest or espionage? Is it possible that someone approached Youssef and Omar in an attempt to recruit them or to temp them to divulge sensitive materials?" Clayton asked.

For the first time Courtney Abuo turned and faced the two cops, her eyes filled with tears, her face bearing the sting of the question Clayton had just asked. She blew her nose and started to speak. "What are you thinking? Surely you don't think our Husbands were involved in something criminal? We're scientists not spies," she said. "And neither of us have a motive to do anything so sinister."

"We're not suggesting anything, but you must admit a lot of people have a legitimate reason for being interested in what goes on here at the NASA complex," Clayton said.

"Then to answer your question, the answer is no. To our knowledge none of us has been approached by anyone for any reason. If we had we'd have reported it at once," Anna said.

"Did your husbands go to many ballgames?" Stillwell asked.

"We have season tickets," Anna Abuo answered. "We usually go to the games together, but Courtney hasn't been feeling well so we stayed here." Courtney Abuo turned to face the two detectives a look of despair in her eyes.

"If we'd only gone with them, this probably wouldn't have happened," she said, reaching for another Kleenex.

"Why do you say that?" Stillwell asked.

"From what we understand about the area where they were found I doubt seriously they would have thought to take us to such a restricted part of the ballpark. For the life of me I can't imagine Omar or Youssef allowing someone to take them to an area like that without some official from the ballpark accompanying them. It doesn't make sense," Anna Abuo said. "It just doesn't make any sense."

"Tell us what either of you know about Vincent Van Gogh" Clayton said.

The two women looked at each other with quizzical glances.

"What on earth are you talking about, Detective?" Courtney Abuo asked. Clayton fished a folded piece of copy paper from his pocket and handed it to her. She unfolded it and held it for Anna to see. Both women shrugged and waited for the detective to give them an explanation.

"We found this painting on another person who had been slain with a knife just like your husbands were, only a month or so ago. Your husbands' bodies were staged to match this scene exactly, so much so that it was easily recognizable at first glance," Clayton told them. "Please, try to think. Does it mean anything to either of you?" Both women shrugged in confusion.

"What does all this mean, Detective?" Anna Abuo asked.

"We don't know, Miss Abuo," Stillwell said softly. "We have very little to work with and almost no clues. We just thought, or maybe we were hoping, that the paintings may have held some significance with you."

"You said earlier that the four of you usually went to the ballgames together, did you have any acquaintances or special friendships that you acquired at the ballpark? Or, is there anyone in particular that you might have suspicions about?" Clayton asked.

Both women shrugged at each other again then turned back to Clayton. "Our seats are in the club level. Most of the people there are business people, engineers, architects, or doctors. Not the kind of people who would do normally something like this. It seems to me that you're looking in all the wrong places," Courtney Abuo said.

"Sometimes our looking in the wrong places leads us to the right place," Clayton answered.

"You said that the two of you were here at the house all evening; did anyone else see you here or know the two of you were here all evening?" Stillwell asked.

"Courtney has had a stomach virus and she was nauseated, so we got our family doctor to call her a prescription for the nausea. I drove to the CVS Pharmacy on NASA Road One around eight-thirty to pick it up. The pharmacist and clerk both know me. While I was gone, Leah Cantor, a neighbor, called and spoke with Anna on the phone. So we can both vouch for our whereabouts, Detective," Anna said stiffly.

"We have to clear everyone who could be considered a possible suspect. If you'll give me the numbers of the doctor and neighbor who called, we'd appreciate it," Stillwell said.

Courtney Abuo left the room quickly and returned moments later with a sheet of paper in her hand. She looked agitated and unnerved when she handed the paper to Stillwell. "I think this is ridiculous; have we been the least bit reticent with you? What reason would we have to want our husbands dead? Even the thought is preposterous," she said, crossing her legs.

"The thought may seem preposterous, Miss Abuo, but I can assure you the statistics warrant our questions," Stillwell told her. The woman raised an eyebrow and looked away as if she were staring at an imaginary object on the wall.

"I have one last question," Clayton said, looking at Stillwell, she nodded. "Was either of your husbands involved in any business ventures? Or were there any pending deals that you might know of that could have gone wrong? Try to think, a property sale or purchase, a stock transfer, anything involving your families' assets?"

Both women seemed to give the question serious consideration and for the first time Anna Abuo was the first to answer. "I can't speak for Courtney but I know for certain that we had nothing financial on the horizon. I know that because we have committed our savings efforts to purchase a retirement home in Colorado. We wanted to live in the mountains and maybe raise horses. Our plan was to retire at fifty, so we'd still have plenty of time to enjoy ourselves."

Courtney started talking as soon as Anna stopped. "Omar and I both had 401K plans at work. We both invested in very safe stocks and it was all done through our companies. This house is the biggest investment we have ever made. Other than our work we had almost no outside interests. We wanted a family and were planning for that, but aside from that, there was nothing."

The two detectives stood and shook hands with the two women and thanked them for their time. Just as they reached the foyer Stillwell turned and asked one last question.

"By any chance do either of you know or have you ever heard of Assam Huleyus, Scheib Al Kour, or Akba Aggerual?" Like Clayton, she struggled with the pronunciation of the names.

The women looked at each other as if the question was part of some elaborate hoax or a futile attempt to make them reveal something sub-consciously. Anna Abuo looked as if she was about to say something, when Courtney held her hand in the air to silence her.

"We both recognize the names as being Arab, or Islamic. We had very little to do with that culture. Our husbands were proud Americans, and all of us worked for the betterment of this country and its ideals. Do not mistake our husbands or us for that matter, as being sympathetic to either of those causes."

Now it was Stillwell's turn to look incredulous. She looked at Clayton then back to the two women before she spoke. "The names I gave you were men with Arab or Islamic ancestry. They were men who were killed in similar fashion to your husbands, all in the last six months. We have reason to believe the killings are related somehow."

"If we jumped to the wrong conclusion, then we apologize. I'll let Anna speak for herself, but I've never heard of any of those people." Anna Abuo nodded in agreement.

"It was a long-shot," Stillwell said, smiling as she stepped outside the door.

Yellow crime scene tape hung loosely from the doorpost. Delores Rucker rapped on the door with the back of her hand then stood away from the opening with her hand planted firmly on the butt of her 9mm. Stacy Cromberg stood quietly on the other side of the door. Seconds later Ryan Archer opened the door and held it open for the two cops. He didn't begin talking until they were both inside the apartment.

Archer was in his late forties and had most of the ill-mannered characteristics of cops with more than twenty years on the force and in the field on a full-time basis. His hair was thinning in front and what was left he combed straight back. He had a tight, grim face, and he chewed gum incessantly, even when he was talking. He closed the door, put his hands in his pockets and rocked back on the balls of his feet as if he were about to jump off a ledge. He clicked his gum and started talking.

"We got three victims," he said, walking them through the living room to the atrium at the rear of the suite. "Two men and a woman. The two men were killed here in the game room," he said, flipping on the light switch. "The man on the left was Lawrence Smoot, age thirty-four," he said, pointing to the taped outline and bloodstains on the floor. "The man on the right, whom we believe to be Smoot's bodyguard, was Mo Freeman, age forty-six. His real name is Morris Freeman. Word on the street is he was a button man for the mob a few years back. Whatever he was, he wasn't overly effective here. His forty-five automatic was still holstered when we found them. He was shot twice in the chest and another time in the head for good measure. We're only speculating but we think the shooter capped Freeman first and then shot Smoot. He apparently knew that Smoot was unarmed and therefore took out the more dangerous of the two first."

"What about Smoot, how many times was he shot; I've never seen so much blood" Cromberg asked.

"Twice, Once in the neck, which the coroner said was lethal, and once in the chest. We can only guess as to what went on here since everyone is dead. But it appears that the shooters came in and stood over near the entrance and got in an argument or some kind of a misunderstanding with one of these two. Before they knew what was happening, the shooter pulled his nine and popped them both."

"You said there was a woman, where was her body found?" Rucker asked. "Through here," he said, motioning in the direction of the hallway. He led them down the hallway and into the kitchen. The light was already on but he reached for the switch and absentmindedly flipped it off, then quickly on again.

"The woman was found in front of the refrigerator with her legs doubled back under her body. We think she was kneeling when he shot her and fell straight backward. The slug we dug out of the cabinet is not the same weapon used to kill the others. That's why we know there were two shooters. Weren't there two shooters in the hold up at the store on Aldine Mail?" Archer asked.

"There was only one shooter, but there were two people robbing the place," Rucker answered.

"Well, I guess whoever the second shooter was got tired of being left out of all the fun and decided to get involved with the business at hand. There wasn't any real reason to kill the woman. She wasn't armed and there's a good possibility she didn't hear what went on outside; they just didn't want anyone around with the ability to drop a dime on them if they were seen."

"Aside from the slugs from the two weapons, were there any other bits of evidence?" Cromberg asked.

"We found several long brown hairs near Smoot's body. The only reason we think there might be a possibility of it belonging to the shooters is that no one else in the apartment had brown hair. Freeman's head was shaved and Smoot had sandy colored hair. Both women who lived here were blondes. The truth is it could have belonged to anyone. People were in and out of here all the time. The man supplied drugs to a lot of people, but one of the hairs was partially embedded in the blood pool on the floor where Smoot was laying. They're convinced the hair fell in the blood from someone leaning over the body. But who knows?"

Archer motioned for them to follow him then moved back into the hallway heading toward the rear bedroom. The room was dark and he flipped on the switch and waited for Rucker and Cromberg to go inside before him.

"Wow," Rucker said as she stopped just inside the door.

"It's just like we found it. Accept for the crime lab dusting for prints and looking for trace evidence; nothing has been moved," Archer said.

"The crime lab had to come up with something with as much work as it took tearing out these walls. I've never seen anything like this," Rucker said.

Archer scratched nervously at a spot on the back of his head and pointed to the chest of drawers to the right of the doorway, after clicking his chewing gum a few times he started talking again. "You're probably right. They took several samples of blood and sweat from around the room. If they got a record and a DNA code on file we'll nail them. This chest of drawers tested positive for drugs; coke, meth, and grass, mostly. We believe the walls in the closet were stacked with money; but there was no evidence of drugs being kept in the walls. From what the little blonde is telling us there could have been as much as a million dollars stashed there in the chest."

"We're going to want to speak to this woman. Are you still holding her?" Cromberg asked.

"We had to cut her loose this morning, but we know where to find her. The DA instructed her not to leave town."

"I hope so. Because I can think of several questions I'd like to ask her," Cromberg said.

"Who did the crime scene investigation?" Rucker asked. "Cassandra Brown and Marge Lomine," he answered. "Do you mean Marge Lamont?" Rucker asked

"Yeah, that's her." Archer said as if he'd pronounced the name correctly. Cromberg and Archer walked back into the hallway but Rucker stayed, mesmerized by the amount of work the killers did in destroying the walls of the closet and bedroom.

"This must have taken hours," she finally said. "Someone must have heard something. I think it would be next to impossible to do this much damage and no one hear something. Who interviewed the neighbors?"

"We were just getting started talking to the people on this floor when ballistics identified the 9mm as the same one used in your case. Peterson and I have two more cases we're working on so we assumed you'd want to handle this yourself," Archer said.

"This is turning into a real can of worms," Rucker said, looking at Cromberg reflectively.

"Thanks for walking us through, Ryan. I suppose we'll take it from here.

Anything else you can think of?" Cromberg asked.

Archer clicked his gum and stared at the floor as if a capricious thought entered his mind and vaporized before he could spit it out. "I know you two have been around long enough to know about what you're up against here. The people who did this are bad to the bone, and given the opportunity, they won't hesitate to do the same thing to you. When you find them, don't try to be heroes. Call me, call SWAT, and call somebody for backup, please. Let me know if there is anything we can do to help."

Archer turned and walked away leaving the two women standing in the hallway. Cromberg watched him for a moment then looked despondently at Rucker.

"What are you thinking? I can see those wheels of yours turning."

"I want to talk to everyone on the floor above and the floor below, I know someone had to hear something, or knows something about what went on here."

"That's not what I'm talking about what are you really thinking?"

"Like I said a few minutes ago, we've gotten ourselves into a can of worms here, and I don't see it getting any better before it's over." Cromberg nodded in agreement.

Redhawk Simmons sipped from his Dr. Pepper and slipped another twenty into the slot machine he was playing. He glanced over his shoulder just in time to catch Snake Lopez whispering something into the ear of a black woman who was playing a machine at the end of the row. She was doing her best to ignore Lopez's line, but he was more than persistent.

Lopez had sucked down enough Jack Daniels over the last two hours that he'd stopped playing blackjack and slots and turned his attention exclusively to hustling every female in Harrah's Casino under the age of sixty. Simmons knew he had to get Lopez out of the Casino soon before thing got any further out of hand, but before he could say a word the alarm bell on the top of the Triple Diamond Machine he was playing began to sound off.

Lopez walked his way staring listlessly at Simmons and the machine as if Simmons had somehow broken the machine and only he could fix it. He whacked at the top of the machine in an attempt to stop the ringing bell and almost fell over the chair next to Simmons. It never occurred to Lopez that Simmons had just hit a jackpot.

Seconds later an attendant appeared and told them that the machine had hit a four thousand dollar jackpot, then quickly started punching numbers on the machine's keypad. Simmons smiled broadly at the news and Lopez slapped him on the back in congratulations.

"Loan me another couple-hundred, since you got plenty now," Lopez said.

He staggered around to the other side of the machine to look Simmons in the face as he slurred the words and spittle collected in the corner of his mouth and ran down his chin.

"You need to ease up on the Jack," Simmons said, fishing three hundred from his wallet and handing it Lopez. The attendant stopped punching buttons on the machine and handed Simmons a piece of paper explaining that he needed to sign the form in order to get paid. When she asked for his driver's license and social security number, Simmons looked around the room for Lopez who'd, vanished in the crowd like the snake that he was.

Fifteen minutes later the attendant reappeared and counted out Simmons's winnings. She asked him to sign an additional piece of paper and as he stood to lean on a flattened portion of the slot machine to sign the form, he saw Snake Lopez leading another black woman through a set of rear doors and onto a covered porch outside the casino. Simmons quickly signed the paper and stuffed the bills in his blue jean pocket and headed for the double doors he'd seen Lopez go through.

Harrah's Casino had been built to resemble a nineteenth century Mississippi riverboat, with broad walkways surrounding each level and wood carved pedestals and handrails protecting the strollers from the water below. When Simmons walked out onto the deck, he realized for the first time that he was on the third floor. He looked in both directions for Snake Lopez and shuddered when he was nowhere to be found.

For a reason he could never explain, he turned to his left and started down the walkway toward the center of the boat. The overhang was lighted with fluorescent lights for the first forty feet then suddenly the porch fell into darkness with only the moon providing a sparse light. He squinted his eyes as he moved slowly into the darkness. His senses were coming alive now. He could hear water lapping at the planks and mooring poles at the bottom of the riverboat, and the sound of an old Eagles song, "Hotel California" being piped onto the walkway through a loudspeaker. His nose filled with the smell of fish schooling near the lights beaming from the bottom of the boat.

Suddenly he could hear the muffled sounds of a woman's voice somewhere in the darkness ahead. Realizing that there was an obstruction in the walkway, he reached out in front of him just in time to feel the metal shroud of a giant pulley with attached overhead cables for lowering a gangplank at the rear of the riverboat. He inched his way around the cowling, stepping over pipes, motor-shafts and welded brackets before reaching an area he assumed was free of obstructions.

As soon as he cleared the machinery, he saw Lopez and the black woman in a dimly lit alcove about thirty feet away. Lopez had one hand covering the woman's mouth and the other busy taking off her clothes. Simmons called out for Lopez to stop, but he continued to rip at the woman's skirt and panties like someone possessed. When Simmons started to move in their direction, he realized that something had clamped onto the bottom of his jeans and he couldn't move an inch from where he was standing.

He watched for a moment, frantically working to shake his leg free from whatever had latched onto him, when he realized that Lopez was becoming more and more violent with every attempt the woman made to free herself from his grasp. Just as he reached down to see if he could loosen the hold on his pants-leg, he saw Lopez' fist go high into the air then strike the woman violently. The first blow was to the woman's mid-section; she gasped for air, her eyes wide and cauterized with fear. The second blow came just as quickly, but this time it was to the center of her forehead, rendering the woman limp and close to unconsciousness.

Lopez was raping her now, but that wasn't what made Redhawk Simmons rip the denim seam from the hook-shaped metal bracket that had been holding him from moving toward Lopez. He saw the metallic glint of a knife blade in the moonlight and knew that Lopez was only seconds away from killing the woman when he was finished with her.

Lopez was holding the knife high in the air above the woman's bare breast when Simmons reached out and jerked Lopez off the woman slamming him against the metal bulkhead.

"Remember what I was in for?" he asked Lopez.

"Take a walk, Chief, this doesn't concern you," Lopez snarled, and began zipping his pants.

"I think it does. I know you remember how much I love a good fight. So, you can go back to work on the woman, but first you got to come through me," Simmons said, throwing the woman's clothes in her direction. The woman took her torn clothes, inching her battered body as far into the darkened alcove as she could.

It was only for a split second that Simmons took his eyes off Lopez, in concern for the woman's nudity; it was a mistake. Lopez lunged in his direction stabbing a deep two-inch gash in Simmons left forearm. Simmons took two steps backward momentarily glancing at the gaping wound in his arm. He never cried out or acknowledged in any way that he'd been stabbed, he merely smiled at Lopez and then assumed a crouch position.

Lopez held the knife in front of him and the two men began to circle each other. "I told you to back off, man. But you just had to get involved with something that was none of your business. Now, she and you both are going to die," Lopez sneered at Simmons.

When Simmons had positioned himself in front of the woman, Lopez lunged at him again with the same quickness as before. But this time Redhawk Simmons was ready for the assault. With his left hand he latched onto Lopez's right wrist and at the same time landed a crushing blow to Lopez's nose. Before Lopez's brain registered the pain from the first blow, Simmons hit him again splattering blood in his face and on the bulkhead behind him. Lopez cried out in pain, and as Simmons backed off, he kicked out with his foot catching Simmons in the right kneecap, sending him to the deck.

Lopez wiped at the blood streaming from his broken nose while he cursed Simmons and planned his next attack. The move on Simmons's bad knee had almost taken him out of the fight. He remembered that Simmons had told him how another Indian had almost cut off his leg with a machete and Simmons had wound up killing the man over a car the two men had just stolen.

Just as Lopez worked himself into the full moonlight, he saw that Simmons, who was still down on one knee, had lowered his head in pain. Lopez decided it was time to end this thing and made one last lunge in Simmons's direction. It was a fatal mistake.

At the same moment that Lopez lunged at Simmons, the big man stood, his reactions were like lightening. He had Lopez's wrist again, only this time twisting his arm, hand, and the blade of the knife into the sternum of Lopez so deeply that his eyes almost bulged from their sockets. For the first few seconds Lopez stood there absolutely stunned by the event. Blood poured from his severed Aorta. He made several steps backward then fell on his bottom and never moved again or said another word.

Simmons stood perfectly still, allowing the events and scene to soak in. He looked at the woman, his mind contemplating his next move. Just for a moment he thought he saw the woman grin slightly. He turned and faced her, blood dripping from his forearm onto the deck of the walkway.

"I'm going to need some time," he said slowly, looking deeply into her dark eyes and praying that she would forget his face.

The woman nodded in compliance and without saying another word, Simmons pulled the knife from Lopez's midsection, moved to the railing and dove in the water twenty-five feet below. The last thing he remembered hearing as his body was hurling toward the water was the last lyric of the song blaring from the loudspeaker; "You can checkout anytime you like, but you can never leave."

"That's what you think," Simmons said, just before he hit the water.

CHAPTER 6

Aaron Phillips had been with the department for just over fifteen years. He was good looking, with a gambler's smile, baby blue eyes and a placid demeanor that never seemed to be confrontational toward any of his co-workers. He was honest to a fault and no one ever questioned his motives or his dedication to the department.

At eight a.m. Tuesday morning, Phillips found the gift certificate and note Ross Clayton had left in his mailbox. After reading the thank-you note he smiled and tucked the gift card in his shirt pocket. When he turned to leave, he almost ran into Delores Rucker who was holding a Styrofoam cup of coffee as she hurried to her cubicle.

"I'm sorry. Didn't mean to run you over," he said.

"No problem. Hope I didn't spill coffee all over you," she said.

"No I'm okay. But I did want to talk with you," he said.

"What's up?" she asked, moping the spilled coffee from her hands.

"I was by the lab earlier this morning on another matter and Art McDonnell said he got a positive match on the two strands of brown hair that the crime lab collected at the Main Street high-rise."

"Great. Anybody I know?" she asked.

"Maybe, his name is Clyde Bonner and he's got a jacket that looks like the yellow pages of crime. To say the least, he's a bad player. He's served two stretches in Huntsville for armed robbery and has been under investigation for at least two murders. We haven't been able to put all the pieces together yet but one thing is crystal clear; this guy is bad to the bone."

He watched Rucker set her coffee cup on a file cabinet, and then write everything he'd told her on a blank page of a black leather notebook.

"Do me a favor, will you?" he asked.

"Sure, if I can," she said.

"When you find this guy, don't even think about being a hero. Call SWAT, call for backup, call me, but don't go up against this guy on your own. He's a killer and he's already made the statement that he's not going back to prison, and I think he means it."

"Any ideas on where we might find this guy?" Rucker asked.

"We don't know. We know he beat up a working girl on Telephone Road a couple of months ago, but she refused to press charges on him so we had to let him go. I hung around waiting to see who came to pick him up. It was another loser by the name of Tony Degas. I think he's from the city somewhere, maybe on the north side; but I really don't know for sure," he said.

"Anything noteworthy on this Degas character?"

"Not like Bonner, if that's what you mean. Several misdemeanors, one B& E, a few fights here and there. His military record shows a dishonorable discharge, but I didn't look any further. It might be worth your time to dig a little deeper into these two and see what comes up."

"Oh, don't worry. We'll check them both out. As soon as Cromberg gets back we'll get over to the crime lab and pick up the reports. Thanks for your help. And don't worry, if we find them we'll get some help," she reassured him.

Aaron Phillips walked away just as Stacy Cromberg emerged from the stairwell carrying a cardboard tray of fresh coffee and bagels. "I got us something to eat," she said, looking at Rucker writing in her notebook. "Did I miss something?" she asked.

"Yeah, we got a lead on the shooting at the high-rise, and we need to get over to the lab. I'll fill you in on the way," Rucker said.

"So much for breakfast," Cromberg said, setting the tray of bagels on the filing cabinet. "I'm taking my coffee. I don't function well this early in the morning without it," she said, hustling to catch up with Rucker.

It never seems to fail, the pre-conceived images the mind conjures on its own when it envisions the face or countenance of a person never actually met or only spoken with on the telephone. Such was the case with Lund Corbel. Clayton had pictured him as an older man in his late fifties, with thinning gray hair and beard, dressed like most intellectuals with a tweed jacket and an out-of-style bow tie that didn't match anything he was wearing. His premonition couldn't have been more off target.

Lund Corbel was in his thirties and clean-shaven, with a full head of blond hair and a pirate's smile. He had a muscular physique, his arms bulging with veins and taut sinew, filling the sleeves of his short-sleeved, buttoned-down, ice blue, Polo shirt. When he stood to shake hands with Clayton and Stillwell, the grip of his hands felt like a vice. His boyish good looks and casual attire reminded Clayton of an advertisement he'd seen for sailing equipment in a yachting magazine. He spoke with a slight accent that was either German or Bavarian, but most definitely European.

"Please sit," he said cordially, pointing to the leather chairs facing his desk. "Can I offer you some coffee?" Clayton declined his offer of coffee, but Stillwell smiled briefly and said she'd love a cup. Clayton gave her a quick glance. You didn't have to be overly intuitive to see the flirtation between Corbel and Stillwell, Clayton thought. Corbel's eyes had been locked on her since she walked into the room.

"I heard about your little adventure here at the Museum on Friday. Are those stitches from the encounter?" Corbel asked, gazing at the yellow and blue bruising above Clayton's eyebrow.

"I'm afraid so," Clayton said.

"You know how it is with some people; even when they don't go looking for trouble, trouble seems to find them," Stillwell said, taking the China cup and saucer from Corbel.

"Nasty business," Corbel said, winking at Stillwell.

"Yeah, well I know how busy you must be so if we can ask you some questions we'll get out of your hair," Clayton said tersely.

"Certainly," Corbel furrowed his brow, like a child caught with his hand in the cookie-jar, then smiled slyly at Stillwell, who was quick to return the smile.

"We're working on a case," Clayton said, popping the end-cap off a cardboard cylinder and removing the paintings. "We're working on an unusual case where the killer leaves one of these paintings on his victim, in what we believe is a clue to his next target. And since none of this information has been released to the public, we'd like to keep it that confidential."

"Absolutely," Corbel said, actually looking at Clayton for the first time. Clayton handed Corbel the paintings and glanced at Stillwell who crossed her legs and sipped from her cup, but otherwise continued to stare at Corbel. "Ah, Van Gogh," he said, his attention now solely locked on the paintings. Clayton and Stillwell watched as Corbel slowly un-rolled each painting, laying them side-by-side. He stood as he uncoiled the last painting, palming his jaw as if in awe of the paintings.

"These are exquisite works of art," he said flatly, still engrossed in the beauty of each painting.

"I guess what we're looking for is some insight into the person who painted them. What can you tell us about the artist, if anything, and moreover, how many people can paint a reproduction like that?" Clayton asked.

"Worldwide, you can count them on one hand," Corbel said. He seemed to be lost in thought as he studied each work. "I noticed that you have a Monet mixed in with the Van Gogh's? Did you come by it the same way? I mean, do you think the same painter painted both the Van Gogh and the Monet?" he asked.

"We did," Stillwell said. "Is that something that strikes you as unusual?" she asked.

"It is most definitely unusual to have so much talent. Both men were Impressionists, but that's where the similarities end. Their styles are so different from one another. The truth is you'd never mistake a Monet for a Van Gogh. This is amazing to say the least. If the same person painted these three paintings, reproducing them almost to the point of perfection, then what you have here is truly a master's work. I've never seen a reproduction this exacting or with so much of the original artist's fervor."

Corbel turned and stepped back to his credenza, pulling an oversized book from one of the drawers. The book was entitled, The Impressionists. As he thumbed through the pages of the book, he begin to speak as someone giving a lecture on a subject that he was so knowledgeable of that it seemed to be an intricate part of his genetic makeup.

"As you probably know, Vincent Van Gogh was a troubled man, given to fits of insanity and psychosis, and many of his paintings reflect these disorders. When the voices in his head reached an unbearable level, he cut off his ear to make them stop. I can't imagine his level of torment, or his lack of grasp on reality." Corbel found the painting by Monet that was an exact duplicate to the one on his desk and turned the book facing Clayton and Stillwell.

"Claude Monet was a man who painted with a sense of elegance and beauty, quite rare among the Impressionists. There were others such as Pierre Renoir, Edgar Degas and Paul Cezanne that certainly knew how to capture beauty on canvas, but Monet did it with a flare that was uncommon, to say the least. Now, that's not to say that the works of Van Gogh weren't spectacular, after all, his portrait of Dr. Gachet painted in 1890, the year of his death, sold at Christie's in 1990 for $82.5 million."

"This painting was found on one of the two men that were murdered at Minute Maid Park on Friday night," Stillwell said, pointing at the painting by Monet. She noticed that Corbel was studying the painting with a renewed interest. "Have you thought of something?" she asked.

"This painting, The Studio Boat was painted by Monet in 1874. Look at the colors in the original and compare them to the ones your killer painted recently."

"The colors on the painting by the killer seem to be brighter, more distinct than the colors of the original," Stillwell surmised.

"Exactly, and that may be how you catch your killer." "How's that?" Clayton asked.

"All three of these paintings were painted with oils and mixed with the oils or certain drying mediums to speed the drying process. Without them, it would take years for the work to dry. There is Oil of Delft, Linseed oil, Amber Varnish, Baroque or Walnut oil, just to name a few. Since these paintings are fairly new and the smells are still present, it should be rather easy for your chemists to analyze the paints and come up with a type and most probably a manufacturer. If the killer used an exotic paint and medium like, Alchemist, for example, the records of who purchased the paints may lead you right to him."

"That was just the kind of information I was looking for," Clayton said. He noticed that Corbel seemed to be captivated more in his own thoughts than by the Monet painting. "Have you thought of something else?" Clayton asked.

"I don't know," Corbel said, almost in a sigh. He was rubbing the back of his neck with his right hand.

"You've helped us a lot already, but if you've come up with something else we'd sure like to hear it," Stillwell said. Corbel walked away from the desk absentmindedly holding the Monet at arm's length. When he turned and looked back at the two cops, he had an austere frown on his face.

"You're looking for this scene, aren't you?" he asked.

"Yes, we think it's where the killer will commit his next murder," Stillwell said.

"I've seen this very scene recently, maybe a couple of months ago. I'm racking my brain to remember where it was. I remember my girlfriend talking on the cell phone and thinking to myself that the boat and lake look like something out of the nineteenth century. I didn't make the Monet connection until now. She's out of town, but I'll be speaking with her tomorrow around noon. I'll see if she can remember where we were. I'm so sorry I can't remember on my own. It's just that it never dawned on me until now that it might be something of importance. If you'll leave me your card, I'll call you as soon as I can speak with her," Corbel said.

Clayton handed Corbel his business card and began carefully rolling the canvas paintings back into the cardboard cylinder. Corbel stopped rubbing the back of his neck and went back to staring at Stillwell.

"I'm not usually so forward, Miss Stillwell, but might I ask you if you're married?" Corbel folded his arms casually waiting on Stillwell's answer.

"No, I'm not," she said blushing, caught off guard by the nature of the question. "I've just ended a relationship and quite frankly I'm not looking to start another one," she said, lying profoundly.

"Pardon my inquisitive nature," Corbel chuckled slightly. "It seems to get me in trouble from time to time," he said, walking them to the door.

It had been one of the longest nights that Redhawk Simmons had ever lived through and one of the most emotional. It seemed impossible for life's events to become so convoluted in such a short period of time. In the last twenty-four hours he had passed through several realms of adulation; renewing an old friendship, sharing a good meal, winning at the casino. And, immersed in the same twenty-four hour period, diametrically opposed feelings and happenstance; he'd fought with Renee, he'd technically violated his parole, and the *coupe de*

grace, he'd killed his old friend in a knife fight and fled from the scene like the common criminal he'd always been.

It was raining when Simmons pulled out of the Livingston Regional Medical Center parking lot and headed for the reservation. His left arm was bound tightly after the surgery and had been placed in a sling. His fingers protruding out of the bandage had a brownish yellow stain from the disinfectant that had been smeared over his arm. And even though he was still groggy from the drugs and painkillers he knew he had to get home and make sure everything was okay.

His mind raced with thoughts and questions about the night before. He tried to rehearse everything in his mind the way it happened. It was the easiest get-a-way he'd ever made in his life. Why were there no cops? Why no ambulance? There should have been roadblocks from Lake Charles to Beaumont, but there was nothing.

Lightening streaked across the horizon as he stopped for a stoplight in the center of town. He could smell fried chicken from the Church's Chicken place on the corner and the streets were quickly filling with water from the heavy rains. He rubbed at his face with his right hand in an attempt to clear his mind and put it all together.

It had taken almost fifteen minutes to swim from the boat, where he plunged into the water, to the shore. It took another fifteen minutes to locate his car and make his way out of the parking garage, all while taking every precaution not to be seen. It took another ten minutes to get on Interstate 10 and head west for Texas. Almost forty minutes of elapsed time, he surmised. How was that possible?

In all that time he'd not seen or heard one siren from the police or any other emergency vehicle nearing the casino. Had the woman done as he requested and waited for him to make a clean get-a-way before she screamed? What did she tell the police when they did arrive? He'd listened to the radio and news channels all the way to Texas for news of the killing, but there was nothing. He'd stopped several times to tighten the bindings he'd made on the cut in his arm, but no one seemed suspicious.

There was one other scenario that was vaguely plausible, and he hated thinking about it. What if Snake Lopez wasn't dead when he'd jumped off the boat? What if he'd somehow regained consciousness and finished the job he'd started, killing the woman? The two could have lain undetected until dawn if he killed the woman then died his self. But that couldn't be, he thought. He'd seen the lifeless death face on Snake Lopez. The shear volume of blood loss would have rendered Lopez helpless, he thought. The only thing even remotely good about that scenario was there would be no witnesses left to finger him for the murder. All he'd have to do is keep quiet and let it blow over.

He turned east on Highway 190 in the direction of the reservation, now his thoughts turned to Renee and the story he'd tell her. He hated the thought of lying and deceiving her, but he couldn't think of a reliable alternative. It had been so easy to lie to the doctors and attendants back at the hospital. The lie was so good he'd almost started believing it his self. He'd rambled on about working on the radiator of his pickup and the fan blade cutting the gash in his arm.

He'd thought of the story after jumping off the boat while swimming back to shore. He'd even raised the hood of his pickup and held his bleeding arm over the radiator and fan blade allowing his blood to saturate both, just in case the authorities wanted to take a look or run some tests to verify his story. The story worked once. Why not use the same story on Renee?

Anthony Degas set up on the couch and tossed the covers on the floor. He could see Clyde Bonner setting at the kitchen table smoking a cigarette and drinking coffee. Bonner was shirtless and the tattoo on his back looked like a cartoon that had been stopped in mid-frame and hand painted on Bonner's back. The tattoo showed a man lying on the floor of a bar room with several bullet holes in his chest. The man standing over him was holding a pair of matching blue-steel revolvers, still smoking from the gunfight. The inscription at the bottom of the tattoo read; Born to Kill, in letters the color of blood.

Degas stood and yawned, clawing at his genitals as he walked toward the kitchen where Bonner was sitting.

"What's up, man? Is something wrong?" Degas asked.

"Does your mother still live in that dump off Homestead Road?" Bonner asked, ignoring Degas' question.

"Yeah, she's been living there for over twenty years now. That's what you're thinking about? You're thinking about what kind of place my mother lives in?"

"What I'm thinking about is how quick we can get there and then get out of town. We can't stay here another day. We left our fingerprints all over that apartment and they got to know who we are by now. I ain't going back to jail. I got everything I ever wanted now and I want to get out of here with it before everything goes to shit. You listening to me, Tony?" Bonner said sternly, looking at Degas for the first time.

"I'm with you, man. We can be at her place in forty-five minutes. I can give her a couple of grand, grab some of my things, and in five minutes we're gone. We still gonna do that boat thing down to Rio," Degas asked.

"Yeah, but I think we need to go over to New Orleans or maybe to Biloxi and catch the boat there instead of Galveston. All we're doing by staying in Texas is asking for trouble. Let's get all of our things and get out of here. How fast can you be ready to go?

"Give me thirty minutes and I'm down for the ride," Degas said.

"Do what you got to do and let's go," Bonner said, dropping his cigarette in the bottom of his coffee cup.

It was almost noon when Delores Rucker and Stacy Cromberg left the Crime Lab with enough evidence to arrest Clyde Bonner and Anthony Degas for the three murders at the drug dealer's apartment on Sunday night. And, with any luck they could tie the two men to the robbery and murder at the Aldine Mail Route convenience store as well. All they had to do was match the DNA of the blood samples taken from the two crime scenes and Degas and Bonner would be spending the rest of their days on death row in Huntsville. The last thing they had to do was pick up the warrants for both men and a search warrant for Silvia Degas' house. There was no reason to believe they were at the Degas residence but it was a good place to start.

The house at 7334 Fawnridge was a single story wood framed house with an awning-covered porch that ran the full length of the front of the house. A red brick wall set on the edge of the porch running the length of the walkway. A concrete driveway on the left side of the house led to an oversized garage at the rear of the property. The front yard was small and fenced with a chain link cyclone fence and the driveway was empty. The door of the garage was open and a red Mercury Tracer belonging to Silva Degas was parked there.

Richey Sneed held the .38 Colt diamondback against the neck of Silvia Degas, the hammer was cocked and his finger was gently curled around the trigger. "I'm only going to tell you this one time. If you do as I say no one will get hurt. We only want our money; when we get it we'll be gone. Just let them in and everything is going to be okay." Silvia Degas nodded sheepishly and opened the door.

Anthony Degas and Clyde Bonner waited until Silvia Degas unlatched the screen door, she could see that Anthony was holding a thick white envelope in his right hand and smiling broadly. The smile faded quickly when the two got inside and saw the foreboding look on Silvia Degas' face.

"Mom, I brought you some money," Anthony Degas started. Then he saw the door close and Richey Sneed holding the gun to the back of his mother's head.

"I was beginning to wonder if you boys were going to show. We've had a fine visit with your mother and some of the best Mexican food I've ever had.

Now, why don't you two back up against that wall and lean on it just like you're holding it up, I'm sure you know the position," Sneed said sarcastically.

"He ain't going to shoot your mother; let's take him," Clyde Bonner snarled.

Beverly Sneed stepped into the doorway at the opposite end of the room and pointed her 9mm at the backs of the two men. "A gunfight is not a good idea, boys. Do as he said and put your hands on that wall." She held the weapon with both hands, waving the semi-automatic in the direction of the wall as she prompted them.

Bonner and Degas began backing slowly across the room. Tension filled the air and everyone in the room seemed to jump when a thunderclap sounded and the rain outside intensified. Just as they reached the wall and were about to turn they heard Richey Sneed curse and grab Silvia Degas around the neck and pull her close to him.

"The cops are here," he yelled to Beverly. You idiots brought the cops here. Keep an eye on them," he ordered Beverly, peering through one of the rectangular windows in the door.

There were two cars, one blue and white HPD squad car, and one unmarked Ford that had pulled in behind Bonner's Dodge Charger. The squad car parked in front of the ditch that paralleled the cyclone fence near the blacktop street. There were two uniformed officers and two women, but only one woman got out of the car. The second woman Detective had positioned herself half in and half out of the car and was carrying on a conversation on the two-way radio. The two uniformed officers and the other woman moved cautiously along the fence and onto the covered porch.

Richey Sneed wrapped his hand around Silvia Degas' mouth and motioned for Anthony Degas to answer the door.

"You hurt her and I swear I'm going to kill you. You understand that, tough guy?" Degas snarled. He could see the fear in his mother's eyes.

"Just answer the door," Sneed said, waving his gun in the air dismissively. Aaron Phillips stood behind Stacy Cromberg who was holding the warrants in her left hand. The second uniformed officer had stepped off the porch and was leaning against the wall that jutted out past the porch; out of sight from anyone who answered the door. Just as Cromberg was about to knock on the doorframe the door opened and Anthony Degas smiled broadly at the cops as if they were old friends. He pushed open the screen door and said, "What can I do you for?"

"Are you Anthony Degas?" Stacy Cromberg asked, allowing her right hand to rest on the butt of her holstered 9mm.

"No, I don't know any Anthony Degas. My name is Jim Rome; want to know how the Astros are doing?" Degas chuckled.

Before Cromberg could say another word Degas pulled his own 9mm from under his shirt and pointed it at Cromberg who was attempting to draw her own weapon at the same time. Instinctively, Aaron Phillips shoved her to the left and Degas' first round caught Phillips just below his badge in the center of his breast pocket, knocking him off the porch and onto the front lawn. The second uniformed officer stepped around the corner firing two rounds from his .357 magnum. The first round caught Degas in his right shoulder and the second round embedded itself in the back wall of the living room. The last thing the officer remembered seeing was a revolver jut out from behind the door blasting a fist size hole in Degas' head. At that exact moment Degas fired again, the round caught the officer squarely in the center of his chest. He landed a foot from where Aaron Phillips was attempting to turn on his side.

The surreal scene took less than twenty seconds to play out, but the gunfight was far from over. Clyde Bonner drew his 9mm and quickly fired three rounds in the direction of Richey Sneed and Silvia Degas. The first and third rounds found no target but the second round caught Silvia Degas in the left breast and she went limp in Richey Sneed's arms. Stacy Cromberg was on her knees when the second round of firing started, she fired three rounds in rapid succession in the direction of Sneed who was firing back at Bonner.

Delores Rucker had seen the horrible sequence of events and had had the presence of mind to put in an officer down call before running to Cromberg's side. Rucker pulled Cromberg from the doorway pushing her over the red brick wall that ran along the porch. They could hear shooting from inside the house and weren't sure if they were being shot at or if another gun battle was going on inside the house. They returned fire through the front plate-glass window but remained low behind the brick wall.

As round after round blasted through the living room, Beverly Sneed fired three rounds at Clyde Bonner who was still firing at Richey Sneed, only one of the rounds found its mark. Bonner fell into the corner with a superficial head wound. The two cops kept firing rounds through the picture window and Beverly Sneed fired three more rounds at the two cops.

Richey Sneed pulled Anthony Degas' lifeless body away from the door and laid him beside his dead mother. Sneed riffled through Degas pockets and found a wad of hundred dollar bills in one of his pockets then picked up the envelope stuffed with cash stuffing them both in his jeans. Sneed fired his last round through the plate glass window at the cops as he darted across the room. He took Beverly by the hand and headed for the back door of the house.

Initially, they had parked the van behind the garage to keep it out of sight, but with the back fence having been torn down by the city Public Works Department to repair a broken water main, it provided the two with the perfect escape. Seconds later they were in the van and rolling. They could hear more gunfire from the house as they sloshed through the mud and puddles of water from the rain.

Several intense moments passed without a shot being fired. Rucker could see Aaron Phillips pulling himself behind the brick wall. She was elated to see that he was still alive and moving to safety.

She inched her way down the wall until she reached Phillips, who was holding onto his chest and grimacing in pain. She unbuttoned his uniform shirt revealing a Kevlar vest with a blackened hole where the close muzzle blast had discharged inches from his chest. She peeled open the vest and raised his tee shirt exposing the fist sized bruise on his upper ribcage. She ran her hand softly over the bruise watching Phillips wince from even her softest touch.

"I'm sure you've got a couple of broken ribs, but at least your going to see that new kid of yours when he gets here," she said, smiling slightly.

"Would you see if Brubaker is okay?" Phillips asked.

Rucker made her way to the end of the wall where the officer had fallen then latched onto his lapel and slowly pulling him behind the brick wall. She placed two fingers on his Jugular vein, but there was no pulse. She looked at his eyes, which were fixed in a cold death stare.

"Bru is dead," she told Phillips. Phillips laid his head on the wet grass covering his eyes with his forearm. A soft rain pelted his arm and face.

Rucker worked her way back to Phillips and gently placed her hand on his chest. "See if you can work your way out of the line of fire toward the end of the porch. I don't know if there is anyone still alive in there or not, but we don't need anyone else hurt."

Clyde Bonner wiped the blood from his face and eyes, crawled across the floor and took Degas' 9mm and examined the magazine. There were at least six rounds still in the clip.

He ejected the magazine from his own 9mm and inserted a fully loaded one then clicked the slide into place. He knew that whatever move he was going to make had to be a good one, and drastic enough to facilitate his escape or death. And he was ready for either.

Rucker and Phillips worked their way back to Stacy Cromberg who was crouched in a kneeling position with her head leaning against the brick wall. She reached out and took Phillips by the hand but what ever it was that she wanted to say never came. The rain seemed to intensify as she stood slightly and peered over the brick wall.

At the exact same moment Clyde Bonner moved from the corner of the room standing in front of the shattered picture window. He began firing with both semi-automatics when he saw Cromberg's head appear above the brick wall. And although his aim was less than what it would have been had he not suffered blurred vision it was good enough. Two of the eight rounds he fired struck the bricks directly in front of Stacy Cromberg's face, exploding the brick and hollow point rounds in Cromberg's face and neck.

Fortunately for Cromberg neither of the rounds was in any condition to make it into her face. But shards of the exploded brick pelted her cheeks, eyes, and neck, cracking two of her teeth and severing a gash above her left eyebrow that would leave a scar for the rest of her life. Rucker pushed her 9mm over the wall and fired six rounds as fast as she could pull the trigger, aiming in all directions. The firing from the house stopped just as quickly as it had begun.

Rucker knelt beside Cromberg her face was covered in blood and fragments of the brick that had exploded from the barrage. Cromberg was unconscious but breathing, and very much alive.

"Help me get her to the end of the wall," she told Phillips. She could hear sirens in the distance and knew that reinforcements were on the way. She ejected the spent magazine and inserted a full one, then began working the two wounded cops toward the end of the porch.

When they reached the end of the brick wall the three cops huddled in the rain like wounded soldiers waiting for a chopper to whisk them to a field hospital. The house was silent now, and Rucker prayed that one of the rounds that she'd fired over the wall had found its mark and killed Clyde Bonner. It was wishful thinking.

Just before reinforcements arrived, Rucker's cell phone sounded and she answered it on the second ring. The call was from Art McDonnell of the crime lab.

"I'm kinda in the middle of something here, Art. I'll have to get back to you later," she said, holding back the tears.

"Well you told me to call you as soon as we had the DNA on the blood that we took off the wooden pole the old woman used to whack one of the shooters. The blood didn't belong to a man it belonged to a woman, and not only that, a sample of her DNA was in our database, and she's got quite a record as well. Her name is Beverly Sneed," he said with the excitement building in his voice.

"Thanks for the information, Art. Like I said, I'm in somewhat of a situation here and I'll talk about it with you tomorrow," Rucker rolled her eyes and disconnected.

A week later Delores Rucker, Ross Clayton, Leona Stillwell and Aaron Phillips sat in a conference room signing the reports that the Inquest Team had demanded before Rucker and Phillips could go back on the streets. Even though the Inquest Team had filmed the entire proceedings, and a Court Reporter had taken a word-for-word testimony from the officers, they insisted on a typed written account, in the officers own words of the events and shootings that left two officers wounded, one dead, and two civilians killed in the gunfight on Fawnridge Street. Not to mention the three armed felons who escaped from the house without a trace of evidence as to their whereabouts.

Ross Clayton signed the last document in the absence of Wade Gorman and slid the papers across the table for Rucker and Phillips to sign. He ran his hands through his hair then palmed his face for a long moment of silence. It was obvious the stress of the last seven days had taken its toll on everyone at the table, and especially Ross Clayton.

With Stacy Cromberg and Wade Gorman still in the hospital; and having attended Ronald Brubaker's funeral on Saturday and spending more than eight hours with his bereaved wife and children he felt about as low as man could get. And as if the grief and suffering of a fallen comrade were not enough, having to sit through an eight-hour inquest into the shooting on Monday and rehearsing the shooting again and again to put it in written form had only added to the stress the cops were feeling.

Forensics and ballistics experts had determined that the only shots fired by officers that actually struck any person were one of the two shots fired by Brubaker that struck Degas in the shoulder. The fatal wounds that killed Degas and his mother were fired from inside the living room and from two different weapons. Ballistics patterns proved conclusively, that the shots could not have been fired from outside the house, and that there were at least four shooters firing from the living room.

But the most perplexing aspect of the shooting, aside from an officer being killed and two wounded, was the absolute lack of an explanation for the escape of the other shooters inside the house. It was as if they simply vanished in thin air.

Trace evidence led investigators to believe that two of the shooters left in a vehicle that had been parked behind the garage. For some unknown reason they left a third shooter behind that was believed to be responsible for firing the shots at Cromberg's face. Everyone concerned was reasonably sure that the third shooter was Clyde Bonner. There was some speculation from the cops at the table that Bonner was left behind to facilitate the escape of Beverly and Richey Sneed. But both Phillips and Rucker testified that they heard shots fired from inside the living room, and that they were not directed at the cops outside. In any event, what was most disconcerting was Bonners disappearance like the others, without a trace.

The only redeeming bit of evidence discovered by investigators was in the bevy of fingerprints that took the portable AFIS computers a matter of seconds to disclose the identity of the criminals who were present in the living room and other rooms of the Degas house. Warrants for Richey and Beverly Sneed, and Clyde Bonner were issued on Thursday morning. Photographs of the three had been shown for the last four nights on all three networks evening news broadcast, and every law enforcement agency in the greater Houston area had made their apprehension a number one priority.

Additionally, investigators uncovered more than $900,000.00 that was stashed in the false bottoms of three suitcases that were found in Bonner's automobile. It is believed the money was part of the robbery and murder at the high-rise apartment on South Main. Investigators also believed that part of the money could have come from the convenience store robbery on Aldine Mail Route.

Just as Rucker signed her name to the document and passed it to Aaron Phillips the phone at the end of the desk began ringing, as did Clayton's cell phone in his coat pocket. Clayton fished the phone out of his pocket and answered it before the third ring. Stillwell answered the phone on the table.

Stillwell retrieved a note pad from her purse and began to jot down notes on the pad as she listened. Clayton began walking away from the table almost as soon as he answered his cell, stopping in front of the window on the far wall of the room. The two cops spoke in low tones and within seconds of each other disconnected from the conversations. Clayton looked at Stillwell and suggested that she go first.

"That was a Homicide Detective with the Louisiana State Police, an officer Fontenot. It seems that there has been a murder on one of the gambling boats in Lake Charles and they want to question a resident of Houston who was filmed walking into the casino with the deceased man. He's an Apache Indian named Redhawk Simmons, who they believe was living in a halfway house in downtown Houston. They've asked us to accompany them to question Simmons around noon tomorrow," Stillwell told the others.

"Have they pegged the Indian as the killer?" Aaron Phillips asked.

"No, they just want to ask him why he didn't leave with the deceased, and why there was no film of him leaving the boat. It was like he came on board then vanished," Stillwell said.

"I hate that word vanished," Rucker said. "We've got way to many folks vanishing these days."

It didn't take more than a second of silence for everyone in the room to turn their attention toward Ross Clayton. Clayton seemed to be lost in thought, looking out the window at two shirtless, black kids sharing a grape soda on the sidewalk that fronted the Police Station.

"Was your call personal or business?" Stillwell asked Clayton.

"Oh it's business," he said, watching the boys walk away. Clayton turned and put his hands in his pockets, still thinking of the boys and their uncomplicated world.

"That was Lund Corbel," he said, walking back to the table.

"Don't tell me, he remembered something on the painting?" Stillwell said. "He remembered where it was he saw the boat on the painting. Just off NASA Road 1 in Clear Lake. He said the boat is tied to a post in the water just like the Monet painting and that it's less than a hundred yards from the bank on the NASA side of the bay. He said it's hardly noticeable from the back side, but from NASA Road 1, it's a dead ringer for the Monet." "We're done here; are we going?" Stillwell asked, looking for her purse. Clayton looked at Rucker and Phillips who seemed eager to have the shooting inquest come to a conclusion. For that he was glad too, but at this exact moment all he wanted was to go home and sit in a quiet place, with no one to ask him questions, or send him in a new direction. He looked at his watch, it was after four p.m. and the evening traffic toward Galveston would be brutal, but he knew they had to go. He couldn't get his mind off the pain he saw on the face of Brubaker's widow. It had haunted him since the funeral and he couldn't shake the feeling of helplessness and loss.

"I've spoken with your supervisor," he said, to Aaron Phillips. "I want you to work with us for a while at least until Stacy is up and ready to roll again. Do you mind giving us a hand?"

"Not in the least," Phillips said.

"Can you two meet with the folks from the Louisiana State Police and get them to this Indian character?" he asked. They both nodded.

"Then I guess we're set to go," he said looking at Stillwell.

"There is one other thing," Phillips said, reaching in his pocket. Phillips handed Clayton a credit card sized piece of plastic with a hole in the center of it. "This was in my pocket when Degas pulled the trigger on me. I'm fairly sure the Taste of Texas won't allow me to buy lunch with it."

It was the first time in the last few days that anyone in the room had seen Clayton smile. He took the card, dropped it in his pocket and for a moment his blue eyes seemed to water and glisten as if he were saddened by what he was about to say.

"I'm glad you're okay. I don't think I could have made it if I'd had to tell Roxanne that you didn't wear your vest. I'll be glad to get you another card, buddy," he said, heading for the door.

The warm southerly breeze carried the smell of salt and spawning fish, and fried seafood from the restaurants along the bay. Clayton spotted the boat rocking along side two wooden poles jutting out of the water, with a forest of Elm and Cyprus trees in the background, just like in the Monet painting. Clayton looked at Stillwell and shook his head in disbelief. Everything was just the way Lund Corbel said it would be.

"He even left the door of the boat open, just like the painting. It's remarkable," Clayton surmised.

Clayton followed the road around the bay until he reached the backside of the waterway. Cars and trucks with boat trailers were parked along the curved roadway leading to the bay. He parked the cruiser near the tree line and the two headed for the beach. When they walked through the clearing that let onto the shoreline they noticed two men wade-fishing no more than thirty feet from the white sandy beach. They turned and looked at Clayton and Stillwell for a moment then went back to casting their lures into deeper water.

They could see two more fishermen on the fantail of a Sea Ray boat that was drifting with the swells not far from the boat that was made to look like the one in the Monet painting. Clayton walked to the water's edge holding his badge in the air and calling to the two men. The men paid no attention at first but after a brief conversation among themselves one of the men cranked the motor and pointed the boat toward the shoreline. Stillwell pulled her badge from her purse and waited for the men to arrive.

Neither of the shirtless fishermen appeared to be over thirty, and both were more than willing to help, especially when it came to assisting Stillwell onto the fantail of their boat. Once the two cops were seated, the larger of the two men took an oar from the gunwale and shoved the boat off the beach, into deeper water. The other man cranked the motor and started slowly in the direction of the boat. The two men who were wade fishing in the shallows had moved closer together, and were straining to hear the conversation between the Cops and the two men on the boat.

It took less than two minutes to reach the boat. Clayton watched it rock from side-to-side in the wake of the approaching fishing boat. Seagulls hovered above the moored craft, darting and screeching at the wind that ruffled their feathers. Occasionally, one of the gulls would land on the roof or railing of the boat, and watch the approaching boat as if the fishing boat were infringing on a claimed property.

Clayton stood as the fishing boat pulled along side, and then quickly jumped from the fishing boat onto the bow of the Monet boat. The two fishermen wasted no time in seeing that Stillwell made it safely onto the Monet boat, and were in the process of boarding themselves, when Clayton stopped them.

"Fellows, this is officially now a crime scene. There's a body on the floor of the cabin and it looks as if it's been here for a while, if you know what I mean," Clayton said. The men looked at each other as if they wanted no part of a decaying body, taking seats on the fantail as far as they could sit from the open door of the Monet boat.

Stillwell handed Clayton a pair of latex gloves and the two put them on before touching anything else on the boat. The smell emanating from the door was breathtaking but both cops went inside to look at the body. It was almost more than they could bear.

The body was naked except for a pair of cotton briefs covering his genitals. He was lying face up, in the supine position, with his arms and legs spread slightly apart. It was obvious that the man's throat had been cut and that he had bleed out where he laid. Hundreds of flies buzzed around the dead man, landing intermittently, and then flying off. Aside from the flies, the man's entire body was covered in fire ants.

The body was so swollen and distorted from decay and ant bites, that it was almost impossible to tell with any certainty what the man might have looked like when he was alive. Clayton held his handkerchief over his mouth and nose, moving it only to speak to Stillwell.

"We have to get Belichec and the crime lab out here ASAP," he said, motioning for Stillwell to head for the door.

"Aren't you going to check the body for the painting?" she asked, before moving.

"I don't have to," he said.

"Why?"

"The killer took the time to frame this one. It's hanging on the wall, just behind his head," Clayton said, pointing across the body to the Van Gogh painting. Once outside, Stillwell took a deep breath and began to rattle off questions.

"It's obvious that he was murdered there on the floor, with all the blood, but how on earth did all the ants get out here?" she asked.

"I don't know, but if I had to guess, I'd say they were living on the boat before it was put in the water. By the looks of this thing, I'd guess it to be at least forty-to-fifty years old. You don't see many of these old wooden boats anymore. Someone went to a lot of trouble to fix it up. It's been repainted, and from what little I saw of the inside, it looked like everything was new. Unless the killer did all of this work, someone around here knows something about this boat that can help us. I want to get these guys to pull it back to shore and take another look inside before the crime lab gets here," he said.

It took more than an hour for the crime lab to arrive, which gave Clayton and Stillwell enough time to go over the boat's interior with flashlights; marking the areas of interest with numerical markers. Just about the time Clayton thought he couldn't stand another minute of the smell, he found an aluminum faced sticker on one of the cushions of a wooden-boxed chair in the corner behind the door.

"I think we just caught a break," he said.

"What did you find?"

Clayton lifted the green vinyl cushion from the frame and handed it to Stillwell. She squinted under the dim light to read the inscription on the sticker.

"Bayport Marina and Salvage, Kemah, Texas. That's not far from here, Clayton. Do you think we could be so lucky?" Do you think they're still open? It's almost nine," she said, looking at her watch.

Clayton got the number of the marina on his cell phone and called. He listened to a recording that told him business hours were from six a.m. to six p.m. then jotted down the emergency numbers on a pad from his jacket. After placing a call to the emergency number he closed his phone and dropped it in his pocket.

There's no answer at the emergency number, just a recording saying they'll be back in the morning. I'd like to be there when they open," he said.

"Well, it's the closest thing we've had to a lead. What time do you want to pick me up?" she asked.

"I'm thinking around four-thirty."

"You'll have to use that American Express card of yours to buy me breakfast if you're going to get me up that early," she said.

"If it turns into anything, I'll spring for dinner, too," he said.

Richey Sneed had never heard of the Lodge Motel in Conroe, a town forty miles north of Houston. But it was off the main highway and obscured by another motel and a lumberyard on the frontage road, and seemed like a good place to lie low, at the time. It didn't take long to realize that he'd made another mistake.

He should have known after the first two nights that the steady stream of cars in and out of the parking lot, at all hours of the night, could only mean one of two things; drugs or prostitution. With the Lodge Motel it meant both. Young girls, mostly white, and all addicted to crack-cocaine, came from all over South Texas and Louisiana to call the Lodge Motel home. And, if they weren't turning tricks to buy drugs they were scheming of ways to obtain them without money.

Sneed sat by the window each night watching cars roll into the parking lot, and young girls stream in and out of their rooms to present themselves to prospective buyers or sellers. An hour later, the same cars would reappear and drop the girls off with enough money for a rock of cocaine, and maybe a hamburger. On Thursdays the girls had to turn twice as many tricks to pay the rent on Fridays. It was a demented lifestyle, Sneed thought, but the alternative was sleeping in one of the dumpsters behind Wal-Mart or Target. It was a vicious and degenerate cycle of inhumanity; and he was caught in the middle of it. So was life in America's drug culture, he thought.

The girl that knocked on his door was bear-footed, wearing white shorts and an oversized, button-down shirt, tied in a knot at the waist. She had dirty blonde hair and hollow blue eyes. An unfiltered cigarette dangled from her lips, and when she spoke, every other word was interrupted by a chronic cough. Her eyes darted around the parking lot as she waited impatiently for Sneed to answer the door.

"What can I do for you?" Sneed asked casually, sticking his head through the small opening.

"Yeah, man, uh, one of my friends just got out of jail. She overheard these cops talking about the drug taskforce making a raid on the Quality Inn, and the Lodge, tonight. If you're not holding,

I wouldn't worry about it much, but if you are, things are about to get interesting," she said, running her wrist and forearm across the bridge of her nose. She flipped her cigarette into the parking lot and was about to leave when she saw Sneed move away from the opening and quickly return.

Sneed handed the girl ten dollars from his wallet, told her thanks, and slammed the door without looking back. How could this be happening, he wondered? Of all the dives between Houston and Dallas, he'd landed in the heart of one of the most decadent drug cultures in the Southwest United States. He didn't know where to start, but one thing he was absolutely certain of; he didn't need another confrontation with the cops.

He threw one of the suitcases on the bed beside Beverly, and began gathering clothes and food from around the room and stuffing them inside. He yelled out for Beverly to wake up, but she never moved. He ran back to the curtains looking outside into the parking lot. There seemed to be a lot of people, mostly young girls, coming and going, but so far, there were no cops. He wondered if the prostitute had gotten some bad information and he was just over-reacting. He couldn't take a chance.

"Get up, Beverly," he yelled again. This time he grabbed her by the arm and shook her roughly.

"What the...," she muttered, and quickly drifted off again.

He knew the coke she'd snorted an hour ago was still working her malaise. They'd made love a few moments after she got loaded; and she'd passed out as-soon-as he was done. Ordinarily, she'd be out for the night, but tonight, any sleep would have to come later, and somewhere else. He rousted her again. This time she sat up in bed and tried to focus her eyes on him. She seemed to smile briefly then started to moan and complain about being awaken.

"Richey, I can't go again. I'm too tired," she said, falling back into her pillow.

"You don't have to worry about taking your panties off, but you do have to wake up and put them on. The cops are on the way to bust this place," he said, throwing another suitcase onto the bed and frantically working to fill it.

He heard the squealing of brakes and tires skidding in the parking lot and instinctively ran to the window to check it out. At the front and rear exits of the complex, two unmarked, oversized panel trucks had stopped and were dumping Conroe police and DEA agents into the parking lot. There were at least two drug-sniffing dogs and he knew that it would only be a matter of minutes before they were at his door.

Doctors and medical technicians had worked most of the evening on Wade Gorman's leg. First, removing the traction devices and pins from his leg, and then casting the leg from his ankle to just above the kneecap with a hard fiberglass cast. They fitted him for crutches and removed the sutures from the lacerations in his face and shoulder. The nurse had given him an injection for the pain before they started, but it had worn off long before they finished. When the last technician left the room the nurse came back and began jotting notes in his chart.

"You know, Mr. Gorman, it's not good for you to lay there in pain," she said, recognizing the lines of stress on his face.

"I don't want to get hooked on that stuff," he said, working to re-position his huge body in the tiny bed.

"Mr. Gorman, if all of our patients were like you, no one would ever become addicted to drugs. Now I'm going to bring you something for the pain, and I don't want any argument. You're going home tomorrow and I want you to get a good nights rest," she said, walking to the door and looking back at Gorman as if she were scolding an unruly child.

"I'm hurting to badly to say no," he said, rubbing his palm over the wound in his shoulder where they had removed the sutures.

"Is something else bothering you, Mr. Gorman?" she asked.

"Everywhere they touched me, I'm itching. I was waiting for you to leave so I could get a coat hanger and run it down in this cast," he said. It was glib attempt at humor, but the truth was the coat hanger thought had crossed his mind.

"Let me talk with your doctor. I can give you something for the itching, but I need to speak with him first. Maybe we can give you something to help you sleep as well," she said, walking away.

"Yeah, when I get well, I'm going to come back down here and arrest you. You've got to be one of the biggest drug dealers in town," he said, under his breath.

Just as the nurse walked away, Stacy Cromberg walked in and feigned a smile. She wore a pair of plum colored scrubs that one of the nurses from her floor had given her, since Rucker hadn't brought enough things from home for an extended stay. And aside from the bruises and missing teeth, could have passed for one of the staff. She moved slowly across the room taking notice of Gorman's cast and the obvious pain in his eyes.

"I heard they were sending you home in the morning and I didn't want you to get out of here without saying goodbye," she said. Each word she spoke carried a hissing sound from the two missing teeth. She put her hand over her mouth, and Gorman could tell that she was embarrassed to have him see her in this condition. Her eyes watered slightly and he could tell that she was hurting in a totally different way from the pain he was experiencing. He took her by the hand and held it gently.

"I want to tell you how proud I am of you. There are not many cops who would stand up to guys like Bonner and Degas the way you did," Gorman said.

"They got away, Captain. We should have had the house surrounded. But the truth is we never expected them to be there. We blew it, Captain. I feel awful that..."

Gorman held his good arm in the air and stopped her in mid-sentence. "You went there to question Silvia Degas. You had no way of knowing Bonner and Degas were going to be there, much less know anything about Richey and Beverly Sneed being there. We'll get those guys; it's just a matter of time. Look, you recovered almost $900,000.00 of stolen money, and stopped those two from getting out of town with it. If you hadn't gone there when you did I'm convinced we'd never seen those clown again. Now, they may be on the run, but they're broke, and when they surface we'll get them," he said, confidently.

"Thanks for the kind words, Captain. But Brubaker is dead and Aaron Phillips could have been killed, and I feel responsible for not being more prepared. I couldn't look at Bru's wife at the funeral. I just can't believe it all happened so quickly," she said.

"Internal Affairs has ruled that you followed basic police procedure. That's all we can ask our officers to do. If you'd known that four armed felons were in the house, and then somehow acted irresponsible, then you may have reason for all the guilt you're feeling. But you didn't know, and you did everything you could to make the best of the situation. Every one of us, including Brubaker, understands the dangers of being an officer of the law. We accept that danger the day we pin on the badge. Most of us never think about it. Its just part of what we do. You didn't do anything wrong, and you've got no reason to feel ashamed," he said.

A nursing supervisor walked to the door and peered inside. "I've ordered your take home meds for first thing in the morning, we should be able to have you out of here by nine, if you want to have someone ready to take you home. We've also got something to help you rest tonight. So, if I don't see you before you leave in the morning, I wish you all the best," she said.

"Thanks for all you've done," Gorman said, waving with his good hand. "I'd better be going too, Captain. I hope the next time I see you I don't look like I've been in a bar room brawl," Cromberg said, holding her hand in front of her mouth. "Thanks again for the kind words, and take care of yourself."

Cromberg kissed him on the cheek and Gorman hugged her as tightly as he could with one arm, and then took her hand, as she was about to move away.

"You just remember what I said. You did nothing wrong, and you have nothing to be ashamed of."

Cromberg turned and quickly walked away. She didn't look back because she didn't want him to see the tears streaming down her face.

CHAPTER 7

Clyde Bonner listened to the branches of a Sweet gum tree scraping against the tin siding and roof of the dilapidated old shed. It had been his home for more than a week following the shootout at the Degas house. He'd ran into the woods not far from the house and found an old cemetery, and a corrugated tin shed that had been used for horses and pigs, a hundred years ago.

Twice in the last week he'd left the hideout, and crossed the tracks to do reconnaissance on the adjacent neighborhood for the supplies he'd steal the next night. So far, he'd stolen a case of bottled water, a first aid kit, six cans of beans, two cans of beef stew, a flashlight, a blanket, kitchen matches, a roll of toilet paper, and a carton of generic cigarettes.

He tried to limit the items to things that wouldn't draw a lot of attention to the neighborhood, or cause someone to get the cops involved in searching for a petty thief. So far, he'd been lucky. But the most fortuitous stroke of luck was when the cops assumed that he had been in the van with Sneed and his wife when they had escaped from the shootout. The dense woods and cemetery had provided the perfect cover. Aside from a few kids playing with air rifles, no one had come looking for him.

He'd never thought of himself as much of a thinker. But with a simple-minded partner like Degas, most of the planning was clearly left up to him. Now, with plenty of time on his hands, very little money, and no Degas to worry about, thinking was about all he had left. He wondered if the cops if the cops had found the money that he and Degas had hidden in the bottom of the suitcases. He thought of ways to disguise himself and steal it back from the police. But of all the thoughts that had crossed his mind, the one that haunted him night and day, was how he was going to find Richey Sneed and kill him.

In his mind's eye, he could still see poor Anthony's face the moment before Sneed pulled the trigger. He was actually smiling as if he'd wandered into an amusement park and all the rides were free. He had the face of a child at play. Or at least he did until the bullet from Sneed's gun ripped through his brain and took off the top of his head. He wanted to do the same thing to Sneed. Stand him in front of a mirror, and have him watch as he slowly pulled the trigger.

And then there was the matter of Sneed's wife. He wanted her dead too; but not in the same way as her husband. He wanted the process to be long and painful. He wanted her to agonize over her impending death. He wanted her to plead and beg for her life; he wanted to rape her, over and over again, he wanted to beat her senseless. She deserved every ounce of pain he could inflict on her, he thought.

Bonner lit a candle and checked his watch; it was four a.m. Wind was howling through the trees and the temperature had dropped twenty degrees in the last hour. He could smell the rain in the air long before it began to sprinkle. Lightening flashed across the sky, illuminating the woods temporarily. He moved his bedroll further back into the shed where he had covered the tin roofing with a piece of canvas that he'd stolen from a garage across the tracks.

He built a small fire with pine needles and branches he'd broken into kindling, and opened his last can of beef-stew, holding the can over the flame with a pair of pliers, and wondering how long it was going to rain. His only other thought was how long it would be before he killed Richey Sneed and his wife.

Black clouds moved over the bay and began drenching the coastline. Bayport Marina and Salvage, Co. sat on a tiny peninsula a quarter-of-a-mile long, with a wide wooden pier with boat slips on either side, leading to an open-faced workshop and dry-dock near the main storefront. Like everything else the storefront and marina were elevated on heavy wooden piers. A covered wooden porch encompassed the store and marina with stairs leading to the pier and boats at the rear of the store.

Clayton and Stillwell watched Richard Tauzin scurry up the front steps and stop on the porch. He was wearing a long, black raincoat, and carrying a thermos of coffee, a briefcase, and what appeared to be a bank bag, full of cash and coins for the cash registers. When the two cops rushed up the steps behind him, he turned quickly, reaching for something in his back pocket.

"I don't know what you folks want, but we're not open yet," he said, turning around and allowing the semi-automatic protruding from his belt to come into full view.

"Since we startled you, we'll assume you have a concealed carry permit for that weapon. We're cops," Stillwell said, holding her badge in the air next to Clayton's.

"Cops? I thought you were all at Duncan Donuts this time of the morning," he said, chuckling at his own joke.

"Are you the owner?" Clayton asked, ignoring the man's attempt at humor. "Rickey Tauzin," he said with a smile, while offering his hand to the two officers. "I've owned this place for forty-two years," he said, proudly.

"We'd like to ask you some questions, Mr. Tauzin," Stillwell said.

"Give me a moment to get things situated, and I'll be glad to help you any way I can. I didn't figure you were here to look at boats," he said, opening the door.

Rickey Tauzin was tall, with a board-straight back and thinning gray hair. Clayton thought him to be in his sixties, but the truth was he was a few days shy of seventy-five. He had steel blue eyes, and capped white teeth and a freshly shaven face. He smelled of Aqua Velva and talcum powder.

Tauzin walked through the showroom and into the office at the rear of the building and flipped on the lights. The walls of his office were lined with trophy game fish, heads of whitetail bucks, and two Russian boar heads mounted side-by-side. There was an oversized executive desk with papers and brochures stacked on one side. A phone and candy dish filled with jellybeans sat on the other. He popped a jellybean in his mouth and leaned back in a leather chair that seemed too large for his body. He looked at the cops as if he were about to go on trial for his life.

Clayton and Stillwell introduced themselves with business cards then sit in leather chairs facing Tauzin's desk. Stillwell pulled a folder from her handbag containing a number of photographs taken by the crime scene investigators, of the boat and it's interior. She handed the photographs to Tauzin, keeping her eyes trained on his face for a reaction of guilt or for a tale-tale sign of a lie that he might be contemplating. What he said next surprised her.

"It's the Monet boat," he said, with a broad smile. He pronounced the name Mo-Net, instead of the French pronunciation. "I've been passing that boat everyday for the last month wondering when they were going to start shooting the movie. But it just sits there in the bay, tied to those two poles, right where I left it. It was so dark and rainy when I passed by this morning I guess I didn't notice it. What happened? Did somebody steal it?" he asked, still entranced by the photos.

"So, you did put the boat there?" Clayton asked.

"I sure did," Tauzin said, innocently.

"Did you build the boat," Stillwell asked.

"Well, yes and no," Tauzin answered.

"Tell us about your level of involvement with the boat; if you would," Stillwell said.

"I didn't mean to not answer your question. The truth of the matter is I don't have a clue as to who actually built the boat or where it came from. We had a hurricane come through here in 1983. Everything, including this building, was under water for several days. There were boats sunk all over the bay. There were others torn loose from their moorings floating around for days waiting for the water to recede. When we came back a few weeks later, this old boat was sitting on the tip of the peninsula. I figured someone would come and claim it sooner or later, but they never did. After a few years it became part of the landscape, and a reminder of sorts," he said, his brow furrowed in thought.

"A reminder of the hurricane?" Stillwell said.

"Well, that too, I suppose. But what I was really thinking of; is that we tend to think that we control things in our lives. That old boat reminded me everyday that we just think we're in control of things. More often than not, life's events are in the hands of something a whole lot bigger than we are," he said, reflectively.

"So the boat has been on your property for the last twenty years?" Stillwell asked.

"Up until about three months ago, yes that's correct," Tauzin said.

"We need to know everything you can tell us about what happened. What all did you do to the boat? Who contacted you? How were you paid? The names of any contacts you might have had? Anything at all will help," Clayton said.

"Can I ask what this is about? I checked with my lawyer about selling that old boat before I ever moved it. He told me that after twenty years, and nobody claming it, that I had as much legal right to it as anybody did. I admit, I didn't have a title to it, but after all this time I figure I had the right to sell it if I wanted too," Tauzin said, defensively.

"You don't understand, Mr. Tauzin. We're not questioning your ownership or your right to fix it up and sell it. We're investigating a homicide that took place on the boat and we need to know anything you can tell us about the person who paid you to work on it," Clayton said.

"Someone was murdered? When did that happen?" Tauzin asked.

"We think the murder happened less than a week ago. And we're desperate for anything you can help us with," Stillwell said.

Tauzin popped another jellybean in his mouth and gazed out the window at the seagulls darting into the morning tide for shad.

"This is going to sound like I've been trying to keep something from you; but I swear, I'm not," Tauzin said, looking back at the cops. "I got a call from a movie producer fellow, who said he was working on a documentary about this painter, Monet. He sends me a photograph of this painting and says he needs me to recreate this boat for a scene he was working on. He told me that he saw the old boat from the road, and that it was very close to the one in the painting. He sent me this picture of how he wanted it to look," Tauzin said, shuffling through his desk drawer.

Tauzin found the photograph and handed it to Stillwell. She looked at it briefly and handed it to Clayton.

"So what happened next? Did he give you an advanced payment? And if so, was it in the form of a check, bank draft or what?" Stillwell asked, excitedly.

"Like I said, I got the okay from my lawyer to proceed and when the man called back, I gave him a price of $30,000.00 to do the job. I know that probably sounds a little steep; but to tell you the truth I wasn't all that crazy about doing the job. I kind-of liked seeing the old boat out there everyday. Anyway, I told him I'd have to have half up front and half when I finished. Three days later a courier pulls up and hands me an envelope with a cashier's check for $15,000.00 in it, and a note to proceed with the repairs. I have a copy of the check here somewhere," he said, absentmindedly.

They waited while the old man sifted through one of the stacks of folders on his desk until he found the one he was looking for and opened it. The words "Monet Boat" was written on the front of the folder with a black marker. He flipped through the bound material until he found a photocopy of the check.

"It's all here, just like I said," he said, folding the pages over the top of the folder and handing it to Stillwell.

Stillwell looked at the photocopy of the check for several moments before handing it to Clayton. He knew instinctively that the check was a dead end from her reaction. The expression on Stillwell's face had turned from one of excitement to a look of despair.

The check was for $15,000.00 just as Tauzin had said. But it was drafted on a Mexican bank called, Banco Popular. The branch of the account was in Matamoras, Mexico, and sent by a Mexican courier to Tauzin. Clayton knew they'd have more luck finding a lost wallet in Matamoras, than trying to glean information from Mexican banking officials.

"It didn't seem a little strange to you that your money was coming from a bank in Mexico?" Stillwell asked.

"Now that I know that someone was murdered on the boat, sure, I probably should have questioned the whole thing. But someone being murdered never once crossed my mind. And the fact is we do business with Mexican salvage companies all the time. They order special parts and send me a check. I wait for it to clear the bank and ship them the part. I never see those people either. So, it just never occurred to me to be suspicious," Tauzin said, holding his hands in the air, as if to convey his innocence in the matter.

"What repairs did you make on the boat? And what happened after you were finished," Stillwell asked.

"I have a full list of the repairs in that folder. But the short version is this: We pulled the boat into dry-dock, then we replaced the rotten wood and fiber-glassed the entire hull to make it sea-worthy. The cabin for the most part was totally rebuilt. We installed a rebuilt inboard motor, steering apparatus and keel, new batteries, running lights, and interiors just the way they appear in the photographs. I tried to sell the guy a custom made trailer to haul the boat. But the man said he didn't need one, so I didn't push it," Tauzin said.

"If you didn't have a trailer, how did you get the boat across the highway and down to the bay on the other side?" Stillwell asked.

"After the last check cleared, which was for $16,000.00 I sailed it around and under the causeway and into the bay. I found the poles and tied it off just the way he asked me to. The last check was supposed to be $15,000.00, but he paid me an extra thousand to sail it over there for him. I did it in one afternoon. I had one of my guys follow me over in another boat and bring me back. Not bad money for an afternoons work, I thought. But I swear to you, I never dreamed of anyone being killed on that boat," Tauzin said.

"When you spoke with the man, did he speak with an accent? How did he sound?" Clayton asked.

"Yeah, he did have an accent, but I just assumed he was Mexican, since the check came from Mexico and all," Tauzin said.

"Would you recognize the voice if you heard it again?" Clayton asked.

"Absolutely," Tauzin said.

"Did the man speak Spanish during any of your conversations?" Clayton asked.

"Well, no, like I said, I just assumed he was Mexican. But now that you mention it, he didn't sound much like the people we deal with in Mexico either. I don't know, I don't hear so well anymore. It could have been another nationality, I suppose," Tauzin said.

"I just have one last question for you, Mr. Tauzin," Clayton said.

"What's that?" Tauzin asked.

"Where did the framed painting come from and who framed it?" Clayton asked.

"I did. A day or two before the boat was ready to go I received a Federal Express package. One of these long cylindrical tubes like engineers mail drawings in. There was a note inside that asked if I could have the painting framed and mounted on the back wall of the boat. Since I'd already got the last check and he was paying me a thousand dollars to drive the boat a few miles; I thought it was the least I could do," Tauzin said.

"If we can think of anything else, we'd like to call on you again," Stillwell said.

"I'm not in any trouble?" Tauzin asked.

"You're not in any trouble," Clayton said.

"Then sure, call on me anytime. I want you to believe me when I tell you this, I don't need the money, I don't need the work, and I'm not really looking for anything new to do. I would never do anything if I thought it would get me in trouble with the law. I'm almost seventy-five years old. That's too old to be starting a criminal enterprise, don't you think?" Tauzin said.

"Any age is too old for that, Mr. Tauzin," Stillwell said. They shook hands with Tauzin and headed for the squad car. As Clayton pulled off the peninsula and onto the main highway, he noticed that Stillwell seemed to be mesmerized by some imaginary object on the bay.

"Are you okay?"

"I thought for a moment, we were going to catch a break. I really thought we were going to get a positive lead this time," she said.

"Well, I still want to get Rucker to call that bank in Matamoras, and talk to the people who handled the financial transactions. What can it hurt at this point in the game?" Clayton said.

"Did you bring that magical, American Express card with you?" Stillwell asked.

Clayton chuckled. "Yeah, I've got the card," he said.

"Then buy me some breakfast. I can't think anymore without food," she said.

Sonny Fontenot and Claude Breaux introduced themselves to Rucker and Aaron Phillips then quickly made their way to the break-room for coffee.

"How was the drive over?" Phillips asked.

"A lot of swamp, rice fields and flatland," Claude Breaux answered.

"I did a background check on your man and he's not living at the halfway house any longer. He's not even in Houston," Rucker said.

"Is he still in the state?" Fontenot asked.

"Yeah, he's not far from here. He moved to a Coushatta Indian reservation between Livingston and Woodville, on Highway 190.

"I hope the scenery is something besides rice fields and flatland," Claude Breaux said.

"I wouldn't know. Neither of us has ever been there," Rucker said.

It took an hour and forty-five minutes to reach the reservation, another ten to find the gift shop and the old storage room Simmons used for a workshop in the rear. Fontenot and Breaux moved from one display counter to another, admiring the custom-made knives, leather goods, hunting pouches, and survival equipment.

When Simmons appeared from the workshop none of the cops realized he was in the room. He was wearing a long-sleeved flannel shirt and jeans with a leather apron extending to his knees. He had a clear plastic, face shield on his head with the shield raised above his hairline like a welder's hood and gloves on his hands.

Rucker had been staring out one of the front windows watching two children chasing a red-bone hound through a sprinkler system, when she saw Simmons reflection behind her in the glass.

"Are you Redhawk Simmons?" she asked.

"I am," he said, watching the men at the counters.

Fontenot and Breaux looked up from the display cases and immediately began walking in Simmons direction.

"Did you make all these knives?" Fontenot asked.

"I sure did," Simmons said.

"Got any discounts for police officers?" Breaux asked.

"No, my price is ten percent higher for police officers," Simmons said, smiling broadly. The two cops looked at each other briefly then began to chuckle. After introductions, Clyde Breaux pulled a photograph from his pocket and leaned on the counter in front of Simmons.

"This man was Carl "Snake" Lopez; he was your cellmate at Huntsville, wasn't he?" Breaux asked, knowing the answer to his own question.

"What's he done now?" Simmons asked.

"He ain't doing much now, partner. He got himself killed the other night at Harrah's Casino, on Lake Charles," Breaux said. Both cops studied the disbelief on Simmons' face.

"Look, we don't want to play any games here, we know the two of you went on the boat together. We know the two of you had several conversations on the boat. What we don't know is how and when you left the boat. We know how Lopez left the boat; in a body bag. Now, we've spent hours going over films and we can't find where you left the boat at all. Did you spend the night on the boat?" Fontenot asked.

"I can't believe Snake Lopez is dead. Are you sure you got the right man? How did it happen?" Simmons asked.

"Let us ask the questions for now, Mr. Simmons. We'll answer your questions when we're done," Breaux said.

"Oh, Redhawk," Renee Harjo said, bursting through the swinging door.

"I'm sorry, I didn't realize you were with customers," she said.

"These people are not customers, they're cops," Simmons said.

"I'm Renee Harjo. I'm a social worker here on the reservation. What's this all about?" she asked, a worried look covering her face.

"We're investigating a murder in Louisiana that happened last week. We have reason to believe that Mr. Simmons can help us with our investigation," Breaux said, smiling broadly.

"Tell them what they want to know, Redhawk," Renee said, lacing her arm into his as a show of solidarity.

"I don't know what happened to Lopez. It's true we went on the boat together, but he hit me up for money about eleven o'clock, and the last time I saw him, he was leaving the Casino with some Black woman. I looked for him a couple of hours after that, and finally decided to come home. I figured he got a room with the woman and would call me when he was ready to come back to Texas. But I never heard from him again," Simmons said, shrugging his shoulders for effect.

"Is this the black woman he left with?" Breaux asked, dropping another photograph on the counter. Simmons held the photograph at arms length and stared at it for several moments before he spoke.

"I don't know. I was playing this slot machine and I hit a $4,000.00 jackpot. When Lopez saw me hit the jackpot, he hit me up for more money. I gave him three hundred dollars and the next thing I know, he's leaving with a black woman. I only saw her from one side. She looked to be maybe thirty, to thirty-five years old. She wore her hair in a short Afro, but I never saw either one of them again," Simmons lied like a pro.

"What time did you leave the boat?" Fontenot asked.

"I hit the jackpot around ten, ten-thirty; it must have been a couple of hours after that. Around midnight, I suppose," Simmons said.

"Well, you must have dived in the water and floated back to shore, cause there sure ain't no film of you leaving the casino," Breaux said.

"I left the same way I came in. I never saw any cameras, coming or going. I was in a crowd of people when I left; maybe that's how you missed me. I think they were part of a tour or something. They all got on a big bus in front of the parking garage," Simmons lied convincingly.

"Did you go straight home?" Breaux asked.

"I tried to go straight home. I had trouble with my old truck. It was over heating. After looking at it, I realized that it had thrown a fan belt. I put the fan belt back on and almost cut my arm off when I was replacing the cowling. I drove myself to the hospital in Livingston and they sewed me up. I didn't get out of there till daylight. I came straight home after that. I'm supposed to get the stitches out in a couple of days," Simmons said, attempting to embellish the story.

"So, you never saw Lopez after eleven? Did you go out on any of the decks to look for him?" Fontenot asked.

"No. I went to every floor though, twice. Like I said, I figured he got a room at the hotel. He looked pretty happy when he was leaving and I didn't want to put a damper on his fun. As much as he had to drink I doubt he was able to do much. I figured he passed out and would call me on Tuesday or Wednesday," Simmons said.

"Didn't you think it was a little strange when he never called?" Breaux asked.

"Snake Lopez doesn't stay anywhere very long. I didn't know what to think when he didn't call. I called the hotel on Wednesday but they said there was no Lopez registered there. I thought he probably went home with the Black woman and crashed for a couple of days. I didn't know who else to call," Simmons said.

"I'm a forensics technician and a detective with the Houston Police department," Rucker said, handing him a card. "I don't have any jurisdiction here and you can say no to my request; but would you mind if I had a look at your truck?" she asked.

"You can look at anything I have," Simmons said, removing a glove and fishing the keys from his pocket. "The truck is parked around back. Just go through the swinging door and out onto the deck. You'll see it parked near the house in back," he said, motioning in the general direction of the truck. When Rucker walked away, Simmons pulled the glove back on his hand.

Rucker took the keys, smiling briefly at Renee Harjo as she worked her way behind the counter and through the swinging door. Aaron Phillips followed closely behind but didn't take the time to introduce himself.

"Your jacket says you did a stretch for manslaughter. Wasn't a knife involved in that killing?" Fontenot asked.

"That was a long time ago and it was self-defense. The man almost cut off my knee with a machete," Simmons said.

"But you did stab the man to death, didn't you?" Fontenot said.

"If I hadn't, you wouldn't be talking with me today," Simmons said. "I like the way you ask me questions that you already know the answers to. Why don't you stop beating around the bush and say what's on your mind," Simmons said.

"Okay, I will. Did you get into an argument with Lopez and stab him to death. Think before you answer the question, because we've got at least three people that seen you leave the casino just after Lopez did," Breaux said, lying through his teeth.

"I never saw Snake Lopez after eleven o'clock. I walked up and down the stairs to each level of the casino looking for him, but he wasn't there. What he did after eleven o'clock is a mystery to me. I didn't kill him. Why would I want to hurt a friend of mine?" Simmons asked.

"What about the Indian you killed? Wasn't he a friend of yours, too?"

Breaux asked.

"He was a "crack-head" who'd kill his own mother if it kept him in pipes and crack cocaine. He wasn't my friend," Simmons said.

Claude Breaux was about to hit Simmons with another question when Rucker and Phillips walked back into the showroom. Fontenot and Breaux looked at them as if they were waiting for a report on their findings.

"I didn't bring a forensics kit with me, but there appears to be blood stains around the cowling of the fan blade and on the radiator. I guess the question I have for Mr. Simmons is; what part of your arm was cut?" Rucker asked.

The question startled Simmons for a moment, because Lopez had stabbed him with a downward blow, cutting the top of his forearm. The only way the fan blade could have cut him in that manner was if he were under the truck when it happened. Simmons took a deep breath and looked Rucker in the eyes.

"It happened when I was under the truck working on the cowling. I was trying to realign it when it slipped out of my hands and the blade cut my arm," Simmons said.

"Why on earth were you working on your radiator with the engine running? You seem like a bright man, but that doesn't sound very intelligent," Phillips said.

"After I put the fan belt back on I started the engine to make sure it was going to stay on. I needed the lights to see what I was doing. With the engine off, the lights were so dim and causing such a drain on the battery, I was afraid the battery would fail and I'd really be in a pickle. You surely don't think I would have stopped on the side of the road and worked on my car if I'd just killed a man a few minutes ago. That don't make sense," Simmons reasoned.

"Do you want me to call a lawyer, Redhawk? Cause I've just about heard enough of this. Just because Redhawk works with knives you think he killed his friend on your dumb boat? You're asking all these questions because Redhawk's an ex-con and because of his acquaintance with Lopez. How many other people from that night have you questioned? Just give me the word, Redhawk. Just give me the word," Renee said.

It was the first time in his life that anyone had ever stood up in his defense. It was just another reason he loved the woman. He'd listen to her too; if there were a next time, and stay away from old cellmates.

"Are you arresting me, gentlemen," Simmons asked.

"No, we're just trying to do our jobs. We're paid to ask questions. Sometimes, the questions lead us in the right direction, sometimes it doesn't. Your friend rapped and almost killed this woman; her name is Thelma Thompson. She's still in intensive care at the hospital in Lake Charles. She hasn't been much help in identifying the man who saved her life," Breaux explained.

"How do you know anyone saved her life? What makes you think she didn't kill Lopez herself? You said that he rapped her; it sounds like self defense to me. It sounds like he got what was coming to him," Renee said.

"That might have been an option, except Thelma Thompson didn't fight back. Lopez beat her senseless before he raped her. She wasn't in any condition to inflict the kind of wounds Lopez took to his face. He had a broken nose and several other abrasions on his face consistent with blows from a good-sized man. And, in the only statement we've been able to get from Thompson, she said that this man appeared from nowhere and saved her life," Breaux said.

"It sounds to me like you need to be questioning the people that this Thelma Thompson came with. Maybe a friend showed up and took matters into his own hands," Renee said, still looking at the cops incredulously.

"Until we can get something more definitive from her, we're running down every lead we can. We just want to clear this thing up. The truth is, if the guy hadn't left the scene, there may not have been any charges filed since he clearly saved the woman's life and could have been attacked by Lopez and fought with him in self-defense," Fontenot explained.

"Then why the third degree on Redhawk?" Renee asked.

"Because the film showed them entering the casino together, but they didn't leave together. If the two men had left together, we wouldn't be questioning Redhawk at all," Fontenot said. "But one of them is dead and there's no evidence from the films we've looked at that Mr. Simmons ever left at all," he continued.

"Show the woman a picture of me. She ought to be able to recognize me from a photograph," Simmons said.

"We did," Fontenot said.

"And?" Simmons asked.

"I think if she'd fingered you we wouldn't still be talking, Mr. Simmons. We've taken up enough of your time," Fontenot said, looking hard into Simmons' eyes. "Don't be too upset with us Ms. Harjo; we have to ask these things. It's nothing personal," he said.

"Well I've got one more question," Rucker said. Everyone in the room turned and looked at her and Phillips.

"Aren't you out on parole?" she asked.

"I have eleven months left on my parole. I've been a model citizen. I've never missed a meeting with my P.O. and I've paid my money just like clockwork. Oh, and I asked for permission to go to the casino for the day," Simmons said, hoping they wouldn't check with his parole officer.

"So you got permission to go? You got permission to leave the state from your parole officer?" Rucker asked.

"I did," Simmons said, convincingly.

"I'm done here," Rucker said. "We were just along for the ride anyway, but if you don't mind, what was your parole officer's name?" Rucker asked.

"Martin Quinn," Simmons said decisively.

"Are you sure you won't reconsider that policeman's discount on one of those skinning knives?" Fontenot asked, smiling broadly.

"When I'm cleared from all this, you come back and we'll talk," Simmons said, squeezing Renee's hand tightly.

The officers drove quietly for several miles before Sonny Fontenot broke the silence.

"You didn't tell us you had a forensics background, detective Rucker," he said.

"I'm working on a doctorate in pathology at Baylor," Rucker said.

"Wow, I'm impressed," Breaux, said.

"Yeah, well, there's something that's still bothering me," Rucker said.

"What's that?" Fontenot asked.

"Simmons wore gloves the whole time he was questioned. You said there was a fight and Lopez's nose was broken. If he'd been in a fight his knuckles would be bruised and cut from a confrontation like that. I sure would like to look at his hands," Rucker said.

Before she could say another word, Fontenot had pulled off the road and was turning back in the direction of the reservation. A few minutes later he pulled back into the same parking space and Rucker and Fontenot got out, leaving Phillips and Breaux in the car. When they asked the clerk where Simmons was he pointed to the back of the building. The cops walked behind the counter and into Simmons' workshop. Simmons was setting at a grinding wheel and immediately stood when he saw the two coming.

"Forget something?" Simmons asked.

"I wanted to look at your hands," Rucker said, noticing that he was still wearing gloves.

Simmons smiled and took his time removing the gloves, a finger at-a-time. He laid the gloves on the workbench and extended his hands, palm up in front of her. His hands were calloused, and rough. Pink scars from cuts that had healed without stitches or medical attention were prevalent. When he turned his hands over, the tops of his hands looked as rough and hard as the palms. They could have easily been the hands of a veteran prizefighter, or a blacksmith's from the old west.

"I make knives for a living. My hands take a beating. It's a tough business," he said.

"Why were you wearing gloves earlier?" Fontenot asked.

"The only time I wear gloves is when I'm working hot stuff, like grinding or working around the furnace. I was honing an edge on a Bowie when you came in; the grinding makes the stainless steel very hot. Sometimes I have to wear really thick gloves, because of all the heat. I never gave it a thought. I have to wear them, so, I wear them" Simmons said, turning his hands several times as if examining them his self.

"Did you see what you wanted to see?" Fontenot asked Rucker.

"I'm good," Rucker said. They didn't speak again until they reached the car and were driving toward Houston.

"Well, did he look like he'd been in a fight recently?" Breaux asked.

"Yeah, he did. Every single day for the last twenty years," Rucker said.

Richey Sneed awoke to the sound of passing traffic out on the four-lane, and a strange smell like a phosphorus match being ignited, and cardboard smoldering. He pushed the layers of flattened shipping cartons to one side of the dumpster and peered through a rust crater in the side of the container.

Standing no more than a foot away from the dumpster was a young boy, probably no more than eight or nine years old, Sneed thought. He was holding a box of kitchen matches in one hand, and tossing the lit matches over the wall of the dumpster with the other. If it hadn't rained briefly during the night he'd have set the whole container ablaze, Sneed thought. Sneed glanced at his watch. It was nine-thirty and they'd been hiding in the dumpster for more than twelve hours. He craned his neck to look back at the Lodge Motel and the cars around the parking lot, if the cops were still there, he couldn't see them from the hole in the container.

Sneed worked his hands under the pile of cardboard boxes until he found his wife's arm. He latched onto her shoulder with his left hand and was about to shake her awake when instinctively, her eyes flew open, as if sensing fear or alarm. She snaked her way toward him then lied very still and alert. Suddenly, there was another voice coming from a direction out of Sneed's line of vision. He could hear a frantic voice yelling at the child.

"You little jerk. What in the Sam Hill do you think you're doing?" the man yelled from a distance.

The kid struck another match, tossed it over the wall of the dumpster defiantly, then broke and ran with all the agility of a runner at a track meet. Seconds later an obese balding man was standing on the container's bottom ledge, peering into the dumpster and talking to himself.

"Stupid little jerk. That's all I need is for some little idiot to set the whole back lot on fire. I'll catch you one of these days," he said to no one. Watching the boy hurdle a chain-link fence at the rear of the property and disappear into the woods like a ghost.

Just when Sneed thought the man was about to leave, he began talking to himself again.

"What's that? Looks like someone threw a good piece of luggage away," he said, looking around the storage lot to see if anyone was watching.

When Richey and Beverly left the Lodge Motel they were in such a hurry they had grabbed only two of their three suitcases, leaving behind the suitcase containing his personal items and clothes. They did manage to grab the case containing what money they had, drugs, guns, and junk food. The other case contained her clothes and personal items, and two of his shirts that he stuffed in just before heading for the door. They had been so worried about getting out of sight that the thought of the other case never crossed their minds.

The obese man worked his way around the dumpster and again looked over the side at the uncovered suitcase. He tried several times to reach the case but couldn't. After one last attempt and a loud grunt he stepped away from the dumpster and walked away. Just when Richey thought the man was gone for good, he came back with a piece of metal re-bar that had a hook formed on one end. He went back to the ledge and began positioning the hook inside the suitcase handle.

Sneed watched from beneath the cardboard boxes as the man strained and fumbled with the metal bar and suitcase handle. It was less than a minute before the man began to pull the suitcase out of the dumpster. Just as the man was about to latch onto the handle with his free hand, Sneed emerged from the cardboard pile and pointed his 9mm at the face of the obese man. The man was so startled by Sneed's appearance that he dropped the suitcase stumbling backward until he hit the ground with a thud.

Sneed jumped out of the dumpster and was on the man before he was able to speak, holding the 9mm just inches from the man's nose. Beverly Sneed stood and propped her elbows on the ledge of the dumpster and smiled at the disoriented man.

"You weren't about to steal our luggage, were you?" she asked, playfully. As Richey helped the man to his feet he tried to speak, but whatever he said came out of his mouth as garble. Richey looked at

Beverly as if the man had invented an esoteric language that no one other than himself was capable of deciphering.

"Do you speak English?" Richey asked, pushing the huge man toward the rear of the dumpster and out of sight. The fat man went at it again.

"Sure. I, I speak, sure I speak, you bet ya, you, you bet, I speak English," the man said, firing the words rapidly, like a machine-gun.

Beverly Sneed collected the other suitcase and made her way to the rear of the dumpster where Richey lifted her over the side and to the ground. She was standing close enough to smell the man's body odor and the awful cologne that he tried to mask the smell with.

"Woo," she said, and backed away from the big man. "I've been sleeping in a dumpster all night and I smell better than you do. Man, you need some help," she said, turning away from the man to focus on some imaginary object in the distance.

"What's your name, big man," Richey asked.

"My, my, my, my, na, na, name, is Norbert Callaway." He only stopped stuttering when he pronounced his name.

"Norbert. Your name is Norbert? What kind of name is Norbert?" Sneed asked. Then quickly decided he didn't need an answer to the question when the man began to stutter again. Sneed held his hand in front of the man's face like a stop sign.

"We seem to have a problem communicating here. How bout I ask you simple yes and no questions and you just nod the answer. I'd like to get out of here while I'm still young," Sneed said. The man nodded but didn't open his mouth.

"Do you have a car, Norbert?" Sneed asked. The man nodded yes.

"I take it that you work here, are you some kind of custodian?" The man nodded yes.

"We're in somewhat of a spot here, Norbert, the police have confiscated our car and our motel room, and we're going to need a place to hold up for a few days. Are you married?" The man shook his head no.

"A, ah, ah, are, are, you going to k, kill me?" the man managed to ask.

"Hell, I been thinking about shooting you just for stuttering like an idiot.

Just be cool, man. I got no reason to kill you," Sneed said.

"Does your place have a bath tub with running water?" Beverly asked.

The man nodded yes but didn't say a word.

"Well, I'm glad we're going to your house then, maybe we can help you figure out how to use those facilities, cause if anybody ever needed a bath, baby you do," she said, waving her hands in front of her nose.

CHAPTER 8

More than two weeks had passed since Clayton and Stillwell had questioned Tauzin. They had spent hours questioning anyone even remotely close to the boat on Clear Lake. It was 6:30 am Friday morning, when Clayton walked into the conference room and caught Stillwell sitting alone.

Clayton stopped at the doorway to the conference room, looking intently in Stillwell's direction. She was wearing a gray pantsuit with a long-sleeved, maroon, silk blouse, and gray suede pumps that she had propped in the chair next to her. The Van Gogh recreation she had propped against a stack of folders on the table. The painting seemed to mesmerize her thought; she was lost in the beauty of the work. Before Clayton could say a word or announce his presence she spoke, without taking her eyes off the painting or turning in his direction.

"Tell me again about this painting," she said softly.

Clayton moved in closer, never taking his eyes off of her, and never really looking at the painting. He sat a cup of coffee in front of her then took a seat to her left, on the other side of the table.

"If there's anything special about the painting, I'm not aware of it," he started. "It's called The Courtyard of the Hospital in Arles. I'm fairly sure this was painted near the end of Van Gogh's life, and by the looks of grounds and overall arrangement of the gardens it appeared to be a peaceful place where he probably spent a lot of time painting. This is a beautiful painting, but personally, I would prefer a painting of a vintage Jaguar on a winding mountain road," he said in an attempt to inject humor into the serene setting.

Stillwell sipped from the coffee he'd brought her then slowly drifted her gaze onto Clayton's stare. Clayton had the irresistible urge to tell her how beautiful he thought she looked, but instead waited for her to speak.

"I spent some time on the computer last night in an attempt to come up with some answers," she started. "If you eliminate the mom and pop storefronts that have no room for a courtyard, there are over twenty thousand businesses in the greater Houston area; I'm including Clear Lake, Kingwood and the Woodlands in our search area. There are several hundred hospitals and institutional buildings, over two hundred and fifty hotels and motels not to mention theaters, museums, opera houses, and buildings owned by the city or Harris County. I couldn't find any statistics regarding buildings with courtyards, but my guess is there are several hundred in Harris County alone," she said, looking back at the painting.

"From everything we've learned so far, it appears that this killer is spacing his kills around three to four weeks apart. That leaves us a couple of days to find a place that looks like this painting, stake it out, and pray that we've got the right one," she said, tapping her nails on the table. "We need at least fifty officers scouring the city and county for this place now, today," she said.

"I have an idea," Clayton said. "There is no way we can get fifty additional officers helping us find this place. But the cops in Metro are on the streets every day, and so are the constables serving warrants. Let's get a good color print of this painting and put it in their hands. It has to help," he reasoned. Stillwell stood, picked up the painting and started for the door.

"What do you say, will a couple of hundred copies be enough?" she asked.

"I think that should do it," Clayton answered.

Clayton had no more than spoken the words when the phone rang. He instinctively looked at the clock on the wall. It was 7:05 when Stillwell picked up the phone and handed it to him. "It's someone named John Williams," she said, handing the phone to Clayton.

"John, this is a surprise. How are things in Cold Spring?" he asked. Clayton had known John Williams since he worked homicide with the Dallas PD and was offered the Sheriff's position in Cold Spring, on Lake Livingston.

"I've been gone from Cold Spring for a few weeks. I took a homicide gig with the Bexar County Sheriff's Department in San Antonio. I thought the quiet life was what I needed. I dang near went crazy in Cold Spring. It was just too quiet, if you know what I mean," Williams said.

"What can I do for you John?" he asked, waving his hand in Stillwell's direction. He wanted to stop her before she left the room.

"Aren't you working a serial killer case there? Someone who's killing people of Arab or Middle Eastern ancestry by slicing their throats?"

"Yeah, we are. Why?" Clayton asked. He finally got Stillwell's attention and motioned her back to the conference table.

"We got a call about four this morning from the Convents Gardens, Mission San Jose'. It's one of those old Catholic Missions like the Alamo. It seems someone killed a man and left him propped up against an oak tree in the garden. He was of Middle-Eastern decent and his throat was cut from ear-to-ear. Sound familiar?" Williams asked.

"It does, but why do you think it has anything to do with our case?" Clayton asked.

"That's why I'm calling. Ordinarily I wouldn't have given it a thought, but the forensics team found a rolled up painting in the man's jacket. I knew from the reports that you were dealing with someone who liked to leave clues to his next victim in the form of a painting," Williams said.

Clayton stood there for several seconds not saying a word; almost as if he were allowing his brain a few moments to digest everything it had just been fed. Stillwell gave him a quizzical look and moved back toward the conference table.

"Clayton, you there?" Williams asked.

"Yeah, yeah, I'm here," Clayton, answered.

"Clayton, the crime scene is untouched except by our forensics team. It's clean. The truth is I've never seen anything like it. There are no prints, none of any kind. There are no signs of a struggle, no defensive wounds. From the lack of blood at the crime scene, and the body lividity we believe he was killed somewhere else and brought here in the middle of the night. The Coroner said he'd been dead for 8 to 10 hours before we found him. I can hold the body a couple of more hours if you want to look at it the way the killer left it. Otherwise, I need to release it to the medical examiners for autopsy."

"Don't hold the body, go on and send it to autopsy. Who called it in?"

"A night watchman said he noticed that the courtyard lights were off. When he flipped them back on and looked into the courtyard he noticed the man leaning against an oak tree as if he were asleep. The closer he got to the man he realized his shirt and coat were covered in blood. He ran back inside the sanctuary and called 911. Do you want to talk to the man?" Williams asked.

"It will take us three and a half to four hours to get there, if you need to let him go be sure and get his address and phone number. We defiantly want to talk to him. John, if you'll stay I'll buy your lunch," Clayton said.

"I'll be here when you get here. Don't worry about lunch; I look forward to seeing you again, Clayton." Williams hung up without saying goodbye. Clayton dropped the receiver back into its cradle and looked at Stillwell.

"Have you been to San Antonio lately?"

Aaron Phillips and Delores Rucker stood away from the front door with guns drawn at arms length. Montgomery County Deputy Sheriff's stood poised; waiting for a signal that everyone was in position. Quiet seconds flashed, a nod was given, and the Sheriff's

Deputy rammed the door latch with a heavy, solid metal ramming tool. The door blew open as if it had been wired with an explosive charge. Seconds later the house was filled with armed officers sweeping from room-to-room.

They found the body of Norbert Callaway in the rear of the house in what appeared to be a den. He was lying on his back in front of a rocker-recliner. A flat-screen Sony television sit on a glass top table near his feet, his arms were folded neatly over his chest, the fingers of both hands were interlocked together. A blue silk pillow was propped under his head and for all practical purposes it appeared that the man had lain down on the floor to watch his favorite program on television took a nap and died.

"There's no sign of a struggle," Aaron Phillips was the first to break the silence. "There's no visible wounds of any kind that I can see, no furniture out of place, nothing out of the cupboard or on the counter, in fact the whole place looks as neat as any place I've ever been in," he said, looking around the room again.

"I agree. Except for an over weight dead man lying in the floor, this doesn't resemble a crime scene of any kind I've ever seen," Rucker said.

Rucker holstered her weapon and knelt beside the body. "He's been room temperature for some time." She continued going over Callaway's body until she was stopped suddenly by one of the Sheriff's Deputies who tapped her on the shoulder and whispered close to her ear.

"You ought to wait on the Medical Examiner before you go too far," he said, smiling at the other Deputies.

"I am a Medical Examiner, or at least I will be in a few months," she said, picking up one of the man's legs to look underneath it. "I didn't bring my bag with me or any of my equipment but I can tell you that he's been dead for at least twenty-four hours. I also don't believe that he's been moved. I think he died here just the way he was laying," she glanced at Aaron Phillips again. "There's nothing on the body that would suggest that he died of anything but something internal, like a heart attack, or a stroke, and we're not going to know for sure without an autopsy. I think we need to talk to the neighbors that called it in before we go any further," she said, dusting her knees as she stood.

The woman who had made the call was standing behind the crime scene tape adjacent to Callaway's yard. Her arms were folded, and she seemed nervous as Rucker and Phillips approached her.

"We're with the Houston Police Department, Mrs. Dunkirk, I'm Delores Rucker and this is Officer Aaron Phillips, we'd like to ask you a few questions." The woman nodded but didn't say anything. Her eyes watered when she started to speak.

"Is Norbie dead?" she asked tentatively.

"I don't know if it's proper protocol or not, but I know you're going to find out soon enough, so yes, Mr. Callaway is dead," Rucker said.

Tears began to stream down the woman's face as she started talking again. "I knew something was wrong," she started, smearing her eye makeup with the inside of her hand.

"Just take your time, Mrs. Dunkirk. Tell us what you know and what you saw," Rucker said.

"It's been over a week now since strange things started happening. Norbie came home in the middle of the day; he's never home before six or six-thirty. I think it was Thursday a week ago, he comes home and I see he's got a young man and woman with him. I should have known right then something was going on. We been living here almost seven years and he's never had no company to speak of, and surely no one as young as those two," she said, wiping at the tears again.

"Did mister Callaway have any friends?" Phillips asked.

"If he did, I didn't know about them. Besides me, and the old woman across the street, he never spoke to anyone in the neighborhood that I know of. Norbie was shy; he wasn't dumb or retarded, just quiet and shy. He was so polite when we did see him that he kind of stuttered when he spoke. Some of the neighborhood kids thought he was retarded, but I let them know real fast that there was nothing wrong with him that a little kindness wouldn't cure." The woman looked at Phillips and stopped talking as if she were waiting for another question.

"You said that he brought a man and a woman home; what did they look like? Can you describe them to me?" Phillips asked.

"I'm guessing they were both in their mid-twenties. Nice looking in a rough sort of way. They both had tattoos and they dressed kind of sleazy. They reminded me of bikers, you know what I mean?" she looked at Rucker for confirmation.

Rucker pulled two photos from her purse and handed them to the woman.

"Does this resemble the two in any way?" Rucker asked.

"That's them. That's them," she said. "Did they kill Norbie?" she asked, wiping at the tears again.

"We don't think so, he may have died of natural causes," Rucker said, taking the photographs from the woman's hand. "Were they doing anything unusual around the house?"

"They did a lot of coming and going. It was always in Norbie's car. Norbie had a late model Cadillac, he babied that car, kept it washed and waxed and always in the garage. Norbie didn't smoke either, and they were always smoking in his car and I figured that he must have hated that," she said.

"Did you ever see the two of them leave together?" Rucker asked.

"Not until yesterday morning when I was leaving for work. They seemed in a hurry, throwing suitcases into the trunk and groceries into the back seat. When I came home from work I knocked on the door and when Norbie didn't answer I figured something was wrong. I waited for a couple of hours before I decided to call the cops. I should have called a couple of days ago, maybe poor Norbie would still be alive," she sobbed.

"None of this is your fault, misses Dunkirk. Do you have any idea if Mr.

Callaway was on any kind of medication?" Rucker asked.

"I don't know. I have seen him at Walgreen's a couple of times, never figured it was any of my business what he was doing there."

"I've just got one more question for you Mrs. Dunkirk," Rucker said, flipping the page on her notebook. "Did either of these two ever say anything to you or you to them? Did you happen to overhear any of their conversations?"

The woman turned slightly and pointed to her kitchen window, which was above the sink. "I spend a lot of time at the stove or at the kitchen sink there," she pointed. "It's to far away to hear much, and as you can see from the angle I couldn't see much either. I didn't go nosing around, if that's what you're asking me," she said defensively.

Before Rucker could say anything to the woman a dark blue Mercedes pulled in front of Dunkirk's house and skidded to a stop. A second later the Montgomery County Medical Examiner's car pulled in front of Callaway's house backing into the driveway.

"That's Norbie's brother," Dunkirk pointed in the direction of the man emerging from the Mercedes.

"Thanks for your help, misses Dunkirk. If you think of anything else please give us a call," Rucker said, handing the woman a card. Both cops turned and headed in the direction of the man in the Mercedes.

Stacy Cromberg ran an index finger across one of the pink ridges on her face where the stitches had been. "Nice teeth," she said to the mirror. Other than that I look perfectly awful she thought. She folded her compact and dropped it into her purse. It had been a long morning. Two hours in the dentist chair to affix her new front teeth, an hour at the doctor's office to make sure the lacerations on her face were healing properly, and an hour at the station; only to find out from a phone call, that Aaron Phillips and Delores Rucker had struck out in finding Richey and Beverly Sneed at Callaway's place.

She dropped what was left of her hamburger into the trash and started for her car. All morning she'd been thinking about the shootout on Fawnridge Street. There was something about that neighborhood that bothered her. Something tucked away in the recesses of her brain that she just couldn't shake. Something about a cemetery, she thought. Then it came to her. She remembered an Aunt that lived on a street called Sundown in the same neighborhood. She had only been there once or maybe twice as a child. She remembered her aunt dying and the family going to the funeral. That's been twenty-two, no twenty-three years ago she thought to herself. She started the car and headed for the neighborhood.

It took thirty minutes to reach the neighborhood. She turned on Shreveport Street slowing at each street sign to check the name. The closer she got to Fawnridge Street the more uncomfortable she felt. A foreboding feeling of despair and loss was tugging at her gut like a virus. When she finally passed Fawnridge Street the uneasiness seemed to lesson, she slowed at the next street, which was Sundown.

She must have passed a dozen houses before she came to the one she remembered as belonging to her aunt. It was a simple, single story, wood-framed home with a narrow concrete drive leading to an old rundown garage at the rear of the property. She pulled off the street into the drive and let the engine idol. She was debating whether to knock on the door and introduce herself or just drive away and forget the whole thing. Suddenly, an old black woman appeared from the garage and headed in her direction. As the old woman reached her door she rolled the window down to say hello but the woman started talking before she had a chance.

"Something I can help you with?" she asked politely.

"I hope so. My name is Stacy Cromberg; I'm with the Houston Police Department," she said holding her badge for the woman to see. "We're investigating the shootout that occurred on the next street over. It happened about a month ago," Cromberg was about to say something else but the old woman cut her off.

"Honey, I sure remember that. I never heard so much shooting in all my life. It sounded like a young war done broke out over there. My friends call me Birdie. I'm Birdie Clark," she said, extending her hand in Cromberg's direction.

"I don't mind telling you that I didn't get a good night's sleep for two weeks after that happened. I was out here in my yard picking up beer cans them hoodlums throw out of they car when I heard the first shot. You were involved in that thing, weren't you?"

"Yes, I was."

"Can I ask you what this has to do with me?" the woman asked, brushing at a lock of gray hair that danced on her forehead.

"Miss Clark," Cromberg said.

"Please honey, call me Birdie," she said.

"Birdie, I had an aunt that used to live in this house. She died over twenty years ago when I was a young girl. Do you remember Cora Hammond?"

"I sure do. She sold me this place in seventy-nine and moved into a nursing home. I heard that she was sick, and that she died shortly after moving to that place."

"You've got a good memory, Birdie."

"Yeah, well that's about all I got left," she said.

"Birdie, this question may seem a little odd to you, but do you remember her ever saying anything about an old cemetery, or do you know anything about an old cemetery around here?" Cromberg asked.

"Everybody around here knows bout that old cemetery. Some of the first settlers in Texas are buried in that cemetery. I suspect a lot of them folks were Negro slaves, by the sound of their names, but I could be wrong."

"Can you direct me there?" Cromberg asked.

"Honey, you ain't a quarter mile away from it. I'll go down there with you and show you around, but first I got to go and turn the fire down on my beans," she said.

"You shouldn't leave your cooking, Birdie," Cromberg said, but the old woman was gone before the words came out of her mouth.

As the woman came back she untied her apron and dropped it on the porch.

She got in on the passengers side and rolled the window down.

"I sure am glad you got one of them unmarked cars; I'd hate for the neighbors to think I was headed off to jail. Just pull out and head back the way you came," she directed.

The old woman was right; it was less than a quarter mile to where Shreveport Road came to a dead-end. Someone had tied a wire rope between two pine trees blocking the rut-filled trail leading to the dense woods. The two women walked around the trees and back onto the trail leading into the trees. The brush on either side of the trail was over grown and pine needles covered the ground as far as the eye could see. Cromberg and Birdie had walked for more than twenty minutes when the old woman pointed to the first headstone.

The headstone was lying on its back and partially covered with brush and dust but the carving was chiseled deep into the stone and still very legible. It read: 'Lizzie Dugan, Born October 14th 1767, Died, November 12th 1821.' There were two additional headstones no more than a few feet away but both were lying facedown, and neither of the two women seemed overly eager to turn them over.

As Cromberg moved further into the cemetery the canopy overhead was so thick it seemed to be late in the evening. She stopped for a moment allowing her eyes to adjust to the scarce light. Then like magic, everywhere she looked another group of headstones seemed to appear.

She followed a tiny trail down an incline that led behind the disarranged headstones, the old woman stayed behind. Suddenly, a shard of light bounced off an aluminum can that was dangling from a tree limb forty feet away. A sense of apprehension came over her and she unsnapped her holster, moving closer to what appeared to be an old makeshift shed and camp.

There was no sign on the camp that said, welcome to the camp of Clyde Bonner, but she knew instinctively that he'd been living here. Bonner had disappeared so quickly after the shootout that everyone assumed that he'd gotten away in a car, the same way the Sneed's had. But the truth was he'd circled the house, slipped across the road and ran the short distance to these woods and hidden from the searchers. Who would have thought he'd have stayed in the same area after being a part of murdering an HPD officer?

Cromberg thought to herself.

Now Cromberg realized that bringing the old woman to these woods was a mistake; she'd put both of them in harms way. She had to get her out of here as quickly and as quietly as possible and set up a surveillance team to surround the place and wait for Bonner to come home. From the looks of the camp, Bonner was scavenging the homes in the area for food and things to keep him occupied until he could come up with another plan, or perhaps steel a car. She made a quick list of everything she could see inside the shed then headed for the old woman.

Before Clayton and Stillwell left for San Antonio, Stillwell was handed an envelope containing the forensics teams report on the boat that Tauzin had rebuilt and parked on Clear Lake for the killer. The report was like all of the others she'd read concerning the actions of this killer. Evidence was non-existent.

"Did forensics turn up anything?" Clayton asked.

"O yeah, those boys are really on top of things," she said, sarcastically. "There were no fibers, no hair, no blood other than the victims, no skin, no body fluids, not even a drop of sweat. There were no fingerprints, footprints, epithelials, or anything else that might closely resemble a shred of evidence. It was like the man dropped in from another dimension, killed a Muslim or two and vanished into thin air like a phantom. We're missing something, Clayton. I don't know what it is but we're missing something. We need a break," she said.

Stillwell folded the report and shoved it back into the envelope. Seconds later she was lost in a malaise of thought and silence. It was five minutes before she spoke again and when she did it caught Clayton by surprise.

"Clayton, how well do you know this John Williams?" she started. Clayton rolled his eyes.

"I hope your not suggesting what I think you're suggesting," he said. "Look Clayton, just hear me out. You said that this man has been living in Cold Spring for the last six or seven months. Whoever our killer is has been killing people of Arab or Muslim decent for at least the last six months. It's certainly no stretch to think of Cold Spring as being too far away from Houston. Now, John Williams moves to San Antonio and like a miracle another murder occurs in a new town where he calls home. You have to admit it is just a little more than coincidental," she said.

"Leona, this guy's a cop. And not just any cop, but one that's clean as snow. I doubt seriously if this man has ever had a reprimand in his jacket. John Williams is straight. John Williams would be the last man on earth I'd expect to be involved in something like this. He's not our man. You're not wrong very often, but John is not our man," Clayton said, emphatically.

"Listen to me a minute. I have theory of my own," Clayton said.

"I'm listening," she said.

"Do you remember that case out in Atlanta where this guy was killing young black kids? Strangely enough this guy's name was Williams, but I think his name was Wayne Williams," Clayton said.

"Sure. Mayor Brown was Chief of Police in Atlanta at the time."

"You're right. If you'll remember this FBI profiler, I can't remember his name, told the investigation team that he believed that the killer was a black man between the ages of thirty and forty. His reasoning behind the statement was that a black man or woman was the only person who could operate so openly, and with impunity, in

180

an all black community. Everybody including Lee Brown got up in arms claiming the guy was a racist, and that there was no precedence to substantiate a claim like that. Lee Brown even went on television and called this guy a racist and an idiot."

"Clayton, can we stop a moment?" Stillwell asked, pointing in the direction of an upcoming exit.

Clayton switched lanes and took the first exit for the town of Seguin.

Seconds later he pulled into an Exxon station and both of them got out.

"Do you want something to drink?" Stillwell asked.

"I'll take a Coke," he said, popping the lever to fill the car with gas. Clayton paid the attendant for the gas then slid in behind the wheel. He was unconsciously tuning the radio from station to station when Stillwell stepped out of the office and headed in his direction. She was carrying two cans of Coke and a Snickers bar. Her face was expressionless, almost childlike. A gentle breeze blew out of the surrounding cotton fields causing her hair to dance like a minuet in the wind. And for a moment he wondered what she must have looked like as a young girl, and how beautiful she was today.

She handed Clayton one of the Cokes, closed the door and sipped from her can then begin to speak. "Okay Clayton, you make a valid point, and what you say makes a lot of sense. And you're right, I don't know your friend John Williams, but he's got a serial killers name," she said, allowing a terse smile to cross her lips.

"What's eating you, Leona? You've been acting strangely ever since we interviewed Tauzin. Do you want to share what's going on in your life that's got you so edgy all of a sudden?"

Stillwell looked away from him, staring out the window at the cotton fields that stretched out for miles in any direction. She didn't want to go where this conversation was leading, and would have changed the subject but Clayton pressed her.

"We've been partners long enough for me to know when something is going on in that pretty head of yours. You're the best friend I have. If you can't talk to me about something that's bothering you, who can you talk too?

"Look," she started. "I spent a lot of money on that dumb trip to New York. Then Rucker needed some money for school, so I loaned her what I had in savings. And if that's not enough the transmission is going out in my old car. It's going to cost at least two thousand dollars to fix it. It's just a money thing," she said with a dismissive wave of her hand.

"Then you don't have a problem. You need money and I have money. I'll write you a check as soon as we get back to Houston. Will five or six thousand be enough?"

"I don't want to take your money, Clayton. You're my partner, and yes you are my best friend. I don't think adding banker to that list is a wise thing to do. It's a good way to end friendships. And besides, I wouldn't feel right taking money from a man who never has more than five dollars in his pocket."

"Leona, just because I don't enjoy going to the bank doesn't mean I don't have money. You know my parents left me money. I can handle it. Believe me it's not a problem."

"Let's talk about it after we see Williams. It's giving me a headache just thinking about it," she said.

Before Clayton had driven five miles and before she had a chance to resume her sullen stare at the passing cotton fields, a billboard appeared on the side of the road. It was an advertisement for the San Antonio and Bexar County Live Stock Show and Rodeo that was to begin tonight at seven. For the first time since the two had left Houston a broad smile crossed her face.

"Are you in a hurry to get home tonight?" "What did you have in mind," Clayton asked.

"I want to go to the Rodeo. It starts at seven tonight. We'll have plenty of time to work the case and still make the Rodeo. You know how much I love the rodeo," she said, sounding a lot like a child working on a reluctant parent.

"Sounds like a plan to me. Do they take American Express?"

Stillwell dropped her Coke can in the console holder and stared at Clayton for a moment before looking back at the passing sign. "Be careful, Clayton. I don't want to have to hurt you," she said.

It was 5:00 pm when Cromberg answered her cell phone. Wade Gorman started speaking at the same time she said hello.

"I understand you think you've got a line on Clyde Bonner?"

"Who told you that, Sir?"

"It's not important. The important thing is that I don't want to get any more cops hurt or killed. Have you set up everything with S.W.A.T.? Gorman asked.

"We've got a team moving in on the site after dark tonight. We want to make sure it's Bonner. If it is Bonner we'll take him down in the morning around daylight," she said.

"Good girl. I don't want any more of my people hurt. Who's running the S.W.A.T. team?"

"Burt Cameron," she answered.

"He's a good man, and he's got a good level head. As soon as he's disarmed Bonner I want you there to read him his rights. You might also appreciate the opportunity to explain to Mr. Bonner that he's got a one way ticket to Huntsville to ride the needle," Gorman said.

"Believe me sir, it'll be my pleasure."

"What time are you going to set up the surveillance tonight?"

"We're going in around nine tonight to make the positive identification. I thought about trying to take him at night but the woods are so thick with brush that it's hard to navigate through it during the daylight much less at night. I just think it's better to wait until daybreak to take him down," she said.

"You're the only one who can assess the situation; I'm leaving that call up to you. It sounds like you've got a good handle on things. Keep me in the loop. I want to know as soon as you've made a positive identification. I don't want to be walking the floors over some vagrant camped out in the woods," he said.

"Roger that, Captain."

"You know, Stacy, you don't have to do this. It's only been a month since the shooting. We've got plenty of people who can handle this if you want to take a pass."

"I'm fine, Captain. If I didn't think I could handle this guy you'd be the first to know. I want to do this. I need to do this. I want to put this guy behind bars," she said flatly.

"Call me," he said, and disconnected.

Cromberg opened her compact and looked at her reflection in the mirror. The scars on her face were still there and would be for a long time to come. Her hands were trembling. She quickly closed the compact and dropped it in her purse. She thought about it for a moment and wasn't sure if the shaking of her hands was from fear or from the apprehension of taking this guy down without shooting him full of holes. There was one thing that she was absolutely certain of; she wouldn't miss the encounter for all the tea in China.

Richey Sneed dropped the keys to Norbert Callaway's Cadillac and two bags of food and drinks on the dresser and listened to his wife humming in the shower. They had both slept until four in the afternoon and woke up hungry. He had driven down to the Chevron Station on Wayside Drive and loaded up on Chester Fried Chicken, French fries, fried fruit pies and sodas. He poked his head in the bathroom door and told her he was back with the food.

"I'll be done in a couple of minutes. I'm famished," she said, and went back to humming.

Sneed opened the blinds and looked out onto the courtyard of the motel. There wasn't much to look at, a dingy looking swimming pool, strewn and tattered lawn furniture, and a couple of glass top tables missing the umbrellas. It looked like something out of the sixties, he thought.

His mind drifted to the stuttering fat man called Norbert, which they had abducted from the back lot of a Conroe lumberyard. He was sorry the man had died in his sleep. How could he have known the man had a medical condition? The truth was both he and his wife liked the big guy. They never had any need to even rough the guy up. All they wanted was a place to stay for a few days and the man's car when they were ready to leave. It was just another chapter of his life that had gone horribly wrong.

Then he thought of Clyde Bonner. He was the only reason that he and Beverly hadn't headed for the border. It was Bonner's fault they were hold up in this fleabag motel with a stolen car and Chester Fried Chicken instead of steak. It was Bonner's fault that the biggest score of his life had somehow turned to shit. It was Bonner and that idiot Degas' fault that every cop in Harris County was looking for him and his wife for the murder of a police officer.

He knew that there was nothing he could do about the money from the convenience store robbery; it was gone for good. There was nothing he could do about the poor fat man who died in his sleep, either. But if it were humanly possible, he would find the hole Clyde Bonner was living in, and kill him.

There in a nutshell was the problem, finding Clyde Bonner. The city of Houston covered most all of Harris County, which meant hundreds of square miles for a person to disappear in. But with any luck and a little help from HPD he might just get his wish. He flipped the switch on the police scanner he'd brought from Callaway's house and tweaked another knob until the dispatcher's voice came in loud and clear.

Redhawk Simmons and Renee Harjo had spent more than a week on Lake Livingston, camping on the lake's north side in a secluded spot away from the tourist, boating enthusiast and homeowners. They swam for the last time in the heat of the afternoon around three, then packed everything in his old truck around five-thirty hoping they could get back to the reservation and get it all unloaded before dark.

He and Renee had spent the week fishing the many slews and bayous that entered the lake for Catfish. Evenings and nights they fished for bass. The only time they hadn't eaten fried fish for a meal was two nights ago when Redhawk decided it was time for some red meat, and grilled up t-bone steaks and fried potatoes for the evening meal. That night they slept under the stars and made love like young kids.

It had been one of the best weeks of his life, he'd told Renee. Aside from languishing away in prison for years at a time, this was the only real vacation he'd ever been on, or earned for that matter. If it had to end, he wanted it to be on a high note.

About a half mile before reaching the blacktop, Redhawk stopped the truck and turned off the engine. He turned and faced Renee.

"There's something I've wanted to say, but you got to understand that this don't come easy for me. I never had a woman before, that is to say, I never had a woman that I cared for before."

"I'm flattered, Redhawk, I…"

"Please, let me finish," he said, holding up his hand like a stop sign.

"I'm asking you to marry me, Renee. I don't even know how to say the words, I love you, but with you in my life it sure comes easy, and I want to say it all the time. Will you marry me, Renee?"

Renee Harjo put her arms around his neck and held him tightly. She kissed him softly, tears streaming down her face. She swallowed hard in an attempt to quell the river of emotion flowing through her body.

"Are you sure this is what you want, Redhawk?" she asked softly. "If you're not sure, I'd be happy to wait," she offered.

"That's just it. A woman like you shouldn't have to wait. I want to get married as soon as we can. I want to speak to the Council tonight and set it all up. Maybe we can do it next weekend."

"Do you even have a ring? Renee wrinkled her brow. "I may be an Indian but I like the ring thing," she said.

"We'll go tomorrow and pick one out. I want you to go with me cause I've never been in a store like that unless it was to case the place. I think women are better than men when it comes to rings and stuff like that.

Renee kissed him again and settled in as close as she could get to her fiancée. Just as they made the blacktop it started to rain and the air smelled clean, of cedar and pine, fresher than she could ever remember. For the first time in her life everything in her universe was perfectly aligned.

It took almost an hour to clean and stow everything away. While Redhawk sifted through a weeks worth of mail Renee pulled a negligee from the top drawer of her dresser and headed for the shower, suddenly she turned and walked back to the kitchen where Redhawk was looking at the mail.

"Why don't you join me?" She stood naked in the doorway as he dropped the mail and watched her walk back toward the bathroom.

"Give me five minutes. I want to check the shop first to see what's come in while we've been away." He didn't wait for an answer; he just headed for the workshop.

He took a deep a deep breath as he flipped on the lights. His workshop smelled of machine oil, grinding dust and leather. His work desk was cluttered with dozens of posted notes from the girls working the counter in the store. There were several orders for custom knives and one order for a commemorative Apache knife from a customer in El Paso. The last piece of paper he picked up was an order form for a knife sharpening. He dropped the paper to the floor and quickly looked back at the workbench.

The curve-bladed knife set among several other knives to one side of the workbench. A white stringed coupon was attached to the handle of the knife just like all the others. He didn't have to look at the coupon to know whom it was from. He knew there would be no name on the tag, just a cell phone number to call when the knife was ready to pick up.

A thousand thoughts raced through his mind as he stared at the weapon. The news hadn't said a word of any new murders. There had been nothing on the radio; he and Renee had listened night and day. He turned abruptly and began sifting through a stack of newspapers. There was no story, not even an article on the string of recent killings in Houston. He ran his fingers through his thick black hair in an attempt to clear his head.

Instinctively he jerked the phone from its cradle and punched in Little-Twins number at the apartment. She answered on the second ring.

"The wild eyed man who brings in that curved blade knife, when did he bring it into the store?"

"Gee Redhawk, oh I'm doing fine, I'm so glad to hear that you had a pleasant vacation," she said sarcastically.

"I'm sorry; I didn't mean to be rude. Can you please tell me what day he brought the knife in? It's really important," he said.

Is everything okay, Redhawk?"

"Please. What day?"

"It was this morning. He was the first customer of the day. We've been real busy, Redhawk. You've got a lot of work to catch up on. How's Renee?" Before she could say another word or ask any more questions he dropped the phone back into its cradle and stood perfectly still, trying to collect his thoughts. This time he had to call the cops. He had to do something before this man killed another person.

He started for the knife then stopped suddenly, remembering the beautiful day and his lovely wife to be waiting in the shower. This would have to wait until morning, he thought. She was so happy. To spoil her happiness on the night of their betrothal would be unkind. It could wait until morning.

Clayton was right about one thing, Stillwell thought; John Williams surely didn't look like a killer. The truth was he didn't look much like a cop either. John Williams was tall and angular with a lean body and big hands. He had a freckled complexion, sandy colored hair and boyish good looks. His broad smile was inviting and when he shook hands with Stillwell she wandered why she ever thought of John Williams as a suspect for anything criminal.

"What did the Coroner have to say?" Williams asked.

Clayton sat on the corner of the conference room table pulling a rubber band off of the rolled up painting.

"A lot of what he had to say we already suspected. The man was killed somewhere else and brought to the courtyard. His throat was cut with a very sharp knife or surgical instrument. Your forensics team turned up the man's name, Ahmad Sepehr. Born in Iran in 1975 and immigrated to the states in 2000, he settled in Houston later that same year. He co-owned a clothing shop on Louisiana Street in downtown Houston with a man named Hobod Taheri. He lived in a small flat above the store and wasn't married. There were no relatives or next of kin known to be in the states. I'm wandering what he was doing in San Antonio?" Clayton closed his notebook and stored it back in his coat pocket.

Clayton turned his attention to the painting and began unrolling it very slowly. The painting smelled of Linseed Oil and Turpentine and depicted a night scene with a covered terrace café and diners eating and drinking while others strolled along the street. The painting was every bit as beautiful and accurate as the others.

"You know, this guy could have made a million bucks just painting for a living, but instead spends his life killing Muslims," Stillwell said.

"Wow," Williams said. "I had heard about the paintings involved with these murders, but I had no idea they were so beautiful. I know very little about art but I know enough to know this guy is a real pro. Who was the original artist, Clayton?"

"It's another Van Gogh. I suppose it's one of Van Gogh's favorite places to paint; it's in the City of Arles. It's called The Café Terrace at Night," Clayton said.

Just then the conference room door opened and another Detective ushered in a man wearing a gray khaki security guard uniform.

"John this is Luis Carmona the security guard that found the body. You wanted me to bring him in."

Carmona was thin and had coal black hair that he combed straight back. He had an olive complexion, and a pencil thin mustache and dark eyes that seemed to dart around the room when he wasn't talking. He shook hands with Williams and Clayton but took his time addressing Leona Stillwell. "Welcome to San Antonio, Detective Stillwell," he said, with a charming smile and half bow. Stillwell blushed slightly at the nerve of the man.

"Do you mind answering a few questions for us, Mr. Carmona?" Clayton asked

"Not at all," he said, keeping his eyes trained on Stillwell.

"What time do you report for work?" Stillwell asked.

"I work the eleven-to-seven shift this month. Next month I work three to eleven and the month after that I work seven to three," he said.

"How long have you been a security guard for the mission?" Clayton asked. "Almost three years."

"Tell us what happened. Tell us how you found the body," Stillwell said. "Like I said, I come on at eleven. I took the time clock and log-book from Ramon and signed in."

"So you have an electronic clock for clocking in at different locations?" Clayton asked.

"We have eight locations around the complex. We have to clock in at each of those locations every two hours. If for some reason we don't make a location or miss one it registers with the guard at the main guard shack and they send someone to see what's going on. When I was going to my locker I just happened to walk past a window with the blinds drawn and noticed the courtyard lights were off. I went to the breaker panel and flipped the breaker to the on position. The lights came on immediately so I didn't think anything about it," he said.

"Are the light normally off?" Stillwell asked.

"No, every courtyard light is normally on."

"You didn't think it was odd with them being off."

"Not really. The old man, Ramon Sanchez, that works three to eleven is seventy-years old, and sometimes he forgets to turn everything on. I've also come in before and every light in the place will be on, and I know he's forgot to turn off some of the lights that are supposed to be off. He's an old man, he's just forgetful," he said.

"When did you find the body?" Williams asked.

"After I turned the courtyard light on, I started walking down the sidewalk to the first check station. As soon as I walked out the door I noticed something strange by a tree on the other side of the courtyard. I walked over to the tree and that's when I saw it. The dead man, I mean. I called my boss right away and he calls you guys."

"Did you take the call from Mr. Carmona?" Stillwell asked Williams. She glanced at Clayton quickly then to Carmona.

"No. I wasn't even in town," Williams said with a yawn. I had to pick up a prisoner in San Angelo. I didn't get back to San Antonio until around five this morning. Everyone was talking about the killing and about the forensics team finding the painting on the body. When I heard that I called you guys immediately," Williams said. Clayton rolled his eyes at Stillwell's question but she acted as if she hadn't seen him.

"Mr. Carmona, have you noticed anything strange around the mission complex lately, aside from last night?" Clayton asked.

"It's a boring job. We occasionally get a few kids necking around the grounds parking areas, but other than that it's a boring job."

"Mr. Carmona, we thank you for coming in. If we need to talk with you any further we'll give you a call," Stillwell said.

"If you need a tour guide for any reason, I'm your man," Carmona said, smiling brightly.

"Thanks for your time. We'll call you if we need anything," Clayton said. Clayton and Stillwell spent the afternoon at the courtyard looking for any evidence that the forensic team may have missed. They questioned workers from an all night Burger King and a Waffle house whose close proximity to the crime scene might have noticed something. Everywhere they turned they came up with the same set of answers. No one saw or knew anything.

At five-thirty they met John Williams for dinner and talked until almost seven. They tried to talk John into the rodeo, but he seemed exhausted from his trip the night before and headed home. All in all, the trip to San Antonio had netted them very little. Except for a painting of the killer's next crime scene they had little more to go on than they did when they left Houston.

They headed to the rodeo arena near downtown, found a parking spot, bought their tickets and went inside. The place was packed with people. Neither of the two cops had any way of knowing what lie ahead. They never gave it a thought. But before this night was over they would experience almost every emotion known to man.

Clyde Bonner watched the cops from a railroad communications tower adjacent to the old cemetery. They each entered the patch of woods from a different angle. He quickly lost sight of them as they moved deeper into the dense wood. Darkness covered his silhouette as he made his way down the tower and onto the tracks. He recognized four of the cops from the shootout on Fawnridge Street. There were six other cops dressed in S.W.A.T. fatigues entering the woods from the back. But the four from the shootout he remembered as if it were yesterday. He wondered how the two who had been shot recovered so quickly from their wounds.

It took him almost half an hour to work himself into position behind Cromberg and Aaron Phillips. He was so close he wondered if they could smell him, because each time the breeze blew he could smell Cromberg's cologne.

Bonner's actions were quick and decisive. He cupped his left hand around Cromberg's mouth and with his right hand delivered a crippling blow to Aaron Phillips head with an aluminum softball bat he'd stolen two weeks ago. He pulled Cromberg to the ground and straddled her back. She was lying face down in the thick brush.

Bonner pulled two pieces of cloth from his back pocket. One he rolled to a ball stuffing it in Cromberg's mouth. The second piece of cloth he wound around her head covering her face and eyes. He pulled her handcuffs from her belt and cuffed her arms behind her. The last thing he done before standing her up was to remove her earphone and two-way radio from her belt and lapel. He took her 9mm and slid it in his belt.

It took another twenty minutes to work his way back onto the blacktop road fronting the old cemetery. He found Cromberg's unmarked car pulled the keys from her pocket, opened the trunk and tossed her inside. He leaned over the trunk until his head was close to hers.

"If you give me any trouble at all and I swear I won't hesitate to kill you. Do you understand me?"

Cromberg nodded and he closed the door. There wasn't any doubt in her mind that Bonner meant business. He was already on the hook for one Cop's murder and he wouldn't think twice about killing another. Right now the only ray of hope she had was that he wanted her alive for some reason, and she'd do what ever she had to do to stay alive and fight another day.

The announcer's voice echoed off the stands of the arena as he told the fans about the five thousand dollar purse that was offered to anyone in the stands who could stay on the horse called Earthquake for an eight-second ride. Clayton had seen the advertisement on the bottom of the billboard earlier in the day, but hadn't mentioned his plan to Stillwell.

It had been three years since Clayton had been on the back of a horse for any reason, and a lot longer than that since he'd been on one trying to kill him. But as a teenager he'd learned from a Cherokee Indian who worked on his uncle's ranch in Sonora, how to ride and break the meanest horses in West Texas. Clayton knew that if the horse didn't kill him and if he could win the purse that Stillwell wouldn't feel so badly about taking the money. At least that was the plan.

Clayton stood up and unclipped his pistol from his belt and handed it to Stillwell. He started down the bleachers without saying a word.

"Where are you going, Clayton?" Stillwell asked. She was standing now, looking at Clayton as if he were from another planet.

"I'm going to ride that horse, I'll be back in a few minutes," he said offhandedly.

"You're going to ride the horse?" Stillwell's mouth dropped open as if she'd witnessed him commit a crime.

"Have you lost your mind? I don't know anything about that horse but they don't offer those prizes with giving the money away in mind. Those horses are mean by nature. You take this gun before I hit you with it. I can't believe that you'd even consider a stunt like this," she said, watching Clayton disappear into the crowd below.

When Clayton reached the judges table they were every bit as incredulous as Stillwell.

"Son, are you absolutely sure you want to ride Earthquake?" The old man was holding a briar pipe with his teeth when Clayton strolled up to the table and told the old men that he wanted to ride the bronco for the five thousand dollars. The pipe slipped out of the old man's mouth and tumbled out of the stands and into the arena.

"Is this where I sign up?" Clayton asked.

The old man didn't seem to be able to make his mouth work; he just slid the forms across the table and stared at Clayton standing there in his pinstriped suit and tie. Clayton signed and dated the consent forms and registration and slid the papers in the old man's direction. Without saying another word he stepped over the top rail and jumped into the arena. He heard the old man telling the other man at the table to call an ambulance. As he walked to the corral he heard snickers from several of the cowboys who knew what he'd just signed up for.

Just before he reached the gate where Earthquake was nervously waiting, a man dressed as a clown tapped him on the shoulder and started talking. "You look like a big strong man, but I'd reconsider this plan of yours if I were you. Your hospital bills are going to run a lot more than five thousand dollars," he said with a sad clown face.

"You're probably right," Clayton said, looking down at the clown. "But I've already promised my friend in the stands that I was going to ride this horse and that's what I intend on doing." The clown shook his head.

"I'll try to keep him off you when you hit the ground," the clown said. He made the cross sign on his chest and slowly walked away.

As Clayton stepped in front of the chute gate, he heard his name being blasted over the public address system.

"Ladies and Gentlemen, we have a contestant that's going to attempt to ride ole Earthquake for the five thousand dollar prize. His name is Ross Clayton, a Detective with the Houston Police department. The rule is he has to stay on the horse for a full eight seconds. We wish you a lot of luck, Son. We just hope you don't wrinkle that fine suit you're wearing." The crowd burst into laughter.

Just as Clayton started working on the knot in his tie, someone accidentally bumped the lever holding the gate and wild animal in check. Without warning he was staring eye-to-eye at fifteen hundred pounds of uncontrollable hysteria. The horse's first move was an attempt to run Clayton down.

With nostrils flared and mane standing on end the horse made a run at Clayton. Clayton's reactions were in every way equal to the horses. Clayton sidestepped the animal and latched onto the horse's mane, throwing his self on the horses back in one fluid motion. The horse went kicking and squealing into the center of the arena, turning like a whirlwind at every bounce. Clayton quickly found the reins and settled in on the horses back like a second skin. No amount of kicking, bucking, or twisting tirades could shake Clayton's hold on the horse.

At seventeen seconds into the ride the horse came to a standstill within a few feet of where it had all began. Sweat poured out of the horses hide and he pounded the dirt a couple of times with his right hoof. Clayton sat there for a moment unsure if the animal was about to start bucking again, but when it was obvious that the horse had had enough he slowly slid of the horse's back and calmly walked him back to the corral. He handed the reins to one of the open-mouthed cowboys standing in front of the pin.

"Man, where did you learn to ride like that?" Clayton ignored the question.

"Where do I get my money?" Clayton asked.

The cowboy didn't say a word, he just pointed in the direction of the Judges table where Clayton had signed the papers for the ride.

Most everyone in the arena had never seen a riding display to equal what Clayton had just done. It wasn't until he latched onto the top rung of the fence railing pulling his self back into the stands that the audience began to cheer. The standing ovation lasted for a full minute. When he reached the Judges table he asked the old man if he could have the check made out to Leona Stillwell?

"Son, after seeing a performance like that, I'll make the check out to Elvis Presley if that's what you want. If you'll print the name here, I'll get the check cut. Have you ever thought about riding professionally?"

"I like being a cop," Clayton said in a low deep voice.

Five minutes later the old man was back with the check. He shook hands with Clayton and posed beside him for photographs for several local newspapers and the Rodeo Association. When Clayton turned and headed for Stillwell she was standing only a few feet away.

"You're the craziest man I've ever met. Are you all right?" "I've never been better," he lied with a straight face.

"Don't ever do anything like that again. I thought I was going to have a heart attack," she said. Then without warning she hugged him and kissed him on the corner of his mouth, but the kiss lasted longer than any friendly jester. Clayton found himself wanting to kiss her back. Suddenly the crowd began to cheer again. He looked away from her for a moment at the crowd of people around them, turned back to Stillwell and kissed her firmly on the lips.

The kiss was more than either of them expected. Maybe it was the moment, or the adrenalin from the ride. As a warm rush of feelings and emotion blew through Stillwell's body like an invisible ray, she tried to gather her thoughts. Clayton was so lost in the moment that he crumpled the check in his hand like a piece of waste paper. He fought with his brain for something clever to say.

"I've got this check for you so you can get your car fixed," he stuttered.

Stillwell looked perplexed, attempting to form her own rational thought.

"Can we get out of here? I can't hear myself think," she said.

Clayton handed her the crumpled check, put his arm around her waist and headed in the direction of the exit. The crowd was still cheering when they reached the parking lot. Stillwell had been trying to focus on the check while Clayton was doing his best to pretend that all of his body parts were unharmed by the torrential ride he'd just endured.

"This check is made out to me? What's going on, Clayton?"

"Please don't argue with me about the check. If you don't want it, just send it back. I just wanted to help you with your money problems and I thought this way you wouldn't feel indebted to me. Please take the check. You need the money and it didn't cost either of us a thing. I hope. Can we just get in the car, I need to sit down."

"You're hurt, aren't you? It's a wonder to me you can still walk after what that horse put you through," she said, walking him to the car.

Clayton slowly took off his coat and tie and slid in behind the steering wheel, wincing from the awful pain in his lower back and hips. Before Clayton closed the car door Stillwell slid in on the passenger's side, put a hand on his face and said, "Clayton, this is the nicest thing that anyone has ever done for me. I promise you I'll never forget it."

Stillwell dropped the check in her purse, turned and kissed him this time. The kiss was hot and passionate, and for a moment there was no pain in Clayton's body and he was lost in her embrace.

People were leaving the arena now and country music was blaring over the public address system through out the complex. The song playing was an old Conway Twitty song called, "I've Already Loved You In My Mind". Stillwell listened to the last lyric of the song as she moved away from Clayton's lips.

"Ain't that the truth?" she whispered softly.

It was a perfectly wonderful moment in their lives, but it was shattered like glass when Clayton's cell phone rang and he said hello. They couldn't have imagined the severity of the call. Clayton glanced at the dashboard clock it was after ten-thirty. Any thoughts of romance the two might have had for the night, were now lost in mental purgatory.

CHAPTER 9

Delores Rucker sat on the bumper of Cromberg's cruiser waiting for Gorman to arrive. It had been a long, trying night. She had escorted the ambulance that took Aaron Phillips to Herman hospital and waited until the doctors told her that Phillips' head wound was not life threatening. She had kept in constant contact with the station dispatch unit that used a satellite link to track the location of Cromberg's car. For some reason the atmospheric conditions had hampered the search until just before midnight.

It was 1:30 am now and she'd just received word that the blood and cloth fibers they found in the trunk of the cruiser belonged to Stacy Cromberg.

In a way Rucker felt relieved by the news, because if Cromberg were dead Bonner wouldn't have bothered taking her body out of the trunk. He wanted Cromberg alive for some reason. That reason Rucker hadn't quiet figured out; but if it was keeping Cromberg alive, that's all that mattered.

Just after she had gotten the report on the blood sample she had phoned Ross Clayton to give him and Stillwell the news. They were frantically racing toward Houston from San Antonio.

A black Lincoln Continental pulled into the parking lot and headed in her direction. As the car pulled closer to the cruiser she noticed that a uniformed officer was driving and Captain Gorman was on the passenger's side of the car. Gorman rolled the window down but didn't attempt to get out of the car.

"I just left the hospital. The doctors say that Phillips should make a full recovery but he's going to be on the watch list for a while."

"Have they moved him out of intensive care?" Rucker asked.

"They're going to wait until morning to move him. He has a concussion and they don't want to take any chances if they have to operate on him." Gorman ran a hand over his unshaven face and rubbed his eyes. He took a deep breath. The night air smelled of night blooming flowers and freshly cut grass.

"Sir, you really shouldn't be out here; there's nothing you can do but worry like the rest of us."

"Have you heard from Clayton and Stillwell?" Gorman asked.

"They should be here any minute. They were just outside of Sugarland the last time I spoke with them. They're worried sick just like the rest of us," she said.

"Any news on any other stolen cars in this area?"

"We haven't heard a thing, Capitan. We think he probably stole a car out of this parking lot. A lot of professors work here all night. It'll be morning before anyone will report a stolen vehicle. He could have stolen a car and another set of plates with all these cars to choose from," Rucker said, glancing around the parking lot. Gorman popped a couple of Rolaids in his mouth and looked around at the parking lot.

"This night has been a disaster. I feel like our whole unit is under attack. Have you been able to think of any reason Bonner would want to take Stacy hostage?"

"Of all the degrees I have, psychology is not one of them. But I know this much, he hasn't killed her or we would have found her in the trunk. From what I've read about Bonner he has narcissistic tendencies, he somehow thinks he's smarter than everyone else. Maybe he is?" Rucker shrugged, "Maybe he intends on using Stacy as some sort of bargaining tool."

Gorman took two capsules from a medicine bottle, popped them in his mouth and took a long drink from a water bottle in his lap.

"In the morning I'm meeting with the Chief and Mayor. I want to turn this city upside-down. If criminals and sycophants like Bonner think they can just arbitrarily start killing and snatching cops off the street, we're done for. I want him brought in or killed, and it really doesn't matter to me which one," Gorman winced in pain and started working on the seat adjustment knobs.

"Sir, will you do me a favor and go home. We need you in that meeting in the morning. I can see you're in pain, and being out here at one o'clock in the morning is only going to make it worse."

"I'm leaving," Gorman said abruptly. "Tell Clayton and Stillwell to get some rest. I want to see everyone in the department at nine sharp in the morning. I want to form a task force and I want to bring this man to justice." Gorman reached out the window and took Rucker's hand. "I'm sick over this. I pushed Stacy too hard to stay in the game and fight. I want you to know I would trade places with her this instant if I could. Take care of yourself. I'll see you in the morning."

A second later Gorman motioned for the driver to start rolling and after a few seconds he was out of sight. She knew from working Houston's hospital wards and from the injuries Gorman suffered in the accident, that the pain he was feeling must have been awful. She thought of Stacy and wondered where she was, and if Bonner had hurt her? She thought of the next few days and could only see a tortuous road ahead.

When Cromberg awoke her senses immediately went to work. She could feel the coagulated blood on her face and neck. It took a few seconds for her eyes to adjust to the soft light in the room but when they did she instantly recognized her surroundings. It was the back bedroom of the apartment where Lawrence Smoot and his bodyguard had been killed. She sat perfectly still listening for noise or for anyone moving about the apartment. The silence and sudden fear enveloped her like a shroud. She wanted to scream for help.

As soon as that notion passed, her first inclination was to move, to feel her face and nose to see if it was broken. She could feel the throbbing pain above her lip and around her eyes. Bonner had thrown her in the trunk so violently that she'd heard her nose crack just before passing out. She had no way of knowing low long she had been unconscious or of the time of day or night. There were no windows in the room, and aside from her and the chair she was in, it was just as she'd remembered it from the murder investigation; the place was in shambles.

As her mind awoke to the full condition of her body, she realized that Bonner had bound her arms and legs to a straight-back chair with duct tape; that much she was able to see for herself. He had also rolled a long piece of cloth, opened her mouth, and tightly bound her mouth with the cloth, tying it with a knot at the base of the back of her neck. For a moment, she wondered how he'd gotten her into the apartment building without anyone noticing.

Now she could hear movement from somewhere in the apartment. It was definitely someone walking around and there was another sound, like the sound of someone tearing into a cellophane bag. It was only a matter of seconds until her questions were answered as Bonner stood in the doorway.

Bonner wasn't as large or as evil looking as she remembered, or as her mind had conjured him since the shooting. He stood in the doorway rustling with a bag of potato chips. He looked as if he'd just gotten out of the shower, combed his hair straight back and put on fresh shoes and clothes, and then headed to the kitchen for a snack.

Bonner stood with a frozen pose looking at her, a stupid grin on his face. He wore tan western boots, denim blue jeans, and a white cotton tee shirt with red lettering across the front, advertising Tony's Bar-B-Que. Under his left arm he carried Cromberg's purse. He had clipped her holstered 9 mm on one side of his belt. On the opposite side of his waist he had clipped on her badge. And, for all practical purposes he could have passed for an undercover cop.

He dropped her purse and the bag of chips on the dresser then turned without saying a word and walked away. He returned a few minutes later with another straight back chair from the dining room and positioned the chair a few feet in front of her. He started talking as soon as he placed the chair.

"I'm going to take that gag out of your mouth but before I do, I want your full and complete understanding of the situation here, and what I'm prepared to do if things don't go my way. If you scream or create any problems, I'm going to hurt you really bad, and there ain't a dentist in the world going to fix you up this time. Have I got your full and undivided attention? Do you understand what I'm telling you?"

Cromberg nodded affirmatively. Bonner moved behind her and began working on the knot at the base of her neck.

"I've been in and out of prison most of my life and I don't have any intentions of ever going back," he said, tossing the bandana to the floor. He sat in the other chair and leaned back, balancing himself on two legs of the chair. Cromberg sat quietly.

"I suppose that you've figured out by now that Degas and me killed Smoot and his bodyguard. Smoot is the one who put us onto Sneed and his wife. He knew that they had just made this big score on some all night convenience store. Degas and me followed them to a motel and boosted their money while they slept. It was also me and Degas that found all of Smoot's money hidden in these walls," Bonner pointed at the demolished walls behind him.

"Smoot got greedy. He wanted half of what we took from those two crack heads. People who get greedy always have to pay for their greed. We hadn't planned on killing the girl though, we just didn't want to leave any witnesses," he said, as if somehow justifying the woman's brutal murder in the kitchen.

Cromberg wondered why he was telling her these things so blatantly. Everything made sense now that he'd confessed to everything so unassumingly. The cold hard truth suddenly hit her like a sharp jab to the midsection. He was telling her these things because he wanted her to know the level of his desperation, and because he had no intensions of allowing her to live when he got what he wanted from her. She wondered how a man could sink to this level of moral vacuity. Clyde Bonner had reached the bottom rung on the ladder of human depravity, and he wasn't about to turn back now.

"What do you want from me?" Cromberg asked.

"I'm getting to that," he said with a glare. "You just sit there and listen." Bonner pulled a half crushed package of Marlboro Lights from his back pocket, tapped a cigarette a couple of times on the back of his hand then lit it. He took a long drag and exhaled a cloud of white smoke into the room. He focused his attention on Cromberg's swollen face and thumped an ash on the carpet.

"This may come as a surprise to you," he started. "I want what you cops stole from my car on Fawnridge Street. I want my money, my clothes, my jewelry and my luggage. Now this may not come as a surprise to you, but I'm not going to stop until I get it, all of it. And just so you'll know that you're not in this alone, I'm going to get your mother and sister and tie them up right here beside you. You may be tough and not care what I do to you to get what I want. But you're damn sure going to care what I do to them," he said, crushing his cigarette under his boot.

Bonner didn't wait for any rebuttal from Cromberg. He could see the horror and despair in her face as he stood up and walked away. Tears filled Cromberg's eyes; she sat with clenched teeth cursing him under her breath. He took her purse and the bag of chips from the dresser and quickly walked out of the room.

Cromberg rocked back and forth in her chair in a silent rage, blood and tears mixing on her face and dripping onto her blouse. This could not be happening, she thought. She could feel the animus building and coursing through her every thought. She should have known better than to leave such personal information in the purse that she carried to work. There was no sense in worrying about it now, she thought. And she didn't dare allow Bonner the satisfaction of knowing he'd just pushed all the right buttons and torn her world apart.

Clayton and Stillwell met Delores Rucker in the University parking lot just after two am. Rucker could tell Stillwell had been crying by the smeared makeup on her face. Clayton pulled the Jaguar beside the wrecker hooking onto Cromberg's cruiser. Stillwell met Rucker and embraced her tightly. Clayton wasn't as quick or as agile leaving the car as Stillwell. Rucker thought how exhausted the two must have been from the trip and the anxiety caused by Cromberg's abduction.

"You guys just missed the Captain," Rucker said.

"Gorman?" Stillwell asked.

"Yeah, Gorman. He was in so much pain that he's popping pain pills like candy. I begged him to go home. He wants everyone in the department at this meeting in the morning at 9 am. He thinks that the mayor and chief will be there to back him up. I guess the pain finally got to him, he just left not more than twenty-minutes ago."

"Speaking of pain, you don't look so good yourself, Clayton."

"Can you just tell us all you know about what happened tonight?" Clayton asked.

"There's not much to tell that I didn't tell you on the phone. We split up into pairs in a large circle around Bonner's camp. We were hunkered-down waiting for Bonner to show up. At the time we were maintaining radio silence until Bonner made it into the camp and one of us could identify him. Then and only then were we supposed to use the radio. Around eleven pm Burt Cameron called Cromberg to see how long she wanted to wait. When she didn't answer Cameron sent a man around to see what was going on. We got an ambulance for Phillips and realized that Bonner had taken Cromberg's cruiser. We figured that he had at least an hours jump on us." Rucker watched Clayton ease himself onto the fender of his Jaguar.

"We had the guys at dispatch run a satellite trace on the car and we found it here a little after midnight. I ran a quick test on the blood we found in the trunk and it matched Cromberg's blood type. We also found blood soaked cloth fibers, and a lot of hair, all of which we've sent to the lab. I took fingerprints we found on the trunk and ran them through AFIS. The prints belong to Cromberg. She wanted us to know she was in the trunk."

"Has anyone reported a car missing from the parking lot yet?" Stillwell asked.

"Not yet. If this is like most universities, people work in labs and workshops all hours of the night, so I'm guessing it will be morning. I'll be surprised if we don't hear something by then," Rucker said. "Are you all right?" Rucker started moving in Clayton's direction.

"It's nothing, I'm just a little down in my back, and riding for the last three hours hasn't helped. I'll be all right I just need some aspirin," Clayton said.

Rucker looked at Stillwell as if she were looking for the truth.

"It's a long story. I'll tell you all about it once we find Cromberg," Stillwell said.

"Do you have a ride or do you need us to drop you somewhere?" Clayton asked.

"I have a cruiser," Rucker answered.

"I don't feel like I can go to bed knowing Bonner's got Cromberg somewhere out there," Clayton said.

"Yeah, you can hardly walk and you're going to do her some good tonight? Look, Clayton, we've all been up for twenty hours, we don't have a clue to go on, and if there ever was a time to rest and regroup it's got to be now. I think just as much of her as anyone here but we've got to use our heads here. Do you want to ride with me, Stillwell? My place is just a few blocks from here and you'll get more sleep that way," Rucker said.

Stillwell looked at Clayton and wanted to touch him. She wanted to take care of him. She wanted to kiss him goodnight and wake up beside him in the morning. But none of those things were going to happen tonight.

"Are you going to be alright?" Stillwell asked Clayton. She hoped that he could read the expression on her face and that all she wanted to do was hold him. "What she's saying makes more sense than anything I can think of," Stillwell said.

"As bad as I hate to admit it I know she's right. If we had anything to go on I wouldn't rest until we did something to help Cromberg, but we're just wasting time here. What about Stacy's Mother, do you think we should call her now or wait till morning? I don't want her hearing this on television," Clayton said.

"I'll set the alarm for six and call her first thing. There is nothing she can do tonight but worry like the rest of us. If we don't get some rest none of us will be able to help her," Rucker said.

Clayton thought about it for a moment before nodding his approval. He was overwhelmed by the events of the night and there was nothing left to say.

"I'll see you first thing in the morning," he said.

Clayton eased himself off the fender of his Jaguar, and waited for Rucker and Stillwell to get into the cruiser before he started the car and headed west for downtown. He turned on South Main and headed towards Herman Park. It wasn't the first time in his life that he had two women on his mind at the same time. But it was the first time in his life that he cared so deeply about the women on his mind. He'd never get to sleep without some help, he thought.

CHAPTER *10*

Richey Sneed flipped off the police scanner and lit a cigarette. The clock on the bedside table said 3 am. He sat there in the dark trying to digest all that he had heard through out the night. He wondered what Bonner was up to. Why would he take this woman cop hostage? It was like signing his on death warrant, he thought.

Was he going to use the woman as bargaining chip of some kind? He tried to put himself in Bonners place. It was no use; there were more questions than answers. He washed his face in the bathroom then lay down on the bed beside his wife, his mind still troubled with questions.

Sneed crushed out his cigarette in the ashtray focusing on what he knew about Bonner, which wasn't much. Outside of his dealings with the drug dealer he knew nothing at all about the man. He knew even less about Tony Degas whom he had killed in the shootout on Fawnridge Street. He had had more than a month to think about the events of that day and had come to the conclusion that the meeting on Fawnridge Street was purely a coincidence. It was true that he and Beverly had gone there in hopes of finding Degas there, but that wasn't the case at all, the Degas woman was telling the truth, she hadn't seen him and didn't know where he was.

Degas had told his mother before ever coming through the door that he had some money for her. Looking back on it all, he believed now that Degas and Bonner were probably leaving town. After all, they had just killed three people and stolen a load of money, if that was what was in the walls of the bedroom. It could have been drugs he thought, but those two were into money, not drugs, and the dealer had plenty from the looks of the apartment.

What was Bonner doing in the University of Houston parking lot? Sneed sat up in the bed and lit another cigarette. He'd never been in the UH parking lot himself, but he knew where it was, it was just off Cullen Boulevard. His mind raced with thought. Cullen Boulevard wasn't four miles from Smoot's apartment. Could Bonner be so stupid as to take the woman cop to the very crime scene where he and Degas had killed everyone in the apartment? Or, was he smarter than he gave him credit for.

Sneed's mind raced with different scenarios and questions. He had been the first person to find Smoot, the bodyguard and the blonde after the killing. The door was unlocked, that much he remembered. What if Bonner had taken a key? Why didn't he lock the door when he left? Sneed left the bed and began to pace the floor as he smoked. Would the police have left the apartment unguarded? How long before the police would turn the apartment over to the next-of-kin, he wondered?"

Sneed thought about the time he'd spent in prison and of the conversations he had had with different cellmates about crimes that they had committed. Only the truly insane ever hung around a crime scene where they had just murdered someone or committed a felony, but he didn't peg Bonner as someone mentally unbalanced. The short time he'd known Bonner he seemed to be an in-your-face kind of guy, someone with a chip on his shoulder. Someone you wouldn't want to fool with unless you were armed to the hilt.

Sneed thought about the shootout on Fawnridge Street, and how Bonner had stayed to shoot it out with the cops even after he and Beverly had fled through the rear of the property. What kind of man would do that, he wondered? Was he that brave? Or was he simply determined not to be taken alive or take a chance on going back to prison.

It was 4 a.m. when Sneed stopped pacing the floors and crushed out his last cigarette. The questions running through his mind were beginning to give him a headache and he needed to sleep. He lay down beside Beverly again and tried to put the thoughts of Bonner out of his mind. That night he dreamed of outsmarting Bonner and taking all of the money that Bonner had stolen. The only problem was that when he sat down to count the money it burned like magic before his eyes. It was a fitful night's sleep and one he wished he could forget.

Clyde Bonner worked on his plan most of the night, then at 4 a.m. he called Joann Cromberg to tell her that her daughter had been in a serious automobile accident, and that he would be escorting her to the hospital and that he would pick her up at her home at 4:30. He told her that his name was Aaron Phillips.

Joann Cromberg lived alone in a split-level home on Lake Houston. The address Bonner jotted down was 14581 Amber Cove Drive in the Atascocita subdivision. Bonner was familiar with the area and parked his stolen Buick in the driveway at exactly 4:30. Cromberg's mother met him at the door dressed and ready to roll.

"Excuse the way I'm dressed Miss Cromberg, I work undercover. I'm Aaron Phillips and I'm here to take you to the hospital," Bonner said.

"Is my daughter alright?" She asked, ignoring what the man said. "Can you tell me exactly what happened to my daughter, and why she was working so late at night? She never told me anything about working undercover," she said.

"I don't have all of the details myself, but there were several of us working on an undercover case until the suspect was somehow informed that we were cops and begin to shoot the place up. There were several cops wounded in the shooting," Bonner said.

"Has Stacy been shot?" she asked, almost in tears.

"No, she hasn't been shot. She was in one of the cars that were chasing the perpetrator," Bonner said, playing the part for all it was worth. Bonner turned off FM 1960 onto Interstate 59 heading south toward downtown Houston.

I can't tell you how many times that I pleaded with that girl to pursue another line of work. She's got a good education, she's intelligent and resourceful, but she always wanted to be a Detective," she said. "What hospital did they take her to?"

"They took her to Herman Hospital, but we have to make one stop and pick up Detective Rucker. She's waiting for us at the crime scene," Bonner lied convincingly.

The woman sat quietly for a moment then began to fidget with her purse. Bonner was driving the speed limit and that seemed to bother her. She kept looking at the speedometer as if she wanted to say something, when she did it took Bonner by surprise.

"Is there some reason you're driving so slowly?"

"I don't suppose so, I just didn't want to upset you, Miss Cromberg."

"I'm going to be a lot more upset if my daughter has to go into surgery without me there with her. Or if, God forbid, something worse should happen and I'm not there. So don't worry about upsetting me, just get us there as quickly as you can," she said.

Bonner took the first downtown exit and headed for Main Street. It was just after 5 a.m. when they arrived at the 2016 high-rise address. Bonner drove to the top level of the parking garage and parked. Seconds later they were in the elevator.

"I don't understand why Delores wouldn't have met us on the street instead of making us come to the apartment. We're just killing time while my daughter is in trouble."

"Don't worry. Rucker couldn't leave the crime scene until I got back. She's going to drive you to the hospital while I stay here at the crime scene and shut things down," he explained it so well that he almost believed what he was telling her.

Once in the apartment, Bonner walked quickly through the rooms leading the woman to her daughter, and to a nightmare she wouldn't soon forget. It had all gone so smoothly Bonner couldn't contain himself. Just as he reached the open doorway, he grabbed Joann Cromberg by the arm, and with all of his strength, threw her into the back wall of the room. She landed so violently that the impact almost broke her neck; she crumbled to the floor in a subdued ball. He hollered and laughed in Stacy Cromberg's face, watching her fight against her restraints.

"I told you what I was going to do," he raved, his eyes wild with anger. "And I'm going to let you in on another little secret," he said, speaking only centimeters from her face. "It may take me a week to kill her, she looks pretty strong, but unless you agree to help me get my money back, you're going to have a front row seat to see hell unleashed on your mother."

Cromberg hadn't prepared herself for what was happening; it was more than she could take in or digest. Her mind and body was experiencing so many emotional and physical gyrations that she was no longer in control of anything. She fought that much harder against the restraints.

Suddenly her breathing became erratic; her heart was pounding so profusely that she was certain it was about to explode in her chest. She felt a wave of heat and nausea rush over her body. The cloth in her mouth was gagging her. It was restricting her breathing, and before she could deal with that she begin to convulse and seizure, inadvertently turning the chair over and crashing to the floor. Her body began to shake violently and uncontrollably.

Bonner was on her in an instant, removing the bandanna from her mouth and setting her and the chair upright. When he was certain that she wasn't going to swallow her tongue or lose consciousness again, he moved away and began working on her mother again. In a few moments she was bound and tied to the chair like her daughter.

Bonner waited for Stacy Cromberg to regain her composure. When the color finally came back in her face and he was sure that she could understand what he was saying, he went after her with a new barrage of threats. The last thing he expected to hear from her lips was what she said next. "If I cooperate with you, will you stop this madness?"

Redhawk Simmons met with Clayton Sylestine of the Coushatta tribal council at 6 a.m. for coffee and to tell him of his plans to marry Renee. The two talked for more than an hour about the fishing trip and Redhawk's plans for the future. After leaving Sylestine he had a late breakfast with Renee and told her about the meeting.

It was just after nine when he made it to his shop and noticed that the curved bladed knife was missing. He walked back through the swinging door and met Joe Parson coming in the opposite direction.

"Hey, Joe, there's a knife missing from my work bench, it's got a funny shaped blade. Do you know anything about it?" Simmons asked.

"The guy came in this morning as soon as the store opened wanting his knife, he was making such a fuss that I sharpened it myself just to get rid of the guy. I've seen that guy in here a couple of times before and I got to tell you he gives me the creeps. I hope you're not upset that I sharpened the guy's knife? I do a pretty good job, you know?"

"It's not a problem at all, Joe. Just between you and me, I don't like the guy either. Say, Joe, while I was gone did anyone collect my newspapers?"

Sure, we put everything in your cottage. I thought the newspapers were with the mail," Parson said.

Without saying another word Simmons turned and headed for the cottage. He remembered looking at the mail last night but he didn't remember seeing any newspapers. He found the mail stacked neatly on the countertop in the kitchen just where he'd left it. He looked around the room and headed for the living room. But before he got there he stopped and walked to the back wall of the kitchen passed the refrigerator and looked at the garbage can. It was full of rolled up newspapers.

There were eight newspapers spanning the days that he and Renee had been away camping. He knew that there was nothing in the papers about any killings for at least a week before the camping trip, because he'd checked every edition thoroughly. He started with yesterday's paper, scanning every section for a possible story of a bizarre killing in Houston, more specifically, a killing where a knife was used. As soon as he finished with one newspaper he folded it neatly and started on the previous day. He breathed a sigh of relief when he finished with the eighth newspaper and finding nothing of any such murder in any of them.

Simmons thought for a moment, it had been over a month since he'd heard anything about any killing by the "Impressionist Murderer" a name given to the killer by the writers at the Houston Chronicle. So, maybe the creep was using the knife for some other purpose and his only crime was a bad disposition. Maybe the other times were just a weird coincidence, he thought.

A broad smile came across his face. He had never been thankful for much of anything in his life, but having this clawing feeling about what the man was doing with the knife gave him pause for thanks. And not having to rat someone out to the cops was an added bonus, he thought. It was truly something to be thankful for.

Maybe there was a God, he thought. Things in his life had never been better. He had a great job and for the first time in his life he had earned some meaningful money. He had this cottage and the love of a woman he couldn't seem to get enough of. That, in and of itself was a miracle, he thought. Now, if the Louisiana Cops would drop their investigation on the death of Snake Lopez he couldn't imagine life being any better. It could be that things were for once in his life going to be okay.

He began to whistle as he bundled the stack of newspapers and dumped them all back in the trashcan. He thought about Renee and about the ring they were going to buy. He wondered how much something like that was going to cost. He'd never bought a piece of jewelry in his life. The truth was he'd never been inside a jewelry store before.

Then he remembered the four thousand dollars that he'd won at the casino. There was only about three thousand dollars left after the casino had made the deduction for taxes, and he'd bought gas for his truck the next morning. But what was left he'd stuffed in an old Mason jar and hidden it under his bed. Surely that would be enough, he thought. This is going to be a great day, he said aloud, and started to whistle again. He had no way of knowing that it wasn't meant to be.

More than a dozen reporters and at least three television cameras recorded every word that Wade Gorman said, as he stood before the crowd propped up on crutches. The pain in his eyes and heart told a story they couldn't record.

Delores Rucker stood with Clayton and Stillwell along the back wall of the media room thinking like everyone else in the room about Cromberg. Suddenly, a loud argument broke out just outside the media room. Clayton left the media briefing and stepped into the hallway.

The hallway way was filled with reporters and cops who couldn't get into the media room. Clayton eased his way through the throng of people, slowly approaching a dark skin man waving his arms about the air and yelling loud enough for everyone to hear what he was saying. He was berating two uniformed officers when Clayton stepped in front of the man. The man ignored Clayton as if he wasn't there.

"I am demanding to see Wade Gormand," the man mispronounced Gorman's name. He didn't give the cops a chance to speak. "My wife was killed almost two months ago and I have not heard one word about the investigation. I am a businessman, I am a citizen and a taxpayer, and I demand to see Gormand. He came to my store once and was in a car accident, and I haven't seen him since. If he has time to do a press conference he has time to speak with me. I want to see Gormand," he demanded loudly.

By now the reporters and cameramen who were unable to get in the briefing room had turned on their recorders and cameras in hopes of gathering a more salacious story than the briefing. Clayton stood at the man's side and put a hand on his shoulder. Clayton towered over the man at least six to eight inches. Clayton introduced himself and asked the man his name. As soon as he was done shaking hands with the man he put a strong hand back on the man's shoulder. The man was not intimidated by Clayton's presence. He gave Clayton a menacing glare and started shouting again.

"I am Nizar Kheif. My wife was killed almost two months ago, and I was almost killed by these madmen who robbed me, and I want to see..." Clayton stopped the man before he could demand anything else.

Clayton tightened his grip on the man's shoulder, leaned over and spoke softly into Kheif's ear.

"I know all about your case, my people are working on it everyday, and I'll get you an audience with Captain Gorman. But before we draw anymore unnecessary attention, let's go down the hall here and into an office where we have a little privacy," Clayton said sternly.

Kheif didn't say another word he just began marching in the direction of the open door down the hall. Clayton followed closely behind. Clayton stopped just before reaching the doorway and stopped the throng of people following behind them. When they begin to walk away he stepped inside the office and closed the door behind him. Kheif was sitting near the corner of the office in a straight-backed chair looking like a scolded and spoiled child.

"That was quiet a performance you put on out there," Clayton said. Kheif stood up indignantly and began waving his arms thorough the air and yelling again.

"Listen to me carefully, Mr. Kheif because I'm only going to say this once. I don't know where you're from, and I really don't care, but if you attack me one more time with that Gestapo attitude of yours, I'm going to arrest you and throw you in a holding cell with about thirty rednecks. If you think you were brutally treated before, you'll pray to be back with the people that robbed you when those rednecks get hold of you. Am I getting through to you Mr. Kheif? Now, you set your ass down in that chair and talk to me with a civil tongue and we'll get along just fine," Clayton said.

There was dead silence in the room for what seemed like minutes before Kheif started speaking again. When he did, the condescending attitude was still there but the tone of his rhetoric had been dialed back considerable.

"My wife was murdered in my store. I was almost killed by these savages. After two months it seems that nothing is being done. I have not heard from anyone and I know that I am entitled to know what is going on here," he said, the sound of anger coming back into his voice.

"I know all about what happened at your store and I am truly sorry for your loss, Mr. Kheif. There's not much I can say that's going to make you feel any better in that respect. But we have made progress. We believe that we know the people responsible for your wife's death. And we did return your money a few weeks ago. Captain Gorman was in the hospital for a month but we've had two detectives working twelve hours a day in an attempt to track these people down and bring them to justice. And, something you may not know, I've spoken extensively with the District Attorney and he believes strongly, as do I that once the Grand Jury hears the case that he'll be asking for the death penalty in the trial phase. If they stay in the Houston area, we'll catch them."

"Are you working on the case?" Kheif asked.

"No, I am working on an unrelated case. But I am on top of everything that's being done and I get involved when I can," Clayton said.

"Then who is working on my case?"

"Detectives Rucker and Cromberg along with several uniformed officers, one of which was killed in a shootout with these people. We're putting our lives on the line everyday on your case."

"These are the women that I spoke with when I was in the hospital?" "They're two of the best detectives in the department. We don't know for sure but we have reason to believe that Detective Cromberg has been kidnapped by these people."

"I prefer someone else, someone that I feel comfortable speaking with. This idea you Americans have that a woman is as capable as a man is unacceptable to me. I want someone like you or Gormand to handle my case," Kheif said flatly.

"Look Mr. Kheif, we have reason to believe that the murder of your wife is related somehow to another group of killings in a downtown apartment building. Since the murders occurred the same night Detectives Rucker and Cromberg have been working both cases simultaneously. We're sure that we've already killed one of the gunmen in the same shootout where we lost an officer. Detective Cromberg was also hospitalized in the same gun battle. She's doing everything she can to stop these men and now she's been kidnapped. I don't know how anyone could say that we're not doing everything we can," Clayton said.

"Are these women under Gormand's supervision?"

"Everyone in this department is under his supervision," Clayton answered. "Then I must speak with him in regards to my wife's case. I apologize for appearing to be insensitive over the loss of your officer. I am very sorry. I am also sorry to hear of the fate of Detective Cromberg. I will sit here quietly and wait for him if you can arrange the meeting."

Clayton left the room and headed back to the media room for the last few minutes of Gorman's talk to the staff and reporters. Behind the podium was a large photograph of Cromberg on the projection screen. Several uniformed officers were passing copies of the same photo around to reporters and newspaper people, with instructions on whom to call and how best to make the report in the event of a sighting. Clayton listened intently to Gorman's last comments.

"I want to make this point crystal clear to everyone hearing my voice," he said. A photograph of Clyde Bonner was shown on the wall next to Cromberg's. "We believe that this is the man who has kidnapped Detective Cromberg last night. We also have reason to believe that this man took part in the shootout that killed Officer Brubaker a few weeks ago. This man is a cold-blooded killer; he is armed and extremely dangerous. Just follow the instructions on the flyer and let us do our job. We believe Detective Cromberg's life is in grave danger. Ladies and gentlemen, we're pleading with every citizen in Houston to join in this search to find Detective Cromberg. Our quest starts by finding this man."

A few reporters asked for answers to additional questions but the Captain waved them off and stepped off the rostrum and headed for the back of the room. Every officer that left the room took a stack of flyers that Gorman and the Mayor's office had printed though the night. By four this afternoon, ten thousand of the flyers would be on the streets of Houston.

The orders were to post the flyers on every convenience store, gas station, super market, shopping outlet and homeless center in the greater Houston area. Clayton had never seen such a consorted and sincere effort by those that were asked to help.

Clayton waited for most everyone to leave the room before he approached Gorman. He watched Gorman stop in front of the podium, pour himself a glass of water and pop two pain pills. He could see the Captain grimace with pain with every step he took, and it bothered him to confront him with the problem waiting just down the hall.

Richey Sneed turned the volume down on the television set, unwrapped a new pack of smokes and lit one. He could hardly believe what he'd just seen. It was like the entire city was arming for an invading force that was setting up camp just outside the city limits. The reporters at the news desk said that they had gotten offers for more than ten thousand volunteers in the thirty minutes since the press conference, and that the phones were still ringing. And what was even more astounding was that his and Beverly's name hadn't been mentioned once, not even as a byline.

Sneed sat on the side of the bed with the remote control device in his hand, his mind at a complete loss for words. In one broad stroke, Bonner had awoken the ire and disdain of thousands of people and law enforcement officials across an area the size of Rhode Island. Without even trying, he had taken the heat off him and Beverly so much so that they weren't even mentioned in the announcement.

For the last hour he had tried to understand the reasons for Bonners insane behavior in taking a police Detective hostage. Was it revenge for Degas being killed? The cops hadn't killed Degas; it was he who had done it. Sneed remembered looking into Bonner's eyes after he pulled the trigger on Degas. If Bonner felt any great sense of loss he sure didn't show it. He almost seemed relieved, now that Sneed had a chance to think about it.

The more he thought about it the more he wished that it was about revenge, because that made more sense than anything else he could imagine. If he was doing this thinking somehow that this would get the cops off his trail he must have abandoned that thought by now, Sneed thought. This was about something else. This was about something so important to Bonner, that he was compelled to do it. It was important enough to risk it all, important enough to throw caution to the wind and lay it all on the line. If that was the case, then it had to be about money, Sneed thought. It had nothing to do with getting even.

Sneed remembered that the newspaper had reported that more than eight hundred thousand dollars was recovered from suitcases in Bonner's car. They assumed that a small part of that money was stolen from convenience store robbery. The newspaper also reported that the department had returned a small portion of the money to the owner of the convenience store to cover his loses. Sneed stood up dropping the remote control device on the bed.

He wants his money back, Sneed thought. He's done this solely for the money. He thinks by taking a Detective hostage that he'll use her to somehow get his money back. That has to be it, Sneed thought. He started to pace the floor.

There was something else tugging at Sneed's thoughts that he couldn't let go of. Why drive a stolen police car from the north side of town to the University of Houston parking lot to just to steal another car? There had to be a hundred places between that old cemetery in north Houston and the University parking lot to steel a car. Why not downtown? A lot of cars were routinely left in parking garages or lots throughout the city, why the UH parking lot? He kept thinking of Smoot's apartment.

What was the police procedure for property where a murder had been committed? Shouldn't the cops leave someone posted at the entrance of the apartment just in case someone came snooping around? It had been almost two months since the murders, Sneed thought. How long would the cops consider a crime scene under their jurisdiction? Surely they would want to keep it the way it was for the District Attorney's office?

Could Bonner be that stupid? Or was it the last place anyone would expect him to return? No one in his right mind would kidnap a cop and take them back to a place where they had murdered three people. That only made sense, didn't it? It could be that Bonner had out smarted them all, he thought. If there was no guard posted it could be the perfect hide out. How could Bonner possibly get in and out with a hostage?

Sneed didn't have enough answers to all of the questions he was asking, but before the day was over he'd know what Bonner was doing. It would be interesting to set on the side lines and watch this game that Bonner was playing, and watch it play itself out. And, if

Bonner got lucky and somehow managed to pull it off, he'd be there to make sure Bonner never got to enjoy one day of his winnings.

Two calls came into the HPD main switchboard after the news conference that almost everyone in the department had expected. The first call was from Martin Richard, a Professor of Economics at the University of Houston. Richard had been working through the night on a project for the City of Houston Planning Commission that dealt with a new Light Rail proposal for the city. Richard reported that his 2002, white Buick Century was missing from the parking lot when he left for home around 9:45 a.m. this morning.

The second call, came in about thirty minutes later, and was from a student named Mark Worth, who was working a part-time summer job with the University Maintenance Department. He and several other workers had spent all night replacing part of the main air conditioning system. Worth stated that when he made it to his car to go home, he noticed that his licenses plates were missing from his Toyota Corolla. The licenses number was BLJ-607.

Over the next twenty minutes every cop in Houston and Harris County had the make, model, and tag number of the car that was most likely used to transport Stacy Cromberg from the University of Houston parking lot to an undetermined location. The orders to every patrol unit were explicit; search every parking lot, public garage, and alley in the city for this car.

Richey Sneed found the Buick Century at 11:45 am in the parking garage at 2016 Main Street; but he had no intensions of reporting it to the authorities.

Stacy Cromberg spent more than an hour explaining the layout of the department storage facility and how things were booked into evidence or held for attorneys and for the State. She made it abundantly clear to Bonner that no one outside of the police, FBI, or District Attorney's office had any access to the items being stored in that area. And that in some cases, when the amount of money reached a certain level it was actually deposited in area banks.

She explained how that in cases involving large amounts of illegal drugs and money that it was sometimes confiscated by other government entities such as the DEA, ATF, or FBI, and the local authorities had nothing to say about it one way or the other. But in almost all cases the money was held in some capacity waiting for the case to be closed. After that the money could be, and many times was divided between law enforcement agencies, in some cases where it was taken over by the feds, they never knew what became of it.

"How can we find out if the money and suitcases are still there?" Bonner asked.

"Well, since you've kidnapped me, and everyone in the county knows about it by now, it's going to be a little difficult for me to check it out," Cromberg said.

"Then what the hell do I need you for?" Bonner spouted.

Cromberg had learned a few things about Bonner in the short time she'd been his captive. She knew that no matter how simple minded he seemed to be, that he was no idiot. She also knew that he had very few limitations when it came to his level of deviance. She believed with all of her heart that he would have no qualms about killing her mother if he thought it was necessary to achieve what he wanted. And, she was convinced that she had to play this game as long as she could to keep her and her mother alive. She didn't want to think of what he might do should they suddenly become expendable.

"Just listen to me for a moment," Cromberg said, her mind working with ideas. "It just so happens that I'm good friends with the cop who works nights at the storage facility. His name is Brandon Ford. We don't see much of each other since he works nights and me days, but I have went out with him a few times. He also has a hard time distinguishing between my voice and Rucker's voice. I could call him and tell him that I'm Rucker. Since she's the one who checked the suitcases into storage it would only be natural if she were checking on something that maybe she needed to look at again," Cromberg explained.

"How's that going to get me in there?" Bonner asked.

"I could explain to Brandon that the FBI is taking over the case and that they want everything moved to one of their locations. They have offices all over town, but I think the Federal Building down town is where they lock everything up."

"So, all we got to do is call him tonight, dress up like an FBI agent, and go down there and pick up my money?"

You know that's not going to happen. Our pictures are being plastered all over this town as we speak. You just saw that for yourself on television and listened to the news conference. Believe me when I tell you that every cop in southwest Texas has a copy of those photos, and that includes my friend Brandon. The only way you or I are going into that property facility is to fly a Hollywood makeup artist in here for a complete makeover."

"I should have known it wasn't going to be that simple," Bonner said. "Nothing is that simple. You also have to have paperwork authorizing the transfer of those items from one location to another. Even if we move items from the storage facility to the courthouse for trial, we have to have the proper paperwork to get it done. If it's the FBI, the paperwork has to be signed by an FBI supervisor. If it's for the city or Harris County the DA has to sign for the move. You just don't move eight hundred thousand dollars around on a whim," she said.

Bonner listened to every word she said as he walked in circles around the dining room table. Cromberg tried to read his face for thoughts or anger, but what ever he was thinking he kept to himself. Suddenly, without warning Bonner stopped at her side turning her and her chair in his direction.

"I hate this bureaucratic nonsense. There has to be a way around it. There has to be a way," he shouted in her face.

"I'm sure in your world of raping, pillaging, and anarchy, that you can do pretty much anything you're big enough to do. But in the real world things are different. I'm just telling you what you're up against here. I'm not saying it can't be done, I'm just telling you it's more of a problem than you might think."

Cromberg looked into his eyes as she spoke to him, and she was sure, at least for a moment that he was going to beat her half to death for what she'd said, but he never touched her. He just turned and began walking around the table again like a man looking for answers to a problem that didn't exist.

"Look," Cromberg started again. "I told you that I'd do just about anything to keep you from hurting my mother or my sister, or me for that matter. I meant that. I personally don't care if you take ten million dollars out of the system as long as it keeps those I love alive and safe," Cromberg lied convincingly.

"Then get my money, and I swear I'll leave you alone."

"Okay. Tonight after midnight, I'll call Brandon and have a talk with him. At least we'll know if the money's even there. They could have moved it a dozen times for all I know. At least we'll know that much. If the money's there we'll figure a way to get it out of there. If it's not there at least we'll know where they've taken it. Does that make sense to you?" she asked.

"I hope you aren't trying to work a scam on me, because if you are, I'm here to tell you it's not going to work out good for you and your mother."

"Get me a cell phone that's not traceable to you or anyone else. One of those types of phones you buy at Wall Mart and download minutes too. At least it won't alert Brandon when he gets the call. It shouldn't take more than a few moments to get the information we need," she said, hoping to steer his confidence in the right direction.

Rucker left Stillwell with Clayton and headed for the hospital to see Aaron Phillips. She met with Phillip's wife in the waiting room and talked for almost thirty minutes until his nurse gave them the okay to go into the room. Rucker stayed behind to call Joann Cromberg for the fourth time this morning. When there was no answer she called Cromberg's sister who was traveling back from Dallas after getting the word earlier in the morning that her sister had been kidnapped. Jeanie Cromberg answered on the first ring.

"I've been calling your mother all morning, any idea where she might be?" "I've called her a dozen times myself and I don't mind telling you I'm worried about her. She wasn't going anywhere that I know of. Do you think that she heard something about Stacy and went to the station?"

"No, I don't. She would have called you or Stillwell by now. What do you want me to do?" Rucker asked.

"Look, I'm right outside of Buffalo, I'm still a good two hours away, you've got to go by the house and see if she's there and if she's okay."

"How do I get in?"

"At the back door next to the garage, there are two terracotta planters, one on either side of the door. The planter on the right has a key under it. Please call me as soon as you're in the house."

"Okay, Jeanie, I'll call you as soon as I know something," Rucker said.

Richey and Beverly Sneed watched Bonner and a woman that neither of them had ever seen before, cross the parking lot, get into the stolen Buick and drive away. Bonner was wearing a white tee shirt, blue jeans, and a white baseball cap.

"Surely that's not the cop that he kidnapped?" Beverly asked.

"No, that's not her. I've never seen that woman before. From the looks of things, it doesn't look as if she knows him all that well," Richey said.

Richey waited until they were out of sight then started down the ramp behind them. Within minutes they were behind Bonner on Interstate 45 heading south towards Galveston. For some reason it irritated Richey that Bonner had brought another player into the game that he didn't know about. It also irritated him that he couldn't come up with a plausible reason for the woman being with him.

"Could they be working together?" he asked.

"How in the hell am I supposed to know?"

"You saw her; does she look like she could be someone that would work with a guy like Clyde Bonner?"

"She looks harmless, like someone's mother, to me. She's at lease twenty years older than Bonner, maybe it's his mother," Beverly offered.

"I don't know anything about Bonner's family, I guess it's possible. He has to know that every cop in town is looking for him, why would he get his mother involved in something like this? It doesn't add up."

Before either of them could say anything else Bonner exited at Wayside drive and stopped at the light on the feeder road. Seconds later they were rolling again. He followed Bonner just beyond the traffic light into a Wall Mart parking lot, parking the Cadillac two rows away from Bonner and the woman. They waited until the two were at the store entrance before Beverly headed in their direction. She pulled a blue silk scarf from her purse and covered her head as she walked; next she added a pair of dark sunglasses to the disguise, hoping it would be enough to keep Bonner from noticing her.

Richey Sneed had lit his third cigarette when Bonner and the mystery woman reappeared and began making their way to the Buick. Beverly was nowhere to be seen. He started the engine and circled to the front of the store just as Beverly emerged and trotted to the car.

"What gives?"

"What do you mean, what gives? She bought a cheap cell phone," Beverly said.

"Is that it?" Richey asked impatiently.

"No, that's not it. I got a good look at the woman, and there is no way she's his mother, and another thing, the woman acted strangely, like she was nervous or scared. She didn't make a move unless he said it was okay. So, if you're asking me, I don't think they know each other at all."

"Who paid for the phone?" Richey asked.

"The woman paid for the phone with a credit card. I tried to get close enough to hear a name or any conversation between the two, but they were talking so low, and the store was playing this loud Latin music over the public address system. I couldn't hear myself think," she said.

Sneed followed the two back to 2016 Main. He circled the block a couple of times waiting for them to reach the top of the parking garage and park. As soon as he found a place to park that was sufficiently out of sight, he fished a twenty out of his pocket and handed it to Beverly.

"Take that elevator down to the street level and get us some sandwiches and something to drink, there's a deli on the corner. It looks like we're going to be here for a while," he said, pointing in the direction of the elevator.

Rucker walked slowly through each room of Joann Cromberg's house. She was in the dining room when she heard the faint sound of a cell phone ringing in another room. She hoped it would continue to ring as she moved toward the sound. When she reached the bedroom she rushed to the phone to look at the screen for the name of the person calling. She jerked it from the charger and started talking.

"Your mom is not at home, Jeanie. Her cell phone is sitting in the charger just where she left it. I've got some more bad news for you if you're up to it," Rucker said, waiting for a response. There was nothing but dead silence on the other line for what seemed like a minute before Jeanie Cromberg started talking.

"Tell me everything, Rucker. I can't stand not knowing; it's killing me," she finally answered.

"I've been in every room in the house and your mother is not here, but her car is in the garage. There's also a vintage fifty-five Chevy in the garage next to her car. Do you know anything about the old car?"

"It was my dad's toy. He loved to fiddle around with old cars. He could make a piece of junk look brand new. My dad's only been gone for a year and mom just can't bring herself to get rid of it. It's probably worth a fortune."

"Any thought on where your mother might be?" Rucker asked.

"Not really. She sometimes goes with some of her friends to Old Town Spring, to go shopping."

"We started calling her just before six this morning; does she usually leave so early? And would she normally leave her cell phone behind?"

"If she was in a hurry she might have forgotten it, oh I don't know, Delores."

"It just seems odd that everything in the house is in perfect order and yet there's no one around. This place is spotless. Got any suggestions on what I should do next?"

"There's a roll-top desk over by the sliding glass doors. It's where my folks paid bills and kept important messages and insurance papers. Open the top and see if there is any notes; mom usually writes everything down on a tablet. She's had to start writing everything down because she's been so forgetful since dad died."

It was the first thing Rucker saw when she slid the rolled top back. The notes were on a white, decorative tablet with Daises and Carnations scrolled across the top of the pad in colors of yellow, gold, and blue. Just below the flowers someone had jotted down three notes, each on a separate line. The first line read: Stacy's been in an accident. The second line read: Detective Phillips to pick me up. The last line read: Be ready at five. There was nothing else written on the tablet.

Rucker could hear Jeanie Cromberg crying on the other end of the phone. She shouldn't have read the message aloud, she thought, but it was too late now. They both knew the cold hard truth; someone had duped Joann Cromberg into believing that her daughter was in trouble, and that she was needed. Rucker could surmise that it was Clyde Bonner posing as Aaron Phillips who made the call. And, since her daughter was a cop there was no reason for her to be fearful or suspicious of another cop.

"I'm sorry, Jeanie. I've been working on my people skills, but it seems I still have a long way to go. I didn't mean to be so blatant. But the truth is this is something we have to deal with now. We can all have a good cry when this is over, but right now we've got to report this and assume that Clyde Bonner has taken your Mom. We're ahead of the game, Jeanie, we know who's behind this," Rucker said.

"I don't know how much of this I can take. First my sister, and now my mother, how can this be happening? I thought these things only happened in the movies. This is so unreal; I can't begin to tell you what I'm feeling right now. Would he hurt my Mom, Rucker? Tell me that he wouldn't hurt my Mom," she sobbed.

Delores Rucker knew only too well the answer to Jeanie's questions. The very fact that he would resort to kidnapping an innocent civilian to further his cause, told her that he was a force without limitations. Rucker knew something else that she would not share with Jeanie Cromberg, today. Bonner had no way of knowing that Jeanie wasn't at home, unless Stacy told him that she was in Dallas on business. He had probably planned on abducting her as well. What his plans were for the women, she could only imagine.

"I really don't think that this guy will hurt your Sister or your Mother," Rucker did her best to make it sound convincing.

Wade Gorman was on the phone when Clayton and Stillwell appeared at his door. He motioned them inside and continued listening to the conversation on the other end of the line. It was clear after listening to Gorman's response for a few moments that he was quickly reaching his boiling point with whoever was on the other end.

"Do you understand that an HPD Detective has been taken hostage and we don't have a clue as to her whereabouts? I frankly don't care if every squad car in this department is running down false leads. When someone phones in a lead, we're going to check it out. We're not going to sit on our ass and do nothing. What do you think this department is going to look like if this guy kills Stacy Cromberg? What would you want me to tell your family if it were you being held captive, Hank? You think about that next time you call me to complain about doing your job."

Gorman dropped the phone in its cradle and took a handkerchief from his back pocket and pulled it across his brow. He reached for a bottle of pain pills on his desk, popped two in his mouth and swallowed them with a full glass of water.

"What's the news on Stacy's mother?" Gorman asked.

"We just talked with Rucker and we have conclusive evidence that she's been taken against her will. We don't have any doubts that it's Bonner, sir," Stillwell said flatly.

"Do we have a time line on when she was picked up?"

"According to the notes Rucker found, she was supposed to be ready around five this morning. There's no reason to believe that it happened any differently," Clayton said.

Gorman palmed his face with his hands and sat very still as if waiting for an uncomfortable moment to pass. When he finally looked at Clayton and Stillwell again his eyes were watering, and he spoke with a solemn voice that neither of them had heard in a very long time.

"I'm at a loss here, and I'm not good at waiting for things to happen. When I was a hostage negotiator we had a well thought-out playbook that we followed like a piece of sheet music. And, for the most part it never failed us, but we don't have a playbook for what's happening here. If one's been written I haven't seen it. So I'm asking, has either of you got any brilliant ideas?" Gorman asked.

He absentmindedly reached for the bottle of pain pills, opened the cap then closed it again, remembering that he'd just taken two tablets not more than five minutes ago. He pushed the pills to the edge of his desk, and looked back at the two cops.

"I'm waiting," he said with furrowed brow.

"Sir, that's about all any of us, can do. We've got a hundred cops on the streets rousting every mouthpiece and snitch in Harris County. Sooner or later we'll uncover something, but right now we're all playing the waiting game," Clayton offered.

"Did any of Miss Cromberg's neighbors happen to notice anything unusual this morning?"

"The house is on a cul-de-sac so there aren't many neighbors. Rucker is going door-to-door as we speak," Stillwell said. Gorman pushed himself away from his desk standing up slowly.

"I have a doctor's appointment in thirty-minutes, but don't let that stop either of you from calling me as soon as you find anything. Keep working the streets and keep me informed every step of the way," Gorman said.

Redhawk Simmons could count on his fingers and toes the number of times in his life that he had had an occasion to smile; there weren't many. In the past few days he was having trouble shutting it off. He was washing his hands when Renee waltzed into the kitchen holding her hand at arms length with her ring finger permanently displaying her beautiful engagement ring.

"Do you see anything wrong with my face?" Redhawk asked with a sullen voice. She stopped looking at her hand and feigned a serious look.

"What's wrong? Do you feel like you're coming down with something?" she asked, running her palm across his forehead.

"It's this thing on my face, I can't seem to make it go away," he said, smiling broadly.

"Are you happy, Mister Simmons?" she asked, moving in close to him.

"I don't' know how to act. I thought happiness was something for pale faces. It's starting to worry me a little."

Renee wrapped her arms around his neck and kissed him on the ear and then on the cheek. "Well, if that's the case I suppose we've got an epidemic breaking out on the reservation, because this squaw has never been more content. You're everything I've ever wanted."

"Another first," he said.

"Another first what?"

"Another first in my life, that's what. It's like all of this is a first for me, my first love, my first wedding proposal, my first jewelry store and my first wedding ring, not to mention my first charge account."

"I been meaning to ask you where did you come up with that three grand? I didn't see you go to the bank.

"I went to the Redhawk Simmons bank and trust," he said.

"Yeah and where would that be?"

"Under our bed. It's the money I had left from the casino. I hid it in a fruit jar under the bed."

"It's not smart to leave that kind of money under the bed," she said, kissing him again on the lips. Are you ready for supper?"

"What are you cooking?"

"I've got green beans and fresh tomatoes from the garden, quail from your last hunting trip and baked potatoes; I bought those from Kroger," she said, kissing him again.

"Dinner may have to wait for a little while if you keep that up," he said, kissing her on the neck.

"I thought you'd never get the hint," she said.

The lovemaking lasted almost an hour. Renee left him half asleep on the bed and went back to the kitchen to finish supper. While setting the table she switched on the television so that Redhawk could watch the evening news. She had no way of knowing that the evening news would do what nothing else could; it would ruin the joy of her lover.

When Stillwell answered the phone and the voice on the other end of the line said it was John Williams, she stood there for a moment trying to remember where she had heard that name. When it finally came to her who the man was, she was embarrassed that the events of the last few hours had clouded her attention span.

"Oh, John, I'm so sorry I didn't recognize your voice. Things have been so screwed up around here that I don't know whether I'm coming or going. Is everything okay, John?" she asked.

"Everything's good here. I just got the news from our forensics' guys that they may have come up with something on the case. It seems that they've been talking with your people and it appears they've found a common link tying the cases together. Whether it's significant or not remains to be seen, I suppose," John said.

"What do you have, John?"

"They found traces of metal in the wound. It could only be seen under a microscope. They got in touch with your team in Houston and sure enough, when they went back over the wounds of the victims there they found the same thing."

"Do you mean like metal shavings?" Stillwell asked.

"Not like shavings, more like a finely ground dust. It was so fine that it could be easily missed. Remember, we didn't catch it either until we photographed the wound microscopically. We all knew that it was the same killer because of the paintings. Now we know that the killer sharpens his knife before every murder."

"John, I know my minds not up to full speed, but how can that help us?" Stillwell asked.

"It's interesting that you asked, because I asked the same question. From a state with almost a million hunters we're taught to sharpen knives as kids. But whoever sharpened the killer's knife was a professional and used professional equipment. It seems that people that do this sort of thing for a living use zirconium wheels spinning in opposite directions to sharpen knives, and, it's somewhat of an art, from what I've been told. Not just any person knows how to use these wheels professionally. This man's knife was sharpened by someone who does it for a living."

"They have people like that?" Stillwell asked.

"Run down blade sharpening companies in your area. I know of several. There's one company in Houston called Circle Saw, I used to carry my chain saw blades and my table saw blades to be sharpened there. Because even if you can do it yourself, you could never do it like a professional does. My guess is they're using the same type blades that produce the same type residue that we've found on our victims."

"I'm going to talk with our people right now. You just may have put us a step closer to finding this guy, thanks, John," Stillwell said.

"Hey, don't' mention it, I'm just glad we found something that can help catch this guy. Oh, before I forget about it, I saw Clayton's picture in the San Antonio paper this morning. You tell him that he's got enough money that he don't need to be working our Rodeos for extra cash," John Williams chuckled in her ear.

"John, that man is a never ending list of surprises. I'll tell him. You take care of yourself, and thanks again for the news," she said, hanging up the phone.

CHAPTER *11*

Buffalo Bayou snakes through downtown Houston just west of the skyscrapers, then circles on the fringe of town to the north before dumping into the ship channel and several other tributaries. In hopes of walking the kinks out of his sore muscles, Ross Clayton walked from the north ridge of Buffalo Bayou to the Star of Hope Mission near Minute Made Park. He stopped every vagrant, miscreant, and homeless person along the way showing them pictures of Cromberg and Bonner.

While it was true that most of the people he spoke with did not have the ability to carry on a meaningful conversation or to digest a rational thought, tips from a few of theses wayward souls had proved quite useful in the past. It didn't hurt that Clayton had flashed a roll of hundreds as a form of enticement for anyone having a worthwhile tip or other useful information for the cops.

It was late August and a grueling evening sun kept temperatures in the mid nineties and humidity at levels close to unbearable. Clayton mopped his forehead with his shirtsleeve and dropped his coat and tie in the back seat of his Jaguar. He cranked the engine and waited for the air conditioning to kick in and cool his face. He flipped on the radio and on the oldies station an Otis Redding song was playing, "Sitting on the dock of the bay. He leaned back in the seat, closed his eyes, relaxing in the coolness of the song and the air conditioning. The peaceful moment wouldn't last until the end of the song.

It was probably a combination of things that caused Clayton to overreact to the sudden pounding on his window. Clayton reached for the door-handle pulled his 9 mm and was outside the car in a matter of two second. The homeless woman who had been beating on his window was inadvertently knocked into the street and sat there with a dazed look on her face.

"Hey man, you're wound a little tight aren't you?" she said, looking at Clayton through a pair of rose tinted sunglasses that had fallen to the end of her nose.

The woman looked to be in her early fifties. She had long frizzy gray hair and a face that suggested that she was probably an attractive woman at one time in her life. But the drugs, wine and chemical inhalants had taken its toll on what was left of her. She began to cough and spit while holding a dirty hand in the air for Clayton to help her to her feet. Clayton quickly holstered his weapon and helped the woman to stand.

"I've never been knocked on my butt so fast in all my life," she said. "You ain't got to worry about nobody getting the drop on you, catlike don't even begin to describe what you are," she said, dusting her clothes as she talked.

"I'm real sorry, I don't know why I did that," Clayton said.

"It's alright. I heard from some of the guys that you're looking for Clyde Bonner," she said. Clayton handed her the two photographs watching the woman's face intently.

"Don't know the woman in this picture, but I know Clyde Bonner," she said, handing the photographs back to Clayton.

"Do you know where I can find Bonner," Clayton quickly asked.

"Slowdown there, lightning. The boys said you were flashing a lot of green. Now I ain't asking for a lot, but I would like to hold onto one of those C-notes for a while," she said, brushing at her nose with the back of her hand.

"How about two?" Clayton said, pealing two of the bills from the stash in his pocket. As the woman reached for the two bills Clayton's grip on the money became much tighter. "I want it all. I want the truth and I want the whole story," he said firmly, allowing her to finally take the money.

"Honey, for two hundred dollars, I'll give you my life history."
"Just tell me about Bonner."

"I wanted to see the beach again," she started. Clayton wondered where she was going with her story but didn't say anything. "So last week I hitched a ride down to Galveston. It's taken me six days to get back here. This morning, I was spare changing in the Wal-Mart parking lot over by Wayside Drive, and I see Clyde Bonner and some woman go into the store. She's not the woman in this photograph, but now that I think about it she did kind of favor this woman," she said, pointing to Cromberg's picture. "Anyway, I'd know Clyde Bonner anywhere," she said flatly.

"Where do you know Bonner from?"

"I haven't always been retired and living the life of the rich and famous. I used to work for a living in Huntsville, let's just say I was in the service industry for a while," she said, looking back in the direction of Minute Made Park. "Bonner always looked me up when he'd get out of prison. The truth is, I didn't like him much back then, and I don't care for him much now. He always played the macho type," she said, making quotation marks in the air with her hands.

"As close as you can get, tell me what time you saw Bonner and the woman go into Wal-Mart?"

"I left my Rolex in San Antonio, but the store was open and the parking lot was full of cars. I know it was before noon because I picked up enough money from folks in the parking lot for bus fare back downtown. I remember seeing a clock on one of the buildings on Travis Street that said it was12:40 p.m. I must have caught the bus around 12:15," she said.

"What's your name?" Clayton asked, handing her his business card. "Velma South. I'm a southern girl in case you're interested." "Do me a favor, Velma."

"I don't do that sort of thing anymore," she said sarcastically. Clayton gave her a long stare. "Alright, what is it that you want from me now?" she asked.

"You take my card and hold on to it. The next time you feel the need to go to Galveston or anywhere else you call me. The next time you see Bonner, I don't care if it's two in the morning you call my cell phone; the number is on the card. One other thing I need you to do, if anybody around here hassles you or causes you any problems, you call me immediately. I promise you I'll take care of it.

"You're a classy guy, Clayton. Can I call you Clayton?" she said, looking at his card again.

"Absolutely, call me anytime, for any reason," "See you around, Clayton,"

Velma South opened her raged purse and dropped Clayton's card inside. She stood there for a moment as if she had something else that she wanted to say, but what ever it was she let it go, and walked away.

Seconds later Clayton was headed for Wal-Mart on Interstate 45. As he darted in and out of traffic he thought of Velma South, and wondered if she'd make it through the night with the two hundred dollars he'd given her, or if he'd just issued a contract for her death. Clayton was fully aware of the statistics regarding street-people and money. It was the law of the jungle that prevailed where only the strong survived. He hoped she would call him.

Redhawk Simmons was thankful that Renee was not in the room when the story aired about the Impressionist killer striking in San Antonio. She would have surely noticed the look of anxiety on his face. The news report hit him between the eyes like the news of a fatal disease. He wondered why, after almost forty years of living on the edge of societal decay, that he'd suddenly developed a conscience. These feelings were all so new to him. Could a life so full of rancor and venom somehow morph into something incisive and meaningful?

He turned off the television set listening to Renee humming in the bathroom. In his mind he could imagine the smell of her body and the intensity of her lovemaking. She was like no other person he had ever met. It wasn't that she was pretty or a great lover that turned his head. She was more than those things. She possessed in her nature, a stability and goodness that he had never known in another person; not even in the family members he could remember.

This man whom he suspected as the Impressionist killer was an evil man; he could feel it in his bones. He had to tell Renee about what he had seen on the television. He wasn't about to allow this to spoil their happiness or to drive a wedge between himself and the only person he had ever loved. He remembered some of the wise men from his tribe years ago talking about honor, and there was nothing honorable about not telling Renee. This would bring dishonor to their home, he thought. He dropped the remote control on the coffee table and headed for Renee.

A fast moving storm blew through Houston at ten o'clock and left the air much cooler than normal and smelling of fresh mulch and roses from the gardens around the Mosque.

The distraught man looked up at a cloudless black sky, tucked the Quran under his arm and walked away from the Mosque. He crossed East Side Street and got into his car, but didn't start the engine. His conversation with the Imam hadn't gone well at all, and he was troubled by it.

For more than twenty minutes he talked aloud, occasionally pounding the steering wheel with his fists. He called on Allah for guidance and wisdom, his mood and voice hovering somewhere between rage and solemnity. The thought crossed his mind for a moment to kill the Imam along with everyone else on his list, but he knew that Allah wouldn't stand for it.

The Imam had told him that he should learn to channel his anger against traitors and infidels into other paths, and into other thoughts. He thought about the Imam's advise and decided that he'd channel as much of his anger as he could into the graves of those he hated. If Allah hated the sins of these infidels why on earth should he have to channel anything positive toward them?

Why was it that no one understood his devotion to Allah? Shouldn't a man of God recognize pure devotion? Maybe the Imam wasn't pure? Maybe he was only masquerading as a man of God and had fallen in love with his American lifestyle. How could a man of God chastise him for killing infidels? What was the word the Imam had used... retribution? He said there would be retribution for the killings he'd committed. How could that be so? Only if he weren't so alone, he thought.

His plan had been so righteous and just, he thought. The men he killed had made a mockery of Islam. They had turned their backs on Allah and the prophet Muhammad. What sin could be more worthy of death? No Muslim on earth could find fault with his decision to kill these men, he thought. He bowed his head. "If I could only speak with," he couldn't bring himself to say her name.

Again and again he pounded the steering wheel in disgust, his anger now raging to a fever pitch. Then suddenly he stopped, leaning his head on the top of the steering wheel. For several moments there was total silence. Then like an epiphany from God he leaned back in the seat folding his arms over his chest. The sedate calm that fell over his body was like nothing before in his life. It was all so clear to him now. It was what he'd been waiting for.

With the curved bladed knife tucked into the back of his trousers he headed back for the Mosque. "You want to talk about retribution? Retribution must begin with the wicked. It's clear to me now that you are wicked. *Subhanahu wa ta'ala,*" as he reached the entrance of the Mosque.

It was 1: am when Clayton awoke from a reoccurring dream that he was having about Stillwell, and decided to call her. He had sat down at the conference table to wait for fresh pot of coffee to brew and fallen asleep; he'd been out for more than three hours. As he sat there thinking about the dream, he wandering what kind of a person could think about something so personal as the relationship between he and Stillwell, when a friend and co-worker was in such grave danger.

Clayton dialed her cell phone and poured himself a cup of coffee. She answered on the fourth ring.

"I don't know where to start this conversation," he said.

"Well let's take it first things first. You were going to check on Joann Cromberg's credit cards to see if there had been any additional charges after the Wal-Mart charge."

"That was the only charge there was. After they were seen at Wal-Mart they crawled back into the same hole and disappeared."

"Has the cell phone been used?" Stillwell asked.

"I must have dozed off in the conference room somewhere around eleven. That was the last time I checked with Fred, I suppose he's gone home by now so I really don't know."

"Clayton, do you know what time it is now?"

"Yeah, it's after one. You and Rucker having any luck?"

"We've been tracking leads all over town. I told you about John calling and about the Zirconium dust that's been found in all the cases. There are over twenty places in the greater Houston area that do sharpening, and on top of that we've rundown at least four leads from dispatch concerning Cromberg. We got nothing, Clayton."

"Well, aside from thinking about you, which I shouldn't be doing, I've been thinking about something that just doesn't add up."

"Why shouldn't you be thinking about me? I've darn sure been thinking about you. And I can't stop thinking about you." Stillwell said.

"Where's Rucker?"

"She's asleep on the sofa," Stillwell answered.

"Write her a note and tell her that your going to Denny's with me for an early breakfast. I'll pick you up in twenty minutes, I'm hungry, I want to see you, and I've got a few things about Clyde Bonner and the Impressionist murders that don't add up. Between the two of us maybe we can come up with something positive."

"Are you leaving now?"

"As soon as I can get to the car," Clayton said.

"I'll write the note and meet you in the parking lot," Stillwell said.

It was 3 a.m. when Bonner walked into the downtown police annex building. He was wearing the same jeans and boots that he'd worn for the last two days but he'd replaced the tee shirt with a light blue, button down shirt that he tucked into his jeans. On his belt he wore Aaron Phillips' badge and handcuffs, on the opposite side, a clip on holster and 9mm Berretta. He had an Astros ball cap on his head and a pair of thick-rimmed, clear lens glasses on his face. He could have passed for one of many cops who worked the streets of Houston in narcotics or on a gang task force.

Bonner had stopped at an all night Dunkin Donuts on the edge of town and purchased a mixed array of fresh donuts that he carried in a white box under his left arm. The smell of the hot donuts quickly filled the elevator as the doors closed behind him. He punched the button for the sixth floor just like Cromberg had instructed and calmly unsnapped the strap holding the Berretta in the holster.

When the doors opened again he was surprised that there wasn't a cop in sight. He could see a long hallway in front of him and one to the right. There was nothing on the left but a dingy beige colored wall that ran the full length of the hallway. He opened the box of donuts and took one of the powdered donuts and quickly took a bite out of it as he made his way toward the fenced area at the end of the hallway in front of him. He could see rows of stacked merchandise and marked boxes on shelves that extended from the floor to the ceiling.

The closer he got to the fenced area the smell fresh paint and roach spray filled his nostrils. Just as he turned the corner he noticed a sign posted on the fencing that read: No unauthorized personal beyond this point. Everyone must sign the Watch Commander's Log before accessing items from the storage area. He set the box of donuts on the metal counter and waited for someone to appear.

Cromberg had given him a description of Brandon Ford and he was startled to see a woman appear from a rest room at the end of one of the rows stacked with merchandise. The woman was probably in her late forties, he thought, and looked nothing like a cop, she looked more like a bean counter, Bonner thought. She wore a dark gray short-sleeved jumpsuit with an embroidered nametag that said her name was Joan. She wore little or no makeup and didn't say a word until she reached the opening in the fence.

"Can I help you detective?" she said, reaching for the logbook on the desk adjacent to the opening in the fence.

"I need to see the contents on case number 1660138891," Bonner said. "You must have been working on that case a long time to have the number memorized," she said.

"No, I just have a thing for numbers," Bonner said, popping the last bite of the donut in his mouth.

"You know, you're not supposed to be eating up here. We have a real problem with rats and roaches," she said, handing Bonner a clipboard filled with forms. "Do you know if what you're looking for is in one of the big plastic containers? If it is, you're going to have to help me get it down, cause of my bad back and all," she said, looking at the box of donuts on the counter.

"Where's Brandon and why isn't he up here doing the heavy lifting?" Bonner asked, as if he'd known Brandon Ford all his life. "Oh, help yourself to the donuts," he said.

"We're not supposed to be eating up here like I said. But I don't suppose nobody's going to say much about it, especially at this time of morning. Besides, I'm pulling a double shift and I'm hungry. Brandon's mother had a bad fall just before midnight and he had to take her to the emergency room. I was on my way out of the building when the supervisor asked me to pull the rest of his shift," she explained.

THE IMPRESSIONIST MURDERS

"I don't remember seeing you around before, which department do you work in?" Bonner asked. He watched the woman pull two of the glazed donuts from the box, neatly placing them on a paper towel on her desk.

"Honey, I work directly for the Chief, Harold L. Hurtt, himself. It's my job to keep track of everything that goes on during the evening shift and write a report for him to see as soon as he walks in the building."

"Sounds like an important job," Bonner said.

"Honey, you can't imagine how much deranged stuff goes on between three o'clock in the afternoon and midnight, especially on weekends. People start getting all liquored up before closing time then all hell breaks loose," she said, taking a bite out of one of the donuts. The woman had her back to Bonner as she munched on the donut.

"Well, honey, you may think you deal with a lot of hell, but you don't have a clue as to what hell is, and how it just walked into your world for real this time."

The woman never saw the blow coming. He hit her with such force using the butt of his 9mm that a stream of blood shot from the side of her head, spattering the walls and pooling on the floor where she landed. For a moment he was sure he'd killed her, but she began to moan and feel for the deep cut just above her left ear.

"Darling, I hate to be as rude as to not let you finish telling me how important you are, but I've got a bit of a time thing here to deal with. I need you to get on your feet and direct me to storage container 1661038891. Now, if you can't manage to do that, then Chief Hurtt is going to have a position to fill and you won't be complaining about how under appreciated you are. Am I making myself clear to you, honey?" Bonner said, holding the 9mm against her forehead.

On the wall opposite of the woman's desk was a cabinet top with a deep sink and faucet. Above the faucet was a roll of paper towels. Bonner pulled the roll of paper towels from the rack and handed it to the woman.

"Hold this against your head to stop the bleeding. I don't need you passing out on me. Just tell me where my things are and you can go to the hospital. Don't waste your time pondering what the alternatives are, because the alternative is that you'll be dead."

"You do know that you're going to lose your job for this," she said, looking at Bonner as if she couldn't wait to tell someone what he'd done to her.

"I'm amazed," Bonner said.

"That I would tell someone what you've done?" she asked.

"I'm amazed that you've got sense enough to get back and forth to work. Let's see how I can put this so an absolute moron can understand it. I'm not a cop; I'm one of the bad guys. I will not hesitate to shoot you. The truth is I'd be doing the public a service for shooting you. The woman began to tremble as Bonner spoke. She pointed at a pad on the top of the desk.

"Can you write the number on a piece of paper for me?" she whispered weakly.

"Sure, no problem."

Bonner wrote the number and handed it to the woman. She stood there for several seconds holding the paper in her hand while holding the roll of paper towels against the wound in her head. When she removed the paper towels and saw that it was saturated with blood, her knees buckled and she began to fall. Bonner caught her just before she hit the floor and moved her to a swivel chair at the desk.

"Look lady, I hate to be a bore, so here's the deal. If you can't or won't show me where my things are; then I'm going to shoot you and look for them myself. So let's go through it one more time. Show me or die."

"There is a red folder in the top drawer. Find your number and it'll tell you if it's here and where to locate it," she said. Her voice was barely audible.

Bonner opened the drawer, placing the red folder in front of him on the desk. The logbook contained over two thousand numbers and it took several minutes to find the one he was looking for. There was no description of the contents, just a row number and a bind number. Bonner said the numbers as he began to walk. "Row 12, bind 132." He stopped abruptly looking back at the woman.

"You'd better come with me," he said, rolling her and the chair into the storage area. "Which way to row twelve?" The woman pointed as Bonner pushed her along in front of him. Bonner saw the two suitcases long before he would have ever found the number. He stopped pushing the woman, stepped around her and jerked the suitcases from the shelf, laying them flat on the floor.

He quickly flipped the latches on the first case opening the lid. The suitcase was filled with neatly folded plastic bags, each marked with numbers and letters that meant nothing to Bonner. He could only suppose that they had tagged and logged every item using an alpha/numeric system. The case contained mostly things belonging to Degas. There was no money. He moved quickly to the second case opening the top.

Again, the suitcase was filled with tightly wrapped plastic bags and larger tags describing the contents with numbers and letters as before. He began to smile as he read the labels. Each tag he examined told the amount of money it contained marked clearly in the center of the tag. The first one read said, 100,000.00 dollars. He began to chuckle as he checked each bag then begin placing the bags back the way they were.

When he closed the case and stood up he realized that the woman wasn't in the chair. His heart began to pound in his chest. He wondered how she could have gotten away so quickly without being seen. He left the case containing the clothes and personal items on the floor. He lifted the case containing the money and started for the front desk.

Just as he made the turn leading to the entrance he saw the woman lying face down with blood pooling on the floor. He assumed she was dead. He walked quickly passed her, heading for the elevator. For some reason, at the exact moment he was about to push the down button, he looked back just in time to see the woman placing the telephone receiver to her ear. Bonner left the suitcase at the elevator and moved quickly back to the fenced opening, drawing his 9mm.

"All you had to do was lay there until I was gone," Bonner started. Total fear gripped the woman now and her eyes filled with tears.

"I'll go back," she managed to say, slowly pulling the phone from her ear. "It wasn't your money. You didn't even know it was here. Did you think that you were going to be some sort of a hero and get a promotion by doing this? She dropped the phone and began backing away from the fenced barricade. "If you had only waited five more minutes, I would have left you alone. I want you to do something for me. When you get to whatever the after life holds for you, and they ask you how you died, you tell them you were killed because you were a dumb-ass."

The woman was about to say something, maybe even plea for her life, but what ever it was, Bonner pumped two 9mm rounds in her chest before she had a chance to say a word. Bonner walked away mumbling something about the woman's stupidity.

Once in the elevator he punched the button for the first floor then thought it would be wiser to leave the building through the basement-parking garage. When the elevator stopped on the third floor his heart began to pound again. Two uniformed officers stepped in the elevator and punched the button for the second floor. Both men were carrying Styrofoam cups of coffee. Bonner leaned his head against the wall and pretended to be half asleep.

"You okay, partner?" One of the cops asked him.

"I've been on a stakeout for three days straight. All I want to do is get home and get some sleep," Bonner said, amazed at how easy the lie came out of his mouth.

"We know all about that, partner." The elevator doors opened and the two patrolmen walked away without saying another word.

Bonner smiled when the doors closed behind them. "The whole place is full of idiots," he whispered aloud.

The dimly lit parking-garage was just what Bonner was hoping for. He darted between the rows of parked cars, moving as quickly as he could before finally making his way up the ramp and onto the street in front of the station. When he made it to his car he threw the suitcase in the back seat before sliding in behind the wheel.

"Piece of cake," he said, starting the engine. Bonner took his time on the way back to the apartment. There was no reason to be in a hurry and take a chance on getting pulled over, he thought. "Why ruin a beautiful operation," he laughed and said.

Bonner never noticed the car that began following him as soon as he left the police station. It never once occurred to him that the car that sat beside him at the light on Louisiana Street was carrying his worst enemy, and it wasn't a cop.

The reason Bonner hadn't paid attention to what was going on with his surroundings was because he was completely immersed in his own thoughts about getting out of the country with his money. And then there was the problem with what he was going to do with the two women in Smoot's apartment. The thought crossed his mind to forget about the apartment and the two women and just head for the border of Mexico. He could be in Laredo in six and a half hours, even if he drove the speed limit, he thought.

Bonner hated loose ends, they had a way of coming back to haunt you later. He could leave them where they were and call the cops when he was safely on the other side of the border, he thought. That thought, for some reason, irritated him and made him appear weak and caring. He wanted the cops to know that he was neither.

"How long could it take to shoot two bound and gagged women?" Bonner said aloud.

"I'm going back to that apartment and shoot them both; that is the only thing to do. But before I do, I want to show that smart-mouthed cop that I got my money, all of it. She said I'd never pull it off, but that was the coolest thing I've ever done," Bonner said smugly.

CHAPTER 12

Ross Clayton's life had always been one of simplicity, or so he thought. He had no financial burdens and more money from his inheritance than he could ever spend. There were no entanglements, no emotional or psychological problems, no fetishes, and no weird idiosyncrasies to wreak havoc with his life. There were no siblings or close relatives, and other than the two people who cared for his home there was no one that he could say he loved. And even though that sounded sad, he had never felt sad because of the way things were.

It occurred to him, just before he reached Rucker's apartment in the medical center, that he'd never had a serious relationship with a woman, any woman; and he liked women. Why all of a sudden was he so taken by his partner after all these years? And why was he thinking about breaking a steadfast rule that his father had taught him about dating women where one worked. Was that what this was about? Did he want to have a relationship with Stillwell? Was this the quickest way to ruin a great friendship?

These questions flashed through Clayton's mind like lights on a passing runway. And yet there was one question that was more pressing than all the others. What if Stillwell didn't have the same feelings for him? What if that life-altering kiss she'd given him in San Antonio was just like the song says, "A kiss is just a kiss," and it didn't have the same meaning for her? What if he had just imagined the romantic nature of the moment? How could that be, he wondered. She was just as breathless as he was, wasn't she? And hadn't she been the one to make the first move?

Amid these mind-boggling questions was the immutable realization that aside from his personal feelings for Stillwell, people that he cared deeply about within his inner-circle were either hospitalized or in grave danger. Not to mention the bodies piling up from Bonner, Richey and Beverly Sneed, and the Impressionist killer. He couldn't remember a more difficult time period, since he'd been with the department.

Clayton turned into the dormitory parking lot and saw Stillwell waiting underneath a streetlight. She was wearing blue jeans, flats, a white, polished cotton blouse and a waste length soft pink jacket with the collar turned up on her neck. She smiled, stepped off the curb and got in to his Jaguar. There was an old Ray Charles song playing on the radio called, *"You don't know me."*

"I love your taste in music," she said, looking at him with eyes so clear and beautiful that for a moment he couldn't form a rational thought. "What's on your mind, Mister Clayton?" she said.

When she closed the door, the car quickly filled with the fragrance of her body and perfume. It was something he had grown accustomed to over the years but for some reason tonight it was almost more than he could deal with. He wanted to take her in his arms and lose himself in the smell, taste and feel of her body. Performing any other normal motor skill seemed almost impossible now as he fumbled with the gearshift knob.

Finally, Clayton shifted the car into gear and headed for Interstate 59. "There're so many things on my mind right now that I can't think straight, and I don't like it," he started without any additional prompting.

"I've always thought of myself as incisive, and able to come up with quick answers when the situation warranted it. But right now, all I have is a head full of questions," he said, and pushed the button for more air conditioning.

"Give me some of the questions," Stillwell said. "I may not have all of the answers, but like they say two heads are always better than one."

"I know that my every thought and action should be on Stacy and her mother, but it's not, and that bothers me a lot. I think about Aaron

Phillips lying up in the hospital, who's lucky to be alive, I haven't been there for him the way I should, and that bothers me. I think about Captain Gorman in so much pain that he's popping pain pills like candy. I've got questions about these cases that I can't put my mind around. And if all of that wasn't enough, I can't stop thinking about you," he said. He saw her smile out of the corner of his eye.

"Why are you smiling?" he asked.

"Because I didn't know if I was part of your brain storming or not, and I'm glad that I am. Did you ever stop to think that I might just be going through the same litany of head games that you are? If there was ever a time in my life that my mind should be on others around me, it's now. And even though it is, to an extent, I find myself wanting to be with you every waking moment. If you hadn't have called me when you did, I would have called you. Rucker is up in that apartment sleeping like a baby and I'm walking the floor, wandering what you're doing," she said.

Clayton turned north on Highway 288 then eased onto Highway 59 north. "I'm going to the Denny's on 59 near the Beltway it shouldn't be too crowded this time of morning and we can talk in peace. "Before we go any further in the conversation about us, I want to run a couple of things by you because my mind may not be so clear later."

"I'm wide awake now and my mind is all yours," she said.

"When we were in San Antonio, I noticed that Mr. Sepehr had a tattoo on his right forearm depicting Jesus on the cross. For some reason it didn't resonate with me at the time, but don't you think that's a little odd?" Clayton said.

"It is if Mister Sepehr is Islamic," Stillwell said. "I don't know the statistical data on the subject but I'd bet there are some men and women who have converted to Christianity from the Islamic beliefs."

"Right or wrong, I just assumed that all of these men that have been killed were of the Islamic faith. If any of the others were Christian, it might just be a motive for the killings. It's certainly more motive than anything else we've had so far," Clayton said.

"Well, you've already said that you believe that the killer is of Middle Eastern descent. You could be right. All we have to do is check with the families and friends of each of the victims to verify it. That's easy enough to do," she said.

Clayton took the Greens Road exit and u-turned on the feeder until he reached the Denny's parking lot. He parked in front of the building where he could see his Jaguar from inside Denny's, but didn't kill the engine. An old sixties tune by the Beatle's came on the radio called *If I Fell,* and Clayton turned up the volume. Clayton was humming along with the song when he turned and looked at Stillwell only to see that she was facing him.

Without saying another word he cupped her neck with his hand, pulled her close and kissed her deeply. Her lips were warm and soft as anything he had ever felt. When the kiss was over, Stillwell caught her breath and whispered an answer, her lips only centimeters from his. "What was that for?"

"I've wanted to do that ever since we left San Antonio. We left in such a hurry and under such horrible circumstances that passion just didn't seem to be part of the equation."

"So, what you feel for me is passion?" Stillwell asked, with a playful smile. Clayton sat thoughtfully for a moment, knowing that the question was a loaded one, and that it could be answered and misunderstood in many ways.

And, for the first time in his life, the thought of getting this woman into bed seemed somehow secondary where it never had before.

As the song on the radio came to an end Clayton turned the volume down and looked back at Stillwell, who seemed to be waiting for the answer to her probing question.

"To my knowledge, in the six or so years we've known each other, I don't think that either of us has ever lied to the other. In my opinion that's not only special it's unheard of these days. You're the best friend I've ever had and I think you feel the same way about me. I also think you know, or maybe you don't, that I've never had a serious relationship with another woman, and for some reason that bothers me a little," he said.

"Why? Maybe you just haven't found the right woman?" Stillwell could see that he was struggling to find the right words to say. She wanted to say something clever and off the wall in an attempt to help take Clayton where he wanted to go with the conversation, but she didn't. What she really wanted to do was lay it all on the line and go for broke, and tell him how she really felt about him. She wanted him to kiss her, she wanted to be held by him, and she wanted to share his bed, but she didn't say that either. What she did say was less than that, but nevertheless straight from her heart.

"I think that the relationship the two of us have is better than ninety percent of the people in the world that are married. I've been with you almost every day of my life for at least the last five years, and you're the first thing on my mind when I wake up in the morning and the last thing on my mind when I go to bed at night. When I kissed you in San Antonio it wasn't because of the money or because I found out that you could ride a wild horse. It was because I've had enough of just being your friend. I want, no, I need to know if there is more to us than friendship. Maybe that's all there is, maybe that's all it will ever be, but I have to know," she said.

"I didn't know you felt that way," Clayton said.

"You said that we were always honest with each other so now I'm going to be brutally honest with you. You're a pretty man, you're a good cop, you're the best friend a person could have, and, now I know that you're a great kisser. But when it comes to women you ain't the sharpest knife in the drawer. As a matter of fact, you ain't even in the drawer sometimes," she said.

"I can't believe you said that," Clayton said.

"Clayton, I get up thirty minutes early every morning just so that I can do something special that I think you might notice. Part of the reason I've been broke lately is because I've bought a new wardrobe that you've never paid any attention to. A few weeks ago I over heard you say that you liked this woman's perfume, so when you went into the restroom, I chased that woman three blocks just to find out what kind of perfume she was wearing. You never said a word when I started wearing it in around you."

"I probably noticed a lot more than you knew about," Clayton confessed. "Are you hungry, do you want to go inside?"

"If you'll kiss me again," she said.

It was four am when the waitress passed by the booth, picked up the check and Clayton's American Express card and carried it away. They had been eating and talking for almost two hours. And while they both should have been exhausted with only a couple of hours sleep in the last two days, their laughter, looks at each other and occasional hand holding shown an exuberance the two had not known for a long time.

Clayton signed the receipt and the two left the restaurant still holding hands. Just as they reached the car Stillwell remembered something she'd been aiming to ask him about.

"There's something I've wanted to ask you," she said.

"What's that?"

"You said when you called Rucker's apartment that there was something about Bonner that you didn't understand. Do you remember what it was?"

"Oh yeah, you're right. I was wondering why Bonner chose the University of Houston parking lot to steel a car. It's probably nothing but it's been bothering me ever since we picked Rucker up. Why that parking lot? Why go there to steal a car? Then it occurred to me that it's only a couple of miles from that drug dealer's apartment. Do you think Bonner could have taken Stacy and her mother there? Or am I just clutching for something that's not there?"

"There's one way to find out," she said.

Before either of them could say another word Stillwell's cell phone rang and she could see on the screen that it was Delores Rucker. She answered the phone and didn't say another word until she grasped Clayton's arm and held onto it tightly. "We'll pick you up in twenty minutes," she said, breathlessly. She kissed Clayton quickly, and started talking as soon as they got in the car.

Clyde Bonner was puzzled by the look on Stacy Cromberg's face, and her mothers Mona Lisa sneer from behind the duct tape made the foreboding feeling even worse. If he didn't know better he would swear they were smiling. It was eerie, and it gave him the creeps.

He lifted the suitcase on the dining room table, checked the restraints on both women to make sure they weren't going anywhere, and then stood back looking into their eyes as if to say, what on earth do you have to be amused about. Don't you know that in ten minutes you'll both be dead?

"I hate to have to shoot the two of you and run but it's the nature of the business. It'll all be over before you know it," Bonner said, snickering as he walked away.

He headed for the back of the apartment to collect his belongings so that his stay wouldn't take any longer than necessary. He was eager to get on the road and put this all behind him.

Bonner never saw the thick porcelain vase that cracked his scull, broke his nose, and temporarily blinded him. Richey Sneed stepped over his limp body as he lay unconscious on the floor of the den, unmoving and bleeding profusely.

"Shoot him, Richey, shoot him," Beverly Sneed shouted wildly. "If you don't shoot him he'll never stop following us."

"Let's just get the money and go," Richey said, heading for the suitcase. Beverly Sneed was wired. It had been over three days since she'd snorted the last of the Cocaine and taken the last of the Quaaludes. All she had left was a handful of sleeping pills. She'd been taking Lunesta tablets to curb the agitation and help her sleep ever since. She'd taken four tablets at nine o'clock last night and when they finally hit her, she curled up in the back seat of the Cadillac and slept while Richey kept an eye on Bonner's activity. Now she could hardly stand still for more than a few seconds, and her head felt as if it were about to explode.

Richey opened the suitcase and pulled one of the bags of money out to examine it. Just as he turned to Beverly to show her the plastic bag filled with hundred dollar bills, he saw her grab a cushion from the sofa and drop it on Bonner's chest. Before he could move a step in her direction, or say another word, she placed the muzzle of her 9 mm deep into the cushion and pulled the trigger twice.

Bonner's body was lifted off the floor by the blasts. Blood spatter covered his white tee shirt beneath the cushion; his body lay lifeless and unmoving.

Cotton fibers from the cushion filled the air and floated around like dust particles in front of a window in bright sunlight. Richey Sneed could not believe what he had just seen, but the madness was far from over.

Before the last spent round from the 9 mm stopped spinning on the floor, Beverly moved away from Bonner and placed the hot barrel of the 9mm to Joann Cromberg's temple, and was about to pull the trigger when Richey dropped the packet of money and dove in her direction. The horrific sound of the weapon's discharge deafened Joann Cromberg. But the fact that she was still alive, and that the bullet had so narrowly missed her head was nothing less than a miracle.

Beverly and Richey Sneed tumbled to the floor; the 9 mm dislodged from her hand and landed six feet away. Seconds later she was kicking and clawing at Richey like someone possessed of a demon. Richey fought off the blows until she bit him on the cheek. He cried out in pain, holding on to the left side of his face. Just as Beverly sat up and was about to hit him again, he clocked her with a roundhouse jab to the side of her face. But to his surprise she came up again with all the tenacity of a wounded animal.

As blood seeped through Richey's fingers, the thought flashed through his mind that perhaps his wife had gone insane and lost it, this time for good. Maybe the years of drug abuse had finally taken its toll on her. Maybe this psychotic behavior was just the onslaught of something worse to come. Maybe the next time her rage would kill him or get him killed.

Richey quickly pulled his own 9 mm from his belt and placed the barrel between her eyes. The expression on her face wasn't one of fear, but of uncontrolled violence. He pulled the hammer back on the weapon, his determination now set in stone.

"I'll kill you right here, Beverly," he said without hesitation. She could see the anger and commitment in his eyes.

"The killing has got to stop. This insanity has got to stop. I don't' know what's happening here, but this madness has got to end, here and now. I swear, Beverly, I'll do it. I'll kill you right here."

Her expression suddenly changed and she began to cry. "Don't kill me, Richey. I don't know what's wrong with me. I'm sorry, Richey, please don't kill me," she pleaded.

He watched her swallow hard then began to gag. She vomited on the floor, her arms clutching at her midsection, she heaved time and time again, until there was nothing left in her system. He released the hammer on his 9 mm and shoved the weapon in his belt. He quickly walked across the room retrieving her pistol from the floor and tucking it in his belt along side his own weapon. From there he went to the kitchen and brought back two wet towels, dropping one on the floor in front of his wife. The other he folded and held against his face.

"Are you going to be okay? Because ready or not, we've got to move now, and I'm not going to wait for you to go through some kind of life altering crisis," he said.

"I'll be alright," she whispered. "Don't leave me."

Richey closed the suitcase and moved it next to the door, then turned back and looked at Cromberg and her mother. While Beverly slowly made her way to the door Richey went back to Stacy Cromberg and removed the duct tape from her mouth.

"Look, you know I can't untie you, but I don't think it's going to be too long before your friends are here to let you go."

"You got what you want, why don't you just take the money and go?" "You know that Bonner had no plans of leaving the two of you alive, don't you?" Sneed asked.

"I know that. And I appreciate the fact that you stopped that nut bag from killing the both of us. You're not a bad guy, Richey, you were right a while ago when you called this madness. You're not going to make it very far with her freaking out on you every step of the way. Why don't you?" Cromberg was in mid-sentence when Sneed put the duct tape on her mouth and headed for the door. Sneed looked back as he open the door shoving Beverly into the hallway.

"You're probably right. But I can't leave her."

There wasn't time to assemble a SWAT team, nor was there time to worry about any reprimands that might come as a consequence of his actions. Clayton made the decision own his own to raid Smoot's apartment as soon as Rucker told them about the murder at the police storage facility and that the suitcase containing the confiscated cash was missing.

Clayton and Stillwell met Rucker at the lobby of the apartment building and took the elevator to Smoot's floor. With weapons drawn they approached the door. Clayton stood in front of the door with Rucker and Stillwell to his sides. He was prepared to kick the door open when Rucker turned the knob and the door opened slowly.

The three cops rushed into the room, scanning every space for danger. Rucker ran to Cromberg and pulled the tape from her mouth then moved to her mother and done the same.

"Is anyone in the apartment?" Clayton asked.

"They're gone," Cromberg said. Rucker and Stillwell worked on the restraints to release the two women. Cromberg stood up and wobbled into Rucker's arms.

"Hold on there, partner," Rucker said.

"I can't hold on, can you help me to the rest room? We've been sitting in this position for over six hours and I've got to pee," Cromberg said. She had been so glad to see her friends that she hadn't looked in her mother's direction. When she did, Joann Cromberg was quietly crying.

"Mama, are you all right? I'm so sorry I didn't," Stacy Cromberg stopped speaking when her mother started to talk.

"I'm okay, but my bladder wasn't as strong as yours. I let it go some time ago. I'm so embarrassed," she said through the sobs.

Rucker stood up and walked the two women to the restroom. Clayton walked to where Bonner was laying and eased the cushion from his face.

"It's Bonner," he said, looking back at Stillwell.

"I'll give you two guesses as to who plugged him," Stillwell said.

"I suppose it could have been anyone who knew he had a suitcase full of money, but if I had to lay odds, my money would be on the other two who were in the last gunfight with Bonner," Stillwell said.

Clayton stood up as Rucker walked back into the room and answered the question. Clayton walked back into the dining room and got on his cell phone calling the dispatcher and ordering police blockades on every major street leaving or entering downtown Houston, and to be especially watchful for a white, late model Cadillac. Stillwell and Rucker stood by Clayton listening to the conversation. The three cops had their backs to Bonner's body.

From the opposite end of the den they heard Cromberg scream out a warning.

"He's not dead and he's got a gun."

Just as the three cops turned toward Bonner he fired a shot in their direction, but his aim was less than perfect. The bullet blasted into a marble statue near the front door then imbedded in the door. Delores Rucker's draw was the quickest of the three, firing two more rounds into Bonner's chest before he could get off another shot.

Bonner was in the sitting position when Rucker shot him. He had had a second weapon in the small of his back, under his tee shirt and decided to use it on the three cops. It was the last mistake he'd ever make. Rucker holstered her weapon but Clayton and Stillwell kept theirs trained on Bonner's body. Rucker moved in Bonner's direction.

"I was so happy to see Stacy and her mother alive; I didn't think to check to see if he was still alive or even if he was still armed. I knew better than that," she said berating her self for the mistake. "If I'd only looked at these wounds, I would have known that there was a good chance that they weren't fatal," she said.

"Forget about it, D. Everyone here is running on empty. The fact is we all thought he was dead. The man's laying there with blood all over his shirt and a pillow covering his face and chest, it was easy not to pay any attention," Clayton said.

Cromberg made her way back to the dining room and sat down. She watched Rucker check Bonner's body, and then smiled when she heard Rucker say that he was dead for real this time.

Cromberg told the three cops about how Beverly and Richey Sneed had strolled into the apartment just minutes before Bonner came back with the money. She told them how strung out Beverly was, and how she'd gone into a psychotic rage and shot Bonner after Richey had already put out his lights with a blow from the vase. She told them how Beverly was only seconds away from killing her mother when Richey tackled her to the floor and the weapon discharged.

"If Richey hadn't have been here we'd both be dead. I thought he was going to have to kill Beverly just to get her to calm down. That blood on the floor over there is from the two of them fighting," Cromberg said, pointing to the bloodstains. "Clayton, they hadn't been gone fifteen minutes when you all got here," Cromberg said.

"They're setting up roadblocks all over the city as we speak. If they are still in the downtown area we'll catch 'em," Clayton said, punching Gorman's number into his phone.

The conversation with Gorman lasted long enough for him to speak briefly with everyone in the apartment, including Joann Cromberg. He ended the call by assuring Cromberg that he'd be at the apartment in thirty minutes to personally escort them home. When Cromberg clicked off with Gorman and handed the phone back to Clayton, it began ringing in his hand. He answered it on the second ring.

The call was from dispatch telling Clayton that Richey and Beverly Sneed had been found, and that they were hold up near a vacant warehouse on McKinney Street. Clayton jotted the address down and disconnected.

"I know you're all exhausted, but they have the Sneed's caught up in an old warehouse over on McKinney; it's not four miles from here," Clayton said.

"They sure didn't get very far," Stillwell said.

"Maybe they stopped to count their money," Rucker said.

The sun was barely visible on the horizon when Richey Sneed pulled the Cadillac into a Shell station for gas. The indicating light showing low fuel was beginning to blink. The light had been on ever since he followed Bonner from the Police storage facility; but he'd been in no position to stop for gas.

Richey hated the thought of stopping before he got out of downtown but he didn't have a choice this time. He smiled broadly when the attendant asked him if it would be cash or credit on the fill up. He bought a small bottle of Advil, two breakfast sandwiches, and two Cokes. He handed the attendant a hundred dollar bill and told him to keep the change. The attendant waited until he had checked the bill to make sure that it wasn't counterfeit before saying, thanks. Richey turned from the counter and never looked back.

Sneed turned on Polk Street and headed east which would take him out of the downtown area and towards their motel on Wayside Drive. Traffic was already starting to build as shift workers were arriving at St. Joseph's Hospital for the day shift. He watched cars pulling in and out of an all night café and wondered to himself if the real world was always on the move so early in the morning. He glanced back at Beverly lying in the back seat, but didn't say anything. He assumed she was still nauseated since she hadn't touched her sandwich or drink.

Two or three lights ahead he saw an extraordinary amount of Police activity beneath a stoplight. He took a sharp left at the next street, drove a quarter mile turning right on McKinney Street, still heading east. He hadn't gone a hundred yards when he saw half dozen squad cars with lights flashing and sirens blasting, heading straight for him. His heart began to pound wildly in his chest as so many thoughts flashed through his mind. Were these cops coming for him? Had Cromberg and her mother freed themselves and gotten the word out this quickly? How was this possible, he wondered?

He saw an open gate to his left and pulled into a vacant lot next to an old abandoned warehouse. Maybe the cops weren't after him. Maybe he was just being paranoid and they were looking for someone else, he thought. Beverly sat up in the back seat just in time to see one of the patrol cars skid sideways and come to a stop in front of the open gate. Several additional squad cars seemed to descend on the site like animals to a fresh kill.

"Give me my gun, Richey," Beverly said, crawling over the front seat. "What? You think the two of us are going to shoot it out with a dozen cops like Bonnie and Clyde? Get real, baby. We ain't going down like this," he said.

Redhawk Simmons was an early riser. He poured himself a fresh cup of coffee and walked out into the dawn, lost in thought. It was the first morning in the last several months that there was noticeable change in the temperature. The air was cooler this morning and had a freshness to it that caused him to notice his surroundings. He watched a squirrel scamper up a pine tree and then saw a leaf fall from a Sweet Gum tree. Things were changing, he thought. He was changing.

He didn't want to think about the knife wheeling man that had been killing people all over Houston and now in San Antonio. He hated the thought of dealing with the Police, but he knew he didn't have a choice with that issue either. He was not about to start a new life with Renee based on lies and half-truths and fear. As soon as she woke up he was going to tell her everything. Even about the fight on the boat in Louisiana. She would just have to deal with it, he thought.

He took another drink of his coffee and headed for his workshop. Except for Little Twin, who was sweeping the floor, there was no one else in the building. He waved at Little Twin but didn't stop for small talk. He wanted to be alone for a while; he needed a chance to think. There was a stack of unopened mail on his desk that he picked up and carried with him to the back of the shop.

He sat down on a stool in front of one of his furnaces that he used to heat metal for hardening, and began sifting through the mail. One of the letters was an advertisement for a bed and breakfast resort in Colorado, a place called Rainbow Valley. The advertisement showed mountain scenery with streams for fishing and trails for hiking or horseback riding, and looked like a great place to spend a honeymoon, he thought. He snickered at the thought of his knowing anything about honeymoons or anything else having to do with marriage.

He let his mind wander to thoughts of his ancestors, and fishing the beautiful streams of Colorado and New Mexico. He wondered if Renee would like it there. She seemed to really enjoy the outdoors, he thought. It was for a moment an extremely pleasant thought, but that thought was suddenly shattered when Little Twin came through the swinging door and ruined his day.

"That crazy guy is here," she said.

"What crazy guy?"

"You know the one you call El Diablo," she said.

A cold chill came over Simmons when she said the words, El Diablo. He stood up and without saying a word and headed in her direction. But just as he reached the swinging door where Little Twin was standing he stopped at his desk and opened a side drawer. There, wrapped in a soft white cotton cloth was a nine-inch Bowie knife that he was making for a customer in Dallas. He quickly unwrapped the knife and carefully shoved it into his back pocket, covering the handle and part of the blade with his shirt. He quickly moved passed Little Twin and stepped into the store. "You stay here," he told her.

El Diablo was dressed in a navy blue sweater with the sleeves pulled up to his elbows, his pants were black denim. He wore a dark colored ball cap pulled low on his forehead. The man looked like he hadn't shaved in several days. His beard was thick and black as asphalt. The man moved toward the counter when he saw Simmons appear from the workshop.

"What can I do for you?" Simmons said.

The man never smiled or indicated in any way that he was interested in making small talk, and he wasted little time in telling Simmons what he wanted. He reached behind his back producing the same curved bladed knife that Redhawk had sharpened a dozen times before.

"I need my knife sharpened, today. I'll pick it up after lunch," he said.

He placed the knife in Simmons' hand then quickly turned and headed for the door. Simmons stood there holding the knife as if he was holding a venomous snake that could bite him at any moment. Before the man made it to the door, Simmons stopped him in his tracks.

"Sir, I'm going to need your name and phone number on the work order before I can sharpen your knife," Simmons said, proud that he'd been able to think so quickly. The man turned sharply and made several steps in his direction.

"You've never asked for that before. Why do you need it now?"

"It's a new procedure," Simmons said nervously.

Thoughts flooded Simmons' mind. Had he overplayed his hand too quickly? Maybe he should have kept the knife and carried it with him to the police. It would be a good thing if they could get some blood or DNA from the knife, he thought. But before he had a chance to think of anything else, the man jerked the knife from Simmons' hand and stormed off for the door.

Simmons waited for the man to get into his car and drive away then rushed back through the store and into his back yard, jumping into his own truck. If he were lucky, there would be other cars on the blacktop and the man wouldn't notice that he was being followed. In two minutes he was less than a half-mile behind the man heading in the direction of Livingston.

The man drove the speed limit until the blacktop ended into the town of Livingston. He weaved through town and then made a right turn that would take him onto Interstate 59 South bound. After an hour and five minutes he was still following the man in the gray Lexus into the city limits of Houston.

Another ten minutes passed and the man eased into the right hand lane then exited the freeway. It happened so fast that Simmons hadn't had an opportunity to note the name of the exit. It was less than a mile to the stoplight where the man in the Lexus turned right and sped ahead, fortunately for Simmons there was another stoplight less than a half-mile away and the Lexus had to stop again. Simmons was six car lengths behind the Lexus and could easily watch any move the man made.

When the light turned green the man sped into the right hand lane turning quickly into the parking lot of a convenience store. Simmons drove slowly past the convenience store watching the Lexus pull to the back of the store and come to a stop. There was a Library on the opposite side of the road and Simmons decided to pull into the parking lot to see what the man's next move would be.

The man sat in the Lexus for what seemed like ten minutes. Simmons watched him moving back and forth behind the steering wheel, and occasionally waving his hand through the air like he was in the midst of preaching an emotionally charged sermon. Simmons had never been sure of much in his life, but he was painfully sure that the man wasn't working on a sermon or talking to God. The man finally left the Lexus and disappeared behind the store.

Two hours passed before Simmons got a glimpse of the man again. This time he walked to the fence behind the store opened a gate in the wood fence and disappeared again. When the man came back through the gate he was wearing different clothes and shoes, much more dressy than before. He had shed the ball cap and Simmons could see that the man had a thick head of black hair to go along with his thick black beard.

The man went back into the store and a few moments later reappeared, got into the Lexus and drove away. It was decision time for Redhawk Simmons. If he was going to keep up this super sleuth routine he'd have to figure out a way to relieve himself inside his truck. After several hours of sitting he knew he wasn't going to be able to follow the man for long without a restroom brake; that last cup of coffee was just one to many.

He allowed the man to get several car lengths ahead of him then pulled out on the blacktop heading back in the direction of Interstate 59. When he reached the Interstate he turned right, in the direction of downtown Houston. Simmons got the name of the road he'd been on and tried to write it down. Aldine Mail Route, he said the name aloud as he scribbled the name on a piece of paper from the glove box.

Simmons followed the Lexus into downtown, snaking his way through the northern portion of the city until the man parked in front of the downtown Police Department building and got out. Of all the places in the world he thought the man might go, the last place he would have ever guessed would have been the police station.

The man had been inside for at least five minutes when Simmons decided that he couldn't wait another minute to use the restroom. He eased out of his truck and trotted across the road, up the stairs and into the building.

When Simmons came out of the restroom he saw the man he'd been following talking with a large Black man resting his frame on a set of crutches. The man he'd been following was every bit as animated as he had been in his car a few hours ago. But whatever the conversation was about they were to far away for Simmons to hear. He thought about moving closer, but if the man saw him, he'd know for sure that Simmons had been following him.

Just as Simmons headed for the door he thought he heard El Diablo say something about his wife being killed and how the police owed him more information than he was getting. Simmons stopped on the sidewalk his mind drifting in consummate thought. Maybe he had grossly misjudged this man? Maybe the man's bad disposition was because someone had killed his wife? What if the man's only guilt was grieving over his murdered wife?

Simmons walked across the road, got into his truck and started the engine, but he didn't move from the parking spot. He thought about waiting for the man to come out of the police station and talking to him, maybe telling the man that he was sorry for the loss of his wife. But the more he thought about it the more he knew that he was involving himself in something that was none of his business. He put the truck in gear and pulled away, as confused as ever.

Clayton and Stillwell stood on the banks of Buffalo Bayou waiting for some word from the wrecker service and the police divers attempting to pull the Cadillac from the cold murky water.

"I don't think I can ever remember packing so much into a twenty-four hour period in my entire life," he said, looking at Stillwell.

"You know, it would be hard to write a report on everything that's happened in the last eight hours, much less the last twenty-four," she said.

"One thing for sure, it seems that things are winding down," Clayton said. It was an observation that later on he wished he'd never made.

Delores Rucker had walked to the Bayou's edge to talk with the officers who had been involved in the chase that ended with Richey Sneed's horrific crash through the barricade and into Buffalo Bayou. When the conversation was over she headed back to where Clayton and Stillwell were standing. Just as she reached the top Clayton extended his hand pulling her to the ledge.

"What happened?" Stillwell asked. "You've been down there long enough to get dates from half the police force."

"We missed a good chase; that's what happened. Have you guys got anything to eat? I'm starving," Rucker said.

"I'll be glad to buy your breakfast, but I want to know what happened first," Clayton said.

"Okay, you got my attention. What do you want to know?" "Everything," Stillwell said.

"They had Sneed and his half-crazed wife trapped in a vacant lot over on McKinney Street. They thought they had enough cars surrounding the place that there was no way they could get out or escape; but they were wrong. Snead puts the Cadillac in reverse and crashes into the radiators of two of the cruisers then takes off back toward downtown. It must have been quite a ride," Rucker said, popping a stick of gum in her mouth.

"By the way, there's something I've been meaning to ask you two. What happened to you guys this morning? I remember crashing on my bed and you were on the couch. When I woke up you were gone and the phone started ringing. What gives?" Rucker asked almost as an after thought.

"Didn't you get my note? Neither one of us could sleep and you were snoring, so we went to Denny's for breakfast," Stillwell said.

"What? You didn't think I would be hungry? Did you by any chance look in my refrigerator? I haven't eaten in almost two days.

Did you bring a doggy bag or anything from Denny's?" Rucker stood there with her hands on her hips.

"I'll buy you the biggest breakfast in Houston if you'll just finish the story," Clayton said.

"There's not much left to tell. They chased them all through downtown shooting up the place like an old west movie. They wrecked half-dozen cars, shot out a few storefronts. Two HPD cruisers plowed into a group of pedestrians and that was a mess. At least four people and the officers had to be taken to the hospital," Rucker looked back at the bayou, and then started again.

"For some reason the Cadillac jumped the curb here at Franklin and plunged into the bayou. We have every reason to believe that the Sneed's are at the bottom of Buffalo Bayou. It's going to take at least another hour or two to bring the car up. They're just getting started. Let's grab something to eat and come back later. There're plenty of cops here to keep an eye on things while we're gone."

Clayton reached in his pocket and handed Stillwell a hundred dollar bill, but didn't take his eyes off the bayou or the divers working at the bottom of the embankment. "I'm not leaving here until that car comes out of the water. You two go on, get anything you want," he said.

Stillwell looked at the money as if he'd handed her the keys to Fort Knox and she didn't know what to do with them.

"What? You've never seen a hundred dollar bill before?" Clayton said. "No, I've seen quiet a few in my life. I've just never seen you with one before," she said, smiling broadly.

Wade Gorman had not had a good night sleep since the accident that left him barely able to walk, and last night wasn't any different. He'd been up since four o'clock this morning; he'd spent four hours taking statements from Stacy Cromberg and her mother before driving them to his home to stay with two other female patrol officers for safety and rest before attempting to resume their lives. Now he was at his wits end with Nizar Kheif, who was drilling him again for answers about his wife's killers.

"Mister Kheif, I'm going to tell you for the last time, we don't know for sure if the people who crashed into Buffalo Bayou are dead or not. But we are quite sure that they were the two people responsible for shooting your wife. We haven't found any bodies and probably won't until the divers bring up the car. The place where the car went in is deep and extremely muddy. The divers are going to have to search the bottom of the bayou an inch at a time. So I want you to listen to me, we've got a lot of officers on the scene, including three of my best detectives; these people will not get away," Gorman said emphatically.

"I pray that these criminals are dead. Bringing them to justice is all that matters to me. My Marta was a good woman. Now my children must face growing up in this heathen country without their mother's guiding hand. How will I manage and run my store, Captain Gormand? How can I manage my business with thieves and murderers coming and going and properly raise three children?" The man looked at Gorman with wild eyes emanating hatred.

"I've never been in your shoes, so I'd be hard pressed to answer your question. Don't you have your mother staying with the children now?" Gorman asked just to have something to say.

"She's an old woman with a bad heart. She could go any day, the doctors say. So that's not much consolation," he said. "I'm counting on you to call me when the bodies of these animals have been recovered. I want to see their dead bodies for myself. I will not rest until I do."

The man turned suddenly and walked away without saying another word, and for some reason it bothered Gorman. That coupled with the fact that he'd shown up at the station before the news of the Sneed's crash into Buffalo Bayou was even covered by the local news people. Most of the television crews were covering the shootout in downtown and were cut off by cops before the Sneed's crashed into Buffalo Bayou.

"Mr. Kheif, I have a question for you." Kheif stopped just as he was about to exit the building. "Just how is it that you come to find out that we had the Sneed's on the run and that they had crashed into Buffalo Bayou? News reports are just now being aired. How is it that you had as many details as I did, and long before it was public knowledge?" Gorman had walked to where Kheif was standing while he asked the questions, and was now only inches away from Kheif.

Kheif's eyes seemed to explode with agitation and were now fixed on Gorman's. It was almost as if his eyes were piercing into Gorman's thoughts and the very fabric of his soul. For the first time in his life, Wade Gorman felt small and inadequate, and even more unnerving he wanted to run from the confrontation with this man. When the man finally spoke again, his voice was deeper than it was before, resounding off the marble walls of the hallway. It sounded like Kheif was speaking from the depths of hell.

"These animals murdered my Marta and you've done nothing until today. Months I've waited. Be careful Mr. Gormand the questions you ask me."

This time Gorman didn't stop the man when he abruptly turned and walked away. And for the first time in two months the pain in his legs and joints seemed secondary to the words spoken by this intimidating man.

Gorman stood there for several moments almost ashamed that he'd allowed this man to so completely unnerve him. In all of his days as a cop nothing like this had ever happened before. Usually his own daunting presence was enough to scare most men silly. But now a man half his size had frightened him like he was a helpless child.

He shuttered momentarily at an invisible cold breeze that blew through the hallway like an apparition, and then headed for the same door Kheif had walked through seconds before. Just as he reached for the door handle his cell phone rang. He fished it from his coat pocket, flipped it open and listened to the voice on the other end begin talking.

"Captain Gorman, we've got a critical situation here," a woman's voice said.

"The pain in his lower back, knees, and hip came alive again causing him to grimace and scowl into the phone. "Who is this?"

"Sir, this is Yolanda Perry, from dispatch. Actually, I was trying to get in touch with Detective Clayton, but his phone just goes straight to voicemail. Any ideas where he might be? Like I said, we've got a volatile situation here, sir," she said flatly.

"Look, Yolanda, I'm not in the mood for guessing games and social graces are not one of my finer attributes. So can you just tell me in the shortest time possible what's happening?"

"There's been another murder of a Muslim, Captain. Only this time it appears that the man that's been killed is some sort of holy man at this Muslim Temple. The address is 1207 Conrad Sauer Drive, at the corner of Westview Drive," she said.

"I don't think they're called Temples, Miss Perry, I think they're called Mosques," Gorman said.

"Well, whatever they're called, it's got a whole lot of people pissed off. They've already beat up one man and set a couple of cars on fire in the neighborhood. The fire department has just pulled a third alarm because one of the burning cars exploded and caught a house on fire. The people that live there said it's going to turn into world war three if something is not done soon. They've barricaded themselves in their neighbor's garage and have started firing on the Muslims. To this point there's only one report of someone being wounded and it's a fireman who was clubbed by one of the Muslims for accidently breaking out one of the windows of his shop on Westview."

"This can't be happening," Gorman said aloud.

"Were you speaking to me, sir?"

"Never mind, I was just thinking out loud," Gorman said. "I'm leaving the station now. I'll get the message to Clayton. How many officers have you sent to the scene?"

"We've had eight calls in the last ten minutes and so far we've sent six squad cars and a total of nine officers to the scene," she said.

"Send another ten officers to the scene now. If it escalates don't hesitate to send a hundred men if you have to. I don't want this thing going any further than it already has."

Gorman disconnected and walked out into the bright sunlight. The day was cool for this time of year and for a change the air had a fresh smell to it, one that he hadn't noticed in a long time. He took a deep breath and began negotiating his way down the steps and onto the sidewalk. The driver of his car pulled to the curb and stopped in front of him. The officer assigned to driving him around rolled the window down and began speaking before the Captain had a chance to say a word.

"You look as if you're ready to head for home, sir?"

"Yeah, I'm about as ready as I've ever been, but that ain't where we're headed," Gorman quipped. "Head for Downtown."

Ross Clayton ran a hand over his unshaved face and watched one of the divers emerge from the murky water making his way to the stern of the boat a few meters away. The diver pulled himself onto the fantail and unhooked the restraints holding his empty breathing tank. The man looked at Clayton giving him a thumbs-down signal indicating that they had found nothing of any importance. Clayton nodded and went back to thinking about how good it was going to feel getting goodnight sleep, when this was finally over.

Clayton had found an old concrete block to sit on while he watched the divers working the bottom of the bayou. Just up the embankment was Franklin Street where the Sneeds' had missed their turn, jumped the curb, and propelled their speeding car headlong into the bayou. From where he was sitting he could see the top of the Old Magnolia Ballroom, which was built in 1894. The old ballroom was a museum of sorts and also served as a place for weddings and other official gatherings. He wondered if anyone had been in the old building when all the commotion occurred.

Just as Clayton was making his way back up the embankment he saw Gorman's Lincoln pull to the curb and stop. The rear window was down and he could see Gorman taking note of the scene and of the divers coming and going from the boats below. Clayton also knew the Captain well enough to know when he was in no mood for small talk.

"Where are Stillwell and Rucker?" Gorman asked impatiently.

Clayton looked at his watch then back at the Captain. "I sent them to get something to eat about an hour ago," Clayton said, knowing that it had been closer to two hours since they'd been gone.

"As soon as they get back take Stillwell and head over to the Mosque on Conrad Sauer Drive and Westview. I think it's called the El Farquq Mosque. It appears that there's been another murder by your Impressionist Killer. Only this time he's killed a Muslim Cleric, and we've got a full-blown riot on our hands. Dispatch said they were burning cars and most of the neighborhood is up in arms ready to start a full-scale shooting war if this is not stopped."

"I know that part of town fairly well. Most of the people that live in the area are of Middle Eastern decent, but there's still enough rednecks living there to cause some problems. Maybe you and Stillwell can sort this out and put a stop to it before it makes the national headlines," Gorman said.

"A Muslim Cleric, you say? Do you mean like an Imam?" Clayton asked. "I wouldn't know an Imam from an Emu," Gorman said. Clayton laughed out loud but Gorman's expression never changed.

"I think one of them is a bird, Captain. I'll tell you something else, it also destroys a theory I had."

"What theory?" Gorman asked.

"Stillwell and I have been kicking around probable suspects and motives for these killings. The man that was murdered in San Antonio had a tattoo on his forearm depicting Christ on the cross. The man was no Muslim, Captain. The man was a Christian. Muslims don't wear tattoos of executed Jews on their arms or anywhere else on their bodies unless they're Christians. My theory was that maybe these men were being killed because they had converted to Christianity. But now with this Cleric being killed, I don't know what to think," Clayton said.

"I'm hurting too badly to give it any real thought, Clayton. But you still may be onto something. Just get Stillwell and get over there as soon as you can. I'm sure the crime scene had already been contaminated to high heaven. Do what you can, and keep me informed. I've got Cromberg and her mother at my house and I really need to check on them and get some rest myself. And don't think I don't know that you guys haven't had any rest either. Go as far as you can then crash somewhere; I know you need it."

"We'll take care of everything, Captain," Clayton said.

Clayton watched the Lincoln drive away then closed his eyes for a moment and dreamed of him and Stillwell lying on a deserted beach somewhere where it was warm and the drinks were cold and plentiful. It was a pleasant thought but it lasted all of one minute. Delores Rucker pulled his Jaguar to the curb and killed the engine.

"Thanks for the breakfast, and oh by the way, if you ever decide to get rid of this car and you're feeling really philanthropic, I want to go on the record today as first in line for the charity. That's one fine ride," she said.

When Rucker got out of the Jaguar he peered inside at Stillwell who had curled up on the passenger's side door and was sleeping soundly. Even as tired and sleep deprived as she was, she still looked gorgeous, he thought. He turned back to Rucker who seemed full of energy and about to head down the embankment when he stopped her.

"Gorman just left here a few moments before you got here. It seems that the Impressionist murderer has started killing Muslim religious leaders now. Gorman wants you to stay here and take charge of the investigation. Stillwell and I have to get over to the Mosque and see if we can calm things down. Call me as soon as the divers bring the car up. Are you going to be okay?" Clayton asked before sliding into the Jaguar.

"Hey, I'm full now and ready for action. This working around the clock thing isn't anything new for me. Try a few years of medical school and see how much sleep you get. This is nothing, Clayton," she said.

Clayton closed the door looking back at Rucker. "Call me the minute you know something." A second later he was out of site.

Clayton made his way down Milam Street then pulled into a parking lot just before he reached Pease Street and parked. He hated to wake Stillwell who was sleeping so peacefully, but he had to tell her what was going on. He put his hand gently on her forearm then kissed her on the neck just below her left ear. She moved slightly but didn't open her eyes.

"If you do that any closer to my ear you'll have to take me home with you," she said softly.

"There's nothing on this earth that I'd rather do than to do just that. I want to be alone with you in the worst kind of way," Clayton whispered back.

"What's stopping you officer? You can even handcuff me if you'd like, but I promise I won't resist," she whispered back, still leaning against the window with her eyes closed.

"You're so beautiful," Clayton said, whispering just inches from her neck. "Look Clayton, you had me at the kiss on the neck. Are you going to take me home or not?"

"As much as I want to, I can't," Clayton said.

What Clayton said ruined a beautiful moment. She opened her eyes and sit up straight in the seat. "Okay, you've got my attention. So if you're not going to take me to play, I've got to assume we've got to go to work. What's up?"

Clayton spent the next five minutes explaining everything that Gorman had told him about the latest killing. She took the news better than he thought she would.

"I want you to promise me something," she said, looking out the window at some imaginary object.

"What's that?"

"If this treadmill that we're stuck on ever stops long enough for you and I to get off, and long enough for you and I to spend some time together, I'd like to go somewhere just for a day or two, where there ain't no treadmills, and there ain't nobody slitting people's throats or gunning someone down. Do you think a place like that even exists?"

"I know just the place, and I promise I'll take you there," he said.

"Don't tell me anything about the place. Just take me there," she said.

"I hope you have a passport," Clayton said.

"I have a passport, and you're on, mister," she said.

Rains from the past few weeks had swollen all of the bayous in the greater Houston area, and Buffalo Bayou wasn't any different. The currents of the bayou became torrents of rushing water in some areas and especially where it dumped into the Houston ship channel and other tributaries and finally into the Gulf of Mexico.

Richey Sneed was fairly certain that he was the only person alive that knew for certain what happened in the final moments of his wife's life, and the sinking of Norbert Callaway's Cadillac.

Sneed had given the cops a pretty good run through the city, darting in and out of parking garages, dark alleys, driving the wrong way on one-way streets, and with Beverly firing more than sixty rounds into the fray as they went, they almost succeeded in shaking the last three cop cars that were still chasing them.

There were wrecked cars all over downtown, and five of them were police squad cars. And, while they had avoided anything major from happening to themselves, they had seen two of the squad cars plow into a group of innocent pedestrians on Louisiana Street, and Sneed was certain that some of them were hurt badly or even killed.

He remembered the chaos and stunned faces after the crash at that intersection and it was horrible.

Looking back on it now, the end came as unexpectedly and as quickly as it had all begun. He remembered looking at the speedometer showing ninety miles per hour just after he turned on Franklin Street. He looked in the rearview mirror and there were no cops in sight. When he looked back at the street, an old woman wearing a red bandanna and eating what looked like a piece of sausage was standing forty feet in front of the speeding Cadillac. The choice was simple. Run her down, or attempt a swerve and hope for the best.

Richey had chosen the latter, which was a fatal mistake. The Cadillac jumped the curb and immediately went airborne. It seemed like it must have sailed through the air for minutes when in fact it was only a couple of seconds. They could have probably withstood the impact had the Cadillac simply plunged into the water. They could have made it out with only a few broken bones and some lacerations. But on the opposite side of the bayou was one of the largest Cypress trees he had ever seen. It must have been there for two or three hundred years, he thought.

Apparently lightening had struck the old tree years ago leaving half of the tree dead. It was just his luck that the half hanging over the bayou was the half that had died. It was an enormous, leafless limb, jutting out over the water almost thirty-feet from the bank on the other side of the bayou. The huge limb blasted through the windshield of the Cadillac and through Beverly's chest, impaling her and the front seat into the back seat of the car. She was dead before either of them knew what happened.

For a moment, and one he would never forget, the Cadillac was suspended in mid-air, like a child's toy car stuck on a pencil; the wheels still spinning at something less than ninety miles per hour. Up until the limb broke, Richey had escaped the whole ordeal without a scratch. But when the limb finally gave way, the Cadillac turned sideways taking out the remainder of the windshield and severing the steering wheel from the column before ripping into his chest like a cannon shot.

The impact of the jagged steering wheel hitting his chest severed his right nipple with all the precision of a surgeon's scalpel, and he was certain, every time he took a breath that he had at least two or three broken ribs. The Cadillac sank quickly in the bayou, but with no windshield and no steering wheel to impede his egress from the wreckage, he surfaced in a matter of seconds.

Fortunately, the massive tree limb had shattered into several large pieces and one of the largest pieces surfaced just in front of him and he latched onto it before it got away. He began surfing with the current of the bayou and was away from the crash site in a matter of seconds.

He managed to stay on the back side of the limb as much as he could, but just before the current pulled them both around a bend in the bayou he surfaced just long enough to see if there was a crowd gathering along Franklin Street. There was no one there. Just the old woman with the red bandanna standing on the sidewalk with her mouth gaped open in horror. He could hear dozens of sirens resonating off the surrounding buildings and heading in the direction of the crash. It was only a matter of time before the place was crawling with cops, he thought.

For more than an hour he clung to the old limb, stopping occasionally at a sandbar, or a sudden twist in the bayou, always checking the banks of the bayou for cops or others looking for him. At about seven miles from the crash site the swift current lessoned and the bayou widened into what Houstonians simply called the Houston ship channel.

He watched as the whole landscape evolved from a muddy bayou circling through the city into a developed industrial complex along the banks that was the envy of much of the financial world. If he stayed in the water long enough he could travel for almost seventy miles to the Gulf of Mexico. But the pain in his chest, the loss of blood from his wound coupled with the frigid waters would never let him last that long.

After another two hours he begin to notice prominent landmarks; the massive bridge spanning the ship channel at Loop 610, and the neighborhood known as Denver Harbor to the south. He watched several freighters pass by as he approached the Galena Park area and the channel widen to almost a half-mile wide. It was when he reached the Washburn Tunnel near Pasadena that he remembered the stories he'd read about the capture of Santa Anna, the Mexican Potentate, in the spring of 1836 near the site of the tunnel entrance. He wondered what the place must have looked like back then.

There were more and more ships navigating the channel now, churning the waters and occasionally spinning the old limb like an amusement park ride. With every passing hour he became weaker and the water seemed colder and more daunting than the hour before. He knew unquestionably that one way or the other his ride was coming to an end. He would have to ride the limb as close to the bank as he could, then swim for it, or simply drown in the foul tasting, nasty waters of the channel.

With every ounce of strength he had left in him, he began to paddle his feet shoving the limb toward the north bank of the channel. It seemed like the most logical choice because the natural wake of water from the passing freighters seemed to be moving the limb in that direction anyway.

Another twenty minutes passed and he let go of the limb when he felt the bottom of the channel under his feet. It was muddy and slow going to the bank. Again, he recognized the area, it was a place called Lynchburg Crossing, a place where ferries shuttled cars from one side of the channel to the other, and because the channel is so wide here, great ships can make a hundred and eighty degree turn in the water before heading back out to sea. He pulled himself onto the bank and into a stand of Mangrove a waist high salt grass, lying flat on his back and staring up into a bright mid-day sun.

He lay there so exhausted from his hours in the water and from the night before that he could hardly move. Then like a vision from a melodramatic play happening in his mind, he saw Beverly's face the look of abstract horror on her face just seconds before she died. She had managed to say only two audible words before death took her; "Richey, I" she gasped slightly, closed her eyes and was gone.

For the first time in years he began to cry uncontrollably, covering his eyes with his forearm and weeping like a child. Somewhere in that moment of despair and self-deprecating torment he went unconscious and would not move again for many hours.

CHAPTER 13

As Redhawk Simmons headed in the direction of the reservation his mind replayed the conversation between the wild-eyed man and the Police Captain. It was only natural to question everything he'd ever thought about the man. But there was one thing that his own inherent instincts would never let him question; he knew the man was pure evil. He had never met another man in his life that had had such an adverse effect on him.

The further he traveled away from downtown, the more he realized that he had a perfect opportunity to do a little investigating of his own. When he reached Aldine Mail Route he took the exit and headed back for the convenience store where the wild-eyed one had spent a couple of hours earlier in the day.

He jotted down the name of the store and the address on a piece of paper he found in the glove box and went inside. He picked up a loaf of bread and a six-pack of Cokes and after mulling around for a few moments headed for the register. The man behind the counter was dark skinned with dark eyes and hair, but he seemed pleasant enough and almost friendly when Simmons' asked him if he carried baking soda.

"We sell very little baking soda here, sir. Mostly beer and cigarettes, but I think we may just have a few cans on the third isle," the man said. Simmons recognized the accent as almost identical to the wild-eyed man. The attendant hurried around the counter and down one of the isles toward the rear of the store. He picked up a silver and red can and began waving it through the air like a winning lottery ticket.

"I was fairly certain we had it, but you were very lucky, we only had two cans left," he said, handing the dusty can to Simmons.

Simmons decided to make the most of the good-natured man's willingness to talk and ask a few questions. He pulled a fifty from his wallet and handed it to the man.

"I'm sorry I don't have anything smaller," Simmons lied convincingly. "Not to worry, no problem. We cash checks everyday for much more," he said, working on Simmons' change. He handed Simmons his change, bagged the items and slid them across the counter.

"Are you by any chance the owner of this store?" Simmons asked.

"No, I only work for the owner," the man answered sheepishly.

"I see. Do you know if this store is by any chance for sale?" Simmons asked, hoping to strike up another conversation. Simmons watched the man's expression change from pleasant to somber.

"To be honest with you, I don't know," he said with a sigh. "There was a robbery here several months ago and the owner's wife was killed. Murdered right here," the attendant said, pointing to the end of the counter and speaking hardly above a whisper.

"That's too bad. I'm sorry to hear that," Simmons said. At that point Simmons wasn't sure if he should continue with the ruse or just go home. It was almost as if the news of the woman being killed took the mystery out of the scam he was attempting to play. But the man made the decision for him when he started speaking again.

"It was terrible. The owner has not been the same man since it happened. He almost never works anymore, and he seems to be preoccupied with other things all the time. But I guess if I were in his shoes, maybe my life would seem meaningless as well," he said reflectively.

"I sure would like to get his name and number so that I could call him and inquire about the store."

The attendant didn't say anything at first. It was almost as if his concerns were more of a personal nature than one of concern for his employers well being. Simmons was intuitive enough to recognize the man's dilemma.

"You seem to be a good caretaker of the man's store; of course I'd have to have some agreement in place to keep a valuable employee like yourself in the event he would sell me the store. I would want that understood if we were to come to an agreement of sale. I will be sure to mention that in my conversation with your employer. Can you help me with the name and number?"

It was obvious the attendant liked the line Simmons' gave him. He pulled a used envelope from the wastebasket and began to write on it. When he finished he handed it to Simmons and stood there smiling broadly. Simmons looked at the name and number and then back to the attendant.

"Is this Mr. Kheif's home number?" Simmons asked.

"No, this is the number to the store. I'm sure Mr. Kheif wouldn't want me giving out his home number. But he lives just behind the store. When you call, we can buzz him at his home and speak with him on intercom. We can even transfer the call if he says it's okay," the attendant explained.

"And the name of the store is, The Pit Stop?" Simmons asked.

"That is correct."

"Please tell Mr. Kheif that I'll be calling him in the next few days. I'm very interested in purchasing if he's interested in selling," Simmons said.

"And your name, Sir?" The attendant asked.

"George Gerber," Simmons said, looking at a row of baby-food jars just behind the counter.

"Thank you, Mr. Gerber. I will certainly tell Mr. Kheif that you called," he said with a smile.

Simmons folded the envelope, stuffing it in his shirt pocket. He smiled back at the attendant and walked out of the store. He drove away from the store thinking how cool it had been posing as Mr. Gerber and how easily the man shared the information with him.

Simmons looked at the envelope pronouncing the man's name aloud, "Nizar Kheif. I wonder what we can find out about you?" he said.

Clayton turned off the beltway onto Westview Drive heading east. He could see flashing lights and smoke in the distance. Stillwell looked at the piece of paper that Clayton had written the name and address on.

"It's 1207 Conrad Sauer Drive; does that road cross Westview?" she asked.

"From the looks of all the commotion in the distance I'd say that it does.

But I'm not that familiar with this part of town either."

Clayton lowered the window placing a flashing, red and white emergency beacon on the roof of the Jaguar. He pulled his badge holder from his belt, holding it out the window as he approached the group of officers at the roadblock. It didn't take long for him to realize that he didn't want to drive his Jaguar any further into the turmoil ahead.

He parked the Jaguar behind one of the cruisers blocking the road and he and Stillwell got out. As they headed for a row of cops in front of the cruisers, Clayton and Stillwell tried to assess the situation and chaos that seemed to be still in progress.

Westview Drive was a divided four-lane street heading east and west, while Conrad Sauer Drive was a two-lane, heading north and south. The property to the south of Westview belonged to the El Farouq Islamic Center. It was fenced with high, wrought iron fencing that extended at least a quarter mile south of the intersection and facing Conrad Sauer Drive.

Across Conrad Sauer Drive, facing Westview Drive was a business strip center. From the sign at the road, it appeared that the Ziller Deli was fully engulfed in flames, and that if the fire department didn't get it under control soon, the whole complex would be a total loss.

To the north of Westview, on Conrad Sauer Drive, was a residential neighborhood, with single-family homes on both sides of the street. Clayton could see that at least two of the homes closest to Westview Drive were burning, and that the fire department was working feverishly to extinguish them.

There were at least three ambulances; one on Westview past the burning deli, and two on Conrad Sauer Drive just north of the burning houses. There were people running in all directions and an abundance of shouting in the distance. At the far end of the strip center, Clayton saw a young boy heave a brick through a storefront, then disappear somewhere beyond the strip center. From where he and Stillwell were standing it was impossible to see any further down Conrad Sauer toward the Mosque and grounds.

There were at least three helicopters circling the area, news trucks from three of the major networks, and at least twenty reporters huddled behind squad cars and ambulances at each roadblock. The scene looked like something out of a Hollywood movie set.

"Who's in charge?" Stillwell asked.

"That would be Captain Rosen. His cruiser is in the parking lot of the small vacant building on the other side of Conrad Sauer. He's the one directing everything on the other side," the officer was pointing across the street.

"Where is the Mosque?" Clayton asked, looking confused.

"There's a red brick building about a block down Conrad Sauer to the south of us, Clayton."

"Has anyone been inside?" Stillwell asked.

"Negative. Until they get these fires put out, and we can get everyone to calm down a little, there's not much we can do but wait. The Muslims who started the car fires and set the two houses on fire have all disappeared behind the fencing. We think some of the neighborhood people set fire to the strip center, because Muslim people own it. We're just trying to keep everybody separated for now till we can get these fires put out."

"We're here to investigate the murder of the Cleric. Can we get in or not?"

Clayton asked.

"I think you need to talk with Captain Rosen," the officer said, handing Clayton a hand- operated radio.

The conversation between Clayton and Rosen lasted for several moments and ended with Clayton waving his hand in the air indicating that he understood everything that Rosen had said. Clayton leaned close to Stillwell's ear.

"Rosen is sending a SWAT team to set up across from the entrance to the Mosque. He wants us to stay here until that's done. There is a Forensics' team already here. They and a group of Rosen's men will accompany us inside the gates if there's no resistance," Clayton said.

"And what if there is resistance?" Stillwell asked.

"I guess that decision will have to be made then, but one way or the other we going into that Mosque," Clayton said.

It was late afternoon when Redhawk Simmons and Little Twin turned off the store's computer and looked at each other with stunned faces.

"I can't believe it," Little Twin said.

"What's that?"

"I can't believe that the man is a business owner for one thing. How does a person with a personality like his, own a convenience store? With his flamboyant personality I figured him to be a prison Warden or an executioner," she said.

"Yeah, my thoughts exactly," Simmons said. "I still can't believe that the man is a prominent engineer. I can't believe that it actually showed pictures of him standing along side Mayor Lee Brown and Governor Ann Richards. I wonder how much graft he had to come up with to get them to stand beside him long enough to take the picture."

"Maybe he just started acting the way he does after his wife was killed? That's a pretty traumatic event for anyone, to have someone that you love murdered like that. I don't know how it could not have an affect on a person," Little Twin reasoned.

"Maybe you're right," Simmons said. He stood and walked to the plate glass window at the front of the store and began staring at some imaginary object in the parking lot, his mind cluttered with thoughts. Little Twin could see the concerned look on his face and didn't want to leave without trying to help.

"There's something else eating on you, isn't there?" she asked.

"Yeah there is. I've been following this story about the Muslim killings for over six months in the newspapers. His wife was murdered roughly two-to-three months ago so if it's him, it wasn't the killing of his wife that set him off or made him crazy. I would guess this has been something that's been going on in his head for a long time. And another thing, I remember a couple of the articles talking about these beautiful paintings the cops found on the bodies of those he murdered, and how that these paintings were clues to the next murder he was going to commit. You know, like he planned these things weeks or maybe months in advance. Did this man, this Nizar Kheif, strike you as an artist?"

"I'm probably the last person in the world you'd want to answer that question. I don't have an artistic bone in my body. I can't even make Indian trinkets with the instructions in front of me. But you can. Anyone who can make a hunting knife a thing of beauty the way you do knows something about art," she said.

"Would you mind turning that computer back on?" Simmons asked.

"Did you remember something?" she said, punching buttons on the computer's tower.

"Maybe, I don't know. You were scrolling through everything so fast; it could be nothing. Go back to the articles we were looking at. Start from the beginning and go slower this time. There was a picture or a painting of one of the bridges that he was the lead engineer on.

I've seen that bridge myself and I've crossed it, I just can't remember where or when. I know it was one of those bridges with the cables coming down and attaching to the sides of the bridge, like that one out in San Francisco," he said.

"You mean the Golden Gate Bridge?"

"Yeah, that's the one. There's a technical name for those type bridges, but I don't remember what they're called," he said.

Little Twin clicked on a dozen articles before she stopped on one entitled: "The Highway 146 Suspension Bridge Spanning the Mouth of the Ship Channel". As she scrolled through the press release they both read silently.

"That's it. That's the one I remember now, keep going. Somewhere in this article is a huge photograph or a painting of the bridge. And if I remember correctly it was one of those artist renderings of what the bridge is going to look like when it's complete."

It took several moments to find the painting, then like a miracle the image lit up the screen in front of them. It was a professional photograph taken of the painting setting on a display easel, with a young, smiling Nizar Kheif standing along side looking like the proud parent of his latest creation. Redhawk Simmons couldn't take his eyes off the painting.

"Can you make this bigger?" he asked.

"Sure." Little Twin moved the mouse and clicked several buttons on the keyboard.

"That's almost it. Can you enlarge just the bottom right-hand corner of the painting, to be more specific?"

"I think so. This is not the greatest computer in the world but I think I can do it," she said, twisting her lips as she moved the mouse from place to place.

When the name Nizar Kheif appeared as the painter's signature, Simmons backed away from the computer screen as if he'd seen a ghost. When he finally spoke, Little Twin could clearly see that the signature had shaken him.

"Can you make a copy of that signature, and also a copy of the full screen showing Kheif standing beside the painting? I've got to show this to the cops. For months I've had a feeling about this guy, and now I have proof that he's the killer. I, I have to get this to the cops before he kills again. God only knows what this man is planning to do next. He has to be stopped. I knew he was the one, I just knew it," Simmons said, pacing around the computer.

"Look, Redhawk, you could be over reacting here. I'm no lawyer but I think this is what's called circumstantial evidence. It may mean nothing. It doesn't make him a killer just because he's also an artist. It doesn't make him anything. I agree the man's a creep, but that doesn't make him a killer either."

"No, I want you to listen to me. Every man that's been killed has been killed with a very sharp knife. The paper said that on more than one occasion that the men's heads were almost severed from their bodies. It takes an extremely sharp weapon to do something like that. Then, like clockwork the next day after he's murdered someone, he brings his knife in to be sharpened. Fate and coincidence is one thing, this is no coincidence. Listen to me Little Twin, the paper said that the killer was an artist. What are the odds that this man just happens to be a great artist? You're right, he's a creep alright, and he's also a stone cold killer."

"So you're going to call the cops?"

"I wish I knew the name of that big black guy at the police station. I'm sure I heard Kheif call him captain."

"Didn't two Houston cops come up here with those two cops from Louisiana? Do you remember either of their names?"

"No, but I've got one of their cards around here somewhere. Now I remember. It was that woman cop. She gave me her card the second time she was here. All I've got to do is find it." Simmons took the two printed pictures from Little Twin and hurried through the swinging door to his workshop.

Ross Clayton breathed a sigh of relief when the Mullah, Abdul Haq Jarrah open the gate and allowed them to enter the grounds and Mosque. The only stipulations made by the Mullah was, that they wait until after the Maghrib 6:05 prayer service, and that Detective Stillwell wear a covering over her head while anywhere in the compound.

The entourage entering the Mosque included four members of the Crime Scene Investigation Unit, Harris County Medical Examiner, Carlin Belichec and his assistant, Clayton and Stillwell, and two uniformed officers for support, in case things got out of hand. Clayton glanced back over his shoulder at Captain Rosen who was standing across the street with the SWAT Team, giving him an uncertain smile as he went through the gate.

They were ushered quickly through the main room of the Mosque that was used for prayer and into a hallway leading to a number of offices, restrooms and classrooms. The hallway was lined with shelves containing books and pamphlets of Muslim literature. The Mullah stopped in front of a closed door then moved away from the opening as if he had second thoughts on being the first person to enter the room.

"If you don't mind, I'll wait out here," he said.

"Has anyone moved anything or touched the body in any way?" Clayton asked.

"No. Everything was just as it was when we called you, and the body has not been touched. It was plain to see that the Imam was dead. There was no need to touch the body." Just as Clayton was about to open the door he felt the Mullah's hand on his shoulder.

"Because of our customs, we ask that the body be released to us as-soon-as possible. We want to send the body home for burial. Also, we ask that there be no further desecration of the Imam's body in the form of autopsy. This man is from Jordan and we wish to make arrangements for his flight home without any further delay."

"Sir, according to our laws, every homicide victim has to undergo autopsy. It's the law, and that's mandated by the State of Texas. The only way that the law can be circumvented is with written permission from the District Attorney here locally, along with written permission from the State's Attorney Generals office in Austin. Neither I, nor Detective Clayton have anything to do about that," Carlin Belichec said.

"I will have our attorneys speak with these people in the morning," the Mullah said and quickly moved away.

There was nothing special about the office. On the floors was a light green Berber carpet, heavy drapes of the same color covering side-by-side windows behind an oversized desk, several chairs in front of the desk, and bookcases on two walls filled with books, two metal file cabinets to the right of the desk and windows, and a private restroom to the right of the entrance door. When the last of the team was in the room Stillwell closed the door.

Clayton stopped at the foot of the body and gave the room a quick glance. The Imam was wearing an expensive tailored, gray pinstriped suit, and a white polished cotton dress shirt. He was laying face down on the floor beside the desk. A crimson bloodstain surrounded the man's head, and there was noticeable blood spatter on the bookcase and on the floor in front of the bookcase four feet away. But aside from that, and the gaping slit of the man's throat, everything appeared to be perfectly normal in the room. There was no sign of a struggle and nothing was out of place. And from a cursory examination of the windows and door there was no tampering of any kind with the locks.

Belichec and his assistant went to work recording body temperature, examining the man's extremities, and checking blood lividity. The Crime Scene Investigators began dusting for prints, bagging hair samples from the floor, and swiping blood samples from the body, bookcase and floor. Clayton and Stillwell took notes of everything happening in the room and everything they observed.

"This man's been dead twenty to twenty-one hours," Belichec said after a while, breaking the silence in the room. "He was also killed here, the body hasn't been moved."

"Any reason to believe he was involved in a confrontation or a struggle?" Stillwell asked.

"In my opinion, there was no struggle at all. His fingernails are cleaner than mine, and there's no noticeable bruising or marks that would be consistent with struggle anywhere on the man's body. There is some bruising on his forehead but I believe it came as a result of the fall when he hit the floor. I'd say that the attack came from someone the Imam knew. And I believe it came as a total surprise. He was probably talking to his killer one minute and the next minute he was dead," Belichec said. Belichec and his assistant began unfolding a dark green body bag next to the Imam's body.

Clayton walked to the door to speak with the Mullah, but he wasn't there. Just as Clayton took a few steps down the hallway, the man suddenly appeared looking quizzically at Clayton.

"Do you keep a log of people coming and going? Or more to the point, did the Imam have an appointment log that he might have kept?

"Nothing that I would know about."

"Do you have any ideas or recollect who might have been talking to the Imam between ten and twelve o'clock last night?" Clayton asked.

"The Imam wasn't a permanent resident of this facility. He was visiting relatives here, and decided to stay for a while on other business. Of course we were glad to have someone as distinguished as the Imam visiting with us. We afforded him the use of this office and access to our classrooms. It was my understanding that he would be returning to his home in Jordan in a few weeks, when he was finished with what he was working on here."

"And what was the Imam working on?" Clayton asked.

"I don't know."

"You don't know, or you won't say?" Clayton said.

"I don't know, and if I did know I would not be at liberty to reveal that information to you or anyone else. The Imam was very private. I did not involve myself in his business; if that's what you're asking."

"Like I said, we believe that the Imam was killed between ten and midnight last night. We're looking for leads to anyone who may have committed this murder, and we need your help. Do you know of anyone who may have been at odds with the Imam?"

"I have no idea," the Mullah said, allowing his gaze to drift from Clayton's face.

"Did the Imam usually work late hours, or see people late at night?" Clayton asked, attempting to make eye contact with the Mullah again.

"Personally detective, I'm usually in the bed shortly after evening prayers, always before ten-thirty. We do have students that occasionally work late.

The library is always open and people study late, I'm sure you can understand that. The Imam's after-hours activity was never part of my concerns. We considered it an honor to have him visit us. If he had a secular agenda or something outside of Mosque's affairs, I wouldn't know about it, and I had no reason to care."

Clayton held up his hand and backed away from the Mullah as if to tell him to not to leave just yet. He moved back to the door and asked Belichec if any personal affects were found on the body of the Imam. Belichec pointed in Stillwell's direction, she was making an itemized list of everything they'd found on the Imam's body.

"We've got a wallet with credit cards, Jordanian identification papers and passport, driver's license, a fair amount of money in US dollars and Jordanian currency, a gold Cross pen, a gold wrist watch, handkerchief, a set of keys and a comb. There's nothing else. His watch is an expensive Rolex, and there's well over a thousand dollars in cash, so I doubt robbery was a motive," Stillwell said.

"Do me a favor, Leona. Run his passport through the FBI, Customs, and Interpol. See if you turn up anything," Clayton whispered.

Clayton closed the door behind him and moved back to where the Mullah was standing. He stood quietly for several seconds as if contemplating what to say next and how to say it.

"I want you to know that I'm not overly concerned with what went on here today. I'm not concerned with a few cars being set on fire or a few houses for that matter. All of that will be sorted out in time by inspectors from the Arson division of the fire department and Captain Rosen. What I'm concerned with is the death of this Imam. Now I guess that I can understand, at least on some levels, your reluctance to help us. But with, or without your help, we're going to get to the bottom of this crime; I want you to know that. Now I'm going to ask you one more time for your cooperation."

"What is it that you expect of me, Detective Clayton?"

"I expect a little more cooperation than what I've been getting. If I have to, I'll fingerprint and interrogate every man and woman inside these walls, and it won't be a pleasant experience. It'll mean shutting down the facility with armed guards everywhere. I can assure you that you're not going to like what I'm thinking about. I'm also sure that you don't want to be a suspect; but right now you're the only suspect I've got."

"You've got to be out of your mind," the Mullah said. "Muslims don't kill other Muslims in holy places. An outsider committed this crime. My guess is that it was a Jew; this town is crawling with Jews.

"That leads me to another question then. Aside from the contingent of American and non-Muslims in the Mosque at the moment, how many non-Muslims or Jews have ever been in here?" Clayton asked.

"I don't know," the Mullah said, dismissing the question.

"Let me tell you what we know as of right now. There was no forced entry, so the killer had to walk through that door. There are no signs of a struggle, not even a little. The Imam didn't put up a fight for his life. He was talking to his killer before he was attacked, and he was absolutely unaware that his life was in any danger. We believe that he knew the man who took his life, and that he spoke with him regularly. That tells me that he wasn't an American and certainly not a Jew. So, I'll let you make the call. In one hour, I'll have five hundred, heavily armed men here to commandeer every corner of this facility and shut it down, if that's what you want. Or, you can help me to find this man's killer, and help us stop him before he kills anyone else. What's it going to be?"

The Mullah folded his arms, and for the longest time seemed to ignore Clayton's stare and his questions. Then with a noticeable hesitation, he turned and moved closer to Clayton's side and began to whisper.

"After the evening prayers and reading, when I was leaving the Mosque, just as I crossed the street, I noticed a man sitting in his car just to the right of the entrance. The man was waving his arms through the air as if he was having a heated conversation with someone else in the car. But the closer I got, I realized the man was talking to himself. There was no one else in the car." The Mullah lowered his head as if he were ashamed for what he was about to say next.

"Go on," Clayton said.

"I had seen the same man earlier, talking with the Imam." "What time was this?"

"Around 9:45. But I saw him leaving the Mosque and crossing the street to his car shortly after that, so I assumed his business with the Imam was complete and he was going home. That is, until I saw him just sitting in his car."

"Did you see the man leave his car and go back into the Mosque?"

"No. When I reached Westview Drive, he was still sitting there across from the Mosque. I did not see him go back into the Mosque."

"You know this man, don't you?" Clayton asked.

"No, I can't," the Mullah looked away from Clayton's glare.

"What's the man's name?"

"I hope you understand that this is very difficult for me. These people depend on me, and I do not wish to betray their trusts. I should have waited to see what this man was going to do, but I just wanted to go home. I haven't been feeling well for some time. I just needed to rest. I swear the thought of a crime being committed never crossed my mind, especially not a crime against the Imam. I just never thought," the Mullah never finished the sentence.

"I need a name," Clayton said impatiently.

The Mullah palmed his face with his hands, turning his back to Clayton. The Mullah began to cry. Clayton's reaction at first was one of disbelief, since the Mullah had seemed so indifferent to the investigation.

"It's apparent to me that you know this man. You have my word that he will never know that I got the information from you," Clayton said.

"I've known for more than five years that this man was moving closer and closer to the edge of insanity. Something happened to him mentally. Something snapped. He began to hear voices from Allah. He would complain that there was a war going on in his head, and that he couldn't sleep. He said that God was commanding him to kill infidels and those who had strayed from the faith."

"We think this man has committed as many as ten murders to date. Give me his name and we can put a stop to this. We can get the man some help and stop the killing," Clayton pled.

Without saying another word, the Mullah whispered softly in Clayton's ear; "the man's name is Nizar Kheif."

When Richey Sneed awoke, he was disoriented and confused, and the pain in his chest stabbed him like a dagger. In the early morning darkness, he could sense the presence of someone setting near him. He could hear the sound and feel the warmth of a crackling fire somewhere near his feet. But the weirdness didn't stop there. There was music coming from a radio or a tape player.

The song that was playing was an old country and western song sung by, Jonny Cash and Waylon Jennings. The song was called; "There Ain't No Good Chain Gang". He listened to the words of the last stanza of the song.

"There ain't no good in an evil hearted woman, And I ain't cut out to be no Jesse James,

And you don't go writing hot checks, down in Mississippi, And there ain't no good chain gang."

Suddenly the music clicked off as he tried to sit upright and see what was happening, but the pain in his chest clawed at him until he was once again flat on his back. What happened next was more than surreal.

In the quiet early morning, a deep soothing voice began speaking to him, and for a moment he wasn't sure if he was dreaming or hallucinating, or both. Then he realized it was neither.

"I wouldn't try to get up just yet, if I was you," the deep voice said, from somewhere near the fire.

Richey's first thought was that it was the voice of some cop that had been trailing him throughout the night. But why would a cop build a fire? And why on earth would a cop be sitting around playing music on a manhunt? The answer to both questions was simple. They wouldn't.

"You're in bad shape, Richey. You just lay there and give me a chance to think," the voice said.

Richey tried to command his eyes to focus, but his vision was blurred, and he couldn't take his mind off the stabbing pain in his chest. With every breath the pain seemed to worsen, and the vicious pounding in his head took away any chance for rational thought. He wanted to heed the man's voice and lay still, but after a while he felt compelled to speak.

"I hope you're finished thinking, Mister. I'm hurt real bad, and I'm so thirsty I can hardly talk. Who are you, and how do you know my name?" Richey managed to ask.

"I know who you are. I know all about you. I know you're hurt, you're hungry, and you're dehydrated. You've probably swallowed some water from the channel, and Lord only knows what parasites you've gotten from that. No, I suppose you're fairly close to death. But you must be quiet for a few more moments while I decide what to do with you," the voice said.

"What to do with me? What's going on? How come my eyes won't focus? What are you doing over there? I know you're not a cop. Are you planning on killing me?" Richey continued to ramble.

"No, I ain't a cop, you're right about that. I'm not here to rob you or to hurt you in any way. If I was of a mind to do something like that, I would have already latched on to that wad of C-notes you got sticking out of your pockets. What I'm trying to do is to decide whether I should help you or not. I don't want this to be a bad mark against me. I want to do the right thing by you, without violating my conscience. The Lord knows you're a fugitive. I know you're a fugitive. I don't want to get myself in trouble with God. Do you understand what I'm saying to you here?"

For some reason, the man's words seemed to have a calming affect on Richey Sneed, and somehow ease the suffering he was going through. All of his worries seem to dissipate with the sound of the man's soothing voice, and whatever it was that the man was thinking about was okay by Richey.

Maybe it was what the man said, or how he said it that led Richey to put his trust in this man with the deep voice. Whatever it was, he realized that he was pretty much at the mercy of the man, and he certainly wasn't going to be much good on his own. Several moments passed before the man spoke again.

"I've decided to help you, Richey," the deep voice said. "I've got a doctor friend over in Orange who can help you, if I can keep you alive long enough to get you there."

"What made you decide to help me?" Richey asked.

"Aside from differences in our ages, which are obviously considerable, you and I are a lot alike. In my younger days I was quiet a boxer. Not good enough for the big time, or for the big purses. So, when I wasn't boxing, I made my living at being a thief. The truth is I was never much good at that vocation either."

"In 1959 I broke into a house in Baytown to see what I could find. What I didn't know was that the owner was at home in the bed, sick with the flu. He caught me in the kitchen going through his refrigerator and tried to kill me with a frying pan."

"I can guess what happened next," Richey said.

"I hit the man one time. He fell backwards and busted his head on the stove as he went down. I tried to stop the bleeding but the man died right there on the floor of his kitchen before I knew what happened. I spent the next 30 years of my life up in Coffield Prison, in Anderson County, for manslaughter. I made myself a promise, that if I ever got out of prison, I'd never hurt another soul as long as I lived. I walked out of Coffield prison in 1989, and I've tried to live up to that promise ever since; I'm eighty-four years old now and ain't much good for nothing no more. But, I can still help folks when they need it, and I recon you could use a little help right now."

"What's your name," Richey asked.

"Frederic Remington Palmer. My mother had a thing for artists. She liked the old west paintings by Remington and named me after him. Can you imagine a black child growing up with a name like that among all these Texas rednecks? Needless to say, I learned to fight at an early age."

"I'll bet you did, Mister Palmer. So, what's your plan for getting me to Orange?"

"My old truck is parked down by the ferry dock. I suspect we better get going so we can get out of here before the sun comes up. This place is going to be crawling with traffic in a few more hours."

CHAPTER *14*

Clayton and Stillwell were already at the station when Delores Rucker called at five a.m. Stillwell answered Rucker's call with a question. "Did you get any sleep?"

"A little. I left downtown at ten-thirty. Everyone was so exhausted and frustrated from not finding the car; it just didn't make much sense in searching for something in the muddy water and pouring rain. How about you, did you get any sleep?" Rucker asked.

"Not much, but that doesn't seem to have a lot of importance right now. All I want to do is take this killer off the streets; that will make it all worthwhile. We left the Mosque just before midnight and worked for another hour setting up our team for this morning. By two o'clock we had all the warrants signed so we got a couple of hours at the station," Stillwell said.

"You know, Cromberg and I interviewed this guy at the hospital after his wife was murdered. He was a total ass. He said that he only wanted to talk with Captain Gorman. I tried telling the man that Gorman was in no shape to help him and that we were working as hard as we could, but he wouldn't listen. At the time I thought he was being so obstinate because of his wife's murder. I have to admit I never would have made him for the Impressionist murderer. What time is everything going down this morning"?

"In a couple of hours. We want to have everybody in place by seven. What about you? When are you going back downtown?"

"We're supposed to meet between seven and eight. We've got two more divers coming to help expand the search. I'm confident we'll find them this morning."

"What's your gut feeling? Do you think they got out of the car?"

"I don't know, Leona. Those two have been pushing the envelope for a long time. Sooner or later your luck runs out. Maybe it's fate or maybe God just gets to a point where he says enough is enough. To answer your question, if they got out of the car they made it a long ways down the bayou. We had teams of cops with dogs walking the banks for at least five to six miles down stream. They never found as much as a track coming out of the water. I think they're still in the car. Maybe we'll get lucky and wrap both of these cases up by noon," Rucker said.

"I hope so. I'm beat. I haven't had a goodnights sleep since I left New York City. I need a break. You be sure to call me as soon as find the car."

"Will do. Hey, you be careful this morning too. By the way, are you and Clayton going to get cozy when this is over?"

"D Rucker, I can't believe that you asked me that. What makes you think Ross Clayton is interested in me?"

"Because I saw the way he looked at you when you were asleep in his car. I may have been born at night, but it wasn't last night. He's got the hot's for you baby; just like you got the hot's for him. There ain't neither one of you fooling me. Hey, I think it's great. I just wish he had a brother."

"Look D, you keep what you know to yourself. I don't want this floating around the department that we've got this thing going on. It could create some problems down the road for both of us, and I don't want that to happen," Stillwell said.

"Okay Misses Jones, your thing is safe with me, but I want all the juicy details when it happens," Rucker said.

"You ain't right, girl. I mean you have to know that you ain't right," Stillwell said, she could hear Rucker laughing on the other end of the line. I'll talk to you when this is over."

"Be cool and be safe. I'll call you as soon as I know something on my end," Rucker said, and disconnected.

It was raining hard when Redhawk Simmons trotted from the back door of his cottage to the rear of his store and let himself in. Five minutes later he was placing a call to Delores Rucker who had accompanied the two Louisiana Detectives to his workshop. Rucker answered on the first ring.

"This is Detective Rucker," she said sharply.

"I don't know if you remember me or not, my name is Redhawk Simmons. I know it's very early in the morning, but I need to talk with you."

"I do remember you. You're the man who makes hunting knives. We interviewed you in Livingston with the cops from Louisiana, right?"

"Yes."

"What can I do for you Mister Simmons?"

"I know who that killer is. The guy that's been killing those Muslim men around the city."

"Okay. Why don't you tell me what you know," Rucker said.

"I know who he is because I've been sharpening his knife every time he kills someone. Somehow that didn't come out right," Simmons said aloud. "I'm kind of nervous," he explained.

"Don't be nervous. Take your time and get it right. Now, does your suspect have a name?" Rucker asked.

Simmons fished the piece of paper from his front pocket, unfolded it, and read the name distinctly. "It's Nizar Kheif," he said plainly. When he said the name, Nizar Kheif, it got Rucker's attention immediately.

"Okay, assuming for a moment that you're not his accomplice, what's led you to this conclusion?" Rucker asked.

Simmons spent the next ten minutes telling Rucker his story. From his description of the unusual knife, to Kheif's background and painting ability, the evidence fell into place like a jigsaw puzzle. He tried to explain his reluctance to bring the evidence to their attention before now, but it sounded more like a case of resentment of authority, than an excuse for waiting so long to say something.

"What made you decide to give us all of this information now?" Rucker asked. For a moment, there was silence on the other end of the line.

"My history with the police has not been a good one. The fact is I've spent a good part of my adult life behind bars. I've made a lot of mistakes, but people do change, and I've found a good and decent woman that loves me, even with my past. I just want to give her a good life and be the kind of man she deserves. That's why I'm calling. I think Kheif is a brutal killer, and I think he needs to be stopped."

"I think you've made some good choices this time, Mister Simmons, and I appreciate you sharing this information with us. It just so happens that we're bringing Kheif in for questioning this morning. Can I call you at this number if we need you?"

"Sure. I'll be waiting for the call. I want to help," Simmons stopped before he finished his thought.

There was something in Simmons' voice that led Rucker to believe he had something else he wanted to say but maybe didn't know how to say it, or how to ask the question that was on his mind. "Was there something else you wanted to say?" Rucker asked.

"When things quiet down and you catch this guy, I'd like to speak with you again, privately?"

"Sure. After we settle this thing with Kheif we'll get together. Is that okay?"

"That will be fine, Detective Rucker. Please call me if there is anything I can do in the mean time."

"Thanks, Mister Simmons, we'll be in touch."

Redhawk Simmons hung up the phone and stood there for a moment looking out the window at the rain pelting the flowers that Renee had planted in the back yard. He missed her, and it felt odd. For the last few nights she'd been staying with a woman from the reservation who was receiving cancer treatments at MD Anderson hospital. It was the first time since she'd moved in with him that they had been apart for more than a day. He missed her, and it was a strange new feeling, since he'd never missed anyone in his life.

There was one other thing he had to do and he wasn't looking forward to it. He had to tell Renee that he'd lied about killing Snake Lopez that night on the gambling boat. In his mind, he had no choice in the matter. It was either stop Lopez from raping and killing the woman or act like nothing was happening. She had to understand that he had no other options but to stop Lopez. There hadn't been a lot of time to think things over when it was going down, not to mention that Lopez had no intentions of leaving him alive when he was done with the woman. She had to understand, he thought.

The wind was blowing out of the north and whipping the rain into sheets as officers from the HPD Tactical unit surrounded the home Nizar Kheif. Additional squad cars blocked any access to the street at Aldine Mail Route. Captain Gorman stood at the door of his Lincoln making a circular motion in the air with his hand, indicating that the operation was on. Everyone assumed his or her positions as an officer with a ramming tool bashed the in the front door.

Six members of the Bravo SWAT team were the first through the front door and into the house. Clayton and Stillwell were only steps behind. Nothing in their training or experiences on the force, could have prepared them for what they were about to find.

Kheif's mother was the first body found in the living room. The television was on casting a scant light on her body and the rest of the room. The sound on the set was muted and the house was silent.

Kheif's mother was reclining in a leather chair; her eyes were glazed over and staring listlessly at the ceiling. Her throat had been cut and her robe and the carpet around the chair were saturated with her blood. The fingernails of both of her hands were dug into the leather fabric of the recliner as if the pain and shock she had endured was more than she had ever known. A foreboding dread fell over the team as they silently moved into the hallway. Though no one said a word, every member of the team knew what was coming next.

There were no closed doors on the hallway. It was as if each door had been left open intentionally to save the cops' time. There was death in every room. The two younger girls were slaughtered in the first bedroom, while the oldest of the girls was alone in the next room down the hallway. Her throat had been cut like the others.

No one said a word, but every last cop in the house silently prayed that they would find Kheif in the last bedroom with a bullet hole in his temple, but it didn't happen that way.

Lights were coming on all over the house. Ross Clayton reached back for Stillwell's hand, but she wasn't there. He turned and walked back to the room where the two younger girls had been murdered. He heard one of the SWAT team vomiting in the back bedroom.

Clayton found Stillwell sitting on the edge of the bed staring at the dead children, tears dripping from her chin. Clayton's eyes scanned the room; blood seemed to be on every surface. Stillwell inadvertently jumped when Clayton gently placed his hand on her shoulder.

"I'm sorry, Leona, I didn't mean to startle you. Why don't we go outside for a moment? I think we could both use some fresh air. I think even the rain would be a welcome relief from this."

"Why, Clayton? Why kill the kids?" she cried.

"I wish I had an answer," he said. Clayton had no more than spoken the words when he heard running in the hallway.

Burt Cameron stopped at the doorway to the room where Clayton and Stillwell were talking. The look on his face was one of terror and duress.

"Clayton, we have to get out of here now. The whole place is wired with explosives. We have to get out now, he yelled."

Clayton looked at Stillwell who seemed to be in a malaise because of the children. He slipped his arm beneath her legs and back, lifting her in one fluid motion and heading for the door. He made it to the front door and took four steps onto the front lawn when the house exploded behind them. The force from the blast hurled them both into Gorman's Lincoln, forty feet away.

They both fell to the ground, bleeding and unconscious.

The carnage from the explosion looked and sounded a lot worse than it could have been. The entire front of the wood-framed home lay in shattered pieces on the front lawn and in the street. Shards of glass from the front windows had caused most of the injuries. Because Clayton was carrying Stillwell away from the blast, she was the least affected by the flying glass and wood debris. Everyone who watched the explosion take place was amazed that the remainder of the house wasn't engulfed in flames as a result of the blast. But only one small blaze coming from the kitchen was all that could be seen.

Stillwell had been momentarily knocked unconscious when she was thrown headlong into the front fender of Gorman's Lincoln. Clayton lay face down, unmoving, his head partially under the body of the Lincoln. The back of his bulletproof vest was pelted with glass shards and pieces of splintered pine from the siding and wall studs that had been hurled through the air like shrapnel.

A few of the projectiles had stuck in Clayton's neck, buttocks, and the back of his head, and he was bleeding from all of them. But the bulletproof vest had saved his life, because one of the larger pieces of flying splintered wood had caught him squarely in the back. It was that blow that had knocked the breath from his lungs and caused him to release his grip on Stillwell, sending her flying through the air and into the front fender of Gorman's Lincoln.

Several members of the SWAT team had suffered similar injuries, but only two were considered to be life threatening. Wade Gorman had almost no injuries at all because he'd dove head first into the back seat of the Lincoln when he heard someone yelling about the bomb. It was his quick reaction to the blast, in calling emergency services that had the sound of multiple ambulances screaming in the distance toward the scene.

The pouring rain woke Stillwell in a matter of seconds. When she opened her eyes she saw Gorman trying to pull Clayton from beneath the car without dragging his face on the concrete and inflicting more damage. She quickly placed her hands under Clayton's face and motioned for Gorman to pull. Stillwell took off her jacket and placed it under Clayton's face.

"He's bleeding everywhere," she yelled to Gorman, the ringing from her ears drowning out the sound of her own voice.

"I see that. We can't turn him over, but we can cover him up. There's a blanket in my trunk. We've got to keep him from going into shock. Can you get it?" Gorman asked, handing her the keys. Stillwell took the keys and headed for the trunk.

For the next ten minutes the scene was one of cops applying whatever first aid they had to their fallen comrades. It wasn't until the ambulances arrived that someone noticed that Kheif's mother and the recliner she had been in, had been thrown into the ditch across the street, almost twenty feet farther than anyone else. Her body was quickly covered by one of the paramedics.

It was 8:30 a.m. when one of the divers surfaced, swam to the fantail of one of the boats, latched onto a long braded cable and went back down again. Twenty minutes later a heavy-duty commercial wrecker was pulling the Cadillac onto the bank. As the front wheels left the bayou, two uniformed officers opened the front doors of the Cadillac and murky water gushed onto the ground.

Delores Rucker walked over and peered inside the car, she couldn't believe what she was seeing. The windshield, the right half of the front seat and the steering wheel were all gone, and Beverly Sneed was pinned to the back seat like a note on a dartboard. Rucker backed away from the Cadillac covering her eyes to shield them from the rain, her gaze scanning the opposite bank of the bayou for the limb or tree that had impaled Beverly Sneed to the back seat.

Then she saw it and began walking in that direction. It was over a hundred feet from where they pulled the car from the water. An enormous old Cypress tree stood at the water's edge on the opposite side of the bayou. The limb that jutted out over the bayou must have been at least a foot or more in diameter. From what was sticking out of the front of the Cadillac, and from what was left hanging over the bayou, it must have been thirty-foot long when they hit it, she thought to herself.

Rucker walked back to where the cops were standing, taking one last look at the broken limb. "I'm guessing the limb took out the windshield and rammed through Beverly Sneed instantaneously. She probably never knew what hit her," she said.

"I want this car taken back to the Forensics' Lab just the way it is," she told one of the officers standing there.

"Detective Rucker, I don't think anybody in the department is going to let us haul this car anywhere with that bloated woman's body impaled to the back seat that way. It just ain't right. And if I know Carlin Belichec, he's going to come unwound over a request like that," the uniformed officer said.

Rucker looked back up the bayou at the broken limb and shook her head. "Yeah you're probably right. I have to admit, I didn't give that much thought. Call Belichec and get him down here. I also want to get the dogs back down here. We've only have one body here; that means that there's still one in the water or somewhere else along the bayou. If Richey Sneed survived the crash he's got to show up sooner or later."

"Detective Rucker, I hate to be the lone dissenting voice here, but I don't think anyone could have survived a crash like that. I know that Richey Sneed's a tough guy, but if his body hit that steering wheel with enough impact to break it off the steering column; I promise you he's dead. He's probably caught on something at the bottom of the bayou. And as for bringing the dogs back out here in this rain, you know as well as I do it's a waste of time," he said.

Rucker looked calmly at the officer then looked straight up into a darkened sky allowing the rain to pelt her face. She had to admit that she had expected to find both of the Sneed's dead in the car. She hadn't thought it through, or expected to see Richey Sneed missing when they pulled the car from the water. She also knew that the smart patrol officer was most likely correct in his assessment of the whole situation. But he was young and way too cute. She just couldn't let it go without having the last word.

"What's your name," she asked calmly.

"My name is Jay Grimes," he answered.

"Well officer Grimes, no question you were right about Belichec, and you could be right about Richey Sneed being trapped on the bottom of the bayou, so I'll have the divers keep looking for his body. But if they don't bring his body up in the next eight hours, then you and I, and six of your closest friends from the department are going to walk the banks of this bayou from here to the San Jacinto Monument, or until we find something positive. Richey Sneed didn't just evaporate like a puff of smoke in the wind. Now, why don't you stand here on the banks and pray for the divers to find him by sundown. Because tomorrow morning, you and your fellow officers better have your walking shoes on," she said.

Rucker waited for Jay Grimes to say something else but he just stood there in the rain looking like a lost animal with no place to go. When Rucker's cell phone rang the officers around her quickly moved away. Rucker could see that the call was from Stillwell and answered it on the first ring.

"Did you catch the bastard?" she asked without saying hello. "You haven't heard anything, have you?" Stillwell asked. "No, but we found the Cadillac." "Are they dead?" Stillwell asked.

"Beverly Sneed is, and it's the most bizarre thing I've ever saw in my life." "So I take it that Richey wasn't in the car?"

"No. We think he's on the bottom of the bayou. We're going to start dragging the bottom with hooks to see if we can bring him up. My gut feeling is that he's dead. He hit the steering wheel so hard that he actually broke it off the steering column. We'll find him," Rucker said confidently. "So, what about you guys? Did you draw a blank on Kheif?"

Rucker stood quietly for several moments listening to Stillwell relay everything that had happened at Kheif's house. Rucker had learned through her work in the morgue to channel her emotions in other directions, or at the very least ignore them until she had moments of solitude and was away from her work as an assistant Medical Examiner. But today for some reason, the thought of Kheif's children being so brutally and senselessly murdered, affected her more than she wanted to admit or think about.

"So all you got is a bump on the head; that's good. Is Clayton going to be okay?" Rucker asked.

"The doctors are still working on him. He doesn't appear to have any internal injuries but he's going to have a boatload of stitches to deal with. D, you should have seen all the things sticking out of that man's backside. Thank the good Lord he was wearing his vest. He looked like something out of a Stephen King novel."

"How did you manage to escape with just a bump on the head?" Rucker asked.

"I was so shook up when we found those two little girls with their throats cut. I don't know. I've seen children murdered before, but for some reason this really got to me. I couldn't move. I just sat there looking at their poor little bodies. I never heard Burt Cameron say anything about the house being wired for explosives but Clayton did. He picked me up and started running for the front door. D, I don't understand any of this, why would the man kill his own children?"

"I don't know. If I knew the answer to that I'd be writing psychology books, but I do know one thing," Rucker said.

"Yeah, what's that?"

"Well, it's fairly obvious that the stakes have gone up now," Rucker said "What makes you say that?"

"The man just cut all of his remaining ties with reality, both literally and figuratively. He's murdered his whole family, walked away from his source of income, and destroyed his home. He has zero reason for living except to keep killing, and taunting us. This man just became public enemy number one in my book," Rucker said.

"That's comforting," Stillwell said.

"What hospital are you guys at?" Rucker asked. "We're still in the St. Luke's emergency room."

"I'm going to stay here until Belichec gets here, then I'll come down." "That might be quite a while; he was still at Kheif's house when the ambulance left with us."

"Well I'm sure they'll send someone else. I'll wait until they get here and then head your way. You take care of him Leona, because if you should decide that you don't want him, I'd like to be the next in line," Rucker said.

"It's a good thing we're good friends, otherwise I'd be all over your bony butt," Stillwell said. She could hear Rucker snickering on the other end.

"Okay, I'll be there in a couple of hours, but if they discharge him sooner give me a call. I'm really glad the both of you are alright," Rucker said, and disconnected.

Redhawk Simmons left his workshop just before noon and walked back to his cottage. He hadn't had a decent meal since Renee had been in Houston, but that was all about to change tonight, he thought. Renee had called earlier to say that she'd be home around four and for him to be ready for a special dinner for just the two of them. Before she hung up, she told him how much she'd missed him since she'd been away, and for some reason it made him feel special. For the first time in his life he felt like he was part of something greater than him self, and that everything had a sense of meaning and purpose to it.

He worked for twenty minutes straightening the cottage, sweeping the kitchen, and emptying the garbage. Then he turned on the television to watch the news at noon. It didn't take long for his festive mood to change dramatically.

The lead story began with an aerial view of a gutted home that had exploded earlier in the morning on the north side of town. Simmons recognized the area immediately. The reporter told how members of the HPD SWAT team, and several Homicide Detectives who were working on the Impressionist murder case had narrowly escaped the home, just seconds before it exploded.

The reporter continued by detailing what had happened the day before at the Mosque on Conrad Sauer Road, and that the murder of the Imam that had caused the disturbance there, had led the Detectives to the home of Nizar Kheif, who was a prime suspect in the death of the Imam. But now, he is also the number one suspect in connection with the Impressionist murders.

"I wish I could say that this was the end of the story and that Nizar Kheif was captured in the pre-dawn raid; but I'm sad to say that's not the ending we'd all hoped for. The Police did not find Nizar Kheif in his home, what they found was shocking and awful," the lady reporter said. Simmons adjusted the volume up and moved to the edge of his chair.

Without skipping a beat the woman reporter went on to talk about the murder of Nizar Kheif's three children and his mother, and that he was suspected in their killings as well. "He was nowhere to be found," she said. The woman ended the report with a sentence that shook Simmons to his core. "Kheif's mother and all three of the children had had their throats cut while they slept," she said solemnly.

An undeniable shroud of guilt enveloped Simmons as he watched the lifeless, covered bodies of the children being carried away on stretchers from the gutted home. He couldn't ever remember wanting to cry so badly at anytime in his life, but this was more than he could stand. "You bastard," he yelled out loud. "Why didn't I stop you a month ago? I should have killed you myself," he ranted. The grief and self-imposed shame was more than he could deal with. He slowly covered his face with his hands and wept like a child.

The light in the room was extremely bright. Richey Sneed wanted to shield his eyes from the light but for some reason he couldn't move his arms more than an inch or two in any direction. He had no idea where he was or even how he got there, for that matter. He closed his eyes and tried to think.

A few seconds later he could hear voices whispering in the distance, but he couldn't understand what the voices were saying. He could also hear music coming from somewhere, it seemed to be all around him and yet the volume was so faint that he could still hear the whispering above the sound of the music. It almost sounded like elevator music, he thought.

The room was very cold, and he had the sudden urge to urinate; and it wasn't going away. When he finally let it go he thought for sure that it would bring someone running to his side, but no one came. His mind began to wander and think of all sorts of possibilities. Had he just died in this strange place, he wondered? He couldn't be dead, he thought, because he could feel his fingers moving against what felt like starched sheets. He could also feel movement from his feet and legs; although he couldn't move them very far. Had Beverly slipped him some type of hallucinogenic drug? It wouldn't be the first time. Where was Beverly? Why wasn't she there beside him? If he knew Beverly Sneed, and he did, she wouldn't be far away if there were drugs to be had.

"Beverly," he called out. That was strange, he thought. He called out her name but he couldn't hear the words coming out of his mouth. What's happening to me? Am I deaf? Have I died? Why can't I hear what I'm saying?

Suddenly, a warm soft hand touched him on his forearm. The tiny hands felt so warm and wonderful. It had to be Beverly, he thought. No one else had ever felt the way she did. Her hands were always rose pedal soft and inviting.

"Mr. Smith, can you open your eyes for me?" the woman with the soft hands asked. She spoke with an accent that Richey thought he recognized, but he couldn't think of where he'd heard it before.

Why was this woman calling him Mister Smith? Where was he? Richey tried to think, but any cognizant thought came and went like an apparition. It was like a ride on LSD, he thought. He strained to open his eyes. Maybe everything would make sense if he could just open his eyes, and see the woman talking with him.

"Open your eyes, Mister Smith. We want to take your breathing tube out but we need to see if you can breathe on your own before we do," the woman said.

A wave of nausea swept over him like a warm breeze on an otherwise cold day. He tried to swallow the urge to vomit back into his throat but his gag reflexes took over, then suddenly it was over. The obstruction in his throat was gone, and the urge to vomit left him.

The woman ran her hand across his forehead then let it rest on his scruffy cheek. "I'll bet getting that breathing tube out of your throat feels better, doesn't it? Can you open your eyes for me, Mister Smith?"

"Why do you keep calling me Mister Smith?" Richey managed to whisper.

"Just open your eyes and look at me," the woman said.

Richey fought the sudden urge to drift off to sleep because the breathing tube was out of his throat and he felt so much better than before. He wanted to do what she was asking, but he couldn't push the right buttons. Finally he managed to open one eye and see the woman's face. It wasn't Beverly, but the woman was drop dead gorgeous. He had to be dreaming, he thought.

"How many fingers do you see?" the woman asked him.

"Two," he whispered.

"Okay, Mister Smith, I'm going to let you rest for a little while but I'll be back to check on you in an hour or so.

CHAPTER 15

It was Monday and a week had passed since the explosion. The massive manhunt for Nizar Kheif had yielded almost nothing. Nerves were on end. Even Muslims in the community were calling for this man's arrest, and wondering when the insane artist would strike again. His name was mentioned on every newscast and the HPD phone lines never stopped ringing with calls of his sighting in one part of town or another.

The fact that Nizar Kheif had vanished without a trace was a lot more than an enigma; it was an embarrassment to the department. The Mayor had even used the word "incompetence" in a phone call with Captain Gorman, and he took it about as personal as anyone could. Everyone, from the Chief of Police to the cops on patrol, was being questioned as to why the man hadn't been brought to justice. No one had any answers.

On Sunday night, after Stillwell had left for home, Ross Clayton checked himself out of the hospital, hailed a cab, and headed for home. He wanted to be the first one in the office on Monday morning to start digging for new answers. But he was surprised to see Stacy Cromberg and Stillwell drinking coffee at the situation room conference table, when he walked in just before seven. Both women stood when he walked in, looking at him as if a dead relative had just materialized to say hello.

"Clayton," both women yelled as he stood in the doorway. Stacy Cromberg was the first to move in his direction, hugging him tightly. Clayton grimaced at the hug. Then Stillwell stood a few feet in front of him with her hands firmly on her hips.

"I thought the doctors told you last night that you could go home on Wednesday? Is this Wednesday?" she said to Cromberg.

"This isn't Wednesday," Cromberg said with a half smile.

"No, this ain't Wednesday, and they didn't say you could come back to work either. You can't be coming in here all stitched up like a used football. I really worry about your mental capacity to pay attention to instructions, Clayton," Stillwell said, and then hugged him too.

The table where the two women were setting was cluttered with papers and folders on the case. Also on the table where Stillwell had been setting was the painting taken from the body of Kheif's latest victim in San Antonio. Clayton Remembered seeing this painting on display in Paris.

The painting depicted a sidewalk café with tables, chairs, and people dining under a moonlit canopy of bright stars. The windows and entrances to the café had an orange colored glow and extended out over the sidewalk. People were strolling along the walkway and cobblestone streets.

"This is a recreation of a painting by Van Gogh. It was one of his most famous works. It's called, *Café Terrace at Night*. And if you had the original here beside it, I swear you couldn't tell the difference. I think you picked a good place to start," he told the women.

"It's all we have to go on," Cromberg lamented.

"Yeah, it is. But it's not enough; where do we look? This could be a scene from along the river-walk in San Antonio for all we know. Who's to say he didn't tie up all his loose ends here in Houston just to set up another rash of killings in San Antonio?" Stillwell said.

"How many sidewalk cafes do you think we have in Houston?" Clayton asked.

"Without really trying, I can think of ten or more," Cromberg said.

"There may be three or four times that many," Stillwell offered.

"How many are open at night?" Clayton asked. "And how many are regularly frequented by Muslims, or people of Arab decent. We're not looking for a sidewalk café for a bunch of Texas rednecks, this has got to be a classy place for dinner, and we're almost certain that the killing is going to take place at night."

"What are you thinking, Clayton?" Stillwell asked.

"I don't think this is going to happen in San Antonio. I think this is going to happen here, in a classy part of town, something high profile. A place like the Galleria, or somewhere on Westhiemer, or Montrose, or right here in the downtown area. And I think we need someone working the evening shifts at every one of these places. I know it's a stretch, but I've had a lot of time to think about this. He's going to do this right under our noses," Clayton said.

"Clayton, what about all the outlying areas like the medical center, Sugarland, Kingwood, The Woodlands and Clear Lake areas? And how many sidewalk cafes do they have at the Kemah Boardwalk, or in Galveston? This guy could be planning this murder anywhere within a hundred mile radius of Houston, not to mention San Antonio," Stillwell argued.

"Look, I don't know why he killed the guy in San Antonio. He could have tracked the guy all over Texas for all I know. I just know the guy wants to do this where we are. We're part of this game he's playing now. He's not going to New Orleans, or Kansas City to pull this murder, because he wants us evolved in the investigation. I think he wants to do it in Houston. And I think he wants to do it right under our noses," Clayton said.

Delores Rucker had left the bayou search party on Tuesday and went back to the Forensic Lab to work on the parts and pieces of Norbert Callaway's Cadillac, in an attempt to figure out exactly what happened in the accident. And contrary to what that good looking young officer had thought of her idea on hauling the car back to the lab with Beverly Sneed's body still in place, it was exactly what happened.

Once Carlin Belichec saw the size of the tree limb impaling Beverly's body to the back seat of the Cadillac, he ordered the limb cut off at the windshield and the car to be wrapped in a canvas tarp, and hauled as it was, to the Forensics Lab. He had made the statement to one of the patrol officers at the site, that this was one gruesome scene that was not going to be aired on the six o'clock news. Rucker wasted no time in giving Jay Grimes a twisted smile and a raised eyebrow at Belichec's orders.

For the next three days Rucker dissembled all the parts and pieces of the Cadillac, including the steering column that had been found by dragging the bayou bottom with hooks. On Friday, she found what she was looking for. There, trapped in the hard plastic cowling of the steering wheel cover, was a densely packed wedge of human issue that she unraveled like an accordion and placed on a white towel.

The swatch of tissue was over a half inch thick near the middle and was almost the size of her hand. In the center of the piece of tissue was the nipple that had been severed from Richey Sneed's chest. She wasted no time in performing DNA test to determine conclusively that the tissue belonged to Richey Sneed.

Now, she knew without question, that Richey Sneed had not escaped the accident unscathed, and that there was a good possibility, with that level of trauma, that he was dead. She tried to imagine the accident and the level of pain he must have endured when it happened. And, although much of it was conjecture on her part, she couldn't imagine him just walking away fromsomething so traumatic without serious medical attention.

Before she called Stillwell to tell her of her findings, she summoned four other members of the Forensics Lab to assist her in calling over forty hospitals in the greater Houston area to see if anyone had been seen or treated for injuries consistent with those suffered by Richey Sneed. The answer from all of them was, no. Finally they faxed over sixty photographs to emergency rooms and minor emergency clinics all over Harris County to see if he could be identified by facial recognition. The answer again was, no.

When Rucker called Stillwell late Friday night, Stillwell's questions ran the gambit of possibilities.

"How much blood would a person lose from an injury like that?" Stillwell asked.

"Well, a man's chest is not like a woman's breast, but there're still a lot of blood vessels there. My guess is he would have bled for as long as he was in the water or until he died," Rucker answered.

"Could he have bled-out from a wound like that had he not gotten medical attention?"

Well, there's no question that if he had enough trauma to his lungs, exsanguinations could have occurred. But from this wound alone, I don't know. I don't see it happening," Rucker said.

"So you think he's still alive?"

"I didn't say that. Richey Sneed was in fairly good physical condition, and if there were no other injuries, a wound like this alone would not have been fatal. But I don't see how that's possible. If he suffered any secondary trauma like a broken ribs or a cracked sternum he's most likely dead," Rucker said.

"Were the searchers able to turn up anything that would indicate that he come out of the water?"

"No, and we checked both sides of the bayou for more than ten miles and there was nothing. I know we had a lot of rain, but there should have been something, somewhere showing where he came out of the water," Rucker said.

"I know this is going to sound a bit wacky, but is there any chance that he could have latched onto a passing freighter and skipped the country, or showed up in another American city?" Stillwell asked.

"I guess anything is possible, but can you imagine the level of pain he would have had to endure pulling himself up a long ship's ladder and onto the deck?" I don't think it could have been done with part of the man's chest missing."

"Any reason to believe he could have made it all the way to the Gulf of Mexico?" Stillwell asked.

"Leona, it's got to be seventy miles to the Gulf. He would have had to be in the water for almost forty hours, maybe more, and with a bleeding chest wound. He couldn't have made it that far. He's either washed up in some bayou slough between here and Galveston or is tangled up on the bottom somewhere we haven't looked. We may never find him," Rucker lamented.

The Vietnamese nurse smiled when she saw Richey Sneed standing in front of the window in his room with the curtains drawn wide. The morning was clear, and a bright sun lighted the room with warmth and serenity. The nurse closed the door behind her.

"So, you must be feeling well today, Mr. Smith?"

When Richey turned and looked at the woman standing in the rays of bright light, the illumination of her white dress and lab-coat appeared almost surreal. He thought for a moment that he was looking at the seraph form of an angle.

Richey Sneed smiled back at the beautiful woman and lowered his head almost in reverence to her beauty. "You know my name is not Smith. Why do you insist on calling me that, when I told you my name is Richey Sneed?"

"Come; let me take a look at your skin grafts. Are you having any unusual pain today? You haven't asked for any pain medication in almost two days. What's up?" she asked.

"I don't want to be high anymore. Does that sound unusual to you, cause it does to me? I've been high in one form or another for the last five years of my life, so yeah it sounds a little weird to me," he joked.

"No. To me, that's a good thing; it means you're getting well. Lie down on the bed and let me take a look at your chest," she said.

"Can I ask you some questions?" he said, slipping into bed.

"I'm not sure if I'll have the answers you're looking for but sure, ask away."

Richey was quiet for a moment, lost in thought about the questions he'd had for days. He took her left hand, holding it gently in his hands; and she let him.

"I don't know where to begin. The last thing I remember was an old black man almost carrying me to his truck. I don't know where he came from, and I don't know why I haven't seen him since I've been here. Why would he help me and then leave me here? I don't even know where here is. And another thing, that's not as important; I remember having some money in my pockets when the old man came along. I remember him saying something about it. Did the old man take my money? And then there's you," he said, looking away for a moment.

"What about me?"

"I've never met anyone like you in my life. You're like no other woman I've ever known. Hell, I'm even worried about getting well, afraid I won't ever see you again. I've only known you for a couple of weeks and yet I can't think of what my life would be without you in it. I mean, my wife has only been dead for these few days and I loved her, I think. But whenever you're around it's like my life with her never existed. Things like this don't happen to people like me," he said.

"Why would you say that?"

"Cause it's true. I've been in and out of jail and in trouble most of my life. Now, this old man saves my life. He got me here, wherever here is. You people have worked miracles on my body. And knowing you for these past few days have been like something out of a fairy tale. I don't understand any of this. I've been on the wrong side of the law for so long that I can't remember ever being a decent person. Why is all of this being done for me when you all have to know I don't deserve any of it?" Richey said.

"Wow, you did have a lot of things on your mind," she said. "Where to begin…"

"Well, I know I'm not dead or in heaven, because my chest feels like someone took an ax to it. Especially when I roll over at night," he said.

"You're definitely not dead, and while you are an amazingly fast healer, you're far from being well. As for Remington, the old man that brought you in, I've never actually met him. But I do know that over the past five years, which is how long I've been here, he's brought a couple of people like you into the hospital."

"When you say people like me, do you mean people on the run, convicts, criminals, or what? And where are we? Can you tell me that?"

"You're in Orange, Texas. And this clinic is part of the Hermann Baptist Hospital. I understand that your friend, Remington and Dr. Thornton are, let's say, old acquaintances, and that the doctor does favors for Remington from time-to-time, with no questions asked. When Dr. Thornton uses the name Smith, or Jones, we always know that the patient is special, and that we're not supposed to ask questions. Oh, and about your money, nothing's happened to it. You'll get it all back when you leave here."

"You said earlier that I'm far from being well; what did you mean by that? Is something else wrong with me? I feel really good."

"We've given you a lot of antibiotics since you've been here, but your white blood cell count is still really high, which means you still have an infection somewhere, and that's a major concern to Dr. Thornton. So I'm going to be in your life for a while longer, whether you like it or not," she said with a smile.

"One more question and I'll leave you alone," Richey said.

"Ask away."

"Are you married, or seeing anyone?"

"No," she said. Her face lost all expression. "My husband and daughter were killed in a car accident two years ago. So in that respect, I'm just like you, I'm all alone," she said.

"What's your name?"

"You said one question; that's two. Maybe I'll tell you tomorrow," she said.

It had taken every ounce of courage that Redhawk Simmons could muster, but as soon as Renee walked through the door, he sat her down on the sofa and started to talk. He spent the next two hours telling her everything he could remember. When he finished telling her about his investigation of Nizar Kheif, and about how badly the murder of his family had affected him, he wasted no time in telling her the truth about what happened with Snake Lopez, on the gambling boat in Lake Charles.

Renee said very little while he was talking. In fact, she'd said nothing at all until he confessed to killing Snake Lopez, and she realized that he had been lying to her ever since it happened.

"I can't believe you didn't trust me enough to tell me the truth," she started. "I feel like getting up and walking out of here and never coming back, but I'm not, and I'll tell you why," she said.

"I didn't know what to do, Renee," he pleaded in defense of himself. Renee placed an index finger on his lips and told him to listen.

"I know that. I also know that this is your first relationship with someone other than a one-night stand. I know that this trust thing is all new to you. But you've got to understand where I'm coming from too. You want my trust? You want my understanding? I can't, and I won't give you either as long as you lie to me. I won't defend, and I won't love a liar; I can't. It's the difference between a relationship that works and one that doesn't. It's all about trust. I don't lie to you and you don't lie to me; it's the fabric and bond that any good marriage is made of, Redhawk," she said, with tears streaming down her face.

"We're not always going to agree. We're not always going to like something that the other one does, but that's life. We're grownups, we learn to adjust; but what we can never adjust to is something built on lies. Let me ask you a question. I've been gone for four days in Houston; do you think that I was seeing another man while I was there?"

"That thought never crossed my mind," he said.

"It never crossed your mind because you know I don't lie to you. It never crossed your mind because you trust me to be faithful. So we're going to make a choice right here and right now. You and I will not lie to each other now or ever. I won't enter into a marriage any other way because unlike you, I've been hurt before. I didn't like it then and I don't like it now."

"You have my word it will never happen again," he said.

Renee wiped the tears from her eyes and hugged him tightly, not only because she believed him, but also because she wanted to believe him. She knew how hard it must have been for a man like him to put himself through this in the first place. She also knew that this was probably the only time in his life that he'd ever apologized for anything. That, more than anything he said, made her feel special and for the first time in her life, truly loved.

The two of them continued to talk while they worked on dinner and never stopped until the dishes were cleaned and put away. They agreed on a plan of action and both were committed to stand and take whatever the law threw at them. But one thing was crystal clear, whatever happened they'd face it together and neither of them would ever be alone again, even if they were apart.

The cab driver glanced at the man in his rearview mirror and caught him looking at his license and identification card posted on the sun-visor. He seemed to have been staring at the information ever since he'd gotten into the car.

"Is everything okay?" the driver asked finally.

"I was just looking at your name, it's very unusual; Mutalib Peter Sulayman." The man pronounced the name Peter with an emphasis on the letter P. He made it sound disgusting, the driver thought.

"I am originally from Saudi Arabia, but I've been here for almost ten years now. I changed my name to Peter when I joined the Baptist faith. I am Christian now, and a legal citizen," the driver proclaimed proudly. The driver thought he saw the man scowl when he told him of his new name and newfound faith.

"Tell me Peter Sulayman, how does a man, especially an Arab, claim for himself a Jewish name? It seems that you've not only dishonored your family but Allah as well. How does one do such a thing and live with him self?"

"One does such a thing when he lives with freedom of religion. That's why I moved to this country. I wanted to be free to worship how I please. In America, no one cares what or how you worship, or, if you worship at all. In Saudi Arabia they cut off the heads of those they do not understand. You should learn to be a bit more tolerant if you're going to live in this country," the driver said indignantly.

"You can never go home. How sad that must be," the man said.

"It's not sad at all. I am at home, and there is no reason for me to ever go back to Saudi Arabia."

It suddenly dawned on the driver that this whole confrontation might have been instigated intentionally. He had read every article concerning the madman who was senselessly killing men of middle-eastern decent, because of their religion. But this man didn't look like the photographs he'd seen in the newspaper or on television. In fact this man looked much older than the pictures of the killer. This man's hair and beard were almost totally gray, he thought.

The driver made a right hand turn onto Main Street and came to a stop in front of the Hyatt Regency Hotel. He reached for the meter pulling down the flag. "The fare is $27.50," the driver told the man, without looking back to see his face.

Suddenly, the man in the back seat guffawed loudly, placing his hand on the Plexiglas partition behind the driver's head.

"I had you going, didn't I Peter?" This time the man pronounced the name Peter with dignity and kindness. "My whole family is Methodist," he said, laughing as he got out of the car. He handed the driver two twenties for the fare and told him to keep the change. The driver took the two bills looking at them incredulously.

"You did have me going," he said with a broad smile.

"I see from the stack of books in your front seat that you must be attending University here in Houston."

"Yes, I attend Rice University, it's a fine school. I'm an accounting major with one semester to go," the driver said proudly.

"That's wonderful, Peter. Allow me to buy your dinner some night. A friend of mine owns a restaurant over on Montrose, not to far from here, actually. Take this gift certificate and have anything on the menu. It's on me. It's the least I can do for giving you such a hard time."

The man handed the driver a white and blue envelope with a hundred-dollar gift card inside, for the Rose Garden Restaurant and Sidewalk Café, at 5454 Montrose.

"I remember when I was in University how difficult it was to have a good meal. Go by there any night you want. You can set under the stars; have a glass of fine wine and enjoy a meal on me. Be sure to ask for my friend Richard, he's the head waiter, and he will take good care of you."

The driver was standing outside the cab now, and smiling as if he had been handed the keys to the city. He reached for the man's hand shaking it vigorously.

"I will do that. I will see Richard, and thank you so much for your kindness. You sure had me going. Look, take my card, please. All you have to do when you call dispatch is ask for me. He will call me very fast. I will take you anywhere in the city, just say the word. What is your name so I'll know when you call?"

"My name is Anwar. You can remember that can't you, Peter?" he said pleasantly.

"I will never forget it, Anwar. You are my best fare ever."

The driver folded the envelope and pushed it into his shirt pocket. He knew just where the restaurant was too, but it had always been far too expensive for his wallet, but not now, he thought. Tomorrow night he'd dine in style and leave the sandwiches and fruit at home. He watched the man for a moment as he disappeared into the lobby of the hotel.

He didn't see the man dropping his business card into a wastebasket just inside the door of the hotel. He just stood there dreaming of the day when he would have enough money for such a noble jester to a total stranger had done with him.

CHAPTER 16

Maurice Couvillion leaned back in his oversized leather chair and reached for a cigarette. He was a gaunt man with prominent cheekbones, deep-set gray eyes, and a tanned complexion. And no matter how many times you were in his presence, he always seemed to be nervous or ill at ease with those around him. He had a habit of pacing the floors when he talked with people, but today, for some reason, he never left his chair.

"Redhawk, I want you and Renee to know that I don't have much sway with the Grand Jury here in Calcasieu Parish. I'm going to be in there with you, but this is not a trial, it's a hearing to determine if you'll be indicted or not." His eyes pinched shut when he lit his cigarette.

"Will Redhawk have to testify?" Renee asked.

"He'll have all the time he needs to tell his side of the story. Then they'll bring in the young lady that was raped and she'll tell her side of the story. If things go our way there won't be any trial, they'll just no-bill you and you can just go on about your business. You may have to do a little time or pay a fine for leaving the scene of the crime, but it could all just go away. What I'm trying to tell you, Redhawk, is that with a Grand Jury, you just never know what they're going to do. I just don't want you to be too disappointed if they return an indictment and we have to go to trial." He tapped his cigarette on the rim of the ashtray.

"I just want to put this behind me and get on with my life," Redhawk said. "If Redhawk has to go to prison, I guess it'll be someplace here in Louisiana?" Renee asked.

"We're not going to talk about that right now. If they return an indictment we'll have at least a year or two before this ever goes to trial, there's a huge backlog of cases right now already on the docket. And like I told you before, the DA on this case is a personal friend of mine. We went to LSU together, and we hunt ducks together. We both know that you didn't go to that casino to murder your friend." Couvillion crushed out his cigarette, leaned over the desk and drummed his fingers on the glass top.

"Look, this case is not a top priority; it went cold case shortly after the detectives questioned Redhawk over in Texas. The woman that was raped claims that the man that killed Lopez saved her life. And that's going to be our defense if it goes to trial; that he was fighting this man Lopez, in defense of this woman's life. The law in the State of Louisiana says that it's a justifiable use of force or violence, to intervene when another person's life is in danger. Certainly this woman's life was in danger."

Redhawk held Renee's hand remembering the fight that night on the gambling boat. He fought the urge to tell his story again, just to make sure that Couvillion understood exactly what happened that night. But he knew that the man was on his side and that anything else he had to say would have to wait for the hearing.

Maurice Couvillion stood up and put his hands in his pockets. He looked at Redhawk and Renee and smiled warmly.

"You folks go home now. Be back here Monday morning at eight-thirty. The hearing starts at nine. It's the fourteenth Judicial District Court, second floor Grand Jury Assembly Room. I can tell you right now, but you probably won't listen, so here it is anyway. It won't do either of you any good to worry about this hearing. We'll deal with whatever happens," he said firmly.

"What about the bad weather brewing out in the Gulf? Is there anyway the hearing could be postponed?" Renee asked.

"I suppose there's a possibility. Most people think it's going in around New Orleans. I've got your cell phone number and I'll be one of the first to know if the hearing is going to be canceled. I'll call you," he said, motioning toward the door.

He walked them to the door and shook their hands. The last thing he did before closing the door behind them was to wink at Renee and smile as if they'd fomented some special kind of bond between the two of them. Redhawk Simmons wanted to punch the man, but didn't.

Richey Sneed watched the weather report on television then went to the window to see if things outside were any different than they were the day before. The day was cloudy and overcast and the wind was out of the south and brisk enough for the flags on the poles outside his window to be flapping tightly.

There was a massive tropical storm brewing in the Gulf of Mexico. Reports had the tropical storm-making landfall on Monday, somewhere between Beaumont, Texas, and Biloxi, Mississippi. The tropical system had all the potential of being a killer storm. Lives along the Gulf Coast were about to be changed, including Richey Sneed's.

Just as he turned to go back to bed, the pretty Vietnamese nurse walked into the room pulling his chart from the holder at the foot of his bed. She seemed troubled or irritated, but he couldn't distinguish which. He thought he'd try something light hearted to change her mood.

"It's been a couple of days and you still haven't told me your name," he said.

"It's Jeanie, Jeanie Nguyen," she said without expression.

"What a nice name. It's great to finally know your name. Did I do something wrong? Is something troubling you?" Sneed asked.

The woman didn't answer his question. She was making a notation in his chart and never looked in his direction.

"If I've done something wrong, I can assure you it wasn't intentional. Have you been watching the news? It looks like we're going to be in for quite a ride with this storm headed for landfall. Do you think it will hit in the Beaumont area, or in Louisiana?"

The woman looked as if she were about to cry. She finished her writing in Sneed's chart and headed for the door.

"Wait," Sneed said. The woman turned abruptly and faced him. "Yes."

"You can't just come in here with tears in your eyes and leave without talking. What kind of person would treat a friend like that?"

"Is that what I am to you, a friend?"

"Well, yeah. But I think over the last couple of weeks it's been so much more than that," Sneed said. He turned and walked back to the window peering through the blinds almost as if he were trying to stall for time. Time to think; time to tell her what was on his mind and in his heart.

"I need to talk to you," she said with a desperate look on her face.

"Good, let's talk. I've wanted to talk to you too," he said.

"Not here. I'll meet you outside, just beyond the flagpoles there's a pavilion with some tables and benches where the staff eats sometimes. Meet me there in twenty minutes," she said.

Before he could say anything else she turned and hurried out of the room. What a strange conversation, he thought. He'd been looking for the opportunity to be alone with her and now she'd suggested it. Now, he wondered what he'd tell her. She had to know that he cared for her. She had to know that whatever he was before, that he had changed. For the first time in as long as he could remember, the thought of committing another crime had not entered his mind. He slipped on his sandals and headed for the courtyard.

Leona Stillwell had been waiting in the stairwell for Clayton to arrive for more than thirty minutes. He was always at work before seven, but for some reason this morning he was late. Then she heard the door open two floors down and she recognized his footsteps jogging up the stairs as he always did. He stopped on the landing when he saw her at the top of the stairs.

She was wearing a white blouse tied at the neck with a soft, hanging bow. Her skirt was cherry red and clung to the curves of her hips and legs like a wetsuit, stopping just below her knees. Her lipstick was the exact same color as her skirt and glistened in the scant light on her face. She moved to the top step and placed her hands on the railing as if blocking his passage to the landing.

"I've missed you," she said seductively.

Clayton never said a word. He just placed both hands on the railing and began moving in her direction. When he reached the next to the last step, they were eye-to-eye. He slipped his hands around her narrow waist, sliding them up her spine, and then he kissed her with all the passion she'd been longing for.

"I like the way you say hello," Stillwell whispered in his ear.

"Did I ever tell you how beautiful you are?"

"You may have, but I've never known a woman yet that didn't like hearing it on a regular basis," she said.

Just as he put his lips on hers to kiss her again, Delores Rucker opened the door to the stairwell and stopped beside them as the door closed behind her. She looked at Clayton and his red lips and smiled as she eased passed them and continued walking.

"That shade looks good on you, Clayton," she said as she disappeared around the bottom landing.

Stillwell grinned, slipped her hand in Clayton's back pocket removing his handkerchief and wiping her lipstick from his lips. She was surprised when he didn't say anything about Rucker disturbing them in the stairwell.

"I guess there's no news on Sneed's whereabouts?" he said casually. "Everybody but her thinks he's dead. If he's still alive he's probably in Mexico by now. It's been over three weeks now and we're no closer to knowing where he is than we did when they went into the bayou. How's Aaron Phillips?"

"I took him home two days ago. He's still having headaches but the doctors said that it's normal for people having concussions like his. He'll be okay; it's just going to take a while." As they walked out of the stairwell together she continued to ask him questions.

"Any news with the arson investigation at Kheif's house?"

"They wrapped up everything yesterday. They found the detonator while I was taking Phillips home. He used C4, and a solid-state circuitry for the trigger. All he had to do was just place the call from a remote location. He could have blown that house up from Dallas. But for some reason I can't get it out of my mind that he was watching us the whole time, just waiting for us to all get inside before he made the call."

"How's your stakeout going? Are your waiter skills getting any better?" Stillwell asked.

"I've checked with everybody but you and Cromberg and nobody's seen a thing. And I don't' have any waiter skills, haven't you heard."

"Heard what?" Stillwell asked, handing Clayton a cup of coffee.

"The owner of the Rose Garden Café wants to fire me. But since I'm working for free and because I have a gun under my apron, he's decided to give me another week," Clayton said, sipping his coffee. Stillwell laughed. "How's your gig going?"

"Unlike you, I wasn't born with a silver spoon in my mouth. I waited tables my whole senior year of college in Austin. I even got a couple of good tips last night. But my gig is about to be over. The Hyatt is closing its sidewalk café on the first of the September. So if he doesn't strike by then I may be helping you."

"I really thought he would have done something before now, Leona." Clayton ran a finger across one of the pink scars just above his right eyebrow.

"It looks like you're healing nicely," she said, moving in close to him.

"Oh yeah, I'm healing fine. It's made shaving a bit precarious. But other than that I'm doing fine. What time is the meeting with Captain Gorman?"

"Eight-thirty," she answered.

She was about to move another step in his direction when a Black man and a tall beautiful blonde woman appeared in the doorway. The man reached inside and feigned a knock on the door.

"Can we help you," Stillwell asked. She seemed agitated by his intrusion. "I'm looking for Ross Clayton," the man said. Clayton moved in his direction.

"I'm Ross Clayton," he said, extending his hand.

"My name is Tyrell Slater. I'm with the United States Marshall's Office out of Phoenix, and this is my associate, Elana Gorrion," he said, shaking Clayton's hand warmly.

"Could we offer you some coffee?" Clayton motioned toward the coffee bar. He noticed that Stillwell had her back to them, staring at a blank wall as if she were lost in thought, but it was obvious that she was avoiding the Marshals.

"No, we can't stay. We've already checked in with the Marshals office here in Houston but we just wanted to give your office a heads-up on our activities while we're here in town."

"What activities would that be?" Clayton asked.

Tyrell Slater took a couple of photographs out of his jacket and handed them to Clayton. Clayton noticed Slater eyeing Stillwell across the room but ignored it.

"Ever seen either of these two men?"

"I don't think so. Who are they?"

"The balding man is Andrew Cain. The man with the bushy eyebrows is Michael Cordelle. We have reason to believe these two killed a Federal Judge in Phoenix two weeks ago. We've been on their trail ever since. We also believe they've come to Houston looking for this man." Slater said, handing another photograph to Clayton.

"This photograph is at least ten years old, but the man in the picture is Howard Pavin. We think he's living here in Houston under an alias, we believe Cain and Cordelle have come here to kill him."

"Did your people put him here under the witness protection program?" Clayton asked.

"No, Pavin disappeared ten years ago while working for the CIA. He just dropped off the face of the planet, and no one has seen him since. We know that Pavin had some dealings with Cain and Cordelle before he disappeared. We know that Pavin tried to turn these two in, and in turn they tried to kill him. When they failed, that's when Pavin vanished."

"Can't say as I blame him for wanting to disappear. You seem to know a lot about things that happened a long time ago," Clayton said.

"Yeah, the Judge was under surveillance and we got it all on tape before Cain and Cordelle whacked him. Look, I've bothered you with this more than I should have. I just wanted you to know that we'll be working with the Marshal's office here in your backyard, and we'll keep you apprised of what we're doing."

"We appreciate that. Let us know if we can help you in any way," Clayton said.

Clayton shook hands with them again and before he could get Stillwell's attention they were gone. He walked to where she was standing.

"Do you know that guy? Is there some reason you're being so rude?"

"No, I don't know him, and I don't want to know him. That man had trouble written all over his face. I got a bad feeling about that guy as-soon-as he walked through that door," Stillwell said.

Before Stillwell could say anything else Rucker walked into the room holding a bottle of orange juice and a box of warm cinnamon rolls.

"I forgot I had these in my car. I stopped and warmed them in the microwave," Rucker said, opening the box and placing it on the coffee bar. "How's your stakeout going, Clayton?" she asked.

"Wonderful. I made a hundred and forty-nine dollars in tips last night." "Wow. Stillwell only made sixty-three bucks and she's beautiful. What's up with that?" Rucker said, and drank from her orange juice.

"I don't know what it all means, but as for me, I've had enough of this waiter gig. I don't have the right build for the job. Twice I've knocked another waiter down while coming out of the kitchen. Both times they've had a load of food on their trays and I've had to pay for it out of my own pocket. I figure if I work there for another couple of weeks they won't need any customers; they'll have made enough off of me to close the place down and retire. I don't wish anybody any harm but I wish Kheif would show his ugly face somewhere so we can put an end to this. I've had enough," Clayton said.

"What did Barbie and the Stud want?" Rucker asked candidly.

"They're US Marshals and they're going to be in Houston for a while working on a case, Clayton answered.

"Case, now that's funny," Stillwell laughed. "The only thing Denzel Washington and the blonde bombshell are going to be working on is making our life miserable," Stillwell said.

"Yeah, I didn't like 'em either," Rucker chimed in.

"Man, I must have missed something here?" Clayton said.

Richey Sneed sat alone the courtyard. The wind was blowing the clouds across the horizon and he could smell rain in the distance. He watched Jeanie Nguyen exit the main building and head in his direction. She had always worn her hair in a tight bun on the back of her head, but today it was long and on her shoulders, the wind blew it across her face but she made no attempt to move it from her eyes. Richey stood up as she neared the pavilion. She sat down and took his hands in hers and wasted no time in telling him what was on her mind.

"Richey, they're going to discharge you on Monday. I overheard the doctor telling the head nurse that you'll be leaving before the storm hits. He said that it would be a perfect time for you to leave. Richey, I don't want to see you go," she said, tears forming in her eyes.

Richey Sneed swallowed hard, he wanted to take her in his arms and hold her, to feel her body next to his. He stood and moved around the table then softly took her in his arms and kissed her.

"I've wanted to do that since the first time I laid eyes on you. There are so many things I want to tell you. There are so many things I want to talk to you about. Things that you need to know about me. You deserve so much more than someone like me," he said.

"I don't care about what's in the past. I want to go with you, Richey. Can I do that? Can I go with you?"

Richey ignored the pain in his chest when he held her even tighter. Over the next thirty minutes he told her everything he could think concerning his tainted past, and Jeanie Nguyen listened to every word. When he was finished, she kissed him and looked up at his face.

"Are you finished?"

"I suppose so," he said.

"Then, answer my question. Will you take me with you when you go?" "Do you understand that I have to leave the country? If I stay here in Texas they're going to kill me. I have to leave the country, Jeanie. Is that something you're prepared to do?"

"It's something I'm going to do if you'll take me," she answered.

"I had money when I came in here. If we're going to start over we're going to need that money."

"We don't need that money, Richey. That money has blood on it. It will only curse us."

"We have to have it to start over. Don't you understand? Without it we'll be right back stealing and running from the law again," he said.

"No, you don't understand. I have money, a lot of it. I received a large settlement when my husband and daughter were killed. I know my husband would want me to be happy. We'll use that money for a fresh start," she said.

"I don't deserve someone like you, but I promise you that I'll never leave you or hurt you. Are you sure this is what you want to do?"

"I am positive, Richey Sneed," she said, her lips an inch from his.

He kissed her as rain began pelting the roof of the pavilion. For the next thirty minutes they held hands and talked about their lives ahead of them and pledging that no matter what happened they'd never look back on the past again.

CHAPTER 17

Monday, September 1st, the storm everyone had been waiting for came ashore between Morgan City and New Orleans. The winds never achieved hurricane strength but the amount of water the storm had sucked out of the Gulf of Mexico was greater than anyone could have imagined. It might as well have been a hurricane with all of the flooding that hit southern Louisiana.

Because New Orleans is for the most part below sea level, major flooding was inevitable. But within hours of the storms landfall, and the five-foot wall of water that came with it, the city of New Orleans was once again under water.

News of the massive flooding, and of those left in peril, was already reaching Lake Charles when Redhawk Simmons and Renee Harjo made their way into the Grand Jury assembly room and found a seat. What happened next could not have been foreseen by anyone associated with the hearing.

It was one of the fastest legal proceedings in Louisiana State history. The woman that had been raped and almost killed, Lushanda Johnson, spent less than twenty-five minutes giving her side of the story. She finished her testimony with a statement that the Grand Jury could not forget.

"I would be dead today if this man hadn't showed up and stopped that psycho from killing me. I owe this man my life. He saved my life," she said with tears flowing from her eyes. And as she left the Grand Jury room, she stopped and faced Redhawk Simmons and then hugged him with every ounce of strength she had.

It was at that point, when Maurice Couvillion made the decision not to have Redhawk testify in his own behalf. The hearing room was emptied, and in less than five minutes the decision was made by the Grand Jury to no-bill Redhawk Simmons for any crimes whatsoever. It was the only time in his life that he had ever left a courtroom a free man. Both he and Renee burst into tears and a celebration of embraces.

As they made their way out of the courthouse and onto the street, southerly winds were blowing now, and a light rain had began to fall. Both of them hugged Maurice Couvillion and thanked him again.

It was a two-hour drive back to Livingston, and Renee snuggled in next to Redhawk for the trip home. Over the next hour they would make two decisions concerning their lives that they would never forget, nor regret, for that matter.

First, they decided not to put the wedding off any longer or wait for a formal wedding to be planned. They would be married on Wednesday night with a handful of friends and acquaintances from their inner circle of friends on the Reservation. Secondly, they decided that after the wedding they'd drive into downtown Houston, get a room at the Hyatt Regency Hotel and stay there until Sunday night for the only honeymoon they could afford after paying Couvillion. After all that had happened to them over the past couple of months it seemed like the perfect ending to a long journey.

Richey Sneed had fallen asleep after breakfast. He was dressed, packed and waiting for Jeanie Nguyen to arrive. When he awoke, Frederic Remington was sitting quietly at the foot of his bed. Richey palmed his face attempting to focus on the image of the old man.

"You're here?" Richey said, finally. "I was wondering if I'd ever see you again. I wanted to thank you for bringing me here and saving my life."

"You sure look better than you did when I brought you in here," Remington said.

"I've never felt better," Richey said, sliding his body to the side of the bed. "I understand that you've decided to take Jeanie Nguyen with you?"

"I wanted to tell you about it myself. But now that you already know, I suppose you're concerned about how I'll treat her, and how that she deserves so much better than someone like me. Believe me I've thought of all of those things. In the last three weeks I've had a lot of time to think about everything. But mostly I've had an opportunity to think about what a mess I've made of my life and how I want to spend what's left of it."

"So you have given this some thought," the old man said.

Jeanie Nguyen had walked to the door and because it was slightly ajar she could hear the conversation as if she were standing on the inside. She stood quietly and listened.

"I don't have all the answers, Freddy," Richey started again. "What I do know is that I love her. She needs me and I need her. I'm not going to tell you that I've got everything figured out, but this woman, this peaceful, beautiful woman, has changed my life. I'm not the same man I was when you brought me in here a month ago. I can't explain it and I don't know that I would if I could, but things are different now."

"I'm glad to hear that, Richey. I don't think that your life expectancy was too good the way you were going," Remington said.

"I agree. If you hadn't found me when you did and brought me in here, I would have died right there on the Houston ship channel. And now my whole life has changed, not to mention that this beautiful woman wants to be a part of what's left of my life."

"Have you given any thought as to what the two of you are going to do? Where you're going to go? And what about taking care of Jeanie, have you given that any thought?"

"Look, Freddy, there's nothing on earth I'd rather do than to stay right here in Texas, get a job, and spend the rest of my life proving to Jeanie that she made the right choice in staying with me. But you and I both know the legal system here in Texas. I killed a man.

And I was part of a shootout where a cop lost his life. If I stay here they're going to try me with that crime if I'm caught. The penalty for that is death, you know it and I know it. I can't stay here. Our only hope is to leave the country. Go somewhere where they don't have extradition, and start over. I know it's not the perfect solution but it's the best one I have,"

"Maybe I can help you with that," Remington said.

Tears were streaming down Jeanie Nguyen's face. She moved away from the door and headed for the restroom. She didn't want Richey to know she'd been listening and that his words had relieved any doubt she might have had about the decisions she'd made.

"You've already done enough, Remington. Besides, you don't need to become anymore involved with me than what you already have."

"That's not a problem. Have you ever heard of a place called Bimini?" "I've heard the name, but I don't know anything about the place," Richey answered.

"It's a beautiful island in the Bahamas. The Lucayans used to call it "Two Islands" because of its configuration. Ernest Hemingway had a bungalow there and rumor has it that he did a lot of his writings from there. But I suspect it was little more than a place for him to escape and do a little fishing. I hear the fishing is great there, and it's a great place to raise a family or to buy a fishing boat and take people on charters. I think you and Jeanie will be very happy there." The old man moved to Richey's bedside, standing only inches away.

"I don't know Remington. I've never been out of the states except for Mexico. I doubt I could find Bimini on a map."

"I took the liberty of getting you and Jeanie some passports. These passports say that you are citizens of the Bahamas. You'll find a birth certificate for you and an immigration status for Jeanie who moved there three years ago from Texas to be with her lover. I even managed to come up with some Bahamian money. This is your home, Richey. All you have to do is drive to Miami and purchase a ticket home and live life the way it was meant to be."

"Look, I know you mean well but there's some holes in your scenario. The US government is going to have a record of us coming into the country. That never happened. And unless you've got some contacts you haven't told me about, we'll just wind up in a Miami jail," Richey said.

"All of that has been taken care of. You and your fiancé have been here to get married and spend your honeymoon here. You'll find the name of a man in Tallahassee who'll not only marry you, but will provide you with a certificate of marriage showing that the wedding took place three weeks ago. Look, you talk it over with Jeanie, if the two of you want to do something else, that'll be your decision."

"I don't know what to say, Remington. How can I ever repay you? Oh, I just remembered, the money I had when I came in here, you can keep that money. Give it to somebody that really needs it. Jeanie said that she had all the money we'd ever need."

"That's good, Richey. I think you and Jeanie are going to be just fine. Don't ever look back and don't try to contact me. It will be better for both of us if we just say goodbye here and now."

Richey looked at the passports, maps, money and directions, his mind lost in thought and gratitude for what the old man had done. He must have been working on this from the day he brought him in to the hospital, Richey thought. No one had ever been so kind or giving as this old man, Richey thought.

"Remington, I want to thank…"

When he turned and looked for the old man, he was gone. He moved the bedside table and ran to the patio doors pulling the curtains back, but the old man was gone from sight. He ran his fingers through his hair just as the door opened and Jeanie Nguyen walked into the room. She moved to his side, tiptoed to his lips and kissed him.

"I was talking to the old man," Richey started to explain. He's taken care of everything, but how he got out of here without me seeing him is crazy."

"Where are we headed?" Jeanie asked.

"Florida, I think. We can talk about it on the way. I'll explain while you drive. Do you have everything?"

"I do. My car is in the front of the building and you're all checked out of the hospital."

"Do I owe anything? Don't' I have to pay before I leave?" Richey asked. "Richey, the payment office said it was taken care of this morning. I assumed you got your money from the old man and paid the bill."

"Jeanie, I never saw the old man until about five minutes ago. I told him to keep the money that you had plenty."

"It doesn't matter. The bill is paid and we're free to go. Where are your things?"

Richey picked up the sack containing his prescription medicine and the old clothes he was wearing when the old man brought him in. He stuffed the passports and documents in the bag, took Jeanie Nguyen by the hand and headed for the door.

"I have so many questions," he said, stopping at the door.

"I'm sure everything will come to us in time. We better be going, Richey."

Because of the closing of Interstate 10 at Gretna and the widespread flooding of the city, people began evacuating southern Louisiana and heading for Texas to stay with relatives or to find motels and wait for the water to recede.

With the summer semester having ended and the convention season coming to a close, Mutalib Peter Sulayman should have had some extra time on his hands. But for the last two weeks he'd been so busy with additional fares that he hadn't had time to eat at all, much less think about the free meal ticket to that fancy sidewalk café in his glove-box. Maybe things were about to change, he thought.

Just after he clocked in, the dispatcher handed him a note to call a man named Anwar. He remembered the old man that had tipped

THE IMPRESSIONIST MURDERS

him so well and given him the free meal ticket. He wasted no time in returning the old man's call.

"Anwar, this is Peter Sulayman, I got your number from dispatch and I am at your service. Where do you need me to pick you up?"

"No, no, Peter. I don't need you to pick me up; I have a business proposition for you. A friend of mine is opening a business here in Houston and is looking for an accountant. I told him that I knew just the man for the position. It would be a great opportunity for you to get in on the ground floor of a business that's going to be big in Houston. Do you think that you would be interested in a position like that?"

"Oh, Anwar, it's truly a dream come true. But I will not have my license for some time. I still have to take the State Exams to be licensed."

"That will not be a problem, Peter. The man wants you to start right away. You can schedule your exam later in the year when there is more time. The starting salary for the position is $65,000.00 a year. I would hate to see you miss out on a deal like this," Anwar said convincingly.

"Oh my, that's more than I make in a year and a half driving the cab. When does the man want to meet?" Peter said, his enthusiasm brimming over.

"On Friday the fifth, be at the same restaurant on Montrose around eight-thirty, I'll bring the man with me, and don't worry about the check, everything is on him. You're going to be an executive now, Peter."

"Anwar, I don't know what to say, or how I'll ever be able to thank you. You're kindness seems to have no end. I have a new navy-blue suit that I just purchased for such an occasion. I will be there early, Anwar, and thank you again."

Peter Sulayman disconnected from the call and dropped his cell phone into the cup holder, his mind racing with thoughts of being a corporate executive. The thought of plunging into the world of big business made him smile. He wrote the date and time on a sticky note and posted it on his dashboard as a token of his good luck. He knew that every time he glanced at the note the smile would return to his face.

It was a night of firsts for Redhawk Simmons. His first marriage, his first suit and tie, his first attempt at being a husband, and in less than an hour it would be his first night to stay in a fancy hotel. He had to admit that he'd never been happier. It was the first time in a long time that he wasn't wanted by the law, or living in fear, and Renee Simmons sat next to him in his old truck with her head on his shoulder. What more could a man ask for, he thought to himself. Just as they turned onto Interstate 59 heading south, a gentle rain began pelting the windshield, but the air was cool and refreshing, and smelled of pine and cedar. On the radio an old love song was playing by the Eagles, called *"Peaceful Easy Feeling"* Renee sang the words to the song and Redhawk listened. When the song was over he turned the volume down and put his arm around Renee.

"I wouldn't mind doing that tonight," he said.

"What's that?"

"In the song, the singer said, I want to sleep with you in the desert tonight, with a billion stars all around. I wish we could do that tonight. There's no place like the desert at night. It has a personality all its own," he said.

"Well, that may be true, and we can do that sometime when we have a little more time. But tonight, I'm glad we're going to the Hyatt. And, as an added bonus, I got us a room with a Jacuzzi big enough for two. Have you ever made love in a Jacuzzi? You can't do that in the middle of the desert," she said softly. "Oh, and another thing, we won't have to worry about snakes crawling around us at the Hyatt either."

"Well, that's another first," he said.

"What's that?"

"That Jacuzzi thing. Not only have I never made love in one, I never seen one of them things either. Exactly what is it?"

"It's a big bathtub with water jets bubbling and blasting you with hot water all over your body. And believe it or not, some of the places it blasts you, feels really good. I think you'll like it a lot," she said.

"What's the speed limit?"

"Sixty-five. Why?"

"I don't want to get a ticket, but I don't want to waste any time getting there either," he said." Renee chuckled, nuzzling into his strong arms.

Ross Clayton rarely drank, but tonight he and Stillwell sat at the bar at The Taste of Texas Restaurant sipping Margaritas, and waiting for the next available table. His cell phone rang and he checked the screen to see who was calling; it was Wade Gorman.

"Yes Captain," Clayton answered.

"Why aren't you and Stillwell working tonight? Dispatch said you were off the clock tonight; what gives?"

"Captain, in case you haven't noticed, it's pouring rain. Sidewalk cafes don't do well in a driving rain. They sent the outside wait-staff home as soon as it looked like it wasn't about to let up. It's just one of those nights, Captain."

"Well, I'm not in Houston, that's why I didn't know it was raining." "Where are you, Captain?"

"I'm in Austin with the Chief and the Mayor. We're working with the appropriations committee trying to get some additional government money for the department. Everyone's questioning me about the Kheif investigation and quiet frankly I don't have any answers. How long are we going to wait for this man to commit another murder? We've got a case load that's building every day, and people want us to find this guy or move on to something else."

"We're on the same page, Captain. If something doesn't happen by Friday night we'll assign everyone to new cases and move on. Is that something you can live with?"

"You don't think he's going to show, do you?"

"I don't know, Captain, but I know this is something we can keep doing indefinitely. No one on earth wants to catch this guy any more than I do, but I have to concede, that up until now it's been a waste of precious time. If you can give us until Friday and he doesn't show, then we'll move on from there."

"I'm not trying to second guess you, Clayton," Gorman said, sounding exhausted. "This thing is costing the department a lot of time and manpower, and that equates to money, which we don't have a lot of these days. I like the Friday deadline, and I'll tell the Chief and Mayor that's what we're going to do. Enjoy your night off," he said, and disconnected.

"You can always tell when the Captain is feeling better," Stillwell, said.

"I can't say as I blame him. This is not like doing surveillance where you're watching some clown who's in the act of breaking the law. This man may never show, and the truth is we don't have a clue as to his whereabouts. All we have is a dumb painting that we think tells us where he'll strike again. This man could be lying on the beaches of Grand Cayman right now laughing his ass off, for all we know. I don't blame the Captain for second guessing us. I'm ready to move on to something else."

"Then let's move on to something else. How about my place?" Stillwell whispered in his ear.

"What about our table? Aren't you hungry?" "I have a king's size bed."

"I'll get the check," Clayton said.

Interstate 10 east of Baton Rouge was closed because of the storm, and with it raining so hard that they could barely see the road, Richey Sneed and Jeanie Nguyen decided to call it a night and regroup in the morning. They must have tried twenty motels before they found one with a vacancy. It was a Comfort Inn just north of town near the airport. It was also one of the few places that still had electricity and running water.

Jeanie handed him an umbrella when they found the room. As soon as he jumped out of the car, the strong wind inverted the umbrella so that it looked like a funnel; he was soaked before he could make it to the door.

He threw the umbrella into the room, grabbed a blanket from the closet and went back to the car for Jeanie. As they rushed for the door she stopped just before going into the room, as if she were apprehensive about going inside. She wiped the rain from her face, looked at Richey for a moment then slowly moved through the open doorway.

"Is something wrong?" Richey asked. Jeanie took his hand in hers.

"Richey, I'm a little nervous, here," she said.

"Honey, we're fortunate just to have found this place. I'll bet we could go another hundred miles north and not find another place to stay," Richey said.

"No, it's not that. It's just that I've never been in bed with anyone but my husband, and that's been over two years ago. You and I have only kissed, maybe you won't like me in the morning and I'll be alone again. So yes, I'm a little nervous."

Richey could feel the trembling of her hands and somehow understood what she must have been going through. He immediately changed the subject.

"Are you hungry?" Richey asked. "I haven't eaten a thing since breakfast and I'm starving."

"At least you had breakfast. I've been so worried that I haven't eaten a thing all day. I didn't know we were going to be stuck in the car for seven hours on that bridge or I would have eaten something. So, yes I'm starving."

"I feel so silly, I don't even know what you like to eat," Richey said. "Richey, I've been living in Texas since I was a little girl. I like everything from chicken-fried steak to lobster, but I'd settle for a sandwich right now if you can find something open. Are you sure you don't mind getting out in the rain again?"

"Honey, I'll be fine. Just give me a few dollars and I'll get us something." Jeanie Nguyen opened her purse that was stuffed with cash and handed him a stack of bills. The banded ring around the bills said $5,000.00. Richey looked at the stack of money as if she'd handed him a sack of diamonds. He handed the stack of bills back to her.

"Honey, I'm not going to the casino, I'm just going to get some sandwiches. Don't you have a twenty?"

She handed him a twenty and told him to hurry back, and that she didn't want him to be alone too long. He took the money and started for the door then turned abruptly and kissed her like she'd never been kissed before.

"Now I'm hungry for something else," she said when the kiss was over. "I'll be back as fast as I can. Lock and bolt the door behind me, and put your purse under the bed. And don't open the door for no one but me. If someone tries to get into the room you call 911. Okay?" She nodded and walked him to the door.

CHAPTER 18

On Friday, Richey Sneed and Jeanie Nguyen found West Madison Street, on the campus of Florida State University and pulled into the driveway of an old two-story colonial mansion that looked like the backdrop for a Civil War movie. Jeanie checked the address, and then stuffed the paper back into her backpack.

"It's the right address, Richey," she said.

"According to these instructions, you're going to have to learn to call me Ronnie. You lucked out and got to keep your name, but I got stuck with Ronnie. Are you going to be okay being married to a guy named Ronnie?"

"When we get to our new home and we're all alone, can I sometimes call you Richey? I like that name," she said, with a soft smile. "And yes, I like the name Ronnie just fine. I don't care what your name is as long as you love me."

"What about the name Burgess, how do you think you're going to like being called Burgess? That's going to be your name too. Ronald Edward Burgess, where did Remington come up with these names?"

"Like I said, I have only one requirement and that's that you love me." "You're too easy to please," he said, and then kissed her.

The man that met them at the front door of the mansion was short and rotund. He had a shaved head, red cheeks and soft brown eyes. He led them to a library off the main hallway and disappeared without conversation. A few moments later, Godfrey Hammond appeared and introduced himself as Judge Hammond with the First District Court of Appeals.

Godfrey Hammond was tall and lanky with thinning gray hair and a full mustache. He was wearing an expensive suit, gray pinstriped with a burgundy tie. On his lapel he wore a Presidential citation medal that had been awarded to the 95th bomber group for its bravery and heroics over Germany and Belgium during world war two. Richey thought it odd that the man didn't look a day over fifty.

"I understand that you kids want to get married?"

"Remington sent us here and said you'd take care of everything," Richey answered.

"May I see the passports that Remington gave you?"

For reasons beyond his realm of understanding, Richey Sneed seemed to be taken with the man and his cool, laid-back demeanor. He got a strange feeling when he handed the man the passports. The feeling was almost electric, Richey thought.

"Everything seems to be in order," he said. "Do you have rings for the ceremony, Mr. Burgess?" Richey Sneed was about to look around the room for someone named Burgess when it dawned on him that the Judge was talking to him.

"Burgess? The ring? Oh, I knew we were forgetting something!" Richey said, a pale look covering his face.

"It's not important, Ronnie," Jeanie said. "There are plenty of jewelry stores in Miami. We'll be there tomorrow evening, Ronnie," she said, holding onto his arm.

"I'm sorry, baby, I should have thought about the ring. But like you said, they do have jewelry stores in Miami. I promise you that before we get on the plane to our home, we'll have a ring on your finger."

The ceremony lasted ten minutes. After the kiss, the Judge handed Ronnie Burgess a sealed envelope.

"This is from Remington. Please wait until you get to where you're going before opening it. I want to wish both of you a long, prosperous and healthy life together, one that is filled with love and happiness. Remember this; most things that are worthwhile are worth working for. Marriage or life for that matter is never a one-way street. If you'll remember these simple things, your lives will be filled with good things; even if you're broke."

The Judge handed them a manila folder and walked them to the door. Ronnie stuffed the envelope the Judge had given him inside the folder and shook the man's hand.

"We won't ever forget this day, Judge. Do we owe you anything?"

"The only debts you have are to each other. Treat each other kindly and you'll do fine," he said, closing the door behind them.

As Ronnie Burgess opened the door for his beautiful wife he kissed her again and said, "This is the happiest day of my life."

As tears welled in her eyes she smiled and said, "Mine too."

Redhawk Simmons knocked on the door to his room and waited for Renee to answer. Since their honeymoon was almost over he'd decided to surprise his new bride with a night on the town.

"Yes," she answered through the door.

"Western Union for Misses Simmons," he said, leaning in close to the door.

"Redhawk, you goof," she said, opening the door.

She stood behind the door as Redhawk peered inside. She was wearing a white terrycloth towel around her head and another wrapped around her torso. She smelled of shampoo and bath-oil.

"Good, I'm glad I caught you before you fixed your hair. They have a salon down stairs and I bought you the complete package, hair, nails, facial, the works. I also rented a limousine to pick us up at six-thirty and take us to one of those fancy restaurants for a dinner under the stars; complete with violins. I figured since tomorrow is our last night here, we should probably do this tonight."

"How sweet of you Mr. Simmons, I have to admit that I'm really surprised. I never thought of you as the moonlit dinner, romantic type. I always thought of you as the outdoors type, a hunter, a knife maker, strong and silent, but you're full of surprises. Can we afford all of this extravagance?"

"I had a few bucks stashed away in my workshop that I was saving for a bigger furnace. But I figured that you only fall in love once in a lifetime, so you should treat that lover really well, and just maybe it will last a lifetime." "Wow. I married an absolute stranger. That's the most beautiful thing I've ever heard a man say, especially coming from a big tough guy like you. Are you sure you've got the right room, and the right woman? My name is Renee Simmons, and I'm married to a big, strong Apache Indian. Maybe you've seen him wandering about the hotel," she said, wrapping her arms around his neck.

"Your appointment is in twenty minutes," Redhawk said.

"Then I'm going to be late. They'll understand," she said, allowing her towel to drop to the floor.

It was just after five p.m. when Ross Clayton arrived at the Rose Garden Restaurant and began changing into his waiter outfit. As he walked out of the changing room he caught Leona Stillwell and Delores Rucker going into the ladies room. Rucker turned and started walking toward him, leaving Stillwell standing in the doorway.

"You got a little problem here boss," she said, reaching for his jacket. "You may not be the best waiter in the house, but you're unquestionably the best armed."

The jackets were the color of a red rose and cut short at the waist. Because of Clayton's height his jacket didn't cover the shoulder holster he was trying to conceal.

"I thought your jacket was rolled up, but it's too short for you. You've got to get a longer jacket or an ankle holster. This looks terrible," she started to laugh.

"Okay, I'll loose the shoulder holster. I'll see you two outside."

The outside portion of the Rose Garden Restaurant had an elliptical shape, so that if you were standing at the entrance, it was impossible to see the guest's tables at the other end of the dining area. A red brick planter with wrought-iron fencing followed the contour of the dining area giving patrons a sense of protection from the traffic on Montrose a few feet away. Colorful roses, mostly of red and pink covered most of the fence and provided a fragrance that everyone enjoyed.

Because of the blind spot at the back of the dining area Clayton thought it necessary that one of them be in that area at all times. As he strolled toward the blind spot he saw Rucker bussing tables near the back fence so he turned back toward the front of the dining area seeing that she had it covered. In that instant of time, Richard Prince, the headwaiter passed him on the right leading Peter Sulayman to a table that Rucker had just finished clearing. The waiter seated Sulayman with his back to the rose covered fence.

"Can I get you something from the bar," the waiter asked.

"No, I am waiting on friends."

"I understand, sir," the waiter said. But before he could turn and leave, Peter Sulayman stopped him.

"I've changed my mind. I'll have a vodka and coke," he said incisively.

"Sir," the waiter looked at him as if he'd just ordered arsenic and cookies. The waiter couldn't help but notice that the man looked out of place and very uncomfortable.

"You're not a big drinker, are you sir?"

"No. But I thought a drink might calm my nerves a little," Sulayman said. He looked at the people drinking around him. "What's that man drinking? That looks good." Sulayman pointed to the table in front of him.

"That's rum and coke with lime. It's called a cubalebra, I think you'll like that, sir, good choice."

As the waiter walked passed Rucker he noticed a couple standing at the entrance. He tapped Rucker on the shoulder and said, "Would you bring the man at table thirty-four a cubalebra."

"Sure. No problem," she said.

Rucker carried a tray full of empty glasses to the bar, placed an order for the drink and watched as the waiter accompanied the couple to a table near the back of the dining area. She couldn't take her eyes off the couple. It was as if she had met them a long time ago but couldn't remember their names or the story behind them. The bartender sat the drink on her tray and she hurried back to table thirty-four.

"You ordered a Cubalebra?" she asked the man.

"I did, thank you," Sulayman said.

When Rucker walked away from the table, she recognized the couple as having something to do with the police. She tucked her tray under her arm, stopping in front of them.

"I almost never forget a face. Don't I know you folks from somewhere?" Redhawk Simmons sat there with a blank look on his face for what seemed like an eternity. Then finally it hit him.

"I know you too. You're that lady cop that came out to my place on the reservation in Livingston. You were with some cops from Louisiana," Redhawk said.

"That's right," Rucker said, snapping her fingers. "It was you that called me a few weeks ago and wanted to talk about something. You also gave me that tip on Kheif. Man, there's been so much happen since then. You know he killed his whole family," Rucker said without thinking.

"We're on the last night of our honeymoon," Renee joined the conversation. She wanted the lady cop to know that she was on the verge of ruining the start of a perfectly good night on the town.

"Congratulations," Rucker said. "The two of you make a beautiful couple. Can I get you something from the bar?"

"No, the man that seated us has taken our orders, thanks anyway," Renee said, hoping the lady cop would leave them alone.

"You folks have a good time. If you need anything just let me know," Rucker said. She took a step back, and then for some reason looked at the table where the man was sipping from the drink she'd taken him a few moments ago. She took several steps around the corner when she saw Stillwell carrying a tray back into the main entrance, and Clayton taking an order from a couple at a table near the entrance of the sidewalk cafe. Then, for a reason that she would never be able to explain later, she glanced back at the man at table thirty-four one last time.

Nizar Kheif had waited for this moment for weeks. Everything was in place. He was about to commit a crime in the presence of the very cops that had been chasing him for months. And if everything went according to plan he wouldn't just be killing a lowly cab driver, he would kill them all.

In the blink of an eye Kheif thrust the curve bladed knife through the wrought-iron fencing and into the neck of Peter Sulayman. But it didn't go the way he planned it. Since he was unable to see the position of the knife, he had plunged the knife to far passed Sulayman's neck, the blade stuck deep into the man's collarbone instead of tender flesh, and the harder he pulled the deeper the blade carved into the bone.

Peter Sulayman cried out in pain. Blood sprayed out onto his shirt and tie as he attempted to latch onto the hand trying to kill him. At that same exact moment, Redhawk Simmons and Delores Rucker saw the attack. The split-second instincts that had served Rucker so well in her past failed her now, but not Redhawk Simmons. In three steps he was at Sulayman's table. In one blow from his huge right hand he paralyzed Kheif's grip on the weapon and Kheif's hand vanished from the fence.

Kheif cried out in pain now, but he had enough presence of mind to remember the plan. He hurried away from the café and down the side street, disappearing into the coming darkness. He could hear the footsteps behind him and he wanted to smile, but it wasn't over.

There were several screams from those sitting at other tables around where Sulayman fell. The moment that Clayton heard the screams he broke in a dead run passed Rucker who was trying to get her 9mm from her ankle holster. Before Rucker started moving Stillwell passed her just as Clayton had done. Several patrons including Renee Simmons rushed to the aid of Peter Sulayman who was now sprawled on the floor, clutching his neck, but still very much alive.

"Where is he?" Clayton yelled.

"He disappeared around the corner. That big man was chasing him," an anonymous man said. Clayton jumped the fence and was gone when Stillwell and Rucker got there. Stillwell looked over the fence and realized she could never jump it without suffering bodily injury. She and Rucker headed for the front entrance at a dead run. Rucker stopped for an instant and told the headwaiter, "Call 911 and tell them what happened here, and tell them that undercover police are in pursuit of Nizar Kheif," she said.

Seconds later she and Stillwell were out the front entrance and following Clayton and Redhawk Simmons.

Redhawk Simmons watched Kheif go into the building through a side door then quickly decided to look for another door at the back of the building. He looked up at the last glimmer of sunlight on the horizon. The voice in his head told him that things were about to get ugly.

Clayton was a hundred yards behind the Indian and Kheif when he saw Kheif go into what appeared to be an old abandon building; the big Indian had disappeared in a nearby hedgerow. He was thankful for what light there was; in another twenty minutes the man could have disappeared anywhere in the neighborhood. Clayton didn't know that the timing was all part of Kheif's plan. He stopped when he reached the door that Kheif had just gone through. Now, with his thoughts racing, he remembered the cunning and daring nature of the man he was after, and for a moment thought about closing the door and waiting for backup to arrive and surround the place. But he couldn't take a chance on loosing Kheif now.

"Take it easy, son. This man's no fool," Clayton whispered aloud.

Clayton wiped his brow, swallowed hard and moved inside the old warehouse, his 9mm drawn at arms length in front of him.

Kheif watched the big cop step into his lair of almost total darkness. He pulled the trigger of his stun gun and the big man went down hard, sprawling on the concrete floor. Kheif wrapped a rope around Clayton's upper body and drug him slowly to the center of the warehouse, hooking the rope to an electric hoist and pushing the button. In a matter of seconds Clayton was suspended six feet above the warehouse floor. Kheif hurried back to the door to wait for the two women who would surely be behind them.

Rucker and Stillwell stopped at the door just as Clayton had done before. Rucker nodded to Stillwell that she would go through the door first and immediately stepped inside the building. As Stillwell eased in behind her, Rucker's keen sense of smell noticed the heavy scent of gasoline.

"I smell gasoline," Rucker whispered to Stillwell.

At that exact moment, Rucker heard a mechanical sound and Stillwell went down as if she'd been shot. When Rucker turned back to see what had happened something touched her hair and she felt the tightening of a noose around her neck. The next thing she knew, she was being dragged like a wounded animal to the center of the room. She fired three shots in the direction of the person dragging her but the rounds missed, and the dragging continued. She dropped the 9mm when it was obvious that she was about to loose consciousness when suddenly the dragging stopped.

Rucker tried to focus her eyes in the darkness. But before enough oxygen could reach her brain for her to react against her attacker, she felt another rope being tied under her arms and hooked into a metal interlock behind her back. The next thing she knew she was being pulled into the air like the carcass of a dead animal. When she stopped moving she listened to the same sounds being repeated, and she knew that Kheif had Stillwell too.

Suddenly a small light from a battery-powered lantern was clicked on and Kheif stepped into the light and began spraying the three cops with water until all three were cognizant of what was happening. Suddenly the water stopped and a deep voice echoed through the darkness.

"I had a fantastic valediction prepared for this moment, but I'm afraid I'm going to have to cut things a bit short. I want you all to know how much I've enjoyed working with you all these months. Now, I have a question for you. I read in the newspaper that one of you had come to the conclusion that the Impressionist Murderer was killing these men because they had turned from the Muslim Brotherhood and became Christians. Which one of you brilliant minds came to that conclusion?" Kheif said, stepping back into the darkness.

"It was me," Clayton said defiantly.

"I should have known," Kheif said from the darkness. "I was always troubled by you and your egregious pursuit of me. You were determined; it was more than just a job to you. But I suppose I can respect that, we're a lot alike. It doesn't matter now. You see, we've come to the end of our little drama, and I've decided to move up north where the weather is cooler in the summer months."

"You're not going to live long enough to reach your northern destination," Stillwell said, softly. "This place is going to be crawling with cops in the next few minutes and you're going to die right here in Houston."

A smiling Kheif stepped into the light when Stillwell stopped talking. His swarthy face looked like a demon. "You are the epitome of infidelity, a typical American whore. Don't speak to me again unless you want to precede your friends to the depths of hell." Kheif continued to walk slowly around them as if he was contemplating his next sentence.

"Which one of you smelled the gasoline?"

"It was me," Rucker said calmly.

"Ah, you're the Pathologist?"

"That's right," Rucker said.

"Well, well. That's what they'll say about you in the morning paper. A student Pathologist was found among the charred remains, but there was no sign of Nizar Kheif. It'll be so official and permanent."

"The only thing that's going to be mentioned in the paper is that you went down in a hail of gunfire. Do you hear those sirens in the distance? In five minutes this place will be surrounded and you'll be dead," Stillwell said.

"Then I must hurry," Kheif said calmly.

"Where're you going?" A deep voice said from the darkness.

Kheif turned quickly, searching the darkness for the familiar voice. He quickly reached for his knife then remembered dropping it at the café.

"There's nothing I like better than a good knife fight," Redhawk Simmons' voice echoed off the walls of the warehouse. Redhawk stepped into the light a few feet away from the suspended cops, their bodies hovering around him like ethereal deities. His 9" Bowie knife planted firmly in his right hand.

"I don't have time for this, Indian," Kheif said.

Suddenly, three shots from Rucker's 9mm rang out and reverberated off the emptiness of the warehouse. Redhawk Simmons fell to his knees and then face down on the concrete, unmoving and lifeless.

"Just so there are no questions when I leave, I want you to know that I've lined the walls of this building with five gallon cans of gasoline. There are over two hundred of them. It's enough gasoline to burn down half of the buildings in this neighborhood. My original plan was to use C4, but we all know where that went. Anyway, gasoline works just as well. I took the liberty of stashing a few cans around the adjoining buildings so that when it gets started the public servants of Houston will have their hands full."

Kheif twisted the knob on a makeshift timer and set it on a table just outside the circle of light. "You have five minutes to live. I hope my next adversarial relationship is as worthy as you've proven to be."

Kheif turned and started for the door. There was a horrid scream and Kheif stepped back into the light; blood from his neck spraying the air like a crimson dye. Renee Simmons had buried her own Bowie knife deep in his neck and chest severing the veins and arteries that pumped life into his body.

Kheif's eyes showed horror and the absolute surprise from the sudden attack. He tried to speak but the words were garbled at best. Kheif fell only inches away from Redhawk Simmons and never moved again.

Renee Simmons rushed to Redhawk's side, turning him over carefully. Tears were streaming from her face. She couldn't tell if he were dead or alive.

"If you'll let me down we may be able to save your husband's life," Rucker said.

CHAPTER 19

At 2:30 on Saturday afternoon the waiting area was full of people going to Nassau, and since there was no direct flight to Bimini, Ronnie and Jeanie Burgess had settled in for the wait like everyone else.

"Are you okay, you seem nervous?" Ronnie asked his wife.

"To this point, everything has gone so well, I'm just afraid that something bad is going to happen. And, I'm also a little nervous about flying. I've never been on a plane before," Jeanie said, taking hold of his hand.

"Well, if it will make you feel any better, I've never flown either. But I've got a passport that says I've flown quiet a bit, so I guess I'm an old hand at this. Don't worry about the flight. Look at all of these people going to the Bahamas; it happens every day. Like you said, just think of all the good things that have happened to us just today. We didn't have any problems getting here. We got a good price for your car, and we bought you a beautiful wedding ring, and all before one o'clock. The plane will be boarding in thirty minutes and we'll be heading to our new home. Nothing could be better than that," Richey said confidently.

"I didn't know you'd never flown before," she said.

"I've flown from the cops. I've flown from my family. I've even flown from a brother-in-law who was trying to kill me. But I've never done any of it on a plane. When you live a life like mine, jetting around the country is not a priority. This passport says I've made two trips to the Port of Spain in Trinidad. The instructions from Freddy say; that if anyone asks, I flew there on business to look at buying a new fishing boat. I couldn't find Trinidad on a map. Man, I sure would like to talk to that guy one last time. I would just like to say thanks for this. Do you know what I mean? No one has ever done anything like this for me; no one."

"I think you're nervous too. You're talking so fast you make me laugh. I love you Richey," she whispered.

"I love you too. You know, I didn't know what to expect when we left Beaumont. It kind of bothered me that I didn't have anything to give you. I mean I'm on the run with no money and no future, and this beautiful woman who's so perfect in every respect is in love with me, and willing to share her life with me; it's more than weird. I keep thinking that any minute I'll wake up. And when I do I'll be back on the banks of the Houston Ship Channel, surrounded by cops, and my life will be over. But now, every moment I spend with you is like the best moments of my life."

"If you're trying to make me feel better, it worked. You say really nice things to me, Richey. I mean Ronnie," she said softly.

"Say, let me use your cell phone; what's the number of that wing where you worked? And what's the name of that x-ray technician that came and took me to get x-rays?"

"I think his name was Marvin. Maybe his last name was Roberts or Johnson, I can't remember. The number is 409-935-5680. This is Saturday, Ronnie, he's probably not working today."

"It can't hurt to try," he said.

Ronnie dialed the number and after a few rings a woman's voice came on the line. He told the voice that he was looking for Frederic Remington. When she told him that she'd never heard of a Frederic Remington he didn't think too much about it. Freddy was probably just trying to keep a low profile, he thought. But when he asked about the doctor who had treated him and saved his life, the answer was the same, and that troubled him. Finally, he asked about the x-ray technician, Marvin Roberts. What the woman told him sent a shiver of cold across his body and chilled him to the bone.

"Sir, I don't know if this is some sort of practical joke or not, but I've been here for twenty-five years and I've never heard of any of these people. Are you sure you've got the right hospital?"

"What about Jeanie Nguyen, do you know her?"

"I know Jeanie Nguyen, but she doesn't work here anymore, and I don't have a number where she can be reached."

Before Ronnie could ask her what her name was, she disconnected. When the dial tone came on the line he flipped the phone closed and stood there with a blank look on his face.

"Ronnie, you look like you've seen a ghost. Are you okay?"

Renee Simmons burst into tears when she came out of the intensive care unit at Ben Taub hospital. Stillwell, Ross Clayton and Delores Rucker headed in her direction as soon as they saw her in the hallway. Renee walked to Rucker and hugged her tightly.

"The doctor said he's going to be just fine. I'm sorry I didn't believe you. I just had to see for myself. Thank you so much for staying with him through the surgery."

"He's a big strong man. He came through everything with flying colors. He'll be walking around in a couple of days and you can probably take him home by this time next week," Rucker said.

"The doctor said that one of the bullets shattered his collarbone and they had to have an Orthopedic Surgeon rebuild it. That's why it took so long. The other bullet went through the side of his left lung, but they saved the lung and he said that he's doing great. He's going to be alright," Renee cried. She hugged each of the cops before heading for the restroom.

"It's been a long night and day. We're going to get out of here, get something to eat and go home. You want a lift?" Stillwell asked.

"No, I'm going to stay here for a while with Mrs. Simmons, at least until he comes out of recovery. They don't have any immediate family and I'm not sleepy yet, so I'll be okay. I'll see you guys Monday."

Clayton pulled a roll of bills from his pocket and stuffed them into the back pocket of Rucker's jeans. "When you do get ready to go home, you take a cab. And thanks for always being there for us. I don't know what we'd do without you." Clayton kissed her on the cheek and waited at the elevator while Stillwell hugged her.

When the elevator doors closed behind Stillwell she kissed Clayton softly and held him tightly. "It's been a long night and day. Why don't we go back to my place and you can tell me about this secret trip you're taking me on."

"Right now all I want is a hot shower, something to eat, and a soft place to lie down."

"How about something to help you sleep?" "That sounds nice too."

They walked out of Ben Taub Hospital and into an evening filled with people rushing from one ambulance to another, wheeling gurneys and patents into the trauma center for the life-saving measures they knew all too well. They walked without talking toward the parking lot. The air smelled of rain and night blooming Jasmine and for a moment, all was right again.

Ronnie and Jeanie Burgess slept until noon on Sunday and had a late breakfast in their room. They left the room just after two o'clock, hired a taxi, and spent the next two hours taking a tour of the island. It was truly everything that Frederic Remington told them it would be. It was as if the two of them had waited for this moment and for this place for all their lives.

Just before they decided to go back to the hotel they spotted a cottage with a white picket fence and a for sale sign on the front lawn. The cottage was on the east end of the island facing the sea, and looked like something from a painting by Norman Rockwell. They took down the number to call on Monday.

"This is the most beautiful place I've ever seen," she told Richey.

Ronnie Burgess smiled and squeezed her hand. Even with all of the surrounding beauty, he couldn't get Frederic Remington Palmer off his mind. He wanted to tell the old man that whatever paradise was, he'd found it, and that it was more than anything he'd ever expected or hoped for. He wanted to solve the mystery surrounding Frederic Remington Palmer, and at least attempt to understand the goodness that he was now blessed with. But, maybe that part would always remain a mystery, and that's just how it was meant to be.

THE END

CPSIA information can be obtained
at www.ICGtesting.com
Printed in the USA
BVHW031622010519
547084BV00001B/6/P

9 781950 540761